PRAISE FOR *THE MAPMAKER'S DAUGHTER*

"The many twists and turns in the life of the mapmaker's daughter, Amalia, mirror the tenuous and harrowing journey of the Jewish community in fifteenth-century Iberia, showing how family and faith overcame even the worst the Inquisition could inflict on them."

—*Anne Easter Smith, author of* Royal Mistress *and* A Rose for the Crown

"Well-researched, evocative, and a pleasure to read, *The Mapmaker's Daughter* offers an intimate and convincing peek into the reconquest of Granada and the expulsion of the Jews from Spain."
—*Mitchell James Kaplan, award-winning author of* By Fire, By Water

"A riveting, often heart-rending tale set against the tragic backdrop of the expulsion of the Jews from Spain. Laurel Corona has crafted a heroine for all ages in Amalia, whose choices define an era of religious upheaval, courage, and sacrifice that still resonates today."
—*C. W. Gortner, author of* The Queen's Vow

"Laurel Corona authoritatively gives the Jewish oppression in fifteenth-century Spain a human face and heart in Amalia Riba, forced to make soul-defining decisions as her world rolls inexorably toward the Inquisition. Peopled with historic figures, her story soars from loneliness to love, tenderness to horror, and from despair to courage. Sentences of startling, hard-won wisdom leap from the page and command our memories not to forget them. Compelling, complex, and compassionate."
—*Susan Vreeland,* New York Times *bestselling author of* Clara and Mr. Tiffany *and* Luncheon of the Boating Party

"A close look at the great costs and greater rewards of being true to who you really are. A lyrical journey to the time when the Jews of Spain were faced with the wrenching choice of deciding their future as Jews—a pivotal period of history and inspiration today. This novel should be required reading for bar and bat mitzvahs, except that makes it sound like a chore whereas it's a delight."

—*Margaret George,* New York Times
bestselling author of Elizabeth I

"The ghosts of the past are never far in Laurel Corona's hauntingly beautiful tale of a woman whose life spans the Spanish Inquisition and the fall of Muslim Granada. Yet despite the dark times, a powerful love story ignites these pages, making the reader yearn for more as they come to know Amalia and Jamil, two of the most compelling characters in recent historical fiction. An absolute must-read!"

—*Michelle Moran, author of* The Second
Empress *and* Madame Tussaud

"I love *The Mapmaker's Daughter:* its compelling, very human characters; its exciting story of exile and love; the heart-rending look it provides into the trials and tribulations of being Jewish; and its empowering message of being true to oneself. Author Laurel Corona has described Jewish rituals and values—honoring family, community, and God—in detail that, as a non-Jew, I found utterly fascinating, and which made me envious."

—*Sherry Jones, author of* The Jewel of the
Medina *and* Four Sisters, All Queens

THE MAPMAKER'S DAUGHTER

A NOVEL

LAUREL CORONA

sourcebooks
landmark

Published by Sourcebooks Landmark, an imprint of Sourcebooks, Inc.
P.O. Box 4410, Naperville, Illinois 60567-4410
(630) 961-3900
Fax: (630) 961-2168
www.sourcebooks.com

Library of Congress Cataloging-in-Publication data is on file with the publisher.

Printed and bound in the United States of America.
VP 10 9 8 7 6 5 4 3 2 1

In honor of the mikveh and the countless Jewish women who have restored their strength and optimism in its waters.

SEVILLA 1432

I hold my hands up for my mother's inspection. "They're not dirty enough, Amalia," she says. Pinching off a burnt candlewick, she smears the black powder around my nails. "There," she says. "That's better."

Little daylight remains on this tawny afternoon as she hands me an empty basket small enough for my six-year-old arm to carry. "You know what to do. And you'd better hurry."

She shuts the door behind me, and I start up the narrow street on the edge of Sevilla, stopping in the apothecary's doorway to smell the scented air. The owner sets down her pestle. "Wait a minute," she says, breaking off a sprig of rosemary, which she tucks behind my ear to protect me from the Evil Eye. Farther up the street, the air reeks from the greengrocer's fly-ridden pile of rotting vegetables and spoiled fruit, and I hold the rosemary to my nose, breathing hard through it to cover the smell as I turn the corner toward the butcher shop.

A severed pig's head looks out into the street with an oddly cheerful grin. The butcher wipes bloody fingers on his apron as he turns to serve me. "Two pork sausages and a few scraps of ham for soup," I tell him, remembering to make sure he sees that, as Friday sundown approaches, my hands are still filthy.

Soon the houses give way to a rocky field. The wildflowers reach my waist as I go down a narrow path of bent and broken stalks. Just before I reach a stand of poplars, I take the meat from my basket, noting with disdain the mosaic of white fat and pink flesh as I fling it all as far as I can into the tall grass.

Spreading my fingers to avoid the feel of the grease, I make my way through the trees to the edge of a small pool. From time to time, someone must come here or there wouldn't be a path, but it is easier to get water from the pumps in the squares than from the springs around Sevilla. In warm weather, my mother brings me with her to stand guard while she immerses the way she is supposed to after the blood stops flowing from between her legs each month, and I think of it as our private place.

A frog splays his legs as he crosses the pool. "Don't be afraid, little fellow," I say as I crouch to rinse my hands of the grease. Mayyim hayyim, my mother calls this pool. Living water, though it makes my fingers look as pale as the dead.

"Baruch atah Adonai," I whisper. "Eloheinu Melech ha'olam." After blessing the Holy One, I add the words for the ritual of washing hands, watching the swirls of water disturb the grass on the edges of the pool. "Vetzivanu al netilat yadayim."

When my hands are so clean they squeak, I splash water on my face to come home looking fresh for Shabbat. I imagine the sausage hidden in the grass, and since there is no blessing for throwing forbidden meat away, I whisper the words I often hear my mother say. "Please accept that we honor you the best we can." I stand for a moment in silence before picking up my basket to head for home.

VALENCIA 1492

I look at my hands, half expecting to see them pink and glistening from the spring, but instead find them corded and rippled. Sixty-six years old. I am a daughter, wife, mother, widow, lover, grandmother, but I sit now in an empty room in a hostile city because I am a Jew. I have been expelled by King Ferdinand and Queen Isabella from the land of my birth for that simple fact.

I should be more precise. I am caught between two impossible choices. I can go to the church whose clanging bells disturb my sleep and allow some cruel-mouthed priest to pour water on me. After he pronounces me restored to God, I will live at the mercy of neighbors suspicious I am not Christian enough. That, or leave Spain with my daughter's family and wander until more hospitable people take us in.

I do not appreciate the service Ferdinand and Isabella think they have done by offering Jews their paradise. Need I say that I prefer the life of comfort and dignity they have torn from me? Or would the fact that I am in the sole chair on a bare floor in an empty room in the port of Valencia say it for me? Isaac, my son-in-law, says that their Catholic Majesties didn't really intend the Jews to leave. They simply want Jewishness to melt away in Spain, forgotten by our children's children for lack of practice.

How little they understand. There's a knowledge deep in our bones that some lines cannot be crossed without becoming unrecognizable to ourselves—the only death truly to be feared. I know who I have been. I know who I am. I know who I will remain.

I am Amalia Cresques, though I have had other names. A Christian name disguised my Hebrew one at my birth. "Ama-lia," my mother would say, deliberately mispronouncing my name so I wouldn't forget. "God loves Leah. That's what it means. It's your real name, the one known to him."

It was the first of many deceptions by which my mother and I secretly lived as what Jews call anusim, the forced ones. "There are two kinds of anusim," she told me. "The ones who say, 'I give up,' and the ones who don't." The ones who don't are called Judaizers, living outwardly as Christians but keeping to the old ways in secret.

Conversos, New Christians—that's what families like the one I grew up in are called. In private, the good Christian folk of Spain call us reformed blasphemers, repentant Christ-killers, unworthy prodigal sons. Even their holy water cannot replace the degeneracy they are sure is in our blood.

"He that fleeth from the terror shall fall into the pit; and he that getteth up out of the pit shall be taken in the trap; for I will bring upon her, even upon Moab, the year of their visitation." The words of the prophets come easily to mind, for I have been awash in them most of my life.

We are the new Moabites, and the year of our visitation has come.

I shut my eyes and feel the memories crowding in again. My breath leaks out and time goes backward with it.

SEVILLA 1432

The sky is coral with sunset, but the shadows are so deep, I recognize my father only by the slight hitch in his gait. I run down the street to meet him and give him the basket to hold, so I can slip my hand in his.

We're late, but I know better than to say so. "Vicente Riba doesn't have any obligation at sundown on the Sabbath," he would snap. "I'm a Christian, and so are you."

At the threshold of our house, he puts his fingers to his lips and touches a crucifix in the doorway. He looks out of the corner of his eye, hoping someone passing in the street sees him make the sign of the cross.

"Rosaura?" he calls out.

My mother comes to the door, looking like the last bloom of summer drooping heavily on its stem. "You worried me. It's almost dark." She takes the basket and turns around. "Susana! Luisa! Come here!"

My twelve-year-old sister Susana comes from the kitchen with my little sister in tow, chewing on a piece of bread the servant girl has given her. "Come along," my mother says, taking an oil lamp from a sideboard. "I need your help." My father's face grows stormy, but as usual, he says nothing.

In the basement, my mother sets two candles on a stool in the middle of the floor, away from anything that might catch fire.

Fishing a splinter of wood from her apron pocket, she lights one end from the lamp and touches it to the wicks. "Blessed art thou, Lord God, king of the universe," she says in a voice between singing and speaking, "who sanctifies us with his commandments and commands us to light the Sabbath candles."

I shut my eyes when she does, taking in the moment. Quiet time with my mother is rare, even if I do have to share it with Susana, who is twice my age and not my friend. I try to make her think I don't notice she's there by crouching down to talk to Luisa, who just turned three. "Baruch atah Adonai," I repeat slowly, emphasizing each syllable. "Rook tadonai," Luisa says solemnly, and my mother smiles.

Susana shifts from foot to foot. She hates coming down here for the weekly ceremony that begins Shabbat. She wants to be like her Old Christian friends, with their honey-colored hair and pale, heart-shaped faces. I catch her glowering into her looking glass, tugging at her drab, brown locks as if they have done something wrong. She wears her crucifix to bed, though my mother tells her she'll strangle on it someday.

"We can't be down here so long," Susana scolds. "Don't you think people can figure out what you're doing?"

I reach for my mother's hand. "Avla bien para ki ti venga bien!" I say, repeating one of her favorite sayings.

Susana glares at me. "Mother, are you going to let her talk to me that way?"

"Amalia is right," Mama says. "Speak well so good will come to you. Ken savi los ke estan sintiendo?"

Who knows who is nearby? Susana should not be so careless. Evil spirits are always lurking, and they might whisper to our neighbors that we secretly light Sabbath candles. The sheddim are happiest when our own words give them ideas about how to hurt us. We refer to them aloud as los mejores de mosotros, the best of us, because it's important to distract them with flattery.

Mother hands Susana a bottle of wine and gives Luisa and me

oranges from a basket, to make it seem as if our trip to the cellar was just an errand. I go up behind my sisters, but sensing my mother is not behind me, I turn at the top of the stairs. She is still in front of the candles, her lips moving as she talks to the circles of golden light.

༽

Luisa slips one hand in mine and wipes the sleep from her eyes with the other as we leave the house the next morning. The lingering cold of winter brushes my cheeks, but the April sun is already warming the air. We hurry behind Susana and my mother, their strides growing longer and faster as they continue a hushed argument that began at the house.

"They act like Jews, Mama. It makes me uncomfortable. You know it does." Mama hunches silently over the covered basket she carries, as if she has not heard Susana's comment.

We arrive at the stables and, after hiring a driver and cart, we are soon in the countryside amid fields of red poppies, dotted with splashes of blue, yellow, and white, as chaotic and wild as if they had been painted by a blind man. Black-and-white magpies fly with wings so shiny they look dipped in water. The scent of newly tilled earth teases my nostrils until I sneeze.

My legs jiggle in anticipation of the chance to run in the open air and to use the loud voice I have to hush at home, calling out to whomever will listen, even if it's just the ducks in the yard or the clouds already billowing in the immense blue sky.

Luisa is squirming, tired of bouncing along the rutted dirt road. "Go to sleep," I tell her. "We'll get there faster that way." She lays her head in my lap, and though I want to stay awake, the jostling makes my head slump, and we doze until the barking dogs in the village wake us.

My grandfather is waiting at the gate to his farm, catching Luisa as she jumps out of the cart. Brushing back a stray wisp of her blond hair, he kisses her forehead. I jump down just as Grandmother hurries up the walk. "Shabbat shalom," I whisper so the driver will not overhear. I feel her arms tighten around me, and my breath is hot against her skirt.

Mama hands our parcels to Susana before getting out herself. "Be back before dark," she tells the driver. He nods, and with a flick of the reins, he heads off toward Sevilla.

"Shabbat shalom, Father," Mama says when the driver is beyond hearing. "Shabbat shalom," she repeats to Grandmother, giving her a kiss on the cheek. Her voice is so loving that I always forget they are my father's parents, not hers.

Luisa and I run ahead to the chicken coop to check if eggs are still in the nests. Just inside the gate, tiny cheeps come from puffs of bright yellow scampering on the dirt floor. "Hold it gently in your palm," I say, picking one up. Luisa's face glows as she holds the chick near her face and talks to it.

Some are still breaking free of their shells, their feathers clinging to them like wet, brown spines. One is making a pitiful little sound, and thinking it might be cold, I blow on its feathers. At the feel of air on its body, it looks around, dazed. I can hear Luisa's soft breath as she puts her chick in the nest.

"Pio, pio," she says, imitating them.

"Pio, pio," I repeat, taking her hand.

"There you are, my little radishes!" Grandfather comes up behind us and picks Luisa up in his arms. He puts his other hand on my shoulder. "How do you like our new additions?"

"They look like they've drowned when they first come out."

"And then, before you know it, they're like old mother hen here, with chicks of their own."

"Grandchicks," Luisa says.

He laughs with a great roar. "Grandchicks," he repeats. "Pollititos." The sound of the word makes us giggle, and we make it a game as we walk back to the house. "Pollititos. Pollitititititos," we say, stopping only when our tongues get tangled up in the sounds.

Inside the house, Grandmother has laid out a bowl of olives

next to the embroidered cloth covering two loaves of challah and is removing hot cinders from around a kettle of stew. She wipes her hands on her apron, and stands next to my grandfather. He pours wine in a silver kiddush cup. "Blessèd art thou, Lord God, king of the universe, creator of the fruit of the vine," he says before taking a sip. He offers the cup to my grandmother and mother before lowering it to me. My cheeks pucker in anticipation even before I taste it.

Luisa stands next to me. "It tastes awful," I whisper, as Grandfather puts his finger in the wine and touches it to her lips. She matches my grimace and shudders the way she always does, causing a ripple of laughter from the adults.

Except Susana, who wants nothing to do with these rituals. "The stew smells delicious, Grandmother," she says, looking away.

"I made your favorite," Grandmother says to her after we have blessed the bread and are seating ourselves on benches around the table. The scent of cloves and cinnamon wafts up from saffron broth as grandmother fills our bowls with white beans, chickpeas, and cubes of beef.

For a while, no one speaks as we enjoy Grandmother's adafina, kept warm from yesterday, because cooking is work, and work is forbidden on Shabbat. We eat the first bites hurriedly but eventually slow down, because Shabbat meals are meant to be savored, and no one will be leaving the table until we have talked about our week, sung a few songs, and eaten all that our stomachs will hold.

A loud knock startles us. "Who's there?" I hear the alarm in Grandfather's voice as he goes to the door.

Grandmother hurries to hide the remainder of the bread, and my mother covers the pot of stew and takes it out the back door. A stew kept warm on a dying fire and a braided loaf means that we are observing the Jewish Sabbath, and no one must know. But it is just neighbors, Bernardo and Marisela, come with a flute and tambourine to be among their own kind making music on Shabbat afternoon.

The bread and stew are brought back to the table, and though we all claim to have had enough, the pot is soon emptied with small tastes, sopped up with the remaining bread. Susana has disappeared, using the excitement of the new arrivals to slip outside.

"You mustn't be so hard on Susana," Grandmother says. "Girls get moody when it's their time to become a woman."

"But she's so scornful!" My mother's eyes glisten. "She says, 'I was born a Christian.' What kind of talk is that? As if we can choose our ancestors?"

"Sensible talk," Grandfather replies, raising his eyebrows. "We are Jews who cross ourselves, eat pork when a Christian puts it on our plate, and buy leavened bread during Passover even though we feed it to the chickens when no one is looking." He shrugs, but his eyes flicker with pain. "We've left behind so much of who we are, perhaps it's no longer worth the trouble to keep to our old ways."

"Jaume!" Grandmother is aghast. "Such talk coming from you?"

"Such talk? I have spent my life paying the price for letting them splash me with their water when I was a young man living in Mallorca. Surely you should know where my heart lies." Above his gray beard, his face is mottled with anger. "I was afraid—I confess to that! I did it to save my life, but I am not one of them. My knees may bend when they wave their crucifixes in front of me, but my mind never will."

He exhales with a snort so loud and horselike I might have giggled if the subject were not so serious. "Stupid fools if they think I believe that nonsense about their Hanged One and their sacred wafers and that wine they say turns to blood that he wants us to drink in his memory." His lip curls. "Drink his blood? What kind of barbarians would do that?"

He stops momentarily, but I know he isn't really asking us to answer. "We live in a terrible place, a terrible time," he goes on. "And if the Holy One means us to survive, how exactly does he mean us to do it?"

I hate these conversations because I know, even at six, that a threat hangs over these afternoons. To Christians, we are Judaizers.

To Jews, we are traitors to the faith of Moses, Marranos, swine. I fight back tears. "Can't you unbaptize yourself?" I say, hearing the huskiness in my voice. "Can't you say, 'I've changed my mind and I'd rather be a Jew?'"

My grandmother smiles wistfully. "I wish it were that simple, little one, but Christians believe that once they've wetted you, there's no turning back."

My mother looks at me, and I know what she is thinking. Immediately after my baptism, she told me she took me to our spring to wash away the water and restore me to our people. The following year, the church burned down and the record of my baptism was destroyed. Mama says that makes me still a Jew in God's eyes, but it's not something we should mention to anyone.

Cleansed with living water and my baptism purged by fire. I return Mama's smile, warmed by our secret. If I should need to say I have never been baptized, no one could disprove it. If I said I was, no one could disprove that either. I don't understand why this is important, but Mama says every secret Jew might need a story someday.

"Best to marry Susana off quickly," Grandfather is saying. "She has excellent prospects. She's healthy, and the Riba family has the means—"

"But she's so young," my mother protests. "She hasn't the hips for childbearing yet."

"Perhaps you haven't noticed," Grandmother says gently. "I think she is growing them now." She pats my mother's hand. "And she'll make you a grandmother all the sooner, if it's God's will."

To avert my mother's darkening mood, we stand for the blessing after meals, after which we burst into song.

Bendigamos al Altísimo,
Al Señor que nos crió,
Démosle agradecimiento
Por los bienes que nos dió.

I have practiced all the verses in bed so I know the song by heart. "Let us bless the Most High, the Lord who raised us. Let us give him thanks for the good things he has given us," I sing, loudly enough to draw the smiles I crave.

Grandfather unfurls his fingers in a loud and decisive strum of the guitar he has fetched from the corner, while the others pick up tambourines and flutes. Eventually Susana comes back inside and stands next to me, clicking castanets with my mother. Watching her, I wonder why Susana wants to be a Christian when Jews have afternoons as wonderful as this.

Grandfather plays the first notes of Luisa's favorite, and we jump to our feet. "Dance, Rachel, and Mojonico sing! The fat rats clap their hands." The song creeps as slowly as a burglar at the start, and we act like statues coming to life. Each verse speeds up, until Luisa and I are waving our arms and leaping in wild circles. At the end of the last verse, we dive into pillows on the floor, holding our bellies and squealing with laughter.

Even Grandmother is persuaded to dance. Though she complains that her joints are stiff and she is too old for such things, I watch her feet flutter like birds taking off from their nests. Finally, Grandfather puts down his guitar. "Praise to the One who has such things in his world as music," he says, signaling our afternoon rest. Bernardo and Marisela leave for home, and Luisa flops on the pillow, her hair plastered brown at her temples with sweat.

Mama and Susana go with Grandmother to lie on the bed while Grandfather settles into his favorite chair. I'm tired, but I don't want to sleep. "Will you show me the atlas?" I ask, widening my eyes in hope Grandfather will find me irresistible. He musses my hair. "All right, but just for a minute. An old man needs his Sabbath nap."

The book is so big it knocks against my ankles as I carry it to him. He sets it alongside his chair and waits for me to hop in his lap. "Tell me the whole story again," I say.

"You've already heard it a hundred times."

I twist my head around to look at him. "But not for a while. I think I might have forgotten something."

He laughs. "You, my little radish, never forget a thing!"

"Tell me anyway," I say, wiggling my legs down between his thighs as he stretches his arms around me and rests the open atlas on his knees.

The six vellum panels in the atlas are almost as long as my grandfather's arms, and as I sit on his lap, the top of the world looms over my head. "Our king, Pedro, knew that the king of France wanted a map of the world. Catalan atlas makers were the best, and my father was best of all. I was a cartographer too, so we made this atlas for Pedro to give to his friend."

"Your father was Abraham Cresques," I interrupt. Now that I've gotten him to show me the map, I want him to know how much, not how little, I remember. "That means Cresques should be my name too."

"Except that in 1391, mobs started killing Jews all over Spain, and I was baptized against my will. They forced us to take Christian names, and I became Jaume Riba. But Jehuda Cresques is my real name, just like yours is Leah even though everyone calls you Amalia."

"Ama-*lia*," I correct him with a smile.

"Ama-*lia*," he repeats. "And when I am gone, I hope you will remember me as Jehuda Cresques, even if that won't be on my tombstone."

"I will, Grandfather."

He doesn't seem to hear my promise. "It was too terrible a thought never to see our work again—may the Evil Eye not punish me for such pride—so we secretly made this copy, which we've kept all these years."

Grandfather thinks for a moment. "We imagine we are on top of the ball of the world but they feel the same in China or Africa." He kisses the top of my head. "Never forget that making a round world that no one falls off is easy for the Holy One. So next time you look around and say, 'this world doesn't make any sense,' just remember that it does to him and be grateful that no one else is really in charge, even those who wear crowns."

"Yes, Grandfather."

The large page scratches my belly as he turns it to reveal the next panel. I know what I'm going to see, but it takes my breath away nonetheless. Navigational lines radiate outward in an ocean of lapis lazuli, like frost on a window against a brilliant blue sky. On the right is Spain. "Sevilla," I say, "Toledo, Salamanca, Valencia." I point to each city in turn, as Grandfather nods with pride. "If I ever need to make another map," he says, "I know who to ask for help."

Mama comes from the bedroom. "Have you kept Grandfather up?" she scolds, but she doesn't mean it. She takes the atlas from his hands despite my protest that I have seen only one page. "It's time for us to get ready to leave. The cart should be here soon."

I crawl down from Grandfather's lap and go to wake up Luisa. "Come on," I say, "unless you want me to say good-bye to the chickens without you." We make a quick trip, and on our way back, we see the cart and driver stopping at the gate. Inside, everyone is gathering around the table for the habdalah ceremony that ends Shabbat.

Grandmother brings a special, braided candle to the table, its tip flaming. "Blessed art thou, Lord God, king of the universe," Grandfather chants, "who separates the sacred from the ordinary." He pours wine into the silver cup until it overflows, then puts the candle out in it. We break out into laughter, not because it's funny but because that's what we're supposed to do to make the start of the week happy.

Grandfather takes off the lid of a small carved-ivory jar, and the aroma of cloves and cinnamon wafts through the air. After massaging the dried spices between his fingers to release more of their scent, he puts the jar under my nose. "May you have a sweet week," he says.

Susana inhales the heady blend next and holds the jar under
Mama's nose. When it has passed to everyone, we stand around
a plate of membrillo, taking turns spooning out a morsel of the
sweetened quince paste and sighing as it melts on our tongues.

Mama and the others start down the path, but Grandmother
motions to Luisa and me to stay. She dips her fingers in the remaining wine from the silver cup. She touches behind our ears for
health, in our pockets for wealth, and on the backs of our necks for
the quick arrival of the Messiah.

As we walk to the gate, Grandmother picks a blossom from
a quince tree and tucks it behind my ear. "Have a good week,
my beloved Leah," she says. Its fragrance fills the carriage all the
way home.

VALENCIA 1492

I wake to the faint scent of quince blossoms and cinnamon, and I think
for a moment it is Shabbat and I am in Grandfather's lap. I feel his spirit
breathing on my neck. "You kept it safe," he says.

"Yes, Grandfather," I whisper. "I showed it to my daughter, to
my grandchildren, and my great grandchildren, just as you shared
it with me."

I don't want to tell him I can protect it no further. Jews may take
no more from Spain than they can carry. Take something useful, my
daughter has told me. A little more clothing, or a piece of leather for
new soles for our shoes. Sell the atlas and sew into my hem the few
coins it will bring. I see the pain behind her resolve. The book is as
much a part of her as it is of me, no easier to leave behind than an
arm or a leg.

I don't know what I will do when my grandson Judah arrives later
today to take me to the boat. I could take the vial of poison I bought
from a gypsy on the road to Valencia and pour it down my throat to
save myself the decision of whether to go or stay behind, but the

thought of Judah finding my body on a day already full of unspeakable loss restrains me.

"Go to the end," my grandfather says, still behind me. I open my mouth to protest that I am already at the end. Go, stay, die, live—it's all the same.

"I mean the atlas," he says, annoyed at my incomprehension. "The last panel, the one that was your favorite." I turn to the Asia of Kubla Khan, a lumpy circle, with people and places lining its perimeter. At the top, the figures are painted upside down, or so I thought when grandfather first showed them to me. "When people think there's only one right place to stand, they say foolish things like 'you're doing it wrong.' All you have to do is go to the other side and look again at how many ways there are to see the world." I am not sure if the solemn voice I hear is a memory or a whisper. "You must act in their world, even when every choice seems as impossible as riding a horse upside down."

I touch the empire of Magog, at the summit of Asia. "Behold a swarm of locusts were coming," the prophet Amos said, "and one of the locusts was Gog, the King." He could hardly be more fearsome than Isabella and Ferdinand. If a mapmaker painted Spain now, it would have boats sinking, refugees drowning, doleful lines of Jews on dusty roads, bonfires with black corpses hanging from stone pillars...

"Grandfather, help me," I plead. "I don't know what to do."

"Go with your heart. You cannot do otherwise."

"But I don't know what my heart is telling me!" I want to protest that I am a confused old woman who can't think straight anymore.

He cuts off my complaint. "It's buried in your memories. Go find out."

2

The windows of the cathedral admit little light on this blustery morning, and the sconces on each massive pillar give up their weak yellow glow into the looming gray overhead. The odor of tallow smoke, wet wool, and incense wafts through the nave as I stand with my family shortly after my seventh birthday, in the long line of people awaiting communion on Tosantos, All Saints' Day.

Father hangs back to let us go first. Susana picks Luisa up so the priest can lay a wafer on her tongue and then puts her down to receive the host herself. They make the sign of the cross, and Luisa looks up at Susana for approval.

I stick out my tongue for the priest, but before the wafer can dissolve, I transfer it to the inside of my upper teeth, as my mother has taught me. When we return to where Susana and Luisa are standing in the nave, I see my mother run the knuckle of her thumb over her lips, and in a few seconds, she has managed to bury the unswallowed host in the folds of her underskirt.

I wiggle the host free from my own teeth and move it to the tip of my tongue. Feigning a cough, I deposit it between my curled fingers. Clasping the other hand over my fist in a gesture of prayer, I wait for the chance to paste the sticky blob inside the hem of my sleeve.

My mother has her own way of going to mass. She says out loud only the things she believes and mumbles her way through the rest. I do the same. The Lord's Prayer is one of the things we both say with fervor. "It's a Jewish prayer," my mother tells me, "taught by a Jew to his own people."

She finds it amusing that Christians hang on everything an ancient rabbi said. "I understand Jesus perfectly," Mama tells me. "I just don't understand Christians, and I don't think he would either." Indeed, my mother seems on quite friendly terms with the Hanged One, as if they are both shaking their heads in bewilderment at what is done and said in his name.

After mass, Luisa clamors for Susana to take her to see the nuns who live nearby. I'm not sure whether it's the little cakes they lay out for visitors that make her so eager to go, or that the nuns create such a commotion over how pretty she is. Though I would rather not, my mother always makes me go too. "It helps us look like good Christians," she tells me with a wistful smile.

Going home afterward, we skirt the edge of the neighborhood where the Jews live. Grandfather told me there used to be a Jewish quarter protected by a wall and a locked gate, but there were terrible riots a while back, and all but a few hundred Jews died or moved away. Christians moved into the vacant houses and shops, and the remaining Jews pay a neighborhood guard to watch over their houses, though all their protectors do is doze in the shade or tell jokes outside the tavern.

None of the guards are in sight when we hear the first screams. Without thinking, we run around the corner to see where the noise is coming from. A group of young men is beating up a Jewish merchant outside his shop, yelling something about how he's defiling Tosantos by being open for business.

"This isn't our holiday," his daughter is screaming. "You want some wine? You want some bread? Who do you think we're open for?"

People are spilling onto the street. A few come to the man's defense, but most seem bent on a brawl. Susana pulls us into a doorway as people stream past. Seeing another Jewish merchant hurriedly closing his shop, two boys pick up fruit from the baskets he has not yet taken inside and stomp it to pulp on the cobblestones.

"Apples for sale!" one says, picking up the whole basket and marching down the street. "Apples for free!" he corrects himself. "Jew apples for free."

Two of his companions drag the greengrocer outside and throw him against the wall so violently I hear his head hit the stones. They are so close we could almost be caught by the backswing of the clubs that suddenly appear in their hands. Luisa is screaming, and I am plastered to the wall of the doorway, my cries frozen in my throat.

Finally the guards arrive, but the crowd is howling for blood. One of them pulls up a man kneeling next to the limp body of the greengrocer and pummels him with his fists. The guard fighting near our doorway pulls a club from his belt, dealing his opponent a savage blow on the head. Blood spatters and the man falls, his splayed arm trailing across the front of my dress. He lies face up at my feet, his lifeless eyes staring skyward as a pool of blood forms underneath his head.

The guard's sweating face is convulsed, and a noise like a wild animal comes from deep inside him as he turns to find someone else to fight. I feel Susana yanking my arm. Carrying Luisa and dragging me behind, she gets us out of the street and in the direction of home. I am sobbing so hard I can't breathe as I hang onto her skirt, and Luisa is clinging so tightly that Susana cannot put her down. She is staggering with the burden of both of us by the time we reach our door.

"A man—" I say, barely able to speak through my sobs. "I saw a man die. He touched me, Mama." I look at my blood-splattered dress, and I run to the kitchen just in time to spew the remains of the nun's cakes in an empty bowl.

"Il Dio ke se apiade de mosostros," my mother whispers, her face ashen. "May God have mercy on us."

Father is heading out the door with a stout piece of wood.

"Lock the door behind you," he commands. "If the fight spreads here, hide in the cellar."

"How will you get back in if I lock the door?"

"Don't worry about me," he says, and then he is gone.

Mama pulls us all to her. "Praise to the Holy One," she says, "for keeping you safe."

Susana breaks away, curling her lip in a way that bares her teeth. "It's people like you that make these things happen," she hisses. "Can't you just call him Our Father? Do you have to give us all away?"

Her knees give out under her, and she falls to the floor sobbing. When Mama tries to put her arms around her, Susana shrinks into a ball, screaming at her not to touch her, not to touch her ever again. Luisa is clinging to me, and I can think of nothing to do but go in the bedroom and hide under the covers with her until the rage in the streets and inside our home has passed.

∽

My father comes back unscathed from the brawl. He says he's sorry he frightened us, but that he took the stick for protection on his way to the palace of his employer, the Count of Medina-Sidonia, to implore him to put a quick end to the chaos. A few of the count's guards arrived on horseback, brandishing swords in streets too narrow to escape the slash of their blades. The crowd scattered in moments, and only the greengrocer and the man at my feet were killed.

"It's fortunate only Jews are dead," Papa says. "If Christians had died, the city would be ablaze. This way it's over, at least for now."

My mother shudders. "Fortunate that Jews are attacked?"

"Rosaura!" My father's words snap the air. "That's not what I mean. You know what Christians say. Jews tempt them to displease God. If shops are open, people will buy, God will be angry, and it will be the Jews' fault."

"And you believe this?"

"What does it matter what I believe? Why look elsewhere when the Jews cry out, 'Here we are! Blame us for everything!'"

I think of the Jewish tailor who gives me leftover pieces of ribbon for my hair, the vegetable man who cracks a pea pod and drops the sweet green balls into my hand. "Papa," I say, "I think Jews are nice."

For a moment, he seems as if he had forgotten I was there, before he crouches down to look into my eyes. "Some are, some aren't, just like other people," he says. "Jews offend Christians. It isn't logical, it isn't fair, but it's true. I don't want to offend people. I don't want anyone seeing me or my family as people it's all right to harm."

He brushes away a stray hair from my cheek, and the feelings I have been holding in come spilling out. "Papa, I'm scared," I say with a huge, heaving sob.

"You have no need to be, if people believe you are a good Christian."

I hear my mother weeping in the corner, but my father does not glance her way. "That's why we go to church. That's why I kiss the crucifix at the door. I don't think about what I really believe. I don't imagine most people do. All I know is that people have to change with the times, or they won't be around to see them."

He stands up and gives my mother a look so hard it sends a shiver up my spine. "You endanger us, Rosaura. I've told you that many times, but you haven't listened."

My mother cowers like a trapped animal in the corner. "What are you saying?" Her hoarse whisper doesn't sound like her voice at all.

"I'm saying that I think what happened today isn't over. I'm saying the time is right for some preacher to come along like Ferrand Martinez did forty years ago and convince Sevilla that every Jew is an offense against Christendom. I'm saying that there aren't enough Jews left here to make one good bonfire, but that doesn't mean they won't try—"

"Vicente—los mejores de mosotros!" Mama says. "They should never hear talk like this."

Papa scowls and puts on his hat. "I need some air," he says, shutting the door behind him on a house stunned to silence.

◦○

That night, I hear my parents talking after I have gone to bed. Our house is big enough to have a sleeping nook for my sisters and me and a room with a door for my parents, but sound travels easily, and I can pick up their voices even over Susana's light snoring beside me.

"You have to give up the old ways, Rosaura," Papa says. Mother murmurs something I can't hear. "Ancestors?" my father replies. "Why are you so sure they would want us to risk our children's lives?" I strain to hear what my mother is saying, but I can't.

"Always done things this way, keep the faith—what kind of foolishness is that if we're all dead?" My father's voice is getting louder. "We changed our ways when the Romans burned the temple and sent us into exile. All the rabbis do now is spout nonsense about holding to the things that make people hate us. I don't call that wisdom, and I'm more than happy not to be a Jew."

The noise from their room has stopped, except for the snuffling sound of my mother's tears. Silence hangs over the house like a judgment, except for the scratching sound of a mouse devouring a piece of grain in the corner. Two cats yowl at each other in the alley, and something crashes to the ground as they fight.

I go to stand in my parents' doorway, but their forms under the blanket offer nothing to comfort me. I tiptoe backward to bed, wanting to trick time into reverse, so today will never have happened.

◦○

I am sitting with Susana in a sparsely furnished room lit only by faint winter sunlight, a small, ineffectual fire, and a candle by whose light a nun is reading. "The Lord said to Peter, 'Whatsoever you shall bind on earth, shall be bound also in Heaven.'" Sister Teresa looks up at me. "Can you tell me what this means?"

"Does it mean if you die tied up, when you get to heaven you still have the ropes around you?" I don't understand any of it, though I have been genuinely trying in the six months since the fight in the street. Afterward, my father ordered Mama not to light Shabbat candles anymore and told Susana to oversee my religious education at the convent. The servant was to see us having both meat and dairy on our table, and once a week, she and my mother were to prepare a dish containing ham or pork.

Mama watches me choke down the same kind of sausage I once threw in the grass and leaves the table uncleared for the servant to see cheese rinds floating in leftover meat stew. She lights one oil lamp upstairs as it grows dark on Friday, choosing a time when she thinks I will not see her mouthing the blessing.

My mother looks pale and her clothes hang on her. She says she doesn't care if she starves to death and makes her supper from only cheese and bread if the soup has even a touch of anything forbidden by Jewish law. "The family is abiding by what you have decreed," she says to Papa in a dull, cold voice, "but I will not." More than once, I have heard her retching in our courtyard after serving food she never imagined in her home.

I hear Sister Teresa's voice through my fog of thoughts. "Only through the church can you be redeemed. That's what 'binding' means. Whoever is bound to God on earth will be bound to him in heaven."

"But why aren't the Jews bound to God? They believe in him too." I avoid looking at Susana. She says I am difficult on purpose when all I really want are answers that make sense.

"Jews say they believe in God but they do not," the nun says. She leans in toward me and I smell her rotting teeth. "Long ago,

God was pleased with the Jews. They worshipped him as One, because they did not know his full nature. Then God made himself flesh through his son, Jesus Christ—King of the Jews!" Her voice grows shrill and her eyes flash. "And who rejected him?"

"The Jews," I say miserably.

The nun takes my hands in hers. Her nails are split and ragged, and her fingers are chapped. "The devil wants to lure you back to your family's cursed race, so you will be lost to God."

I want to pull my hand away, but hers are too strong. "You're scaring me," I whisper.

"As well I should."

The God Mama speaks to seems so different. That God scorns the proud, not the Jews. That God raises up the downtrodden and pours his wrath on those who persecute them. That God loves those who believe in him. Why does Sister Teresa think he doesn't love me?

I look at a statue of the Virgin Mother in a niche across the room. My mother's gentleness makes her a bit like Mary in my eyes, and when I told her that, she was pleased. "Mary was a Jew," she said. "We could have been good friends, talking about our children and husbands."

Susana's and the nun's pitiless eyes bore into me. Jesus was a Jew, and I don't understand why he would hate me for being like him. I look away again toward Mary, hoping that maybe she knows me, maybe she understands. I wait for a smile, a wink, a nod, but if she responds, even the mother of the Hanged One does not have the power to penetrate the gloom.

My mother's back is turned, but I can see she is holding the crucifix that usually hangs outside our front door. She startles when I come up behind her, and for a moment, she tries to cover up the hollow channel she is carving out of the wood. I unroll a curled paper on the table and see tiny Hebrew writing on it. "What's this?" I ask.

"Get me a piece of tree bark from the courtyard and I'll show you," she replies. "And be fast about it. I have to finish this before anyone else comes home."

When I return, she puts the rolled paper in the recess she has carved and tacks the bark over it to hold it in place. "It's a mezuzah now, with the words of the shema inside," she says. "I bought the paper from a rabbi. The Holy One commands Jews to put these words on their doors." She picks up her handiwork and replaces it on the door, matching it up exactly with the faded outline on the painted stucco. "Hear, O Israel, the Lord is our God," she whispers. "The Lord is One."

That night, Papa, Susana, and Luisa put their fingers to their lips then touch our new mezuzah as they come into the house. Mama and I exchange furtive grins, and I know that I will never trade such moments for anything Sister Teresa offers—even salvation itself.

ᔕ

I do everything I can to ease Mama's misery, but it's harder to know how to please my father. He makes maps for the Count of Medina-Sidonia, but he's also his astronomer, astrologer, natural philosopher, and translator. Papa knows both Latin and Arabic, and though he won't admit it, I'm sure he knows Hebrew too from having grown up with my grandparents.

He's proud I have taught myself to read and write. "It's time you learned to write on paper," he says one day, spilling onto our table a bag of sheets spoiled by the count's secretary. "Wax tablets and slates are fine for some things, but you should learn to do it well enough to keep."

By my tenth birthday, I will have learned to read and write Castilian, Latin, Arabic, and Hebrew. I don't know why languages pour into my mind so effortlessly, each one more easily than the last. I feel sometimes as if I am not learning them at all but remembering something I had forgotten. "It's a gift from the Holy One," my mother says. "He plans to use you for something. It's too bad you're not a boy."

Would I please Papa then? He's not home much now except to sleep and have his meals. My mother and he barely talk, and Susana and Luisa get his attention more easily than I do. Perhaps if I were a son…

I look down at my ink-stained overskirt. But I'm not.

Please Papa? I don't know how. A lump rises in my throat. How can I please someone who hardly knows I'm there?

VALENCIA 1492

"I loved you, Amalia. You were my favorite. How could you not know that?"

Is my father here? It can't be a memory, because he never once said such a thing.

"Not then," I say into the quiet. "Not when I was little and needed it most."

"I loved your spirit, your mind. The others were easier. They accepted everything, but I never knew quite what to make of you. You always gave me joy, even if I didn't know how to show it."

"Why didn't you say so?" My heart still twists with pain at how much I wanted reassurance then.

"I didn't know a father was supposed to. I was always working. That's how I showed my love."

"You didn't love Mama. Not at the end."

"I always loved your mother. I tried to stop her because I couldn't have lived with myself if any of you were hurt by her Judaizing. I had nightmares."

I know his nightmares. I've seen them now myself.

"You wanted a son. I tried to make it up to you."

Susana was my parents' first child, born a year after their marriage. In the six years before I was born, three baby boys preceded me. One was stillborn, one died in his sleep a month after his birth, and one was struck down by a fever around the time he began to walk.

I heard the laments of women who had borne only daughters. I heard the rejoicing over every birth of a boy. I heard what women always wished the pregnant ones—"Ijo de buena ventura ke te se aga." May you have a son with a good future.

Three sons dead, and then there was me. How could I not feel I had failed?

All those years I spent reading every book in the house, huddled over slates, wax tablets, scraps of paper, trying with scratches of pen or stylus to cast a spell that would bring his love to me. All those copied bible verses and pages of scientific and philosophical treatises—were those my offerings to my father, to soften his disappointment?

He reads my mind. "It was never that way. I wanted a boy who would live—who doesn't?—but I never wanted you to be anybody else. And look at all you became."

Perhaps if I hadn't believed I needed to atone for his disappointment, I might have settled for less from myself. But my mother was right. The Holy One had a plan, and in trying all those years to be something I wasn't, I became the person I am.

3

The news from the court of Henry the Navigator in Portugal is so astonishing that my father is making the trip to my grandparents' farm to share the news. I am eight, and in my years of weekly visits, I can remember only a few times when he has been sitting beside us in the cart as we leave Sevilla.

"Tell me again about Cape Bojador, Papa."

Annoyance flickers in his eyes. He wants to be left alone, and I have been pestering him since he came home yesterday with word that Gil Eanes had finally rounded Cape Bojador on the west coast of Africa.

My mother intervenes to keep the peace. "Why don't you tell Luisa and me what you remember? Papa will tell you if you forget anything important." I sigh loudly, but this is so exciting, I don't mind telling the story myself.

The first of Luisa's teeth is coming loose now that she is nearly six, and she wiggles it solemnly. "Tell me!" she says in a voice muffled by the finger in her mouth. I could make up crazy details just to watch her eyes widen, but this story is so fantastic I can't think of a way to embellish it.

"Everyone said Cape Bojador was the end of the world," I tell her, "that a boat that sailed past it would never return."

"The end of the world." Luisa nods. "We would fall off."

"We will not fall off," I growl. "People thought the sea was boiling there like the mouth of Hell, but it turns out—"

"No one wants to go to Hell," Luisa interrupts. "If I were on that ship, I would turn around." She looks at Mama and Papa for approval, but they are both looking away.

"Well, if it really were the mouth of Hell, Gil Eanes wouldn't have been able to come back, would he?" I retort. "The devil would have sucked him right in." Luisa is starting to annoy me as much as Susana does, but she's just a little girl and there's no pleasure in baiting her.

"Sucked him right in," Luisa repeats.

"But it turns out the ocean south of there is like everywhere else. He saw places where the people were black as night and they have piles of gold and treasure."

"Jesus is the treasure."

I sense my mother's weight shift. She is only pretending not to listen, and she doesn't like what she hears. I am so mad at Luisa I turn my back to her and cross my arms. "I was going to say more about the boiling water," I sniff, and with a jolt, I recognize Susana's tone in my voice. But I'm nothing like her. She's always glowering about something, but it isn't every day that a man sails beyond the end of the known world and comes back to tell the tale.

"Look, Mama!" Luisa holds aloft a little white pearl. Blood smears her fingertips, and she makes a smacking noise to keep the pink saliva in her mouth. Mama takes out a handkerchief and dabs the blood away. Luisa's astonishment quickly gives way to fear. "I have a hole in my mouth," she whimpers. "We have to bury my tooth right now!"

"We'll do it at Grandmother's." Papa has been brought back from his thoughts by the commotion.

"No!" Luisa says. "I can't grow another until it's buried!"

"Look!" Mama takes Luisa's finger and shows her that the stub of her new tooth is already protruding.

"No! Now!"

"We'll be there soon," Papa tells her, "and a few minutes won't make any difference."

"It won't make any difference if we get there a few minutes later either," Mama says in the clipped tone she now uses with him.

Papa sighs. "Stop the cart," he tells the driver.

The wheat fields are dotted with oaks as dark as ink on a yellow page. A hawk circles, following something moving below. Papa and I stay in the cart while Luisa and Mama climb down. I see the outline of Mama's pregnant belly as she stands watching Luisa cover the tooth with loose dirt. Soon, Mama tells me, she will be too big to make the journey, and our Shabbat visits will have to stop.

Luisa and Mama climb back inside, and we are off. I lean against the side of the cart, and my thoughts drift off again to Cape Bojador. I wish I had been on Gil Eanes's ship, even if I quivered in my shoes the whole time. Papa told me that plumes of foam and mist shoot into the sky at the cape, and the breeze from the shore is so hot that the water roils and hisses. Even if the sky is blue, great clouds hug the coast and make the shoreline invisible, so any boat that comes too near is dashed to splinters.

There's a ship painted off Cape Bojador in Grandfather's atlas, with a mermaid following behind. It would be wonderful to be her. I'd have sapphire blue eyes, waving gold hair, creamy skin, and a tail I could flip and go off into the deep without worrying about drowning. I would be the most important thing any sailor had ever seen.

I sigh. Luisa looks more like a mermaid than I do. I have dark hair and muddy gold eyes. Over the course of the year, my skin goes through all the shades of honey, into a hue as dark as almond skins by the time summer ends. My nose is small and straight, but I know that when people praise your nose, there isn't much else they can think of to say.

No, I think, casting a glum look to where Luisa has drifted off to sleep, snuggled against our mother. She'd get the attention in the ocean too.

As usual, Grandfather is waiting at the gate. His jaw drops when he sees my father, and then he breaks into a grin. Putting his arm over Papa's shoulder, he starts toward the house, with Luisa and me trotting alongside as Papa shares the news.

"It was Eanes's fifteenth attempt to round the cape," Papa says after he and my grandfather are settled in. "They continued south until they ran short of provisions. Prince Henry plans to send expeditions to see how much farther it goes."

Grandfather strokes his beard, mulling what Papa is saying. "I spent several years with Prince Henry in the Algarve, at Raposeira," he says. "The man's curiosity is unbounded. He will want maps."

"I know," my father says, glancing at my mother. She puts down the jug she is carrying and moves closer. "I am thinking of writing to offer my services."

Portugal? On the atlas, it looks close to Sevilla, but I know it has to be a journey of many days from here. "Would you be gone a long time, Papa?" I ask.

"If I go, it would be all of us, to get out of Spain." I know he has been worried about our safety since conversos were killed along with Jews in riots in Toledo. All I can think is that I would be rid of Sister Teresa if we went to Portugal, although I suppose Susana and Luisa might find more nuns there.

"Would we have a nice house?" I ask Papa.

"The best that Prince Henry's money can buy."

"It's true, little one," Grandfather says, looking at Grandmother. "We lived well there, didn't we?"

She nods. "And there's less ugliness about Jews, praise the Holy One. At least less that shows." She lifts the lid from the stew pot. "Come and say the blessings, Jaume. It's time to eat."

By the time my mother is ready to give birth, my father has received an invitation from Prince Henry to come to Raposeira, a town near Lagos on the southern coast of Portugal. It's fall now, and with a new baby, we will not leave until the following spring.

The best part is that Susana will not be going with us. She is betrothed to a Christian man, Roberto Salas de la Cruz, from a family of textile merchants. Though Susana is only fifteen and my mother thinks that is too young for marriage, her wedding has been set for April, before we leave.

I am so happy I could float away. In Portugal, Mama won't have to hide her Shabbat candles in the basement. Papa will have fewer distractions and can spend more time with me. And with Susana gone, Luisa will stop being so stubborn about everything the nuns tell her. In Portugal, I will have the family I want.

When Mama's water breaks, I am sent with Luisa to gather rue and garlic to protect her and the baby. By the time we come back, it has already been born. Susana acts as if she's always been aware it doesn't take long when women have had several children, but I don't see how she could know unless she'd just been told. Grandmother and Susana take the rue, placing some of it over the baby's crib, some in Mama's tangled hair, and the rest at the foot of her bed. The garlic is tucked under her pillow and beneath the baby's mattress.

"Is it a boy?" I ask. Grandmother holds her finger to her mouth. "Don't bring the Evil Eye! Pretend nothing happened today." She takes me to the baby's crib and unwraps its swaddling, and immediately a tiny appendage lets out a stream of urine. I look up at Grandmother and smile, knowing how happy everyone must be that it's a boy.

"He's very pretty," Luisa says, trying to be polite, since the wizened creature is nothing of the sort. Susana gasps. "Take it back, Luisa! He's not pretty at all. Look at that ugly little thing. Who would want it?"

Luisa's face crumples. Grandmother rubs a clove of garlic between her palms and touches them one after the other to the baby's forehead. "It will be all right now," she says, pressing her warm palms to Luisa's and my face as well.

Susana takes a tiny bracelet of blue beads from which dangles a hamsa charm in the shape of a hand. She puts it around the baby's wrist, then holds up her own hand, palm out and fingers straight. "Cinko!" she says, for the number five, which has the power to keep away evil spirits looking for babies to steal.

My mother gives the baby a lick on the forehead. "Te pari, y el espanto i el ayin arah ti kiti. I gave birth to you, and the fright and the Evil Eye I remove from you." She licks him again. "The cow licks her calf because of love, and I lick away your fright and the Evil Eye."

Susana, Grandmother, and neighbor women stand watch over the next few days in the room where Mama and the baby lie. Neither of them is left alone, for it is when no one is looking that spirits come to lay a curse on a mother's milk or make a baby sicken and die. I am too young to ward off the Evil Eye myself, but I spend almost every minute in her room, fluffing her pillow and bringing whatever she wants.

Like all Christian babies, the child, whom my mother calls Abraham and my father calls Benito, will not be circumcised. "It's why the others died," I hear her whisper. "I didn't claim them as Jews, and the Evil Eye thought I didn't want them."

When I come in her room the morning of the baptism, I am surprised to see her out of bed. "Let Leah stay," she tells Grandmother.

She shuts the door as my mother takes out a sewing needle. "We are doing what needs to be done," Grandmother tells me. "Don't make a sound."

"Blessed art thou, Lord God, king of the universe," the two of them whisper as Mama unswaddles the baby. "Who has commanded us to bring him into the covenant of Abraham, our father." I watch in shock as my mother makes a shallow prick near the top of his penis. He lets out an angry howl, as a tiny jewel of blood rises at the site.

"This is what we do when we can't circumcise a boy," she tells me.

Grandmother murmurs in Hebrew, looking furtively toward the closed door. "Just as he has entered the covenant, so may he enter into the Torah, the marriage canopy, and the performance of good deeds."

"Ken y'hi ratzon. May it be so," my mother says, holding the baby close until he quiets. "You can take him now," she says to Grandmother. "We've done the best we can."

I follow her as she carries the baby to my father and Susana, who are waiting near the front door. "Rosaura is not feeling well enough to attend the baptism," Grandmother says. "The rest of you go ahead. I'll stay with her." As I leave the house, Grandmother whispers in my ear, "Just go along and look happy. We fixed it, so don't worry."

When I get home, my mother is in bed looking ill again. The count of Medina-Sidonia, the baby's godfather and Papa's employer, is throwing a dinner this afternoon in honor of the birth, and Mama asks Grandmother and me to stay home with her. My sullen mood at missing the party vanishes when, to my surprise, the minute they are gone, Mama jumps out of bed, wearing her regular underclothes beneath her nightgown. She puts on her dress and places Abraham in an empty basket lined with a towel. Grandmother and I leave the house first, and Mama follows with the baby, covered by loose folds of cloth.

The way is as familiar as my own feet. At this time of year, the field is dry, brown stalks, and the path is stomped to a dirty pulp. When we reach the spring, Mama begins pulling off her clothing. Naked, she steps into the pool, and Grandmother hands her the baby. She crouches to submerge him, whispering something in Hebrew too soft for me to hear. Then she stands again, lifts her eyes skyward, and recites the Shehechiyanu, a blessing we say for special or long-awaited days that will not come again. "Blessed art thou, Lord God, king of the universe, who has created us, sustained us, and enabled us to reach this day."

Abraham cries at the shock of the water but quiets when Mama puts him to her breast. "Take off your shoes," she tells me. "Put your feet in."

Mayyim hayyim. Living water. That's how it feels as I submerge my toes in the cold, crystalline water. Mother puts on her clothes, and while Abraham sleeps in his basket, the three of us sit together, dangling our feet and making ripples with our toes. We recite every blessing we can think of and make up a few more—for the shelter the trees provide, for the smell of harvest burning in a nearby field, for the blue of the sky, for the sun and the water, for each other, for the new life sleeping on the bank.

"You need to learn our ways well, Leah," my grandmother says. "When we are gone, you must pass them on to your own children— the ones who will listen. May there always be some of those."

When the baby cries, we get up and head for home. "You know why we came," Mama says as we cross the field. "We undid the baptism, but no one must ever know."

God's love radiates from the heavens as we cross the field. Only when we reach the streets and can be observed am I back in a world where the best things must always remain the deepest secrets.

Abraham is so warm and strong, and his eyes are bright, but Mama and Papa seem worried, as if he will disappear if they look away. We keep quiet about how the baby is doing. No one speaks of how well he feeds, how much he has grown in the six months since his birth, how easily he survived an unusually cold winter. "Hello, Abraham," I whisper in his ear, though I am careful to call him Benito when other people are listening. He calls me Mahyah and wets my hair when he puts it in his mouth. He laughs and bangs the floor with his toys. "Pum! Pum!" I say. "Buh buh!" he says back, smacking his lips.

But the Evil Eye has many ways to strike a family. That spring while hunting with the count, Papa slams his head against a rock when he is thrown from his horse. He is brought bleeding and limp to the palace, where he drifts in and out of consciousness for days, with a fever so terrible he moans and cries out as if seeing a terrifying vision of the beyond. We take turns sitting with him day after day until his fever breaks and the count's physician says he can come home.

He complains that everything sounds as if he is under water. "It will pass," Mama says, but it doesn't. By midsummer, Papa can hear only his own pulse in his temples and muffled sounds when we yell or clap to get his attention.

Our troubles mount when the summer brings renewed hostilities against conversos all over Spain. Though Sevilla is quiet, we're all afraid.

I try speaking with my fingers in my ears to understand what it must be like for Papa, and everyone tells me to quiet down because I am yelling. His voice has grown so loud I'm afraid people will make fun of him if he goes out.

Mama and I act out simple things, like shaking a basket to say we're going to market, and I use wax tablets to write what we can't communicate any other way. No one has to say the obvious, that he will not be able to function at Henry's court. Papa has written to the prince already, putting off his departure for Raposeira until the following spring, while we hope for improvement.

Papa and I develop a system of hand and finger signs I use to supplement the movements of my lips. We only communicate simple things at first, but by the time winter has passed, we can converse almost normally, using signs for most things and spelling the rest with finger shapes we invent to stand for letters. We go out so Papa can practice talking with people through me, and though he often comes back frustrated and glum, I know he is relieved.

"Will we still go to Portugal?" I ask him one day after a meeting with the count. By now, I am invisible at my father's side, and business goes on as if I am not there. Papa's face clouds. He points to his forehead and shakes his head to say he doesn't know.

"But I can help!" I touch my chest and grasp my forearm. "You can work with the count—why not with Prince Henry?"

Papa barely tries to speak anymore, having seen the distressed looks on people's faces at his loud, nasal mumblings. He shakes his head, puts two fingers to his mouth, and draws P-O-R in the air.

He doesn't have to finish before I know what he means. "I can learn Portuguese! I'll translate for you!" More than anything, I want him to be glad again. I want him to pick me up and spin me around, telling me what a wonderful girl I am, how proud he is, and how much he needs me.

But he doesn't. His face grows pensive. He spins his finger, our sign for the future, then points to his eye. "We'll see."

That's all. He looks away so I won't see the sadness flitting across his face, but I see it anyway and recognize it better than he knows.

༄

Mama doesn't want to leave Sevilla. There's a one-year-old baby to think of, and with Susana marrying in a few weeks, she will need her mother while she adjusts to being a wife. Mama is not confident things will work out well at Raposeira. After all, Henry might reject Papa's services if he sees how limited he is, and what would we do then, so far away from home?

"Remind her that I am one of the best cartographers in Europe," Papa signs, his face darkening at the insult of her fears.

"Well then, see if the count will compensate you better so we can stay here," Mama replies.

"Henry doesn't want to talk with me. He wants my maps. He wants my charts. I could work in a…" He stops to spell on his fingers. "M-O-N-A-S—" I nod. "Monastery, for all he cares."

Mama is adamant. The Riba family is at home here, Susana needs her mother, and my father is deaf. We are not going to Portugal, and that is that.

The night Susana goes off to be the wife of Roberto Salas de la Cruz, I lie awake wondering if it will be different now that I am the oldest child in the house. When neighbors talk about what a good wife I would make because I am so devoted to my parents and the baby, sometimes I want to cry out that they don't understand. I don't care about making some man happy—all I want is for my mother and father to say what a good job I am doing, to notice how hard I try.

In any case, I am too important to Papa's livelihood to consider letting me marry when I'm older. It's my little sister whose future hips get talked about, how she will bear some man's children and shop for his vegetables someday. I glimpse pity when the neighbors look at me, as if it is already decreed that I will end up like the shriveled-up old crone at the end of our street, the one whose house Luisa and I hurry by.

Why doesn't anyone ask me what I want? I catch myself grousing like Susana, but the truth is I don't know what I would say if anyone asked, other than I'd like to feel a little happier right now.

How could I forget that the sheddim are always lurking, ready to turn idle complaints into fateful wishes they love to grant? "You think other people are happier than you?" the Evil Eye whispers. "You selfish child—just see what I have in mind for you."

One day shortly before my tenth birthday, Abraham's nose is running and his bottom is scarlet from watery messes. By the next day, his eyes and face are bright with fever. By the third, they seem drained of life, and he sags in our arms. No one sleeps that night. We cover his bed with amulets and sprinkle his bedding with rosemary and rue and dozens of cloves of garlic, but to no avail. All day, his breath is shallow and infrequent, and as quietly as if he were falling asleep, at nightfall, he dies in Mama's arms.

She wants to bury him the Jewish way, in a simple shroud, but Papa will not hear of it. Benito Riba is buried in the Christian cemetery, his name carved onto the stone below my other lost brothers.

A day after the funeral, Mama wakes me after everyone has gone to bed. "Come with me," she says.

She carries a cloth-covered basket as we make our way to the Jewish cemetery. Once there, she goes to the top of a rise and crouches under an almond tree. In the moonlight, its blossoms look like hundreds of tiny, luminous angels hovering above us. Mama gets out a trowel, and when she has dug a hole, she pulls out something wrapped in a small white cloth.

"I cut a lock of his hair before we buried him. It's inside." She gives me a package so weightless it could drift away with the slightest puff of breeze. "I did this for my other babies too."

I nod my head, silenced by a moment that feels too weighty, too sacred for words.

"On the eve of Yom Kippur, the Day of Atonement," my mother goes on, "I ask the Holy One to have mercy on me for all the ways I have been unable to honor him—for food I was forced to eat, for the festivals I didn't keep. And each time I lost a child, I've come here to bury a lock of his hair and ask for forgiveness that he sleeps with a cross over his head. I ask God not to be harsh with me, but…"

We are both crying as we place the packet of hair in the soft, cool earth under the tree. We sprinkle dirt until the cloth is heavy with it, then we push the rest of the soil back in the hole, patting it down as gently as when we held Abraham over our shoulders to coax the air from his stomach.

She brushes a fallen petal from my hair, and I pick one off her sleeve. "Is there a blessing for burying hair?" I ask.

She smiles. "There are many that will serve." She raises her voice in a plaintive call. "Blessed art thou, Lord God, king of the

universe," she sings out, "who restores the souls of the dead." I
want with all my heart that he would do that for Abraham, but
Mama has taught me that it is not proper to pray for what cannot
be undone.

Day is breaking, and we will soon be missed. Hand in hand, we
walk back to a home that seems no more part of the living than the
tiny grave we left behind.

∾

That summer is the hottest in memory, and the churches are full
of people praying that the plague spreading across the country will
spare our city, or at the very least that the Angel of Death will visit
someone else. We don't have the outbreaks they had a hundred
years ago—the Great Mortality, when whole towns died overnight,
when wolves came down from the hills to finish off the dying,
when people spit up their lungs and smelled their own bodies rotting. The fluxions, agues, and poxes that have visited Sevilla in my
lifetime are frightening enough, though they lay low no more than
one neighborhood and sometimes just a few households.

No one in our family could imagine for whom the angel would
come, and how.

An upturned pot of stew burns my mother's arm, making it
blister and weep, but Mama assures me she has seen worse. She
applies a poultice of figs mixed with yarrow and chervil and then
goes about her work, stopping from time to time to chew poppy
seeds for the pain.

Within a few days, angry red lines shoot outward from the
wound, and her whole arm is hot to the touch. Mama says this
is because she had put a ham bone in the stew that burned her.
"Swine flesh is poison," she mutters. "Do you need any more
proof than that?"

By the time her whole arm is discolored and swollen, she has
taken to bed. She throws her blankets off, complaining she is too

hot, and then moments later, she shivers with cold. By the fourth day, her body is raging with fever, and she vomits the elixirs the apothecary gives her to drink.

Grandmother has come from the farm to tend to her. "I know what's wrong with her," she says. "We've been treating her arm, but it's espanto that's making her sick."

Espanto. The fright. It disturbs the blood as surely as witches' spells do.

"When Rosaura burned her arm, it gave her quite a scare," Grandmother says. "The Evil Eye took possession of her when she was momentarily weak. We have to calm her blood before her burn can heal."

She sends me to the apothecary for a fistful of cloves, which she passes in circles over my mother's head, chest, and shoulders. She takes the cloves to the fire and heats them in a large metal spoon. Their sweet aroma fills the air, and my grandmother nods. "The scent will discourage los mejores de mosotros," she tells me.

"I remove from you the ojo malo, the ayin arah," she says in a stern, commanding voice as the cloves wiggle and puff from the heat. "In the name of the Temple in Jerusalem and all the prophets, such a woman should not experience harm."

She examines the cloves again. "I think it worked. When they popped, they took the Evil Eye with them. We'll make your mother tea with these, just to be sure, and she should be getting better by morning."

She is no stronger the next day, and Grandmother takes a handful of salt and passes it over my mother's body. "Pour some water in a bowl," she tells me, and when I have done so, she rubs the salt from her hands into the water and puts it on the floor. "Piss into the bowl," she commands. "The urine of an innocent makes the potion stronger." I crouch over the bowl and do as I am told. Grandmother examines the pale yellow fluid. "The evil is dissolving," she says. "Watch it."

She carries the water out into the courtyard and tosses it in three directions to confuse the spirits, then takes the remainder and throws it in the gutter outside the front door. "Al la undura de la mar ki si vaiga todu il mal," she says. "It will make its way to the sea now, and the evil will sink into its depths."

We go back to sit by my mother's bed. She groans and tosses her head, arching her back feebly in pain. "There's one more thing to do," Grandmother says. "We'll change her name so the Evil Eye will think it is in the wrong place." She incants the formula for changing a name, calling her Vida, while I stand by the bed trying to convince myself that no one named for life could be dying.

The next day, Mama cannot be roused at all. As the day goes on, her moans grow softer and then disappear into a deeper sleep. Sometime that night, she slips away.

When I wake from my makeshift bed on the floor, Papa's face is slack and his eyes are unfocused and distant. Susana's are nearly swollen shut with tears. I look at Mama's closed eyes and peaceful expression, and I feel my whole body shudder. "Grandmother?" I ask in a tiny, pleading voice.

She shakes her head. "She's gone, Leah. Baruch dayan emet. Blessed be the one true Judge."

"No!" I scream. "Get more salt! We need more cloves!" I shake Mama's shoulder. "Vida! Vida!" I cry out as I crawl in next to her. I lay my head on her chest as if nothing has changed, but her cold, still body is so unnerving that I jump up in horror and rush into my Grandmother's arms.

I feel my breath burning circles in her overskirt. Though my eyes are scalding, my sobs seem locked inside, and when I pull away, I am surprised to discover her skirt is wet. "Should I wake Luisa?" The question comes from the blackness enveloping me, and I barely recognize my voice.

"It has to be done," Grandmother says. "Help your sister braid her hair before you come back, and do your own as well. I want clean faces and hands." Though I can't imagine why it matters, I go off to do as I am told.

"Luisa," I whisper, going to the bed and jostling her shoulder. I want to crawl deep under the covers with her, to take in the breath of someone who hasn't yet had her world turned upside down, but I know Grandmother is counting on me to get back quickly.

I shake her again. "Wake up," I say. "Mama is—" I can't get out the word.

Luisa sits up. "Mama?" she asks. Her eyes are sleepy but wide open. I nod my head, and she starts to cry.

We return looking as presentable as I can make us. A lace on Luisa's dress is undone because my fingers don't feel as if they belong to me and I couldn't tie it. Grandmother has been arguing with Papa and Susana, but they stop when we come in.

"Very well," Grandmother says, "I'll do it then, if you won't." She motions to the two of us to come stand near Mama. Grandmother places Mama's limp hand on top of first my head and then Luisa's and gives us a last blessing.

"We are conversos," my father replies when she turns back to him. "She'll have a Christian funeral and be buried in the Christian cemetery, and that's the end of it."

My heart lurches. Her body will wait for the coming of the Messiah far from where she wants to be, next to the mementos of her four little sons, among the Jews of Sevilla. I imagine a cross on Mama's grave, pounded deep enough to stab her heart, and I think my own will break with sorrow.

⁓

Within hours of my mother's death, Papa leaves with Susana to discuss Mama's funeral with the priest, but Grandmother asks me to stay behind. She sends the servant off to get two buckets of water. "Find someone at the pump who can bring back two more," she says as she hurries her out the door.

"I'm not going to let anyone tell me what to do, especially not someone who once nursed at my breast, even if he is a grown man now," Grandmother mutters as she bustles around our kitchen. "And if the church wants to tear me in pieces for what I'm doing, that's my business, isn't it?"

Once she has her water, Grandmother sends the servant home for the day and closes all the windows and doors so no one can hear or see what is going on inside. Before Papa and Susana left, they laid Mama's body out on the kitchen table, and Grandmother stands looking at the sheet-draped form.

"I told my son that if his wife has to be buried as a Christian, she should at least have taharah first. It's the ritual washing Jews receive when they die. I knew you would want to help."

She soaks a cloth in the water and twists it to release the water over Mama's head. "In the beginning, God created the water and the land," she repeats, continuing the prayer as she rinses Mama's head seven times.

Grandmother washes every bit of Mama's body, removing the dirt from under her nails and sponging the folds of tissue in the private place between her legs. "Everyone should go from life unencumbered and pure," she tells me. "I am anointing her for the beyond." I follow her, moving the bucket as she goes, but I keep a respectful silence. When the washing is finished, Grandmother picks up a cloth cap. "Take one last look at your mother," she says.

Mama's face is as dewy as a child's. "She looks peaceful," I say.

"The dead are happier than the living," Grandmother replies. As she covers Mama's face, I look away so as not to see the moment I lose her forever.

"You're a good girl, Leah," she says as she puts two eggs in a small pot on the hearth. "Very brave." While we wait for the water to simmer, she tells me to strip down to the chemise under my dress. When I have done so, she takes the tip of a knife and tears the fabric over my heart.

"It's called kriah. Jews wear clothing torn this way as a sign of mourning. Don't take this off for seven days, and the next time I see you, I'll help you mend it, so no one ever has to know." She helps me wiggle back into my dress. "Normally we would tear your outer garment, but it's obvious why we can't do that."

The eggs rattle in the boiling water, and when they are done, she peels them and lays them on a plate alongside a few olives and a slice of bread.

I go to the table, but she motions me to sit on the floor. "It's part of our mourning. For the next week, I will do this at home and ask God to accept that I am also sitting shiva for you. But since we are alone now, you can do it properly at least once."

We sit on the floor and eat what she tells me is the traditional meal of eggs, olives, and bread. Through our tears, we share stories about my mother, and though I think my throat is too tight to eat, I manage to swallow my share. "You see, my Leah," she says, pointing to my empty plate, "life does go on. Min hashamayin tenu-hamu." She pats my knee. "May you be comforted from heaven."

A thought comes to me, and I get up. "I know something that would please Mama."

I take the knife Grandmother used to cut my chemise and cut a small strand of my mother's hair. Taking a piece of white cloth and colored ribbon from her sewing basket, I wrap the hair into a package.

"What will you do with that?" Grandmother asks me.

"Come with me tonight and you'll see."

Then I think of something else. I run to the front door, take down the crucifix, and pull out the tiny scroll. I lodge it into Mama's curled fingers and put the cross back on the wall.

When my father returns with the coffin, Mama is placed inside, not in a shroud, as Grandmother had hoped, but in a dress, as if she is just off to market instead of returning to the Holy One's earth. I check before the lid is nailed shut to make sure the scroll is still there, clutched in her hand until the Messiah comes.

❦

Within a few days, our future is decided. Papa says the pain of Sevilla is too great for him, and he will take his position with Prince Henry as soon as he can get his affairs in order. Luisa can't go with Papa because he doesn't know how he will take care of her in Raposeira, and he needs me with him at court rather than home with her. "May I board at the convent?" Luisa asks, grabbing Papa's sleeve. "Please? Lots of girls do!"

Susana is still getting used to running a house, and her belly is already beginning to swell with the baby she is expecting. She seems relieved not to have to take Luisa in, assuring my father how easy it will be to look out for her and bring her home from time to time for a visit. Papa balks at the idea of leaving his youngest child without a mother or father, but Luisa pleads with him. "She does love the nuns," I remind him, and finally he gives in.

I lay awake all night wrestling with guilt. I wanted to be the most important child to Papa and now I will be. The cost? The lives of the two people I loved most. Now, the only member of our family left to go with my father to Raposeira is me.

4

The sunlight makes a path across the covers of my bed as I sit up and pull a strand of hair out of my eyes. The air inside my room is cool, but I can feel the summer heat seeping through the window. I throw on a dress over my muslin undergarments and go out into the main room of the cottage.

My father, heedless of how the incessant wind makes the window behind him rattle, is at a table positioned to give him the best light for his work. Two oil lamps add to the light streaming through the window, setting the table aglow. The whitewashed walls cocoon us in peaceful, still air but can't entirely mute the sound of the waves slamming against the cliffs in cracking booms and the shorebirds crying overhead.

Our servant, Tareyja, has left a breakfast of orange juice, bread, and a wedge of cheese. Papa has already eaten, I can see, by the crumbs on the breadboard. His cup is on the table, and I come over to ask if it needs filling.

He looks up, his eyes watering from the intensity of the work. "Are you well this morning?" he signs.

I nod my head. "Do you need anything?" He points to his cup, and I take it to the pitcher of orange juice and mix it with water, just the way he likes. When I bring it back, I come to his side to look at his work.

This map is not nearly as big as the atlas. It's one piece of vellum, weighted down at the four corners with smooth beach stones. At the top is the southern end of Portugal and Spain, and at the bottom is the land just beyond Cape Bojador. Papa has added details from Gil Eanes's logbook about the land south of the cape, but most of the new information comes from sea raids on Moorish fortresses north of there.

A few days ago, Papa painted a tiny gold-and-blue banner and crown at Raposeira to mark Prince Henry's court, and just yesterday, he indicated the point at Sagres, where we now live, by a whitewashed stone tower like the one near our house. He hands me his magnifying lens, and I see a man and girl next to the tower. She looks like me, but so small he is using a brush with a single hair to paint her features.

"I'm on the map!" I sign to him, grinning. He makes a sad face, our sign for "sorry," and taps the map at Cape Bojador. I had asked him to put my face on a mermaid, but there aren't going to be such creatures on this map, or monsters inland either. The prince isn't interested in any of that.

Prince Henry's mind is occupied with only three things: what riches lie south of Cape Bojador, whether the Moors have gotten to them first, and if the people of those lands can be turned into Christians. He says he is sending his ships out to bring the word of God to the savages of Africa, confident that this will make them willing to trade exclusively with him, which will make him rich and starve out the Moors. The fact that all his goals work so well together, he says, is all the proof anyone should need of God's will.

I make the sign for horse and raise my eyebrows to ask Papa's permission to go riding. There's not much to do here out on our lonely point, since most of the books and papers I used to read belonged to the Count of Medina-Sidonia and were left behind in Sevilla. Papa doesn't worry about me being out on my own though. I am ten now, and in the two years we have lived here, I have come to know every patch of the peninsula at Sagres as well as I know my own bed. If I should get into trouble, someone will see me home. It's so different from Sevilla, where what I did had to be carefully considered in case the neighbors were watching. Here, the only prowling eyes belong to the sea eagles soaring in the glorious sky.

He nods and goes back to his paint and brushes. When I go out the door, the wind finds me, and I lean into it forcefully in the direction of the stable. The sky is huge and blue, with a few low clouds hugging the horizon at sea. The cluster of buildings on the promontory—two cottages, a walled garden, a stable, a tiny chapel, and a watchtower—are so white they hurt my eyes.

I can see Tareyja's husband Martim in the corral. He is about my father's age and small like him, but strong and light on his feet. He and Tareyja are serfs who came at the prince's orders to live in the caretaker's cottage and tend to the needs of the deaf mapmaker and his daughter.

"Can I take Chuva out today?" I ask him. I named my Andalusian mare after the Portuguese word for rain, because her gray shoulders and haunches look like dust spotted with raindrops. A carriage transports Papa and me to Raposeira in bad weather, but I learned to ride when we first arrived, and we go everywhere we can on horseback.

Martim saddles up Chuva and holds the bridle while I get on. The wind-scoured rock is uneven and slippery—too hard on Chuva's hooves to do anything more than pick our way forward, but beyond the promontory the footing in the scrub flowers and low grass is better, and I ease her into a trot. "Do you want to run on the beach?" I ask her, sure she understands because she tosses her head and nickers.

A gentle, sloping path leads to the water. The beach is a half-moon of sand, bounded on both ends by low cliffs and surf-carved rocks. The gentle breakers shimmer like strewn handfuls of jewels. I let out a laugh that comes from the deepest place within me. "Go, Chuvita!" I call out. "We're the wind, you and I!"

Chuva's stride lengthens when she reaches the packed sand near the water's edge. Back and forth we gallop, her hooves splashing through the edges of the waves. I sing loudly to the sky, because in these moments, I am so free nothing can stop me, not even the ends of the world itself.

I dismount and leave my shoes and stockings on a rock while Chuva wanders over to a ragged patch of grass. Making my way to the water's edge, I let the hem of my dress lift up as the surf hisses and crackles around my feet. It tickles my toes as it washes in and out, sinking my feet into the sand. The water is so cold it takes a moment to be comfortable enough to wade in up to my knees, soaking the back of my dress as I squint into the sun in the direction of the watchtower on the cliff top. Then, as always, I walk up the beach until I am too close to the cliff to be able to look up and see the buildings.

If Papa or Martim or Tareyja were to come to the cliff's edge to look for me on the beach, they couldn't find me. I feel reborn in these moments, and my imagination runs wild. If a stranger came along, I could make up any story at all, because no one would expect me to be the Amalia people know. I could be a gypsy girl, or perhaps a Moorish princess washed ashore from Africa, or a mermaid who suddenly discovers she has lost her tail and must live in the world of humans.

Even more than these stories, I love having nothing at all in my head except a feeling of comfort in the world. It's not too hot or too cold, I am neither hungry nor uncomfortably full. I am out of the wind and the midday sun. Everything is perfect.

I tip my face to the sky. "Baruch atah Adonai," I whisper. Saying a blessing at such moments still feels natural to me, although I'm really neither Christian nor Jew now. Living our solitary life at Sagres, I rarely go to mass. I would not have known it was Passover a few months ago if I hadn't been at Prince Henry's court for the day and overheard a Jewish visitor refusing to eat leavened bread, or Eastertide if the prince had not spent most of his time praying in his private chapel.

One day is like another on the cape—although I know I've missed Shabbat if we come into Lagos, the only real town near us, and I hear the Sunday bells ringing. It makes me sad to have drifted away from Mama's ways, because it feels like losing her a second time, as if there is a place beyond the grave where the dead disappear only when they become strangers to the ways of the ones they left behind.

The rock I am sitting on feels jagged and hard now, and my throat is dry. I shift my weight, and my bottom feels numb. Tareyja will worry if I am late for dinner. I start back toward Chuva. "Are you ready to go home?" I stroke her nose and lean my head into her mane, and she whinnies to say she loves me too as we head up the path for home.

When I come back to our compound, I see a horse wearing the regalia of Prince Henry's court tied up outside my house. I leave Chuva with Martim and hurry to see who is here. I feel guilty for being gone so long, because my father will have trouble communicating with whoever has come from Raposeira to see him.

Papa has rolled up his new map and is slipping it inside a leather case when I come in. "He's been summoned," the messenger tells me.

Before Martim has a chance to remove Chuva's saddle, I am back astride and accompanying my father to Raposeira. We ride past white-sailed windmills and small farms, through grain fields and pastures dotted with cork oaks, across creeks and along ridges looking down to the sea, until an hour or so later, we arrive at Prince Henry's palace.

It's really no more than a large house, nothing like the Duke of Medina-Sidonia's residence, where I used to interpret for my father. The first room is a vestibule with a stone floor covered with fresh straw to catch the dirt from people's shoes. Except in the worst weather, the heavy palace doors are open, and dogs wander through, sniffing in the corners for scents and making water to mark their spot.

Anyone can come in this first room, but except for petitioners during set hours, only Prince Henry's guests can cross the threshold to the antechamber. Inside, wall sconces and heavy iron standards hold lit torches day and night, but the light is dim enough that I have to stand close to the wall frescoes to see the details. One shows caravels heading across blue seas, carrying the banner of Portugal atop their masts. Here and there, a sea monster lifts its head and mermaids cavort—scenes that must have been painted before Prince Henry decided such things are foolish. The other fresco shows the Moorish ramparts at Ceuta, on the north coast of Africa. Led by the prince himself, Portuguese troops with banners and shields blazoned with crosses are routing the Moors, and flames rise from the besieged citadel.

Off the antechamber is a banquet hall big enough for no more than ten or fifteen people, because the prince does not entertain large groups. He is always dressed exquisitely and expects the same of those in his service, but a meal at Raposeira is no grander than at the inns where we stopped on our journey to Portugal, with pewter plates, soup, and heavily watered wine. I've heard Prince Henry wears a hair shirt next to his skin, and I suppose the meager fare and the shirt are part of something God demands, though I don't understand why the Holy One would make someone a prince and then not let him enjoy it.

If I were a princess, I would have a huge palace. Perhaps if Prince Henry had a wife, she would insist on it. It seems odd he isn't married, and I think he must miss having sons, since he seems partial to several of the young squires who attend him. A few go with so little protocol into the most private recesses of the palace that it seems as if it is their home as much as his.

My father told me that Henry chose a life of chastity as a young man, and he has never known a woman. He's the head of the religious fraternity known as the Order of Christ, and though he hasn't taken vows, he thinks he should set a good example by being chaste like the others. It would be rather pleasant to see women at court though. If he had a wife and daughters, someone might notice that I have outgrown all my dresses and need new shoes. As it is, I am invisible at my father's side.

The squire ushers us out of the antechamber into the bedroom, the largest room in the palace, where the prince holds his audiences. Around a large table are a half-dozen men, most of them middle-aged like the prince, except one, Diogo Marques, who looks to be eighteen or twenty.

Prince Henry is standing in the middle of the group, poring over a roughly drawn navigator's chart. I recognize three of his sea captains as frequent visitors to Raposeira.

"Senhor Riba," the prince says. "Show us what you have, even if it isn't finished." I point to Prince Henry, then to my eyes, then to the leather case where my father stores his work. He pulls out his new chart and lays it on the table.

"Our latest ships went a hundred leagues beyond Cape Bojador and still haven't found the mouth of the Gold River," Prince Henry says, smoothing down the curling edges of the vellum. "It must be there. We have it on good authority in our sourcebooks." My father has drawn the north and west coasts of Africa, including a river known as the Gold, which extends deep into the continent below Cape Bojador. Near the middle, it parts around a huge island Papa has labeled Insula Palola, a place some travelers' accounts say is rich with gold.

Prince Henry's face is long and square. Green eyes look out from under a broad-brimmed, velvet hat from which a few curls, gray at the temples, have escaped. His most notable feature is his hands. His fingers are thin and fragile for a man, and his nails are always well trimmed. He tents his fingers when he is lost in thought and touches his palms together in a single light clap when he has thought of something that excites him.

He is looking at the blank bottom of my father's new map, devoid of anything but a rough outline to the south, representing the unknown reaches of the coast of Guinea, as the area below Cape Bojador is called. After running his finger off the lower edge of my father's chart, the prince traces a straight line to the east. As he turns north and comes back onto the chart, he stops and taps his finger. "We should try to round Guinea—it cannot be much farther south than we have already gone."

He makes a semicircle inland to indicate a large bay whose top is just below where my father has painted Egypt. "The Sinus Ethiopicus," Prince Henry says. "I don't understand why none of the Saharan traders has heard of a bay that is supposed to be as big as a sea."

He looks at the group as if someone might have an explanation. "Perhaps there is no such place," one of the men replies. "The traveler who described it has been wrong before. Some people doubt he visited many of the places he wrote about."

"Perhaps," Henry says. "But the Saharan traders' camels are laden with gold, and they get it from somewhere."

"Not from the sand," another says, "unless they have greater alchemists than all of Christendom."

Everyone laughs, but Henry is too intent on my father's chart to hear the joke. "If the Gold River is here," he says, "we could sail almost all the way across Africa. We could set up outposts here"—he taps the farthest reach of the Gold River—"and here." His finger marks the shore of the Sinus Ethiopicus. "Connect those two by a road over land, and we will unite the coasts of Africa. With that, we will control all trade with Europe from Africa and the Indies. More than that, we will have reached the kingdom of Prester John, and together we can drive the Moors out of Africa."

Prester John, the only Christian ruler in Africa, is said to have a standing army of ten thousand men and so much wealth in his empire that his foot soldiers go into battle with swords of gold. Prince Henry wants to join forces with him against the Moors, who control North Africa and still hold Granada. It's a very good dream, but Papa tells me that until explorers find the bottom of Africa, it's best not to count on sailing around it so easily. Until Henry's men find the Gold River, it's fruitless to think of getting to Prester John that way, if indeed such a river or such a man exists. "I draw what the prince tells me to," he says, "and if he wants me to show a river that may not be there, I'll do it. But even a prince can't make something real just by putting it on a map."

I am on Chuva, staring out to sea, when I glimpse the masts of Henry's latest expedition growing tall on the horizon. I hurry back to tell my father, who sends Martim at full gallop into Raposeira with the news.

Within a few weeks, Father has a new logbook to examine, with drawings and descriptions of more than a hundred leagues of newly explored coast. The Gold River, it seems, must be pushed even farther south, and the bottom of Guinea as well.

The prince is undisturbed by this news and is not pressuring my father to finish. His attention is now focused on something else—the capture of Tangiers, a day's ride from Ceuta on the north coast of Africa. Prince Henry is famous for having captured Ceuta from the Moors, but twenty years is a long time to see no further triumph for Christendom.

He has been in Lisbon the last few months, convincing his brother, King Duarte, to attack Tangiers. Now that he has gotten royal approval, he is too busy to summon my father, and with no translating to do, I have little to occupy my time except day-dreams. These I weave into fantasies about the life I would have if I weren't an eleven-year-old girl living a solitary life on a cape at the end of the world.

When I leave the house to go riding, it takes me awhile to get used to noise. My voice sounds foreign when I greet Martim, and

Chuva's soft whinnies seem to come from another world. Then, as my ears adjust, my senses start to tingle, and I feel the heat on my skin, the wind in my hair, the soft leather reins in my hand as if I were experiencing them for the first time. Then I am gone into a world of colors, textures, and sounds, where I roam, dizzy with imagination and spilling over with all the yearnings of my heart.

Everything is music. I understand this in the drum of Chuva's hooves, the syncopated crash of waves inside sea caves, the crackle of foam as waves recede around my toes, the calls of birds on the wing. Out here in the world of the hearing, I inhabit the place music comes from, part of one great soul from which Martim, Tareyja, and their friends pull their joyful cries and pained laments as they make music outside their cottage on summer evenings.

Colors seem like living things, the spirits of ancient gods per-haps, lingering in the world like a taste on the tongue long after the food is gone. The sea, the cliffs, the beach, the point at Sagres change by the hour as if they are passing thoughts in the mind of something, someone, beyond all comprehension.

The Holy One. I have never stopped believing in him. I don't understand the idea that God wants to be worshiped one way alone, and when I feel overwhelmed by the immensity and beauty of his creation, I am glad my mother taught me to bless and praise him everywhere.

My prayers and dreams are wrapped up together, vague and contradictory. "Let me leave my mark in the world," I say to the air around me. I don't want to feel so invisible, yet I'm torn between wishing to move away from this place and wanting it to be me and I it.

I spend my days talking with lizards and birds, watching the clouds change shapes overhead, and acting out stories where I am a queen with magical powers, a warrior princess, or the only female sea captain the world has ever known.

"Looks like a storm's ahead." I hold my spyglass as I peer at the horizon, my legs planted wide on the beach to withstand the rolling waves

splashing over the bow of my caravel. "Steer away from shore!" *Cape Bojador is half a league off the port side, and I see surf breaking off shore.* "A reef! A reef! We'll be dashed to pieces." *I leap below deck to take the tiller and use my powerful arms to turn the boat away. I see the cowering ship hands' admiring eyes, for I am the famed Amalia of the Deep. My flowing locks whip in the wind, and my ample breasts heave inside my bodice. It's up to me to save the crew and bring the ship back, its coffers overflowing with gold—*

"What are you doing?" Diogo Marques is standing on the beach a few paces away. He's well dressed, as always, and though he is slender and not much taller than me, his shoulders look powerful. His calves, under the short, ballooning trousers and tight stockings favored at Henry's court, are strong and muscular.

"I—" My eyes fall to the ground in embarrassment. "I'm acting out a story."

"It must have been quite a tale." To my relief, his smile seems curious rather than mocking.

"Was I talking out loud?" I ask, fearing the answer.

"No, but it looked as if you had something rather fearsome to do battle with."

His light brown hair is sun streaked, and his eyes are between green and brown, like moss. They glint as if thoughts are streaming through his mind too quickly to hang on to. His cheeks are rosy, and he is pretty like a girl.

I've studied him so carefully because he is the only man at court younger than my father's age. He is being groomed as a commander and has been named captain of one of the vessels in Prince Henry's next expedition.

"I really should be getting home." Here on the beach, he seems unfamiliar and formidable.

"Perhaps I could accompany you," he says. "You live at Sagres, I believe?" He is acting as if I am a young lady, and I wish I had done a better job lacing my dress and braiding my hair before leaving the house.

If only I were a little older and didn't have a flat chest. If only my hands were milky white rather than covered with sand and calluses. But I'm just a girl who Diogo Marques would not notice if anyone else were here.

I try to behave as grown-up as I can. I keep Chuva to a trot, holding my back very straight and doing my best to look knowing and imperious. I am exhausted from the effort by the time my house is in sight.

Diogo points to the tower. "That's what I came to see," he says.

"It's hardly worth climbing the stairs. You get as good a view walking out to the point." No one but me ever risks the tiny, slick steps, and I do so only when I am a captive princess or a witch brewing powerful spells from atop my domain.

"I've been told that," Diogo says, "but I thought I might see if the prince should post a lookout here. It's not the best vantage point to watch for the Moors, but then again, we haven't been about to go to war until now."

We reach the stables, and Martim helps me down. "Thank you for the pleasant company," Diogo says, setting off without another word. I watch his silhouette in the tower as he takes in the sea and sky, and when he comes down, I run quickly for home so he won't know I have been watching him.

For the next few days, I stay close to the house, not wanting to miss Diogo if he comes for another visit. Then, just when I am about to shake away the fuzz in my head by taking a long ride on Chuva, I see a horse and rider go past our window. I jump up, spilling the contents of a cup of water on the front of my dress. I massage the spot until the moisture spreads enough not to be visible and make what I hope looks like a casual exit from the house.

I see Diogo inside the tower. The excitement is too much for me, and before I can stop myself, I have climbed the steps and am standing next to him. "What are you doing?" I ask, realizing to my chagrin how obvious the answer is.

"Prince Henry said to leave this here," Diogo says, gesturing to the looking glass he is mounting. "He's sent for a more powerful one for the harbor. He said that since there's not much to do out here, perhaps your father could be a sentry."

My father could never handle the tower steps, and I am stunned that the prince would suggest it. It's disrespectful, as if he doesn't understand my father's gifts and assumes any task would be suitable. I say nothing, determined that if my father is assigned this new duty, I will handle it myself, and no one at the palace will ever have to know.

Diogo looks through the glass, pointing it here and there. "Would you like to look?" he asks.

I squint into the eyepiece. Though the horizon is empty, white-caps are visible far into the ocean, and if a boat were to sail into view, I would see the color of the sailors' caps before I could see the ship at all with my unaided eye. I turn to say something and am startled that his face is close to mine. "It's quite good, isn't it?" he says, backing away. "At sea, it's how we sight land."

"If the Moors come, we will have plenty of time to prepare for them," I say, trying to sound calm after having been so close to him.

He smiles. "We'll send you to that beach to lead the battle."

Embarrassed, I murmur something about Papa needing me and head down the stairs, taking pains not to tumble to the bottom in a heap.

༄

I spend hours watching the horizon through Diogo's spyglass, wanting to be the first to spot a Moorish invasion. I spend as much time looking down the road toward Raposeira, to see if Diogo might be coming to check on his spyglass.

It's been more than a month since he was last here. At Raposeira, the talk is of Henry's imminent departure for Lisbon, to lead an army massing for the assault on Tangiers. The idea of a lookout seems to have been forgotten, but nonetheless, I come up here every morning and again before sunset in hopes of sighting the Moors on the horizon.

Diogo will be captain of one of the expedition's ships. No one knows how long they will be gone, but it's the beginning of August now, and since Tangiers is only a few days' journey by sea, everyone hopes for a triumphant return by the end of September.

I spend much of my time practicing being grown-up, hoping that my body will go along, and that by the time Diogo returns, I will have budded into a young woman. We have one silver tray in the cottage, and I take it into my room to look at my reflection. I turn my head from side to side to see how I might look if I were Diogo's true love, awaiting his victorious return.

I put down the tray. "Stop it," I whisper.

Susana has a husband, a little boy, and another child on the way. Luisa is only eight, but from Susana's letters, it sounds as if she has settled on becoming a nun. I won't be able to leave my father as long as he lives, since someone must take care of him.

My cheeks flush with anger at the unfairness of being the only one who won't get to choose, but I don't want to leave Papa anyway. I love him. He's my responsibility. I wanted him all to myself, and that is exactly what I got. I return the silver tray to the cupboard, vowing not to take it out again.

VALENCIA 1492

I remember the reflection I pored over that summer at Sagres. At the gawky age of eleven, I could not see much to be positive about, and I had to admit defeat about blooming overnight. The loose hair constantly around my face made me look unkempt, and my eyes were a mix of colors adding up to an unremarkable shade of brown. In the distortions of the silver tray, my mouth seemed too small and my nose comically large.

I was alone at the end of the world, except for Martim and Tareyja, who were too old and too busy to play, and Papa, who was too idle to be happy company and looking older by the month. The palace at Raposeira might just as well have been boarded up after Prince Henry left for Tangiers. I settled into the routine of spending mornings with Papa before going off for long rides on Chuva.

As the days grew shorter, the word reaching us from Tangiers worsened. The Portuguese troops were poorly supplied and too few for a successful assault, and in early October, Prince Henry was forced to sign terms of capitulation, cede the fortress at Ceuta he had won from the Moors in his youth, and send his army home. Nevertheless, when King Duarte died the next year, the blame for the debacle at Tangiers was shifted by Prince Henry's minions onto the dead king's shoulders, and the disgraced prince emerged again to wave the flag for Portugal's rising greatness in the world.

Henry the Navigator. How little I understood his secrets at the time!

I go to the window and see no signs of life except a scrawny dog sniffing at garbage in an alley. Even looters of Jewish property need a break from the pounding sun. By increments too small to notice, the room has become suffocating, and I stay by the window hoping to catch even the smallest hint of a breeze. In the distance, I hear the slow roll of thunder, and the street darkens for a moment as a cloud passes across the sun.

Perhaps this day will end in rain—welcome except for those like me, whose armful of remaining possessions will be soaked as we make our way out of Spain. May it ruin everything stolen from this house. May torrents sweep through Spain washing away everything, making us the Noahs and Torquemada and his army of benighted souls the victims of God's wrath.

Everything but the atlas. I cannot bear the thought. Sitting down,

I pick it up before succumbing to a listlessness so great I can't make the effort to open it. Instead, I gaze at the floor and listen for even the smallest sounds, relishing a silence as deep as I remember at Sagres during those rare times the wind died. I remember my last days there, the faint crack of surf against the cliffs, the nicker of horses in the corral. The muted sound of Martim and Tareyja's voices drift through the air, blending with the soft scratches of father's quills, and the clicks and taps of his brushes...

SAGRES 1438

Papa finishes wrapping his pens and sets them into a woven basket next to his inks and pigments. His maps and charts are safely rolled inside their stiff leather cases while his tiny pots and dishes dry after Tareyja's washing.

My belongings are packed and we are waiting now for the escort that will take us away from Sagres. It is August, shortly before my twelfth birthday, and Prince Henry has been back in Raposeira for a little over two months.

"It's different now," Papa signed to me one night when I grew tearful, thinking his moodiness was caused by discontent with me. "He's not the man he was before he went to Tangiers."

Defeat has made the corners of Henry's mouth surly and drooped his eyebrows into a permanent scowl. There's no mention of new military crusades against the Moors, though his hatred of the infidels makes spittle fly whenever he speaks of them. Now all the talk is of Guinea and the opportunities for profit wasted in the past by his strategy of going farther south rather than bringing back more from the areas already explored. He is determined not to allow Guinea's wealth to fall into the hands of people despised by God. Every coin that Guinea can put in Portugal's coffers will be his answer to the Moors and to his critics at Duarte's court.

As usual, I am too wrapped up in my own world to pay much notice of Papa's growing unease at court. He does not inform me when he sends a letter to Prince Henry asking to be relieved of his role as mapmaker, but within a few days, he is summoned to discuss the request, and I go with him to interpret.

Prince Henry does not press Papa to change his mind. It will be good, he says, to have a younger man who can go along on the voyages and create notebooks and sketches on the spot. We make a dejected journey back to Sagres, and only after supper do I broach the subject hanging heavy in the air.

"Papa, why did you want to leave?"

Papa's face clouds. "All the prince talks about is—" He pauses to think of a sign before reaching for the wax tablet to write the word "slaves."

Slaves? I know Prince Henry gave away the first few Africans his commanders brought back, but I can't imagine what he would do if he had more. Where would he keep them and what would they do?

"Slaves at Raposeira?" I sign, knitting my eyebrows to show confusion.

Papa makes a circle to signify everywhere. He picks up the tablet again, because we don't have a vocabulary for such things. "Thousands. To sell. For profit."

"Why would they come?"

"They are captured and brought in chains."

I smooth out the wax, but I don't know what to say. It's one thing to enslave captives after a battle—everyone does that—but to steal them from their homes? "That's wrong," I sign, adding an angry downturn of my mouth for emphasis.

He nods agreement. "I don't want to help him," he signs. "I told him I wanted to finish my new atlas and then take no more work. I told him I was getting old, and God knows that's true too." His eyes cloud, and he reaches down to rub the knee that has given him a decided limp in the last few months.

Several weeks later, we are spending our last hours at Sagres. Papa will finish his atlas at King Duarte's court in Lisbon. It will be a gift from Henry to his brother, and after it is done, the famed mapmaker Vicente Riba will retire at the court's expense, in honor of his service.

Chuva is trotting around the corral as if she knows something is about to happen. A cart sits to one side, ready for the draft mules coming up from Raposeira. I go up in the tower to see if the party is on the road, and suddenly I comprehend that I am seeing the ocean from Sagres for the last time. I want to rush down and go to my beach, to every spot I love, but how could I say good-bye? Overwhelmed, I begin to sob, not bothering to wipe my tears.

I see the cloud of dust on the road from Raposeira, and I go down to tell Martim to saddle our horses. Tareyja has to be coaxed out of the house to see us off, and I can tell she has been crying. I bury my head in her ample breasts and let her rock me in her arms until the horses come down our road. Then, because the sun is past its apex and we have little time to linger, I get on Chuva, and in a matter of minutes, we are headed down the path away from Sagres. I don't look back—can't look back—for fear I might shatter with grief.

5

SINTRA 1438

We are not the only travelers to Lisbon that summer. Nearing the city, we hear rumors of people dying of plague in cities to the north, and on the outskirts of Setúbal, we see columns of people leaving the city. "Don't go in," they tell us. A man points to the haze on the skyline behind the city. "They're burning corpses. The cemeteries can't keep up with the dead."

One of our guards is sent ahead. He tells us that no one in Lisbon has fallen ill, but as a precaution, we will make our way west of the city to the king's summer palace at Sintra.

I toss that night on a straw mattress in the sweltering attic of an inn whose windows are sealed tight to keep out the disease. The rats scurrying across the roof sound as big as squirrels, and the droppings on the floor make my heart pound at the thought that they have a way of getting in. The vision of their yellow teeth, beady eyes, and wormlike tails is so unnerving that I sleep the rest of the night in a chair with my feet curled up so they can't run across my toes.

The ferries across the Tagus River are full of people escaping from Lisbon, and we skirt the riverbank, hoping we can find a boatman to ferry us across farther downstream. By nightfall, we have found only a deserted farmhouse, where we devour a bottle of wine, half a round of cheese, and a few dry sausages we find in the larder. The next day, we leave a few coins to reassure ourselves that the owners must be briefly away rather than lying dead some-where of the plague.

East of the fishing villages at the mouth of the Tagus River, we see a family huddled by the side of the road. The woman is slumped in her husband's arms, while next to them a small girl holds a crying baby. The man's shirt has been torn away, revealing horrible black swellings on his neck and back. His eyes are haunted and wracked with pain. His wife turns to me, and I see a bloody froth escaping at the corner of her mouth.

Our guards cry out in horror and send their horses at a gallop. I call out after them to stop. How can we leave children there, with their parents dying? My father's expression is a mix of revulsion, fear, and grief. He makes a cutting motion across his throat and gestures to me to follow as he gallops away behind the guards.

He is right, I know. Taking the children with us will not save them, and I can't comfort them without dooming all of us. Still, I see the little girl's terrified eyes and hear the baby's wails for hours.

The disease has killed several in the next village we reach, and those who have been spared are at the cemetery burying the dead. One old sailor scoffs, saying he has survived so many plagues that God must plan to drown him instead, though he is certainly taking his time about it. Our guards tell him that if God isn't brewing up a storm to remedy the oversight right away, they will pay him to take my father and me as close to Sintra as his boat can manage. He casts a momentary glance at the horizon and scans the sky over-head. Then he holds out his hand, rubbing his fingers together to ask for payment.

In minutes, I watch from the boat as our guards, belongings, and horses recede on the distant shore. The rest of our party will find a way to get across the river and bring everything to us at the palace. We have nothing but ourselves, some food and water, and Papa's map case. The fisherman will leave us on the coast below Sintra, and we will have to find our way from there using prayer and our own two feet.

We sleep that night on the other side of the Tagus. Lights from a fort blaze on the promontory above us, but the abandoned fishing hut we find is safer than risking human contact. The following morning, the old man roasts fish over a driftwood fire. He looks at the dark clouds out to sea and decides he can't risk taking us around the point because the windward coast will get the worst of the coming weather.

He points toward steep hills so thick with trees they look more black than green. "Sintra is up there," he says. "You can walk from here, but it would be better to take the coast path until you come to a village where the road goes up the other side of the mountains. It's an easy climb from there." With a loud hacking cough, he brings up thick phlegm that he spits onto the sand. "You can stay there tonight, and get to Sintra tomorrow."

"Tomorrow?" I say, casting a glance at my father. I've noticed how weak he is getting, and I assumed we would be put ashore close to the palace.

"I'm just telling you what people who live around here would do." He shrugs. "Go whatever way you want." Without another word, he readies his boat and shoves off into the surf, leaving me looking around, astonished at how alone we are in an indifferent world.

By afternoon, my father is struggling to keep going, wincing whenever he moves his knee. Finally we see a village where wisps of smoke rise from chimneys and laborers toil in the fields. Although both are signs that life is going on without the plague, I know not to expect a warm welcome. For all they know, we are carrying the disease to them.

At the first house, a woman tells us she has no room and shuts the door, but a passing neighbor sees our worried faces as we turn away.

"I'm a Christian," she says, "not like some who just say they are." She glances at the shut door behind us. "Mistreat a stranger and you turn away the Lord himself." She gestures toward a distant farmhouse. "I have a barn you can sleep in. We'll get some bread in both of you right away and a cup of milk from our goats, and later you can eat supper with us. It's not much, but with a little wine, it will get your strength back."

I feel the burdens of the day lift and my fears vanish. "Thank you," I say.

"We do what we can for Our Lord's sake, don't we?" she says. I feel the phantom outline of the crucifix I took off as we left Sevilla and never wore again, and I pretend I did not hear her.

The woman's husband, Manuel, is taking vegetables to Sintra the following morning. He lets Papa ride in the cart to rest his aching bones and blistered feet. I am tired too, but far too excited to sit still, so I walk alongside. "Is that where we're going?" I point to a mist-shrouded peak, where square-notched watchtowers look down to the sea.

"Praise God, no. We don't go that high," Manuel replies. "It's a ruined Moorish fort. No one lives up there—except for a few Jews when the king decided he didn't want them in Sintra."

"Jews?" My heart jumps in my chest. "Jews live up there?"

Manuel whacks the mule with his switch. "Don't know. They have houses in town again, that's all I heard. Just don't send them to our village, my wife and I say." He points to a tree-covered hill. "You see those chimneys sticking up? That's where we're going." Two white chimneys shaped like inverted funnels protrude above the trees. We're almost there, and the man's troubling words about Jews vanish from my mind.

We pass the first houses on the edge of Sintra and continue along the ridge that leads from one cluster of buildings to another until we reach the main square. Manuel leaves us in front of the royal palace and goes around to the kitchen entrance, while I swallow deeply and walk toward the uniformed guards standing at the bottom of the wide stairs.

A guard orders me to halt. "No visitors allowed," he says, "on account of disease." My heart sinks. Have we come all this way only to be told we aren't welcome?

I set my shoulders and spend my last bit of strength. "This man is Vicente Riba," I say, "from the greatest mapmaking family in Spain. We've come from Prince Henry's court at Raposeira, by appointment to the king. Our belongings are coming with the rest of our party. We came on foot as quickly as we could." I hesitate. "On account of how sick they are in Lisbon."

"Ah, that's the problem," the guard says. "No one enters, for fear they will bring the mortality with them."

My fatigue gives way to rage. "What are we supposed to do? Wait outside until we can prove we aren't sick? Or until we are?" I point an accusing finger at the guard. "What would the king say about that?"

The guard shifts from foot to foot, and I press my advantage. I give him a smile I hope is charming, despite my disheveled appearance. "We don't want to bring the mortality inside either. Isn't there somewhere we can stay for a few days until—" I don't want to acknowledge that if we do fall ill, we will be herded like livestock at the end of a stick to find a place outside the city to die.

The guard's face is troubled. Finally he speaks. "I suppose you'd best come along."

Two sleeping pallets and a chamber pot are brought into a gardener's shed built into the wall at one side of the palace grounds, and we settle in amid the rakes and shovels. The garden is bound on three sides by walls and on the fourth by the palace itself. I can see people looking out, so we spend the next few days in plain view, to make sure they can see we have not fallen ill.

I strike up one-sided conversations with the marble sea goddess who stands at the center of the garden. Symmetrical paths converge on the statue from all directions, and I go up and down each one, touching heel to toe, until I have walked them all. Because the garden is small, I can do this in a few minutes, and it does little to ease my boredom.

Our good health soon wins us a reprieve. How strange it is, after days on a dirt floor in a tiny shed, to step into the sparkling rooms of the king's summer palace and see high ceilings adorned with elaborate candelabras, tapestried walls, and furniture upholstered in fine damask and brocade. Our rooms look fit for the king himself, although they are probably the most modest in the palace.

No one seems to notice we are here, and we pass the first day exploring the ground floor and reading books from King Duarte's library. When our evening meal is brought to our quarters, we learn the king is not in residence and only a few servants remain. The maid tells us that shortly after we took up residence in the shed, plague broke out in the little town where we had slept the night before our arrival. At the news, the king left in a panic for the Convento de Cristo at Tomar. "He feels safer among all those religious folks, I suppose," she says, "although praying hasn't helped anyone that I can see."

Alarming news comes a few days later that plague has breached the walls of the monastery at Tomar. On the ninth of September, word arrives that the king is dead. "What will happen to us?" I ask Papa, but he doesn't know. The heir to the throne of Portugal is Duarte's son Afonso, but he is only six years old.

Perhaps my father won't have a position after all. Will we have to go live with Susana in Sevilla? Will Prince Henry let us return to Sagres? Could we find a little house here in Sintra and exist like mice on whatever money Papa has?

My mind whirls for a few days. Then, with great trepidation, my father breaks the seal on a letter that has come from Duarte's widow, Eleanor of Aragon. As Afonso's mother, she has been named regent.

"I understand you have been waiting at Sintra," she writes from Tomar, "and I regret the inconvenience these difficult times may have caused. Rest assured of your position at court, for you have a strong advocate among my husband's advisers. Please stay at Sintra until the danger is gone, at which time we will send for you."

We have an unexpected friend at court and Eleanor's permission to stay. I can stop being afraid.

6

The Castle of São Jorge at Lisbon is bursting with children. King
Duarte left behind five, as well as a pregnant wife. His brother Pedro
and his family have arrived, and that's another three boys and three
girls. Another brother, João, has settled in with his three daughters.
His oldest, Elizabeth, is eleven, just two years younger than I am.

All told, there are five young princes and ten princesses here,
the rest of whom are too old or young to matter to me. I've never
really had a friend before, and I don't think Elizabeth has either,
unless her silly nine-year-old sister Beatriz counts.

Eleanor sent for us when she returned to Lisbon after Duarte's
death, and since then, Papa has worked slowly on his atlas. Our
journey, now five months in the past, took a great toll on him. He
tires easily, spending much of his day dozing in his study or reading in the royal library. I keep him company in the morning, and
then, after he has his midday dinner, I am free for the rest of the
day, which I spend in the royal apartments where Pedro and João's
families live.

There are three worlds in the palace, one for the men, another
for the women, and a third for the children. I don't know much
about what the men do, but the women visit Eleanor when she is
not busy with affairs of state and make the rounds of each other's
quarters. There they are entertained by bards and musicians, read
aloud, and gossip constantly.

The children have their own nursery, except for Elizabeth and Beatriz, who are old enough to have a separate apartment. Everyone attends morning mass in the royal chapel, and then all but the youngest spend a few hours with tutors learning Latin, religion, literature, and science before dinner at midday. All the children take this meal together, with their governesses standing over them, because even rules for breaking bread are important matters for the princes and princesses of the realm.

Afternoons are for outings in good weather, as well as music and dancing lessons, fencing practice for the boys and embroidery for the girls. Late in the day, they all pay a visit to their mother, after which they return to the nursery for supper, prayers, and bed.

The women treat me like a poor relation, welcome to join in whatever Elizabeth and Beatriz are doing, as long as I know my place. Perhaps the ladies pity me. My father is so reclusive, it must be easy to forget that I am not an orphan.

I like my two worlds—my silent cocoon as Papa's companion and my busy life as Elizabeth's best friend. Life in Sevilla as Mama's conspirator was intimate and cozy, and with Papa in our little cottage at Sagres, it was solid and secure. Now everything seems as light and airy as the dancers and jugglers who entertain us in the evenings, as sparkling as the women's jeweled crowns in the reflected torchlight of the banquet hall.

And as fleeting. Elizabeth is here in Lisbon because of the rancor among the nobility toward Eleanor, who is from Aragon and does not speak Portuguese well or know the customs of this land. At twenty-five, she is young for a regent, even if she does have nine children and her belly is swollen with another. She married at twelve and had a baby almost every year, though several died as infants. João, Elizabeth's father, is here to support his brother Pedro's bid to replace Eleanor. He has summoned a meeting of the Cortes, the national assembly, to end the dispute. If Pedro becomes regent, Eleanor will return to Aragon, Elizabeth will leave for home, and I will stay behind with Papa.

Elizabeth and I are tired of the gossip in the women's quarters, so we spend our free time in the palace gardens acting out stories with her tagalong sister Beatriz. For her birthday, Elizabeth received a copy of *Amadis of Gaul*, Portugal's greatest epic poem, and as we read, we dramatize our favorite scenes.

Today, Elizabeth puts her hand to her heart and flutters her eyelids as I walk through a break in a manicured hedge and stride toward where she stands on narrow stone steps leading up to the palace ramparts. Never mind that I am wearing a dress—for the moment, I am Perión, the King of Gaul, and Elizabeth is the beautiful princess Elisena. I am tall and bony enough to play the men's roles, and since they do more interesting things than swoon, I don't mind. As usual, Beatriz is sulking in her perpetual role as the servant.

Amid the squawks of the parrots and macaws roaming the palace gardens, Elizabeth drops a ring from her perch on the stairs. I pick it up, and she bends with a graceful sweep of her arm to take it from my outstretched hand. "Thank you, King Perión," she says in a breathy voice.

"It shall not be the last task I do for you," I say, lowering my voice to a manly pitch as I bend my knee to the ground. "All my life will be spent in your service."

I hear the sound of a throat clearing behind me and look up to see several of Pedro's advisers looking at us. One of them, a portly, full-bearded man in his thirties, is dressed differently from the others. His cloak is well-cut from a plain but lustrous fabric, and he's wearing a black skull cap. Solemn brown eyes look out at me from below dark brows so thick they intrude on the tops of his eyelids.

I know who he is—Judah Abravanel, our advocate after Duarte's death. The Cresques family's mapmaking is a source of pride for Jews, and even if my father is a converso who no longer bears the family name, I am confident we will not be sent away as long as Don Abravanel has any influence at court.

I am embarrassed to be acting so silly. I shake off the dirt that clings to my skirt and stare at the ground. "We were just playing a game," I say.

"And an excellent one at that, it would seem," one of the men replies.

Something about the way Judah Abravanel looks at me pierces to my core, as if he knows all my secrets. I look back and see he is still watching as Elizabeth makes an embarrassed withdrawal and drags her sister and me back inside the palace.

⁓

That night, I lie awake, reviewing what I know about the intense man in the garden. I interpret for my father when they meet privately, and I know that Don Abravanel was one of the late King Duarte's most important advisers, raising money and lending his own treasure to help finance Henry's expeditions and the failed military campaign in Tangiers. As a reward, Don Abravanel is a wealthy man, granted by the king a house and land in the nearby town of Queluz.

He is proud of my father's new work, accurate far into Africa and more detailed to the east than any atlas before it. "We should limit ourselves to what we actually find," he said one day, tapping the side of his head and looking at me. "Knowledge. That's the key to conquering fear. And fear is the greatest enemy of man."

Judah Abravanel has a home where they light candles, where they sing special songs on Shabbat afternoons—precious things I have lost. Christians keep their distance from Jews on the streets, but I always try to pass as close as I can, hoping to catch their words. Often I know they are near before I see them, as if a force in the air connects us.

I know why I can't get my mind off him. I have drifted too far and too long from what my mother taught me. I am a thirteen-year-old girl who lives in a Christian world. I should accept that. Still, I find no rest until the night has crept all the way to dawn.

∽

"'The Child of the Sea remained fifteen days in that castle, where the damsel tended to his wounds, and then, though they were hardly healed, he departed.'" Elizabeth traces her fingers over the words in *Amadis of Gaul.*

"He was very brave," Beatriz says solemnly.

"But such things have to be done," Elizabeth says. "If a maiden needs to be avenged, any good knight is obliged to do it." Her eyes drift away dreamily. "Even if it costs him his life."

I look out the window. It's a week after Easter, and I am in the private compartment of one of the royal barges, heading up the Tagus River toward the Convento de Cristo at Tomar. The day is warm, and the curtains flutter as the scent of blossoms wafts around us. The oars creak as twenty or more rowers strain against the current, but the only other sounds are the riotous calls of birds and the occasional buzz of a dragonfly that has left the riverbank to investigate the brightly colored barge.

So much has changed in the two weeks since Eleanor had her baby. People had been waiting to see if it was a boy, for if so, he would be second in line to the throne, and Eleanor would be harder to get rid of. Luckily it was a girl, baptized Juana, and quickly forgotten.

Only a few days later, Pedro became the new regent, appearing with great fanfare next to Prince Afonso for Easter mass in the cathedral. Now Pedro and Elizabeth's father João are taking Afonso for a ceremonial stay at the headquarters of Prince Henry's Order of Christ at Tomar, and their families are coming with them.

Elizabeth hands the book to her sister. "'He thought of his lost love,'" Beatriz reads, "'and said to himself, "Ah, child without lands and without lineage, how dare thou fix thy heart upon her who excels all others in goodness, beauty, and parentage? I, who know not who I am, must die without declaring my love."'"

Elizabeth sighs. "Wouldn't it be nice to be loved like that?" She lies back on the ornate upholstered couch on which she has been lounging for the last hour while Beatriz and I sit in stiff and uncomfortable matching chairs. She lifts her hand, dangling her wrist as if it were a delicate wisp of gossamer. "Take this handkerchief, brave knight! It has rested against my breast all these years, waiting for someone worthy of my love."

Her face grows somber and she sits up. "I wish I lived then."

"If you lived then, you'd be dead," Beatriz replies, a bit too cheerfully.

"I might as well be dead now." Her voice is suddenly hollow. Elizabeth can be like that, full of cheer one moment and despondent the next. "I'll end up betrothed to some little boy in an awful place where they don't speak Portuguese. Or some old man who wants a young bride to make a son because he's about ready to die and only has daughters."

The barge is slowing to a stop, and I hear voices on the riverbank. I look out the window and see saddled horses. One man waiting for our party turns toward our barge as we step on the dock. My jaw drops. Diogo Marques? Here? Elizabeth's eyes dart between Diogo and me. My cheeks are so hot they must be red as coals. I've given myself away, I realize with a sinking heart.

Diogo's expression eventually shows that he recognizes me as the girl who roamed Sagres with hair as wild as her horse's mane and hands and feet caked with beach sand. After months of acting out fantasies about knights and maidens, part of me believes he should fly to my side and cover my hand with kisses, but instead, he turns away without acknowledging me, and I wonder which of the two things, Diogo's indifference or Elizabeth's crazy ideas about love, will be the cause of more unhappy moments for me at Tomar.

Elizabeth conspires ceaselessly to maneuver me where I am likely to run into Diogo. I don't tell her that I see him more often than she knows, for he comes every few days to talk with my father about the new atlas. The western coast of Africa bulges out farther than in previous maps, before dipping sharply to the east. Along the coast, my father has used sailors' charts to fill in dozens of place names, add islands, and draw bays and inlets on the shoreline.

The interior is mostly blank, and the southern coast of Africa remains a rough line, but Cape Verde and Cape Rosso are marked, as are the Senegal and Gambia Rivers, neither of which seems to have an island of gold. Papa has ended these rivers not far from the coast, but not for long. Diogo's new commission is to go upstream to see what might be of value there.

"What is of value to me," Papa says, "is information." Diogo admires my father for that, and Papa in return likes the dashing young mariner who shows such interest in his work. Diogo is polite to me but no more, asking my opinion about things like the Gold River, Prester John, and the true length of the African coast. "You know as much as anyone else, Senhorita Riba," he says. That's what he calls me, making me feel so grown-up that I have to keep myself from looking down ruefully that I still do not have the body to match.

My breasts do stick out a little, finally, and my hips are less bony than they used to be, but I am not beautiful and I am already too tall. Elizabeth's maids can make my hair and her castoff clothing look quite nice, but even after they've done their best, I am hardly worth singling out.

The royal quarters are small at Tomar, and most of the party, including Papa and me, are lodged at the bottom of the hill. On this day, Diogo and I leave my father at the same time for the palace, I to join the princesses and Diogo to meet with the men.

We walk in silence through an arched gateway that opens onto the palace grounds. "I must leave you here," Diogo says, putting one foot forward and keeping his leg straight as he bows to take my wrist. Time whirls as he brings my hand to his lips. I feel a pleasant stab in my belly, and my head spins with astonishment as I watch him disappear down the walk.

He kissed my hand! My heart pounds so furiously I wonder why the laces on my bodice don't pop. I look up at the windows of the royal apartments, hoping Elizabeth is watching, before deciding I am glad she isn't. I want to keep this moment to myself, rather than giving it to her and Beatriz, like another bauble to play with as they wish.

༄

I go up the hill every day to visit Elizabeth and Beatriz, but there's still plenty of time to explore Tomar by myself. One day, I notice a doorway with a menorah carved above it. Though I play an endless game of fetch with a stray dog, waiting for someone to go in or out, eventually I give up. The next day and the next I walk by, but still see no one.

The afternoon shadows are growing long one Friday when, after a visit with the princesses, I make my daily trip down that street. My heart jumps to see a man go inside. I hurry to the door and hear the sound of men's voices. "Shema, Isroel," the men chant, and memories of my mother lodge painfully in my throat. I don't know how long I stand there, but eventually the door opens, and two men go out.

Judah Abravanel sees me immediately and stops. "Shabbat shalom," he says to the other man, who heads down the street.

He sees tears welling in my eyes. "A wish for Sabbath peace makes you cry?" He means it as a joke, but I have to fight the urge to blurt out how much I miss hearing those words. His gaze is as intense as it was in the garden when he saw me acting out stories with Elizabeth and Beatriz.

"I should go," I say.

He knows why I am there. "Would you like to look inside?" he asks. "This is the synagogue of Tomar, humble as it is."

"Yes," I whisper. "Yes, I would."

"I think it's best if you stand in the doorway and look only for a moment. It would be unwise for you to appear too interested."

I take in the small, square room, no more than eight paces across. A few men talk among themselves, but otherwise it is deserted. In the middle is a raised wooden platform with a rail around it and a table in the center.

"That's the tebah," Judah tells me. "It's where we read from the Law." He gestures to a niche in one wall, covered by a curtain. "That's the Aron Kodesh, the Holy Ark, where we keep the Torah scrolls." He points to four evenly spaced pillars holding up an unadorned stucco ceiling. "You see those? They're for the four matriarchs—Sarah, Rebecca, Leah, and Rachel. The pillars remind us that women enable men to become all we are capable of."

"Do you have a family?" I blurt out.

His face lights up. "A wonderful family in Queluz. My wife and I have two girls and a baby boy."

"You must be proud to have a son."

He looks at me quizzically. "I am proud of all my children."

We start up the street. "Don't let this quiet little town fool you, Senhorita Riba," Judah says. "People have an eye out for conversos who seem too interested in Jews. I wouldn't come up this street again, if I were you." He stops at the corner and bows politely. "The loss will be mine." Without a word, he turns down the cobbled street and disappears around a corner.

"Esteemed Senhorita Riba," Elizabeth reads aloud. "I would be most grateful if you could arrange an opportunity to meet with your father again before my departure for Lisbon." She stares at me. "Again?"

Diogo left a week ago, and I have forgotten I slipped his note into *Amadis of Gaul* to hold my place. "He met with my father a few times," I say with a shrug.

"Did he kiss you?" Beatriz asks. "Did he put his lips to yours in a passionate embrace?" The question is so fanciful, I wonder for a moment what strange creature would ask it.

"Of course not!" I reply.

"Well, that's disappointing," Elizabeth says, in a tone that implies such failure is entirely my fault.

To distract her, I pick up where we left off. "'At the entrance of the valley, a Squire met them, and said, "Sir Knight, you pass not on unless you confess the mistress of yonder knight to be fairer than your own."'"

Elizabeth opens her eyes and looks at me. "We must get Diogo to fight like that for you. It doesn't matter that you aren't beautiful."

"And it's even better that you can't marry him," Beatriz adds.

"Much better," Elizabeth says. "This way, he can be tormented."

I curl my lip with indignant scorn. "That's just silly."

Elizabeth's face clouds, and she falls silent. I see the faraway look that comes over her sometimes, and I brace for a change in her mood. "Fine," she says in a clipped voice.

Beatriz and I exchange glances. It's just like Elizabeth to go from giggles to curling up around herself as if she wants to disappear. Her eyes seem blank and distant as I continue to read, but eventually she lifts her drooping head. "It isn't about beauty, it's about love." Her voice is flat, as if she were reciting the Hail Mary for the thousandth time.

"Angriote has to die now," says Beatriz. "He has no other choice."

I read on. "'"Your Lady will be ungrateful if she acknowledges not thy pains in her defense," quoth Amadis. "I swear to do all I can on your behalf."'"

Revived by disbelief, Elizabeth sits up. "Help an opponent? Angriote won't think Amadis is much of a knight if he's going to do that."

Beatriz nods somberly. "He should have killed him while he could."

I'm impressed with Amadis, though it's best not to argue with the princesses. What would Diogo do? I think for a moment but set those thoughts aside, because I have no way to know.

What would Judah Abravanel do? That, I tell myself, is far more worth pondering.

7

LISBON 1439

By late June, the court has drifted west to Sintra, where sea air and lush forests create a haven away from the Lisbon summer. Elizabeth and Beatriz are no longer in residence at court because their family's lands are nearby, but they come and go between their home and Sintra when the mood strikes them.

I miss Elizabeth, but not too much. Her moods go from laughter to gloom so deep it seems like death then back again, and I get tired of guessing which person she will be. Once Beatriz found Elizabeth in her bedchamber naked from the waist up, a dagger to her chest. Another time, the three of us climbed a tower, and she went on about how just one little jump would solve everything. Soon she was cheerful again, seeming to remember nothing of her bleak mood and exhausting me with her determination that Diogo carry me off to a life of wedded bliss. Or, better yet, die of unrequited love because he cannot have me.

Papa and I now live away from the palace. He finished the atlas while we were at Tomar, and in appreciation, Pedro gave him use of a pleasant house in Sintra, where he will live out his days at the crown's expense. I keep Papa company morning and evening and go off on my own in the afternoon. Though occasionally I ride Chuva to visit Elizabeth and Beatriz, most of the time, I prefer to be alone.

I left Sagres nearly a year ago and am almost fourteen now,

but I still marvel at how two places could be so different. On our promontory, nothing grew more than a few inches because of the incessant wind, and only plants that could worm their roots into crevices survived at all. The trees were mostly cork oaks scattered in fields, and I can't remember a time when a tree blocked my view unless I deliberately stood behind it.

Here, on the mountain slope exposed to the ocean, fog and mist hang over us, and the frequent summer rains feel as cold as winter. It's dark most of the time, like a weight I can't shake off. Even when I urge Chuva to gallop along the paths around Sintra, I don't feel airy and free the way I did on the beach at Sagres.

It's beautiful, though, like being in a bed with green blankets underneath and on top of me, from the tips of the pines to the moss covering the ground. My heart lifts when I see rays of light in a clearing, and when the fog burns away, my face turns toward the sun like the yellow sunflowers I remember in the Algarve. I yearn to run across open land, but here there's no straying from the paths, for lichen-covered fallen branches make a barrier too dense to cross.

Coming home one day, I hear the sound of hooves on the path. Judah Abravanel comes up astride a beautiful chestnut-colored horse large enough for his substantial girth. He settles into a trot beside me.

"Senhorita Riba." He gives me a deferential nod. "All alone?" He looks into the dense forest, although I don't know what he expects to see.

"Yes," I say. "I have no one to ride with."

By now, we've reined in our mounts and stopped in the middle of the path. "I've been told it's safe," I add. "Chuva wears the colors of the royal household." I reach down to stroke the side of her neck. "Don't you, girl?"

"Chuva?" Judah says.

"I named her that when I lived at Sagres. She belongs to Prince Henry, but everyone at the stables thinks of her as mine."

Chuva nickers and bobs her head, making Judah smile. "It appears Chuva agrees with the stablehands." He looks down the path. "May I accompany you?"

I had been hoping for a chance to meet again after our encounter outside the synagogue at Tomar, but since my father no longer works at court, it hasn't happened. "I'd be most pleased," I say.

"Your father is a remarkable person," Judah says as we go down the path, "and he has a daughter to match."

"Me?"

"A daughter who handles every language spoken at court and turns it into signs. I've watched you, and I think I've picked up a little." He points to his chest, to his head, and finally to Chuva. *I think Chuva…* He takes one fist and cradles it inside his other open palm before pointing to me. *Belongs to you.*

I grin. "That's very good, but can you sign it in Arabic?"

He gets my joke immediately, throwing back his head in a hearty laugh. "Signs are all languages at once, aren't they? Perhaps everyone should learn them. It might be easier for us all to get along."

I don't know what comes over me, but suddenly I am stammering in Hebrew about wanting to hear that language again. He is so startled he pulls up his horse and turns to face me. "You know Hebrew?"

I feel my face growing hot. Papa would not want me revealing this. "I'm sorry," I say. "I was just trying to impress you. You know my family are conversos."

"But perhaps you are not so converted after all."

I think for a moment I should cross myself and recite the Pater Noster to prove something to him. What kind of Jew is Abravanel anyway? Is he one of those who despises converts, or would he be happy to know someone in the Cresques family isn't entirely lost?

"You're afraid." His voice is so soft, I turn to look at him. Under his thick brows are the most compassionate eyes I have ever seen.

Though I feel tears welling, I manage to shrug. "I don't know what you mean."

He holds up his hand to cut off my nonsense. "This is too

serious a conversation to have on horseback," he replies. "Queluz is not too far from here for a good rider like you. Perhaps some Shabbat, you could point your horse in the direction of my home." He pauses. "If your father permits, of course."

My father would not permit it, and I think Don Abravanel knows that. I suspect he knows I will come anyway. "Thank you," I say, feeling like a drowning person being pulled from the sea.

When I reach Judah Abravanel's home the following Shabbat, the family is just getting up from the table after the midday meal. His wife, Simona, insists that I sit down and have some challah and lamb stew, although I ate with Papa before I left. She is as small and wiry as her husband is portly, as animated as he is calm and reserved. Their two daughters, Chana and Rahel, are beautiful girls of about ten and eight, with eyes like black olives and their mother's gleaming, dark curls. The youngest child is a moon-faced boy of two named Isaac, who watches the world with the contemplative eyes of a sage. His father holds him on his knee while he settles in to read with two men who are visiting for the day.

When Isaac fusses and Simona takes him from his father, I follow her into the bedroom, leaving the girls to play with their dolls. She lays Isaac on the bed and unties the string holding a cloth between his legs. When she takes the cloth away, I notice the flared tip of his penis, so unlike my little Abraham's soft peak of skin. With a few expert motions, she has folded a dry cloth around him and secured it with the string. "There you are," she says, standing Isaac up on the bed and holding him while he jumps up and down with a happy grin. "You won't be needing this much longer, little man."

I glance out the door. "What are the men reading?" I ask.

"The Zohar," Simona says, in a voice so offhand she must think it's obvious. Seeing my confusion, she tells me it's a book by an ancient sage, a guide to unlocking the deepest meanings of the Torah. "Can you show Amalia your teeth?"

Isaac thinks for a moment then puts his finger on a lower tooth. "Where's your nose?" He misses and grazes a nostril. "What do you say when you go to bed?" Simona asks.

"Mema," he says.

"That's shema," she tells me with a smile.

"I know," I say. "I have a little sister who said that when she was first learning. She wants to be a nun now." My eyes well up. "I had a baby brother who didn't live long enough to say it at all."

She gives me a quizzical look. "Judah told me you might come," she says. "He was surprised to hear you speak Hebrew, since anusim don't learn it."

"I taught myself when I was young," I say. "My father had some books. He's a Christian, and the books were from before. My mother taught me—" My voice catches in my throat. "Taught me the things Jews do. We—"

Simona puts Isaac down on the floor. "Go to Papa," she says, and the little boy toddles off. "Where is your mother now?" she asks softly.

"She died," I whisper. "Almost three years ago." I try to swallow the lump in my throat. "I miss her. I miss Shabbat."

The room squeezes around me, and my head feels hollow. "Would you excuse me?" I ask, not waiting for a reply.

I rush through the back door to the garden. Orderly paths lead outward from a mosaic-tiled fountain at the center. Sparrows flutter around the rippling water, filling their beaks, while a crow squawks from its perch on a stuccoed wall. The smell of roses and drying grass suffuses the air. My mind is in turmoil, and I barely sense these things as I fight the urge to heave the contents of my two dinners into some out-of-the-way spot.

I don't know what came over me. It is more than a wave of longing for my mother, for I feel that often and haven't reacted like this. Perhaps being here, I'm realizing all the candles I haven't lit, the songs I haven't sung, the blessings I haven't proclaimed. Or perhaps it is the love Simona shows her children, love that will never shine on me again.

The sparrows desert the fountain as I approach. My whole body aches and I want to fall in a heap and be gone from here, from everywhere, like a drop of water absorbed into the ground.

"Senhorita Riba?" Judah Abravanel is standing a few steps away. "My wife sent me to see if you were all right."

I dab my eyes with my sleeve. "I'm sorry," I say. "I'm not a very good guest."

"You are the guest I expected you to be." His eyes are solemn. "Does this have to do with what you started to tell me the other day?"

"I'm not sure what that was."

"Perhaps I can help. I think what you pretend to be is not who you really are." He gestures to the mosaic design in the fountain. "Like this," he says. "You might say, 'this is a fish,' or 'this is a flower,' but they're shattered pieces put together to look like what they're supposed to be."

"I am supposed to be a Jew," I tell him, surprised that I have said it aloud. "Since I lost my mother, I've been—" I think for a moment. "There hasn't been a me since she died." Before I know it, I have told him everything—the sausages, the secret mezuzah, the prick of Abraham's penis, his ritual washing at the pool, the burial of his hair inside the tiny shroud. I have been crying from the beginning, but I almost cannot get the words out between sobs as I tell him about Shabbat afternoons at my grandparents, the singing, the dancing, the wishes for a sweet week over the spices.

When I finally fall silent, Judah speaks. "Your mother was a brave woman. Sevilla dislikes its anusim, even the sincere converts, and it dislikes the false ones even more than it does the ones who remain Jews."

"I know," I say. "I saw men die."

"And more is coming, I fear. You are better off in Portugal, at least as long as Pedro is regent. After that, it will depend on what kind of man Afonso becomes."

"My sisters don't have any trouble believing in the Hanged One, but I can't. I tried for a while, but it didn't work."

"And now you can't be either a Jew or a Christian, while all around you everyone seems to care a great deal about which one everybody is."

"I think I would like to live as a Jew someday," I blurt out. "Openly, I mean."

"Your father should live his remaining days in peace. He's done everything he could to keep his family safe, and you should respect that."

"But when he's gone?" I ask. "What about then?"

"Don't do anything drastic that you can't take back."

I feel as if he has stolen something from me, but then again he doesn't know my secret. "Actually," I say, "my baptism might not count. My mother washed it away in the mikveh, and then the church records burned. Maybe I can still choose for myself."

Judah's face is grave. "There are people who would drag you to church to splash you with their water the minute they hear this. You're best off never mentioning it again."

He thinks for a moment. "The Holy One works in strange ways. Perhaps you have a different fate from what seems possible now."

Chana and Rahel run into the garden. "Papa," Chana says, her arms reaching only part way around his belly. "What's taking you so long? We've been ready to sing for hours!"

"Well, then," he says. "We won't keep you waiting any longer." The girls' laughter is like music as they lead him into the house.

VALENCIA 1492

The scent of roses warmed by the sun nudges me awake. "Is that you?" I ask, but I know it is Judah by the faint smell of cloves that was always on his breath.

As I grew into a woman at Sintra, I rode almost every Saturday afternoon to Queluz, as if I were visiting my own family. Isaac eventually pulled up his own chair to study with the men after dinner. He was a solemn child, showing none of a seven-year-old's tendency to squirm or get distracted. Chana reached her fifteenth birthday and was betrothed to a second cousin from Lisbon, and Rahel at thirteen was as lovely as a spring blossom and not far behind her sister in marriage.

The princesses remained part of my life as well, but only occasionally. Their lessons largely at an end, they spent most of their time gossiping with the ladies and attending court events. Their foolishness no longer amused me, and as I lost interest in them, they did in me. Papa was clinging to the loose threads of unraveling life. His eyes were too weak to read, so his life turned even more inward. Always small and thin, he shrank into something no more substantial than a seed drifting on a bit of fluff. His mind floated away with his body, and he showed no signs of remembering what he once had been.

And then there was Diogo. When the court was at Sintra, he visited my father frequently. Papa knew every bay and inlet on the African coast, but in time, he had trouble remembering Diogo. I thought the visits would trickle to nothing then, but they didn't.

I close my eyes, as if this can protect me from unbidden memories. The scent of cloves is fainter now. "Judah," I whisper. "Did you see it coming?"

Since I couldn't have the life I wanted, I didn't think about my future at all when I was young. I suppose that's why I couldn't see at first that a man was courting me. Diogo was a wave that began offshore as a bump in the water, and then rose to a crest, hanging for a moment before tossing me, his shocked and gasping victim, onto shore.

"Did you see it coming?" I ask again.

"Life is always coming. Best to act in the moment because it will be gone regardless of what we do." I sense him shrugging. "The woman who is reluctant to make bread because it might burn has nothing to feed her family."

"Or herself."

Judah's chuckle makes my heart glad. "And you ate burned bread as a result."

"We all do." I smile, knowing that even with all I have endured, I would willingly taste the charred and bitter to be filled again with the bliss of that sweet, soft interior, those moments in which everything seems perfect.

SINTRA 1444

On the Feast of Corpus Christi in late May, church bells ring out over Sintra as Papa and I leave church. He leans on my arm as I guide him to the edge of the crowd. He is tired from the strain of the outing, and we make our way immediately toward home.

"Senhor Riba!" Diogo is standing beside us. "May I?" He puts his arm through the crook of Papa's elbow, relieving me of the weight. "It would be my pleasure to walk you home."

"How long have you been back?" I ask.

"My ship docked a week ago, and I've been at the palace ever since."

"Did you find an island of gold?" I arch my eyebrows to show him I am teasing, and he laughs.

"In a sense. We found thousands of people, black as night. We turned back only when we ran short of supplies and the men objected to eating nothing but the monkeys and snakes the natives brought us."

We climb a staircase in the warren of tiny lanes above the square, to get to our street. "I have only a few weeks to stay in Sintra," Diogo says. "It would be a pleasure to spend time with you."

I look at him, dumbfounded. My father is standing on the step of our house waving Diogo inside. "Would you care to join us for dinner?" I ask, knowing what Papa is trying to say.

"I would be delighted," Diogo says, taking my arm as we go into the house.

Papa enjoys the talk of sea over dinner, but it tires him, and when he goes off to his room to rest, Diogo and I are alone.

"How much you have changed in the years since I saw you on the beach at Sagres," Diogo says with a tip of his chin so precise I think he may have practiced in a mirror. "You were just a little girl then."

Is he flirting? The idea seems preposterous. Diogo is a dashing young commander, sure to be favored when Prince Afonso comes of age. He'll get a share of the treasure he brings back and most likely a title and lands someday. I have scant beauty and no wealth. I don't have the charm to assist a man in gaining favor at court, and I'm only suited to the quiet life I have now.

To avoid looking at him, I busy myself stacking the dishes, but when I glance in his direction, he is staring at me. Something about his look gives me a momentary chill, but I decide it's just the deepening afternoon shadows obscuring his face. "Now that's something else to like about you," he says. "You're dutiful. Look at how well you have cared for your father all these years."

"As you said, it is my duty, and I should hardly be praised for it."

"Amalia, look at me," Diogo says, and I force myself to meet his eyes. "A man has a great deal of time to reflect when he's at sea, and on this last voyage, I decided that the time has come for me to marry. It will help me rise at court, and I need someone to look after my interests when I'm away."

"A man needs a wife," I say, sounding dumb as an ox.

He doesn't seem to hear. "You have a quick mind and I imagine you would be quite good at business." He speaks as if he is checking a list. "You are quiet and gentle, and I want a peaceful home without conflict. And don't you think it would be pleasant to be rich someday—perhaps tremendously so?"

Is he talking about marrying *me*?

"Amalia, if you are not opposed, I would like to ask your father for your hand."

I feel disembodied, as if this day is happening to someone else and I am merely watching. "I—I can't," I sputter. "My father needs me and—" Attended now by palace servants, Papa wants to see me married before he dies, but he seems so frail and helpless, I can't bear the thought of leaving him.

Diogo shrugs. "He could live with us, I suppose. I'll be leaving in a few weeks, and you can tell me your decision when I come back if you prefer."

I want to tell him I am speechless only because this is so unexpected, but he doesn't seem eager for a reply. "Well," he says, looking at the fading light outside. "I'm due at the tavern." After he helps me to my feet, he touches my hand to his lips but does not take me in his arms or press me for a kiss. Perhaps, I think, a gentleman does not. I am no longer a silly girl expecting to be swept away by passion like the beauties in *Amadis of Gaul*.

"Send for me at the palace if you want me to pay a visit to your father." Before I know it, I am staring at an open doorway wondering what just happened, as Diogo disappears down the street to meet his friends.

༨

Terrible news from Sevilla pushes Diogo to the back of my mind. Two thousand people are dead of the bloody flux, among them Susana's husband and baby. The convent where Luisa is now a postulant nun lost many sisters, but she was spared.

Susana is coming to Sintra with her six-year-old son Pablo and four-year-old daughter Ana Maria. Her letter is so cloying and full of self-pity I can barely read it, although Papa hangs on every word. I send word to Diogo that our house is in upheaval and I can't answer him now, and for the next few weeks, I ride with heavy heart to Queluz on Saturdays, knowing that Susana will put her nose into my affairs when she arrives, and she won't be fooled for a moment why I make these trips.

I picture retorting that my life is none of her business, that I've gotten along fine without her and won't let her tell me what to do now, but I feel myself growing smaller, as if I already know I won't be able to stand up to her abrasive ways. Maybe she's changed, I tell myself, but I can't imagine it.

I have bigger problems than Susana's visit. When I look at my father huddled under a blanket even on warm days, the bones of his skull under his papery skin, I know that his body cannot support life much longer. After he is gone, I don't know what I will do, since our house belongs to the crown and was provided in honor of his service, not mine. What then? Return with Susana and be under her command in her own home? I would have no place else to go. Our house was sold when we left, and the proceeds used to maintain Luisa in the convent. I don't see any way out of marriage, but I am facing the prospect not with the honor of being chosen by a handsome and successful man, but with dread I can't quite explain.

"How serious a Christian is this man?" Judah asks as we sit discussing my dilemma in his courtyard one Shabbat afternoon.

"He takes communion every week," I say, "but he doesn't seem to care." Diogo's conversation is never pious before or after church, and he is a step behind others in crossing himself, as if he has been thinking about something else. It doesn't seem to bother him that I don't go to confession and thus can't take communion, since he probably would have said something if he thought I was endangering my immortal soul.

"I suppose I might be safe with him," I say to Judah. "And he's gone a lot."

Judah frowns. "Men have ways of watching even when they're not around. I must tell you, if he forbids you to come here, I would have to go along. A Christian commander bringing back treasure to Portugal would not be the one sent away if there were disharmony at court. After all, regardless of how friendly things may appear, deep down most Christians think even one Jew is too many."

I try to smile but I can't. "And I think there is one Jew too few."

Judah's eyes search mine. "You will be lucky to find a tolerant Christian husband, but that's all you can hope for."

I cover my face with my hands and weep, softly at first and then with abandon. "I feel forsaken," I say, when I finally can speak.

He shakes his head. "Even the Hanged One said as much when he was on the cross. But God doesn't have to do what we want. He doesn't have to prove that he's listening. Don't forsake him, Amalia. That's what you should be concerned about."

The sound of a guitar being tuned drifts from the house. "It's time to go in," Judah says, heaving himself to his feet with a groan. "And in case you don't realize it, the Holy One has never forsaken you. He gave you your mother. He knows you cannot serve him as you wish to, but your mother showed you how to do the best you can."

He casts his eyes upward, taking in the trees, the birds, the sky. "When you feel her presence, you accept his continuing gift. Say the shema, say the blessings, even if only to yourself. Turn the ways you feel forced to dishonor him into praise that he continues to sustain you."

He seems to know my question before I have a chance to ask it. "Ask your mother if you should marry Diogo," he says. "Perhaps she will find a way to answer."

Within a week of Susana's arrival, my life is so noisy and chaotic that if my mother tries to speak to me, I don't know how I will hear. Susana thinks it's my fault Papa has grown so feeble, and she busies herself in the kitchen cooking what she says are the right foods, of which he has apparently had none since leaving Sevilla. She rearranges the house, moving a lamp from one side of a table to the other, as if where it sat was proof of a failure on my part and where she put it was a sign that finally things are being set right.

One afternoon, I get away to ride Chuva long and hard, and

when I return, I find supper unprepared and Susana in a rage. "I fired the servants," she says. "I need ones I can talk to."

I'm not sure I have heard correctly. "How do they know they're fired if you can't talk to them?"

"I stood at the door and waved them out with an angry look."

Her face turns purple as my snicker becomes a hearty laugh. "They'll be back tomorrow," I say. "Appreciative, I'm sure, of their afternoon off."

"Well then, you fire them."

"They're assigned to us by the court," I tell her. "Maybe you should learn to speak Portuguese."

My pleasure at her distress is short-lived. "He won't last a month," she says coldly. The disdainful turn of her chin in the direction of Papa's room chills me to the core. "Who knows what will happen to me then?" Susana adds. "I'm not going to bother learning that ugly language unless it's worth the trouble."

How old she seems, when she is only a few years my senior! Perhaps the downturned lines around her mouth and eyes come from having no sense of humor. I've tried to get her to laugh or just offer up a smile that doesn't seem self-righteous or predatory, but so far I haven't succeeded.

I change the subject to another I'm sure will distress her. "Do you remember how we used to sing zemirot at our grandparents' farm? Those were so much happier times."

"Don't speak of that!" she hisses, clapping her hands to get her children's attention to order them outside. "Our family is not Jewish, and Mother did us no favor by acting as if we still were."

The first few nights she was here, she had to help her children with even the simplest bedtime prayers, although she's put on quite a show about her family's piety. "They've had a great shock," she explains, and perhaps that's why they don't seem to remember. They're far too small to understand death. The older one asks when Papa will arrive and the younger one goes through the house looking for where her baby sister is taking a nap.

I remember what it is like to lose a parent, and my heart goes out to Pablo and Ana Maria. I want to hold them in my arms, but Susana stops me every time. "It's best not to spoil them," she says. "They'll grow up expecting things to revolve around them." She sniffs. "Rather like you did."

"Me?" I burst out in incredulous laughter. "You were the one always telling Mama what to do."

"It was for her own good, and Mama came to see it my way in the end."

I open my mouth to retort that Mama just became better at disguise, but there's no use in prolonging the argument. "I'm going riding," I say, trying to hide the anger in my voice.

"Of course!" Her voice is like spilled vinegar behind me. "Leave me to deal with all this. When you're married, Diogo won't allow such selfishness."

Diogo makes a point of being charming to Susana, and she is relentless in her efforts to use him to improve me. "You just don't understand how lucky you are to have attracted such a man," she says, making it clear she isn't going to let me ruin everything by being myself.

I make a game of it now that Diogo is setting sail and she won't be able to conspire with him. I lie with ease about how Diogo likes me to take Chuva out for long rides by myself, appreciates my hair unkempt, prefers exactly how I water the wine or trim a candlewick. She knows I'm making it up. If she were to say Diogo likes his new cloak, just to be contrary I would say he had sworn off wearing clothing altogether.

As I wait for the groom to finish saddling Chuva, anxiety sets in again. Susana may be right that I should put some effort into keeping him interested, but if Diogo doesn't like me the way I am, isn't it better if he loses interest?

Chuva is ready, and I mount her with the same flood of relief as always, shaking off my burdens as we leave Sintra behind.

By the time Diogo's ships sail up the Tagus River and dock at

Lisbon, I have resigned myself to his proposal. When he comes to visit, Papa is roused from what seems like a perpetual nap. *Marry*, I wonder. *How do I sign that?* I slide my fingers over the ring finger of my other hand, before pointing to myself and Diogo. Papa bursts into a smile. He beckons to us, joins our hands, and nods his head.

౪ა

On the eve of my wedding, one day after my nineteenth birthday, I kneel in the confessional. "Bless me Father, for I have sinned," I murmur. "It has been two months since my last confession." It's been so long I can't even remember, but what does that matter when everything about my life feels like a lie?

I mumble through some bad thoughts I've had and mean things I've done and wait to be assigned my penance, but the priest wants to talk with me first. "You'll be married tomorrow, Amalia," he says. "You must remember to treat your vows with the respect God demands."

"Yes, Father."

"Man and woman are different creations, but God intended that they complement each other, and it is your responsibility to make sure there is harmony in your home."

My heart is in the pit of my stomach. It feels as if he is talking about somebody else who will go off tomorrow to live in a strange house with a man she barely knows. *I can't do this*, I think, and for a moment, I consider throwing myself at him, begging him to stop the wedding.

"Entering marriage without the intention of having children is a grave error in God's eyes. Will you take this obligation seriously and raise your children in the one true faith?"

The tiny confessional booth closes in around me, and my mind goes blank. Then suddenly, my lips are moving. "It goes without saying, does it not?"

I feel a glow on my back, as if my mother is standing behind me. Judah was right that she would come, for she must have put in my head those clever words, neither lie nor truth, that satisfy the smug man behind the woven cane screen of the confessional and get me out of making a promise I hope I won't have to keep.

She wants the marriage to happen. Why else would she be here helping me?

"I have a wedding to prepare for, Father. Please excuse me, but I must go." I race through a penance of a few Pater Nosters and Ave Marias then take the town steps two at a time for home.

Papa is not strong enough to go to church and there will be no music, no mass, no crowd watching us exchange our vows. The house is filled with flowers, courtesy of Elizabeth and Beatriz, for our small ceremony at home. Wine, joints of meat, and platters of fowl and fish have been sent by Afonso's regent, but his real gift is conferring on Diogo the title of Lord of Esposende in honor of his wedding. This gives him a tenth of all taxes collected on his new lands and the right to levy new ones to build a palace.

Every worry I had was put aside when my mother rescued me from the priest. I'm marrying a handsome sea commander, I remind myself, and a lord of the realm. Susana adjusts the wool velvet dress we ordered from the best tailor in Lisbon as I stand in my bedroom with my hair flowing in waves to my waist. It's the only time, by tradition, that I will wear it this way, and Susana brushed and brushed until her arm ached.

I can tell that Diogo and Susana are disappointed that the day won't be filled with important guests and entertainment, but I am shaking almost too hard to stand, and I am glad to need only to take the few steps from the bedroom.

Diogo has no family to speak of, having been orphaned young with no living siblings and raised by an uncle who is now dead. His only guest is another expedition commander, Lançarote de Freitas, a barrel-chested man about ten years older than Diogo, with a nose so bulbous Susana had to silence her children to keep them from asking what was wrong with his face.

The priest clears his throat and begins. "Do you, Amalia Riba, take Diogo Marques as your lawful husband?" he asks. I whisper that I do. After Diogo says his vows, the priest puts a cloth over our joined hands and blesses us. *I'm married*, I think, trying to believe it.

Diogo gives me the traditional kiss at the end of the ceremony, and then turns away. "So, Freitas," he says, "you thought I would never do it! What do you think of me and my bride?" He kisses me again, but his lips are pulled into a hard line and our teeth click uncomfortably. Lançarote de Freitas's expression is a mix I can make no sense of—curiosity, perhaps, or amusement. Or maybe, though it hardly seems possible, contempt.

Sunlight pours over the palace square in Sintra as the clouds momentarily clear. Though the muddy carriage wheels spoil the effect, the gilded coach waiting to take me to Diogo's home in Lisbon glows like something out of a childhood story. I see a rainbow over the wooded hills in the direction of the city, and my heart soars. Surely these must be signs that everything will be all right.

I watch through the coach window as the men mount their horses and ride off ahead of us toward the city. Regent Pedro's wife, the Countess of Urgell, has sent two of her ladies-in-waiting to be my escort, and my sister is coming as well. Susana prattles on with uncharacteristic cheerfulness in the coach. "I just hope all the riding hasn't"—she searches for words—"ruined her."

Lady Lionor's eyes flicker with concern. "You mount your horse astride?" she asks me.

"I've ridden that way since I was a little girl."

"Oh dear," Lady Violante says, looking down nervously. "Your maidenhead is a shield to prove you are a virgin."

"I am a virgin." I never knew I had some kind of shield between my legs, and I shift my weight to see if there is something hard and uncomfortable inside me I had failed to notice.

"Yes," Lionor says, "but being jostled by a horse with your legs parted can break you open in a way that is not desirable."

Break me open?

Violante puts out a hand to pat my knee. "Lionor," she chides her friend, "don't scare the poor girl." She takes my hands in hers. "The countess was concerned that having no mother, perhaps you knew little of—womanly things—and that's why she asked us to come with you today."

What hasn't Susana told me? She stares out the window to avoid meeting my eyes.

"You are aware of the marriage act, I assume?" Lionor's eyebrows arch.

I nod my head. "It's what—" I was going to say it's what animals do in barnyards and pastures, but I think better of it. "It's what a man does to a woman."

"Yes," Lionor says, "and you should expect the first time to be painful." She touches the bridge of her nose. "Imagine your maidenhead as something hard, but not solid like bone. It must be broken for your husband to enter you, and that must happen for your marriage to be consummated."

Tears spring to my eyes as I massage my nose, imagining what it would feel like to have something forced up it so hard it broke the top. "It's not that bad, dear," Violante says. "We all lived." She smiles. "Although you will bleed."

"Bleed?" I whisper. "How much?"

"Oh, I don't know," Violante says. "It differs."

"On my wedding night, it was a flood," Susana says.

Lionor frowns at her. "The important thing is that there should be some. You may have ruined your chance to prove your virginity, although I am sure your husband will not doubt it."

I am shuddering, and Lionor puts an arm around my shoulder. "What men do, women must endure. You'll find after the first few times, it doesn't hurt anymore."

"When I was married," Susana adds, "the priest told me that if I found it unpleasant, I should concentrate on becoming with child from it."

"Now, it is true that some women find the encounter pleasant," Violante says, ignoring her, "but I would suggest that if you are one of those, you don't appear to enjoy it too much. Your husband might think you will look elsewhere for more, and since he will be away so often, perhaps it's best to fight off any...excitement...you may feel."

"Oh my goodness," Lionor says, looking out the window. "We're almost in Lisbon!" My heart sinks even further. Much as I want to get out of the coach, away from the torment of this conversation, I know that when the coach stops, the inevitable will be one step closer.

Diogo's front door is open, and the pathway has been strewn with flowers. Two servants come out at the sound of the carriage and wait near the front steps. One of them helps me down, introducing himself as the butler, Alvaro.

The other servants assembled at the door are a blur of names and faces. The last is Catellina, my new maid. She looks a little younger than me, with cheeks that blotch when I speak to her. She and Alvaro usher us into a room where Diogo is waiting with a few of his friends. They all rise, and Diogo comes to me, flushed with wine I can smell on his breath. "Welcome to your new home," he says.

After supper, Catellina takes me upstairs to my quarters, with Susana and the ladies following behind. In the dressing room, a silk nightgown has been laid out from an open chest of linens and undergarments. "Whose are these?" I ask, worrying for a moment there is another woman in the house.

"Senhor Marques has kept all the seamstresses in town busy preparing a trousseau for you," Catellina says. "The tailor will be coming tomorrow to fit you for your dresses." The chest contains more clothing than I have owned my entire life. "You can choose another nightdress, if you prefer," the maid tells me, misunderstanding my silence as displeasure.

"No," I say. My voice sounds so small I hardly recognize it. "This is beautiful."

While Susana and the ladies watch, Catellina helps me remove my dress and undergarments. I cling to my chemise, because I have never undressed in front of anyone since I was a little girl. They wait for me silently, and I know I must do what they expect. After a moment of nakedness, I am covered with the nightdress, and Catellina pulls back the covers to help me into bed.

I pull a blanket up to my chin, but Lionor shakes her head. "You must not look like a frightened child," she says, pulling it gently away. The pink of my nipples shows through the thin fabric, and I struggle to keep myself from crossing my arms.

Diogo comes into the bedchamber wearing a robe, which his manservant helps him remove. Clad only in a night shirt, he settles himself beside me. One by one, the guests wish us well and leave.

Diogo puts his arm around my shoulder. "Are you afraid?" he asks. I nod, unable to speak.

"Perhaps it's best just to take care of it." He doesn't remove his shirt or my gown but simply pushes fabric aside as he gets on top of me. He pumps his hips for a while before rolling off to lie on his back. "I guess I'm too drunk," he says. "Or maybe it's all the excitement. Would you mind if we got it done tomorrow?"

I don't know what to say. I've been rescued from the horrors I have been imagining, but they'll still be ahead of me. I want to say I'd rather it be over, but Diogo has already blown out the candles. "Good night," he says, turning his back on me without another word.

8

I lie awake for hours listening to Diogo's shallow breath. The next thing I know, the room is filled with sunlight, and birds are chirping in the trees outside the window where Diogo is sitting.

I pull back the covers and see a bloodstain on the sheet. "How did that get there?" I ask, wondering if it is possible to sleep through such an event.

"I did it," he says, shrugging his shoulders.

"Why?"

He gets up and looks out the window. "To preserve your honor. So no one would think there wasn't any blood."

"But we haven't—" I say. "We didn't—"

His loose sleeve comes up his arm, and I see blood seeping through a white bandage. "For your honor," he repeats. "Tonight, we'll try again."

He rings for Catellina, pulling back the covers to make sure the blood is visible from the door.

The maid is there before the sound of the bell has died. "Help my wife dress," Diogo orders, "and see to the bed right away." Her eyes dart to the stain. She curtseys, and I follow her into my dressing room.

Catellina helps me into a dress and finds me a pair of matching slippers. "Your hair, Donha Marques," she says, going to a drawer and taking out a white cloth that she pulls tight around my forehead and smooths over the top and sides of my hair.

Of course—this is how married women look. I picture my braid flying in the salt air of Sagres. Gone. In its place, I can picture nothing at all.

$$\sim$$

Diogo and I don't succeed the next time, or the next. When two weeks have passed, I can think of nothing else. I sink into self-recrimination, telling myself I am not pretty enough, womanly enough, charming enough, something enough. He spends most of his time out with his friends, and when they are at the house, they are in his library, a room I have been told he would prefer me not to visit. I get in bed looking as attractive as I can and force myself to remain awake, but if he comes to me at all, he soon quits in frustration and goes to his own room.

By the time a month has passed, I am grateful that Diogo had the foresight to bloody the sheet so no one will know there is anything amiss. Then one night, I wake to hear him breathing heavily by the bed. Without a word, he presses on top of me. I feel hardness between my legs, and though part of me wants to protect myself, in sheer relief I open them willingly.

He wastes no time, driving hard into me, then lets out a grunt as he thrusts once, twice, three times. I feel sharp pain as my body stretches to accommodate something so big. Almost immediately, I feel hot liquid coursing inside me, and just as it stops, he does too, freezing in place before falling over on the bed with a groan.

Is that all there is to it? All the stories of lusty knights and forbidden passion—had they no truth to them at all? Shocked and betrayed, I am overcome with loneliness so deep I want to cry.

Voices rise from downstairs. "I must go back to my guests," Diogo says. When he is gone, I touch between my legs and find only a smear of milky liquid and no blood. Lionor and Violante were right. I had been broken by my time on Chuva, but they were wrong about my husband caring. I roll over and pull the covers up around me. It's done, I think. At least it's done.

The next morning as I dress to go out to visit my new neighbors, a messenger arrives. "Senhora Marques," he says with a deep bow. "I have word from Sintra that you should come as quickly as you can."

When he averts his eyes, my heart sinks. "It's my father, isn't it?"

"I am to inform you that your father died last night," he says. "Your sister is waiting for you." My knees buckle, and Alvaro catches me before I collapse. Did he die while Diogo and I were—? The possibility seems so horrible I can hardly take a breath.

Within an hour, I am in a carriage headed for Sintra, and it isn't until I am out of the city that I realize it didn't occur to me to leave word with Diogo that I was gone.

Papa's body, laid out on the dinner table, seems impossibly small, as if death were only the final diminishment in a process that had taken years. The house is empty. There is no sign of the children, and Susana is at the church arranging for the funeral mass and burial.

My eyes fill with tears as I take his still graceful-looking hand in my own and kiss it. Such works of art, such knowledge flowed through these fingers! How hard he worked to make his contribution. I wish there were some way I could honor him, send him off with the love and admiration he deserves.

Memories of my grandmother preparing my mother's body for burial come to mind, but all I can remember is how much water it took and how gentle and thorough she was. I get a bowl and fill it. At least I can wash his hands. I slide each of his fingers between my own, working by feel because my eyes are blinded with tears. I cup his cold palm in my own and stroke the top of his hand, feeling the bony protrusion of his knuckles and the corded sinews underneath the cold, pale skin.

"Blessed art thou, Lord God, king of the universe…" My voice trails off. Papa wouldn't want a Jewish blessing. Or would he? I never knew how he really felt about being a Jew by blood. Perhaps he didn't either.

Would he want to be joined to his ancestors now, having done his duty by protecting his family? Had he too honored the Holy One in the only way he could? I continue the blessing, knowing I am really saying it for me.

"What are you doing?" Susana's voice breaks the stillness, and I whirl around to see her standing in the doorway. Behind her are several men carrying a wood coffin. "The Hail Mary," I say, unconcerned with the obviousness of my lie. "Holy Mary, Mother of God," I intone, continuing to wash his hands. "Pray for us sinners now and at the hour of our death."

"Amen," Susana says by rote.

"Pray for us," I whisper to the mother of the sad and betrayed Hanged One, and this time I mean it.

Papa is buried the next day in the Christian cemetery. Susana has by now realized that the house is not his, and she can remain in it only long enough to settle his affairs. She storms around in a barely subdued fury about the pains she had taken to be with her father and how ungrateful everyone is.

I have never known such loneliness. I don't want to be in Sintra now, but Diogo's house in Lisbon is so bleak that I can't make myself go back. I send word to him that I will be gone a few days, and I tell Susana I am leaving that afternoon. There's only one place that can comfort me.

Shortly before nightfall, as rain is turning the roads to mud, my carriage pulls up at the Abravanel's house in Queluz. The table has just been laid for supper, and another soup bowl is brought for me. The girls squeeze in on their bench to make room, and Isaac bangs his spoon to get my attention. After the blessings have been recited, Judah prays that I will find comfort in my father's memory and peace in God's will.

The children are uncharacteristically quiet, and we soon finish the simple meal of soup and bread. Simona takes Isaac to bed, while the girls clear the table and wash the dishes. Judah lights a candle at his desk, says the blessing for study, and opens the Zohar. I follow Simona and sit as she sings to Isaac until he dozes off.

When she gets up to leave, I ask her to stay a little longer. I struggle to hold back sobs as I tell her about the delayed consummation of my marriage and how it and my father's death are linked in my mind.

"You feel unclean," Simona replies, and I realize that's exactly the right word. "I think I know something that will help." She takes two large pieces of plain cloth from a chest. "Come with me."

A temporary break in the clouds casts pearly moonlight onto the courtyard. I hear the fountain spilling water and raindrops falling from the roof into buckets, but other than that, the night is quiet. It's cold enough for me to see my breath, but Simona, to my surprise, is stripping off her clothes. She unpins her hair and shakes it loose, and then, wrapping a sheet around herself, she goes barefoot to the fountain. "Come on!" she says. Incredulous, I take off everything and follow her. The soles of my feet burn on the cold tiles, and I hop back and forth to relieve them.

"Mayyim hayyim," Simona says. "Do you know what that is?"

"Living water," I say, trembling from both the cold and the memories.

Simona puts her sheet on the wall, climbs in the fountain, and waits for me to do the same. "Usually women go to the mikveh alone," she says when we both are standing naked and shivering in the water, "but I thought you might not know how to do it."

"I used to watch my mother," I say, crouching to splash my thighs and belly in preparation for the shock of sitting down. Cold sears my buttocks, my spine, my shoulders as I immerse. My scalp feels pierced with needles as my head goes under, and my hair balloons out. We immerse ourselves three times as Simona intones the blessings, after which we scurry out to cover ourselves.

Just as we do, a cloud bursts overhead. Despite the cold, a warmth suffuses me, and I begin to laugh, really laugh, from somewhere deep inside. Simona laughs too. Draped in useless wet sheets, with hair like matted rope, we turn our faces to the sky and let the rain pelt us as we catch the drops on our tongues like children.

~

Inside the house, Simona lends me some warm clothing, and we brush our hair by the fire. When she's no longer shivering, she gets up to take care of some mending in her basket, and I stay there, letting the heat penetrate my skin as I watch her and her husband absorbed in their activities.

I hear the girls giggling in bed and feel a pang of regret that I never had a sister I could do that with. Luisa was too young, and Susana was Susana. Even in this perfect moment, Susana would find something lacking, and I am glad she is not here.

Simona was right. The mayyim hayyim made me feel clean, but it did more. I am open to life again. My burdens seem lifted, although I know nothing has changed except in my mind. I imagine my spirit soaring above this house, looking down on a nimbus of golden light surrounded by cold rain and darkness. I am inside the light with Judah and Simona, because their love expands so effortlessly, because they saw me suffering and took me in, because they are my friends.

Everything you need is within your reach. The thought flows through me with such intensity that I sense Papa and Mama's spirits hovering nearby, telling me not to be afraid and that whatever happens, I am strong enough to deal with it.

I close my eyes, enfolded in a world where blessing and breath are one. A belief seeps into my heart that I can handle anything, even Diogo, and that perhaps my mother saw that I would find a way to work my life out whether I married him, someone else, or no one at all.

I open my eyes to see Judah watching me. "Forgive me for staring," he says, "but the Zohar was revealing itself through you." His eyes are shining. "Would you like to see something?"

As I move away from the fire, the warmth on my back feels as if I am sprouting wings. He shows me a pattern of circles and inter-connecting lines at the front of the book he is reading. "It looks like the design for a garden," I say. "With fountains and walkways connecting them."

He smiles. "It is a garden, in a way. It's the key to understanding the word and the being of the Holy One."

I am puzzled. "I thought the Torah was the word of God."

"The Zohar tells us how to find the Word inside the words." His face glows. "Did you ever wonder what it means that man is made in God's image?"

"I haven't given it much thought."

He shrugs. "Most people don't. They settle for the flattering idea that God must have two legs and one head. But of course, that's not possible, because God is formless. If he looked like something, there would have to be other things he did not look like, and of course there is nothing that God is not."

He makes a circle with his finger over the page. "This garden, as you put it, represents the ten aspects of God, the sefirot." He touches the circle at the top. "This is Keter—the crown. Part of Ayin."

I recognize the word. "Nothingness?"

He nods. "In this state, God is understood only as whole. It is his different aspects that complicate things for our feeble minds. I suppose Keter could be called 'everythingness,' but then we might picture it crowded with things, when really it is simple, pure, all."

He gives me a moment to think before going on. "The sefirot correspond to parts of the body. The arms, the legs"—he points to four of the circles—"and the womb and phallus, because God encompasses both masculine and feminine."

"We're walking symbols of the Holy One," I whisper, in awe of the staggering thought.

Judah is obviously pleased. "Made in his image." He touches the two sefirot immediately below the crown. "Some think the Zohar is only for men, but they misunderstand. This is wisdom." He touches the circle on the right and then draws his finger to the left. "And this is the womb—Binah—the understanding that flows from wisdom. Many of my friends disagree, but how could the Holy One not be telling us that those with wombs are wise enough to understand the Zohar?"

He points to other circles. "The Zohar speaks of love and power, and how when they are in harmony, the result is Chesed, compassion."

Simona looks up from her work and smiles at her husband and then at me.

Compassion, I realize, is why this house glows. It's the reason I always go away stronger than I came.

"Love that crumbles in the face of power is not compassionate," Judah goes on. "You have to be brave when people are taking sides against each other—or against you. You have to assert yourself to avoid snuffing out your own light."

Simona puts her work away. "Speaking of snuffing lights, it's time to go to bed," she says. Judah yawns and gets to his feet. "We don't have an extra bed," he says. "You'll have to push Chana and Rahel over a little, but they won't mind."

I go into the little room the girls share and marvel at their lovely heads on the pillows, their fresh faces at once so substantial and ethereal. Judah and Simona have protected them well, but soon they will go out to face the surprises of being a woman, just as I am doing. I sigh and settle in bed beside them. Their softness and warmth envelop me as I drift off to sleep.

❧

The jostling of the two girls getting up wakes me the following morning. I lie in bed for a moment after they have gone, thinking about all that happened the night before. The mikveh in the fountain, the Zohar—somehow all the threads tied themselves together as I slept, for I now know clearly what I must do.

My small traveling chest had been brought into the house the night before, but I put on the same dress I was wearing rather than bothering to open it. It's Friday, and Simona is in the kitchen cracking eggs to make the Shabbat loaves. "I'm going back to Lisbon," I say. Simona does not look surprised, nor does she urge me to stay.

A carriage is brought, and the chest is put aboard. I hug Simona and the girls and give Isaac a kiss on his ruddy cheeks. Judah watches with approving eyes, but he keeps his hands clasped behind his back, in case I forget that touching him would be inappropriate.

The trip to Lisbon is not long, but December days are so short that I can't linger, and the coach is off the moment I sit down. Just yesterday, I would have dreaded my return, but now I'm ready to start over, to walk into that house in Lisbon as a married woman, not a girl crying and cowering in bed, not a specter wandering around lost.

Diogo is taking his dinner elsewhere. After all, he is not expecting me. I ask the cook to prepare me something simple, and when I have eaten, I take a two-pronged candlestick from a shelf and bring it and two new candles to my quarters.

I close the latch behind me. After lighting the candles, I motion the warmth toward me as my mother did. I've been away too long, I tell the Holy One. I haven't honored him the best I can.

The candles flicker, releasing black tendrils of smoke. "It will be different now," I whisper. "I won't forget you again."

9

LAGOS 1445

Diogo is gone again before the first buds form on the trees, saying only that the prince has chosen him for a new mission in Africa. Within a few weeks of his departure, I wake up ill every morning and realize I am with child from one of his brief nocturnal visits.

By the time my belly has begun to swell, Diogo has summoned me to the port town of Lagos, near Prince Henry at Raposeira. He tells me to bring only Catellina and enough to stay through the summer. After the baby is born, we will move the household to Lagos because it is more convenient for his voyages.

I arrive on a day sparkling with hope. Shorebirds dive and swirl over a bay dancing with whitecaps, and the breeze is warm enough to hint of the languid summer ahead. Diogo has bought a small house, situated about halfway between Lagos and the lighthouse at Ponta da Piedade, which he intends to expand to befit a man of his rising stature at court.

The point is long and narrow, making Lagos, on its lee side, one of the most sheltered harbors in Portugal. From my new home, I can walk west a few steps and see the windward coastline in the direction of Sagres and the vast sea beyond, or walk east the same distance and see the busy port on the other side. Already Diogo has workers building a lookout at one end of the house, and soon we will be able to see everything in all directions without leaving our home.

The years I spent in Sagres as a child made me comfortable with my own company—a good thing, because I see almost no one. There's little reason for townspeople to come out here, and the only passersby are the lighthouse keeper's family and the sentries manning the bulwark at the point.

I touch my stomach at the flutter in my womb. Things will be better here, I tell myself as I rest each afternoon in the shade of wind-sculpted trees inside the garden walls while Diogo is off at sea. Mornings I walk out to Ponta da Piedade, where waves crash onto spiky rock pillars in astonishing hues of ochre, rust, maroon, and violet. I walk back along the edge of the cliff, looking down at tiny beaches that no one can reach except fishermen in boats tucked among rock arches and pinnacles in the jewel-like blue water.

On one such walk, I notice several dots on the horizon, which over the next few hours turn into sails with the square cross of Prince Henry's Order of Christ emblazoned in the middle. My belly is still small enough to disguise my condition under a loose-fitting dress, so I ready myself to go down to the docks.

By late afternoon, the first of three ships my husband commands has entered the harbor. Two boats put down anchor, and I wait at some distance while dockhands struggle with heavy lines to get the third secured at the wharf. When the gangplank is laid, Diogo walks off the ship to greet several of Henry's courtiers.

He nods to a group of men approaching the boat, clubs and whips in hand.

I don't understand what I am seeing. Naked people, black from head to foot, are coming down the gangplank. Most are men, but a few women and girls are scattered among them. They keep coming and coming until sixty or more of them are standing bewildered on the dock. The men are yelling at them, shoving them into a single file column before marching them away into the blinding light of the square.

Diogo looks pleased to see me when I finally come to him. "Successful, very successful," he says before turning back to

Henry's courtiers. I look back toward the ship and am surprised to see there seems to be little else to unload. I know about slaves, but surely bringing back people is not the only reason Diogo would brave the sea.

I wait until Diogo and I have had supper and are settling in for the night. "So," I say, swallowing hard, "tell me about your voyage. You said it was a success."

"A few more like it and you can have any house in Lisbon your heart desires."

"I rather like it here," I tell him.

"Good. That will make it easier for me. We can get to the coast of Guinea from here in less than three weeks, now that we know the way. Henry plans one voyage after another, now that everything is in place."

"In place?"

"The gathering point on the coast. The captives are brought there. No more going up the river to find them ourselves, like we did with the first few. Henry is planning a new design for the hold so we can bring back more each time."

"Your only cargo is people?" My heart sinks. "You aren't looking for gold anymore?"

"Not people," he says smugly. "Slaves."

"Diogo!" My jaw drops. "What have they done? Were they captured in battle? Are they hostages?"

"Just unlucky, I suppose." He shrugs. "Guinea is full of them."

He notices my crestfallen look. "Just wait," he says. "Before too long, you'll see them the way I do, a row of gold coins marching off the boat straight into my pocket."

I stand up to get away from him. "It's not right, Diogo. It's not—compassionate."

He laughs. "Compassion toward beasts? Save your compassion for lepers and orphans." He shakes his head. "Since you are feeling so compassionate, you should remember that we are saving their souls. Don't you think that's important?"

"I didn't see priests taking them to church."

Diogo's face grows stony, and he points to my belly. "Show some compassion for the child. If God wishes to provide a better life for our family, are you refusing the gift?"

I shut my eyes to try to quiet my mind, but all I feel is a deep, stabbing ache behind my eyes. "Perhaps you're right," I say, desperate for the conversation to end. He must be too, for he gets up with a yawn and heads off to his bedroom, using the baby in my womb as an excuse for not touching me.

Diogo is gone again within a few weeks. He and Lançarote de Freitas are competing for the admiralty that will go to the one who brings back the most slaves in the first year of Prince Henry's new project in Guinea. Soon, square sails with red crosses again appear on the horizon, and Freitas's boats are in the harbor. I am ready for them this time.

I have arranged for barrels of water to be brought to the docks on donkey carts. My household staff comes with me, and as the first slaves come off the boat, we call out to offer them water. One man with wide, desperate eyes is struck across the back with a club for approaching me, and I wince not just at his pain but because I have caused it.

Enraged, I stride over to the men herding the slaves. "They need water," I say, "and you are not marching them off until they get it."

The leader makes a move as if to strike me, but then he remembers who I am. "Does your husband know you are doing this?" he asks.

"Does Prince Henry know his cargo is dying of thirst?"

His eyes flit to the other men, who look equally perplexed. "Well then," he says, "at least let's be orderly about it."

The slaves are herded into a line, and each receives a ladleful of water from Catellina and me at the first barrel and another from the servants at the second. We're not all bad, I want to tell them, praying it won't be the last time they see evidence of that.

To my surprise, Diogo is not angry when he returns. Henry heard what I had done and told the nuns at the convent in Lagos to take charge. I no longer risk my health in the summer heat by coming to the dock, which is just as well, for I could not bear to watch the priest, on a newly erected platform overlooking the procession, making the sign of the cross and thanking God that light has come to those who lived in darkness.

I sleep most of the afternoon now. It's July, and Diogo is preparing to leave again. He's the only energetic person in the house, thinking of one last-minute need after another and making me pity the servants who have to do his bidding. I am too lethargic to do anything in this heat, and even the baby isn't moving much anymore. I press my hand into my side to see if I can get it to respond, but it just slips away as if it is too tired to play such games.

Diogo and his friends go to a tavern in the cool of the evening. As his departure approaches, the carousing spills over to our home, lasting well into the night. The noise in the house often keeps me from sleeping, and I lie in bed drenched in sweat from the lingering heat. The only remedy is to take a walk to cool down and shake the discomfort of my massive belly from my bones.

Wisps of clouds drift across a nearly full moon as I look down on the harbor. A gust of cool air caresses the damp hair clinging to my neck, and I brush it free with my fingertips. Boats bob at anchor in water dancing with moonlight, and Diogo's ship is a faint silhouette as sailors prepare for departure by the glow of lamps.

The quiet of the world is broken by the sound of my husband roaring with laughter inside the house. Time to go back, before I embarrass him by having his friends see me outside in my condition. I close the garden gate behind me, and as I reach the house, a ragged urchin I've seen on the docks runs out. He collides with me, and a coin drops from his fingers.

Through the open doorway, I see one of Diogo's friends adjusting his private parts before fastening his belt. Diogo and Lançarote de Freitas stand next to him, their faces red and glistening.

"Dios mio!" I whisper. Suddenly I know why he can only penetrate me when he rushes in from his parties. How could I have been so oblivious to the reason he is not interested in me?

I am the perfect wife for him, I realize with a horrified, convulsive shudder. I have neither dowry nor beauty, no family to cry to, no one to make demands on my behalf. Peace in the house. He could count on it. And Henry, with all those pretty young men going in and out of his private chambers. What might Diogo have offered to make the prince favor him?

I feel sick to my stomach and rush upstairs. Diogo's guests must have left right after the boy, for the house is suddenly quiet. When he comes to stand by my bed, I turn away from him.

"I'm sorry you saw that," he says.

"I am too." I pull the coverlet from under me with a violent yank and throw it over myself like a rampart.

"I don't want to—to fail you as I have." I hear what sounds like trembling in his voice. "It's just that I—that men are—" He doesn't try to go on.

"Men?" I sit up to look at him. "You call that boy desperate for a little money a man?"

"My friends are the ones who do those things. I only watch."

"Well, that makes everything much better," I hiss. I don't know whether to believe him, and I'm not sure I care.

"I made a baby, didn't I? That's all you really wanted." The momentary vulnerability in his eyes disappears as they narrow to slits. "At least I'm fairly certain it's mine."

I gasp at the callousness with which he insults me to turn the subject away from himself. "I waited night after night for you!" Spittle flies as my anger boils over. "For what little you have offered!"

He steps back. "My goodness," he says. "The bitch can bite."

I get up out of bed and put on my robe. "If you don't leave my room this minute, I will be gone from this house tomorrow—"

Suddenly I feel as if my body has been pierced by a sword. The pain is so great I crumple to the floor. I feel a flood of warmth between my legs as Diogo calls for Catellina to come to me. The pain subsides and I pant for breath. Then it is upon me again. For hours, I writhe on the bed, trying at the same time to hold the baby in and force it to come, to end a pain so intense I am sure it will kill me.

I try to remember all the invocations to keep the Evil Eye away, and I scream them again and again. Then, with such surprising ease it seems little more than an afterthought, a slippery package comes out between my legs. It's a bloody and impossibly small baby inside a pale caul. It never takes a breath.

ↄ◠

Catellina is busying herself in my room when I open my eyes to the morning light. I lie on fresh sheets, but the smell of blood still rises from the bed. "Where is my baby?" I ask.

Her brow is furrowed as she rushes to me. "They've taken him away to—" She sees my stricken face. "Your husband thought it best to bury him quickly. Lord have mercy and take him to heaven, even though the baptism wasn't in time."

I lean back against the pillows, staring blankly at the ceiling.

A boy.

Baptized.

Buried.

I haven't done what I could to enter him into our covenant, even if it was no more than the pin prick my mother had given Abraham. My firstborn child, torn from my body, is even more lost than I am. I put my hands over my face and weep.

ↄ◠

Diogo sails for Africa the next day, and I remain in Lagos only until I stop bleeding. In our grief, we speak no more of the argument we had been having when the baby came, and I never tell him I cannot bear to stay in the house where I experienced such a night. I remember nothing of my agonizing journey back to Lisbon with Catellina, and once there, I sleep for days to gather my strength.

The Evil Eye has felled me. It sought me out in a comfortable house at Lagos with an admired and successful husband and a baby on the way, and it laid me low. How else could I explain why in a few months, a place that seemed so inviting became a nightmare of sweating slaves, predatory men, and my own dead child? I will never return to Lagos. Whatever Diogo wants from a wife, he will have to come to Lisbon to get it.

10

When Diogo returns and finds me gone, he comes straight to
Lisbon. I am ready to counter his recriminations with my own,
but to my surprise he is contrite. He wants me to know that I
haven't done anything to drive him toward men, and that he has
never been more successful with whores in the taverns than he has
been with me.

He tells me that what I saw that night was part of life at sea,
one of the many uses of a cabin boy. Men seek outlets for their lust
when there are no women around, and I shouldn't be surprised
that some of them choose boys even when they are on land.

Diogo thinks that my knowing this behavior is widespread
should be enough to brush aside my disgust, but his shrugs of
explanation only deepen it. Still, he is right that I don't know
much about the world. Perhaps all wives have wounds and aston-
ishments they keep to themselves.

I think of Judah and Simona and grieve that the thousand invisible threads that link them, the loving secrets they convey with
their eyes, will not be mine. Diogo and I are linked too, by silent
anger and loathing, although I seem to be the only one hurting. I
feel as if I am made of lead, and only at Queluz is my spirit light
enough to smile.

Diogo will be in Lisbon two months. He and Lançarote de
Freitas will resume their rivalry in the spring because Prince

Henry does not want to run the risk of ships being lost at sea in harsh weather. My husband's contrition is only for having upset me, and though he promises not to bring boys into his library to entertain his friends, he tells me what he does away from home is not my business.

Because we want a child, he uses his hand to prepare, but I ask him to do it in his room. Hearing his breath quicken sends chills through me because of what he might be picturing. Still, I welcome his visits, because we are partners in a conspiracy, and it is the only way I feel close to him. We are going to make a baby, and no one has to know how we did it.

We keep an uneasy peace until I mention Judah over dinner. Diogo frowns. "Why do you know so much about his family?" he demands. I tell him I go there from time to time, and that I hope our children will bring us as much pleasure as Judah and Simona's have them.

"Jews?" Diogo arches his eyebrows. "You're comparing our children to Jews?"

"That's not what I mean," I protest. "They're well behaved and healthy—that's all." But of course it isn't, not in the slightest.

Diogo scowls. "It's not good for you to visit them. I already took a risk marrying a converso, and people might get ideas about your sincerity as a Christian."

"I've never heard anyone suspect my sincerity. And this isn't Spain, after all." I arch my eyebrows, as if my meaning should be obvious.

"Don't be so sure. The people of Portugal don't like Jews or conversos any more than Spaniards do, and it will come out soon enough."

My body tightens. "Come out? How?"

"You know what happens when people get it in their minds that a Jew has wronged them."

"And you?" My mouth is suddenly dry. "How do you feel?"

Diogo shrugs. "Abravanel and the others are useful at court. If they're helpful to me, I can put up with them." He spears a piece of mutton and chews it once or twice before swallowing hard to force it down his throat. "They are the best educated, that's for certain. No foolishness about how God wants people to show they trust him by remaining ignorant."

A bit of sauce wets the side of his mouth, and he wipes it away with his sleeve. "I've contracted with a converso to collect taxes on my new lands." He laughs. "I'll grow rich, but the people of Esposende will hate him more than me. Now there's something Jewish blood is good for."

∽

We get along by avoiding each other and speaking little at meals. I go to Queluz only when Diogo is visiting his new lands, but that isn't enough for him. One evening I mention Simona, and he dents his favorite pewter mug when he throws it against the fireplace.

"I thought I made it clear I didn't want you to mix with Jews," he says.

"You told me no such thing," I say, which only makes him angrier.

"Couldn't you figure that out for yourself?"

Despite wanting to put on a stony front, I burst into tears. "I have no friends, no family," I sob. "And I feel more alone when you're here than when you're not."

He ignores my criticism. "Go out and make some Christian friends, why don't you? Or are only Jews good enough for you?"

I storm from the room, and within a few hours, I am on the road to Queluz, leaving word with Diogo where I am going and saying that I will not be back until he apologizes.

He does not. Two days later, guilt drives me home, and I arrive around dinnertime to find Diogo and a group of his friends enjoying their meal. They are jolly with drink, and no one is happy to see me. I go to my room and bolt the door. I am at my window getting some air to calm myself when I see two boys skirting the edge of the house. Below me, a door opens and they are ushered inside.

∾

By summer, I am pregnant again, but I say nothing about the baby aloud, for fear the Evil Eye is close enough to strike. Diogo stays in Lagos when he is not at sea, and I visit Judah and Simona whenever I wish. Their son Isaac is a studious boy with solemn and soulful gray eyes, and at eight, he has lost the blond curls of childhood. I love the way he absentmindedly chews on a ragged strand of hair as he pours over his books, lost in another world.

Judah is away at court more than ever these days, and Isaac, hungry for someone to talk to, explains to me the science of the Muslim doctors Averroes and Avicenna, the philosophy of Aristotle, or whatever he is studying at the time. He reads Portuguese and Hebrew with ease, and I help him with Arabic, which I learned while translating for my father.

Chana was married last summer to a soft-spoken young man from an old Jewish family in Lisbon, and she lives in the aljama, the Jewish quarter there. She is expecting her first child around the same time as mine. Rahel is almost fifteen, and several families with marriageable sons have made inquiries about her.

Judah's time is taken up with a new business importing textiles from Flanders, a license he was given as a reward for service to the crown. One of the Portuguese princes recently died, and in his will, he repaid a large debt to Judah. Astute as always, Judah saw the regent's longing eyes and lent most of it back to the crown, using the rest to build a larger house at Queluz.

The chaos, dust, and noise of the workers drive Simona to distraction, as does the increased flow of visitors. Judah is the leading figure among Portugal's Jews, and though they might look to rabbis for spiritual advice, it's Judah they come to for everything else. The Abravanel family is among the few Jews exempt by royal decree from having to live in the aljama, so most of his visitors ride out for the day from Lisbon and are back in the city before the curfew for Jews at nightfall.

Like most homes in Portugal and Spain, the new house looks inward to a courtyard that supplies light and air. Though the outer walls are solid with only a few high windows, there will be another wall around the compound, because one never knows when or how quickly life can become unsafe for Jews caught outside the aljama.

As I reach the outskirts of Lisbon one August afternoon, I feel the baby fluttering in my womb, annoyed perhaps by the jostling of the road. I remember how still my first baby was in the days before I lost him, and I'm relieved that this one, with several months yet to go, seems so much stronger. "Go to sleep," I whisper, but I'm glad it doesn't. Those little kicks are the best company I will have until I am at Queluz again.

The carriage pulls up in front of the house, and my heart sinks when I see Diogo's lawyer's horse tied up outside. Perhaps he's come home, I think, hoping it isn't so. Alvaro meets me at the door. "Senhor Montes just arrived." He motions toward the library. "I told him you weren't here, and he asked to write a note to send to you."

Montes looks up from his writing at the sound of my shoes on the stone floor. His face is as grave as Alvaro's. "Donha Marques," he says. "I'm afraid I have some bad news."

Time stops—for how long I don't know—and I find myself alone in my room as the afternoon shadows lengthen over the street. Diogo is dead. On its way home, his boat broke apart during a storm, on a shallow reef not far from Cape Bojador. Some men scrambled to safety but Diogo's body washed ashore the following day.

The image is horrifying, but calming in its certainty. Most who die at sea simply vanish. I will be spared wondering whether somehow, years from now, he will walk back through the door. I'm a widow, I tell myself. I'm rid of him.

I stand at the window with the door bolted behind me and let my heart go wild. Diogo isn't coming home. I'm not yet twenty and I'm a widow. Baruch Hashem, this baby will be mine, to raise as I wish.

I swing between silence and sobs that are a mix of horror and joy. I picture the splintering boards, the rush of water in the cold night. I see waves pounding over the rocks. Did Diogo know how the water claimed him, or did it happen too fast?

Free.

He was my husband, despite his faults, and I try to keep my mind on him, but I can't.

Widowed.

I am sure his last thoughts weren't of me, but why should they be? He was fighting for his life, and now I can stop feeling as if I am in a battle with him for my own.

I am entering my ninth month of pregnancy by the time the leaves start to fall. The carriage ride to Queluz is too difficult for me now, and though I haven't seen the Abravanel family in more than a month, all I really want is to curl up in my bed and sleep like a bear.

Senhor Montes is handling the estate. Since my husband had no family to speak of, many decisions have been left to me, and the first thing I did was cancel a scheduled new tax in Esposende. None too soon, for I hear from Montes that people in the north have been rioting over just such increases, and collectors have had to be rescued from attacks on their barricaded homes. If unrest spreads here, I may not be seen as a grieving young widow, but a grasping converso who only cancelled the tax out of fear for her own skin and would show her true colors soon enough.

Am I safe in Lisbon? As if worried too, my baby turns in my womb.

The news grows grimmer over the next weeks—Jewish houses torched in one town, the beating of Jews in another, an effigy of a rabbi burned in a third. When Catellina tells me that in a town just across the Tagus River from Lisbon, not only Jews but converso families are barricading themselves in their homes, I have had enough.

I picture myself in the throes of labor as rioters attack my home. I imagine delivering my baby by the side of the road as I flee Lisbon. I envision sticks, daggers, fists—anything a mob can do to harm me and my child—and I know I can't risk staying in this house. Catellina helps me pack a few things, and I heave my huge body into the carriage to make the trip to Queluz.

Night has fallen as I leave the city, and though the driver must go slowly in the dim moonlight, I cry out with every bounce. I spend most of the journey moaning from grinding cramps in my back and from fear of who or what could lie in the road ahead. As we reach the first houses outside Queluz, fluid gushes into my underskirts. My back cramps again, and I realize that the jostling of the carriage has disguised the beginning of my labor.

My knees buckle as I get down from the coach, and Simona helps me into the house. She throws back the covers on her bed. "I gave my birthing chair to my daughter," she says. "You'll have to do the best you can."

She straddles me from behind, holding me under my arms as the pains get closer together. When there is no time between them, Simona lays my head on a pillow and clears the garments from my legs. "I see its head," she says. "With the next pain, push hard."

"I can't," I moan. "I don't have the strength."

"Of course you do!" I bear down so hard I think I will rip in two as the baby's head strains the entrance to my body.

"One more," Simona says, and with everything I have, I deliver my daughter into the world.

I hear a loud, healthy wail. Simona holds up the tiny body for me to see, and then lays her down while she cuts the cord and delivers the afterbirth. Finally, slick with sweat and dressed with little more than a mane of matted hair, I hold my most cherished dream in my arms.

Simona covers me up and opens the door to the bedroom. Isaac and Rahel are standing wide-eyed outside.

Isaac gets to the bed first. "Would you like to see the baby?" I turn her so he can see her face.

"What's her name?" Isaac moves closer.

I feel a wave of love for this sweet boy, and I pull him to me with my free arm. "I can't say yet. I don't want the Evil Eye to know she's here." Isaac nods, patting the baby on the head as if to reassure her it's all right not to have a name quite yet.

But she does. The Holy One sent her to me when I was lost. I started this day full of doubts about myself, about my past decisions, about my future, but it's as if his hand scooped me up in Lisbon and set me down here, as if he were saying I wasn't listening well enough, that I hadn't yet figured out what he has in mind for me.

Eliana. In Hebrew, it means "my God has answered," and I know he has. We were both delivered today. He brought me to the Abravanels to have my child in a Jewish home, where we both belong.

I lie back and shut my eyes. *It's settled then*, I think. No matter what comes, Eliana and I will face it all—joy, hope, pain, sorrow— reunited with our people.

I feel my parents' and grandparents' spirits hovering near me. "Our exile is over," I whisper. "I've brought us home."

11

VALENCIA 1492

I take the vial of poison I bought from a woman in an alley before we came to Valencia, and I pour it out the window, letting it run down the wall so it doesn't touch anyone in the street. I haven't come all this way to give up on life. I shut my eyes and thank the Holy One for the memory of Eliana's birth and for the many reminders that he always answers, even if sometimes we can't hear.

The room is full of ghosts of the Mallorcan family I never knew—of Abraham Cresques, who created the atlas with my grandfather, of the wives, parents, brothers, sisters, aunts, uncles. "I was wrong about bringing my baby home," I whisper to them. "Our exile will be over in God's time, not mine."

I know now that the Evil Eye can wait for years, and it is just now exacting the price for my arrogant belief that I could choose Eliana's destiny and my own.

The air in the room shifts, as if the spirits have stepped back in surprise. "You're in exile in Spain now," they tell me.

"Here?" My incredulous tone echoes off the bare walls. "Spain is my home!"

I picture my people wandering through the desert, weeping by the rivers of Babylon, expelled from England, France, Aragon. "Anywhere you can be a Jew is home," they remind me. "And exile is anywhere you cannot."

"But—" I want to know what I should do today, whether I should sail from here with my family or stay and defy any mortal—even a king and queen—to keep me from being who I am. Whether I die in exile, at the stake, or alone in my bed, the one thing I am sure of is that I will die as a Jew, because I will not forsake myself or my people again.

QUELUZ 1450

Eliana lets out a sigh so long and slow she must be wondering if it's possible to deflate completely and disappear. She rocks her body back and forth as if every minute were an eternity. "Isaac promised," she whines. "No one keeps their word to me."

Growing up as part of the Abravanel family, Eliana has seen nothing of the sort, and I say a silent prayer she may be so fortunate her whole life. Of course, I think with a smile, it's not possible for a four-year-old girl to understand what the men huddled over the Zohar could possibly find more important and exciting than what she wants to do.

Newly a man under Jewish law, Isaac is studying outside with Judah and his guests, and I hear his husky thirteen-year-old voice drift in from the courtyard. "When you sit in the sukkah, the shade of faithfulness, the Shekinah spreads her wings over you," he reads. "Abraham, five other righteous ones, and King David make their dwelling with you."

I see Eliana's downcast look and put down my quill. "I'll do it with you." Only the first two days of the fall harvest festival, Sukkot, require rest from all labor, but it's not in the spirit of it to spend as much time as I have at Judah's desk.

We walk into the dappled sunlight of the courtyard, the front half of which is taken up with our sukkah. It's a temporary house with roof and walls made of leafy branches, where during the week of Sukkot we take our meals, spend our leisure time, and sleep if we wish. We build a sukkah every year not just in gratitude for the harvest, but to remind ourselves of both our displaced ancestors and those who live now without our comforts and security.

I call it our sukkah even though Eliana and I don't live with the Abravanels. After Diogo's death, I sold the houses in Lisbon and Lagos, never wanting to set foot in either again. I used the proceeds to buy my own home in Queluz and turned the rest of the money over to Judah to invest in his textile business. He says I am becoming quite the wealthy widow, but I don't care, other than to be sure I have a good dowry for Eliana.

Judah doesn't like that my house sits outside the walls of his new compound. In the years of Pedro's regency, laws limiting Jewish rights and activities were not strictly enforced, and by the time Afonso became king two years ago, the people were angry enough to revolt. Last year, riots broke out in Lisbon, and a mob attacked the Jewish quarter, intending to burn it down. Afonso cracked down hard, claiming the Jews of Portugal as his personal property and saying he would show little mercy to anyone who damaged anything that belonged to him.

Remembering those frightening days still makes my heart race. Someone came from the compound to tell me to hurry to safety there. I carried the atlas in one hand and clutched Eliana's hand with the other, for in my haste I could think of nothing else that mattered. We stayed together inside the compound for several days, and Eliana and I came home to find our house untouched, except for a shattered clay mug knocked to the floor by a cat that had gotten in through a window. Queluz, praise to the Holy One, is still a sanctuary.

Sukkot is too pleasant a time to dwell on bad memories, I remind myself, as I look around the courtyard. Some of the furniture has been moved outside, and Simona sits in her favorite chair, bouncing Chana's eight-month-old baby on her knee. Chana stands over a flower bed watching her four-year-old son and two-year-old daughter giggle as they pick blasted flowers from wilted stalks and poke them in each other's hair. Rahel, married last year, sits next to Simona, looking miserable in the final weeks of her first pregnancy.

"Grandmother," Eliana says, "where did you put my basket?" Simona produces a small covered box woven from rushes and hands it to my daughter. She pulls her close and buries her face in Eliana's brown curls, kissing her on the top of her head until they both are grinning ear to ear.

Eliana and I go to the place of honor in the sukkah, a chair covered with the finest Flemish cloth from Judah's inventory, on which his most treasured religious texts are placed. The chair shows we are ready for the arrival of seven biblical guests, the Ushpizim, whose presence casts an aura of holiness over the sukkah. Eliana already knows their names and the attributes they represent. "Abraham for love and kindness," she says, swinging my hand, "Isaac for serenity and strength, and Jacob for..." She scrunches up her face as she tries to remember. I make the sound of the first letter and her face lights up. "Beauty and truth!" she says, continuing through Moses, Aaron, and Joseph without faltering.

"And David, for the kingdom of heaven on earth," Isaac says with her, having left the men to come over to us. He crouches beside Eliana. "I'm sorry I made you wait so long." Eliana gives him a shy, pleased look, and I am amazed that my daughter already seems to know more about flirting than I've learned in twenty-four years.

"Let's see what you have today," Isaac says, opening the lid. I look inside as well, wondering what treasures Eliana will want to offer Jacob, the visiting spirit of honor today. There's a small, pink pebble rubbed to a glow and a huge tuft of goose down. Of course there's always a biscocho de huevo, a Sukkot cookie Simona bakes just for her.

I suspect she has kept to her ritual so diligently because she's gotten so much attention from Isaac for it. I remember his wide eyes as he stood in the doorway the day Eliana was born, and I feel a rush of tenderness for him as I watch the two of them looking through her box.

Isaac's quiet piety bears none of the marks of arrogance I find so annoying in many educated men. He studies at a yeshiva in Lisbon during the week, but he never boasts about what he has learned or insinuates that he is better informed than most people. Instead, he examines rocks and feathers with my daughter, as if he knows that the real connection with the Holy One comes in such moments. Perhaps the young see better than the rest of us, who clog our minds with knowledge we think will make us wise, but often brings nothing but greater bewilderment.

"Shall we do the blessing?" Isaac asks. This is what Eliana has been waiting for, the part she thinks an adult must do, although I've told her it isn't so. She knows I used to say blessings when I was her age, but she still doesn't know about the crucifix I wore or the sausages I threw into the grass. Someday I may tell her about living a lie, but that day hasn't come, and I am glad of it.

"Blessed art thou, Lord God, king of the universe," he chants. Every day, he makes up a different Sukkot blessing just for Eliana, and today his words bring a lump to my throat. "Who commands us to love all his people as parents love their children." My daughter turns to look at me with a confident smile.

The sages say that the sukkah radiates such intense bliss that the seven Ushpizim are lured away from the Garden of Eden, where they await the arrival of the Messiah. They come to earth to dwell inside the sukkah, which is the closest the living ever get to Eden. Watching Eliana and Isaac, I see a special light radiating around them, and more than ever I see how deeply I, and all of us, are blessed.

"He was a fool!"

I hear one of Judah's neighbors raise his voice, and I know the Zohar study is over. Eliana does too, and she runs to take Judah by the hand. "Grandfather! Come and look what I left for Jacob!"

Distracted by what the man has said, Judah doesn't hear her. "A man is hardly a fool who weds his daughter to the King of Portugal," he says, referring to the marriage of thirteen-year-old

Crown Prince Afonso in 1445 to a cousin of my childhood friends Elizabeth and Beatriz. Their uncle Pedro finished his regency when Afonso was crowned king, but not before ensuring his legacy by marrying his daughter to the young king.

"And look at how he paid for it," one man says. "All because he tried to be gracious to a rival who turned around and betrayed him." It was the talk of the court for several years, how the Duke of Barcelos, Pedro's half-brother, had worked his way into young Prince Afonso's heart. Knowing that Barcelos might be working against him, Pedro used his power as regent to create a new duchy for his half-brother as a way of creating an alliance, however uneasy, between them.

Overnight, the first Duke of Braganza became one of the richest and most powerful men in Portugal. Despite this, he could never forget that Pedro had denied him the real prize, a daughter as queen and his own descendants as heirs to the throne. When the new king was crowned and Pedro lost power as regent, the Duke of Braganza was bent not on gratitude but revenge.

The uprising that caused me to scurry to safety at the Abravanels several years ago was sparked when Braganza persuaded King Afonso to overturn all the laws Pedro had established during his regency. The fact that the newly crowned king was unready to announce policies of his own made many think the time was right to settle old scores with the Jews.

Chaos reigned, and with the Duke of Braganza whispering in his ear, King Afonso became convinced that the unrest was Pedro's doing. Declaring him a traitor and a rebel, the king dispatched troops to capture and kill the man who had served him loyally and well as regent. Pedro fought back and was killed, or as some whisper privately, murdered by an aide in his own camp.

"No one at court is a hero," Judah tells me, especially when he hears me express sympathy for Pedro. For Judah, what matters is how those with power treat Jews. For generations, there's been a struggle between the nobles and the king. For a ruler to undermine the nobility, he needs the support of the Cortes, the people's assembly. To have this, he must show that he is the enemy of the people's enemies. What better way to do that than taking aim at the Jews?

Sukkot has so excited Eliana that she is unable to nap, and by nightfall, she is crying at imagined slights and acting as if every touch hurts her. We eat quickly, and after I pack up the papers I am working on, I take her by the hand. "Say good night," I command, ignoring her wails of protest.

The full moon bathes our path with light as we return to our house. The crisp air calms my daughter, and by the time we have closed the door behind us, she is too tired to help me get her undressed. She flops in the bed we share, pleading for me to lie down with her until she falls asleep.

I hold Eliana close to me in bed, cradling her small shoulders in the pit of my arm and taking in the hint of dust and sweat in her hair. I shut my eyes, marveling how a power as strong as love doesn't burst us open like melons, spilling its sweetness into the world, because to keep it inside even for another moment is more than we can bear.

When I open my eyes again, I realize I have slept. I get up and put on a thick robe, shivering a little but glad the night is not so cold it will numb my fingers. I leave the door to our bedroom open in case Eliana wakes, and I put a log on the fire. I watch the bark glow before breaking into tiny filaments of gold that caress the wood and coax it into flame, and then I open my portfolio and take out several sheets of paper.

Judah tells me the Duke of Braganza is a great lover of poetry. I don't like the way he treated Pedro, but Judah finds it hard to believe anyone who appreciates poems could have a truly dark soul. When Pedro declared Arabic poetry to be the finest of all, Judah tactfully disagreed, explaining that he might feel otherwise if more Hebrew poetry were translated into Portuguese.

Delighted, Braganza challenged Judah to convince him, but my friend doesn't have the ear for such work himself, or the time. He showed me a book by Samuel Hanagid and asked if I could try my hand at it.

I open the book and read the poem I had been working on earlier at Judah's desk.

> *Think: the skies are like a tent,*
> *Stretched tight by loops and hooks;*
> *And the moon with its stars,*
> *A shepherdess on a meadow*
> *Grazing her flock;*
> *And the crescent hull in the clouds*
> *Looks like a ship being tossed;*

I dip my pen and continue.

> *A whiter cloud, a girl in her garden*
> *Tending her shrubs;*
> *And the dew coming down is her sister*
> *Shaking water from her hair onto the path…*

How could anyone have such beautiful thoughts? I have been holding my breath at the sheer magic of his lines, and suddenly I need to go outside to see the night sky for myself.

In the still air, the sting in my nostrils hints of approaching winter. The sky does look hooked overhead, and there she is, the shepherdess moon tending her flock of stars. Feathery clouds streak across the sky like a girl on horseback, her hair loose in the wind.

I wish there were someone to tell how I used to be that girl. I wish that person were a lover. The thought ambushes me with its cruel clarity. The only man I have known in that way would not have stood with me looking at the clouds, and I would never have risked sharing any private thoughts with him.

I pull my robe tight around me. Don't ask for too much, I tell myself, remembering the treasure who lies sleeping in the house and the refuge I have with the Abravanels. "I'm sorry," I whisper into the night. "Please don't think I'm ungrateful." Still, as I go back in the house and take up my pen to finish Hanagid's poem, my heart cries out with every beat for something more, and I cannot make it stop.

I put the translation aside and take out a new piece of paper. I stare into the dark room, composing my thoughts. Then I write.

> *The clouds blanket the cold moon,*
> *saying, "My love will warm you."*
> *The trees cast shade on the panting doe,*
> *saying, "My love will cool you."*
> *The sun beats down on spring mud,*
> *saying, "My love will firm your steps."*
> *The grass covers the parched soil,*
> *saying, "My love will soften you."*
> *And I, by turns too cold, too hot,*
> *too heavy, too soft.*
> *Where is the love to comfort me?*

I don't know if my first poem is good. I only know it's mine. My eyes sting from the low light, and I am suddenly so tired I have to summon new strength to go to bed. I crawl in next to Eliana and put my hand on her arm, just to be touching her, as I lie awake, aching and restless, until dawn.

❧

Over the next few days, I finish the poems for Judah. Only after he leaves do I realize that in the rush of his departure, I accidentally included my own. I fret for a day or two, wondering if Judah will be upset by what he will think is my presumption. Or worse, if he will laugh. Still, there's so much to do after Sukkot, and with

Isaac's departure for his yeshiva in Lisbon, Eliana is so clinging and needy that I have little time for any thoughts at all.

Simona and I are making the last preparations for Shabbat when we hear Judah's voice in the courtyard. We drop what we are doing and hurry out. Eliana is dancing in circles around him. "Shabbat shalom!" she sings as she reaches out to grab each of our hands in turn to wish us the peace of the Sabbath. "Where's Isaac?" she asks, looking toward the gate. The sun has nearly set, and if he doesn't arrive soon, he will not arrive at all, since traveling is forbidden by Jewish law from Friday to Saturday sundown.

"Sorry, little one," Judah says. "He said he couldn't get here, but to be sure to give you this." He pinches her nose, and she wiggles away laughing.

As we head back inside the house, Judah asks to speak with me. I see the quizzical look on his face and my heart sinks. The poem. It must be about the poem.

"Did you include something extra in the portfolio for Braganza?" Judah asks. Before I can explain it was an accident, he holds up his hand to stop me. "From the way the duke was sniffing about the poems, I was sure he didn't like them. Then he started reading one aloud, and I wondered why I didn't recognize it. Then it came to me that it wasn't one of Samuel Hanagid's at all." By now, Judah is seated at his desk and he leans back with a chuckle. "You, my dear, are the Duke of Braganza's favorite Jewish poet."

"Mama? A poet?" Eliana giggles.

I stare at Judah, dumbfounded. "No, Mama's not a poet," I tell her. "I wrote one poem, and the duke saw it by accident."

"You've never written another?" Judah asks.

"It just came to me one night. I did it to see if I could, that's all."

"Braganza's favorite Jewish poet has written one poem!" Judah laughs, but I can't manage a smile.

"Did you like it?" I ask, my voice nearly a whisper.

Judah turns to my daughter, his face suddenly serious. "Eliana, would you see if your grandmother needs some help?"

He waves me toward a chair after Eliana has run off. I perch stiffly and wait for him to answer my question. "It's a fine poem," he says. "I pondered it all the way home."

"Please don't think that I feel unloved," I rush to say. "I am the luckiest woman in Portugal, to be part of your family, and to have my daughter—"

Judah doesn't seem to hear. "The duke wants you to write poems for him. And when I told him more about you, he is most eager to make your acquaintance."

"Meet me?"

"I think you should say yes. No one can force you to write poetry if you don't want to, but it would be good to make yourself known at Braganza's court."

"I—" This whole conversation is so unexpected it is making me dizzy.

"You've been hiding in Queluz long enough," Judah says.

"Hiding?"

"I don't mean it as a criticism. You had wounds to heal, and you needed a place where you were truly welcome, among people you could trust. You had to learn to be a mother, and a Jew. You've done all those things now. We've been enjoying your company so much that we haven't noticed that God's gifts are being squandered here in Queluz."

"Squandered?" From someone else, I might take this as an insult, but Judah speaks with such love and wisdom that I lean forward, intent on what he has to say.

"Squandered," he repeats. "I remember you as a girl, turning Arabic, Portuguese, Castilian, even Latin into signs, so your father could understand the people around him. I remember you on that horse, speaking Hebrew as we rode back to Sintra. And your translations of Hanagid—they're superb."

I look down at my hands, embarrassed at such attention. "I haven't given up on the duke's literary tastes," Judah says when I don't reply. "I hope you'll translate some of Halevi's work next, or perhaps Moses ibn Ezra's. Braganza may eventually come to see there are good Jewish poets other than you." This time I smile with him.

"Amalia." Judah's voice is commanding. "Soar, don't settle." I recognize the first words of a poem by Judah Halevi.

Soar, don't settle for earth
and sky—soar to Orion;
And be strong, but not like an ox or mule
that's driven—strong like a lion.

We recite the poem together, falling silent when we have finished. Finally Judah speaks. "I hope you'll continue to write," he says. "In Hebrew or Portuguese—English, for all I care, if you choose to learn it. Use your voice. I imagine the Holy One is pleased finally to hear it again."

∽

I use that cold and rainy winter as an excuse to stay home to write. Eliana goes back and forth to the Abravanels, heedless of her mud-caked boots and soggy hems, leaving me precious hours to write a few words, pace, poke the fire, pace some more, and write another line.

By the time the hills are green again and the swallows are building their nests under my eaves, I have ten poems I am willing to share with the duke, and many more I am not. I feel different now, less lonely, as if the true Amalia had knocked and the shadow I had been was opening the door to let her in.

I bring the poems to the duke a few at a time, whenever I have cause to make the two-hour trip to Lisbon. One day in early May, Eliana and I have come on errands and stop first in the aljama to visit Chana, Rahel, and their children. We pass through the gate and I am struck, as always, by how different it feels to be inside among the Jews. Children chase each other down the crooked streets, avoiding by a hair's breadth the wares outside the greengro-cer's and the other shops. On a balcony, a woman is shaking a rug from a window while gossiping with a neighbor in the window across the narrow street. It's a warm day, and through the open window of a yeshiva, I hear the voices of boys chanting the Torah.

Though Lisbon's streets are familiar to me now, the aljama is the only place where I feel at home. Here, being a Jew is ordinary. Every store is kosher. The holiday greetings are for our festivals—Rosh Hashanah, Passover, Shavuot. The smell of meat stews and challah fills the air on Fridays, while silver is polished and fresh cloth-ing is put on. The streets on Saturday are filled with people singing as they come from the synagogue to dinner with family or friends. Men converge on a door leading to a small synagogue to form the minyan for prayers. It's a place with a wall that works both ways: to keep us in, and to keep out those whose fondest hope is that such sights, smells, and sounds will vanish from Lisbon soon, and forever.

Judah has come with us, and once we leave Eliana with Rahel, he and I start the climb to the palace. My visit does not take long. I read my poems and leave them with the duke's secretary for copying. After a few pleasantries, I excuse myself so the men can continue their business.

I sit waiting for Judah on the shaded walkway between the palace and the outer fortress walls, so we can enjoy the walk back to the aljama together.

Behind me, the city of Lisbon stretches out along the banks of the Tagus, which shimmers in the mellow light of late afternoon. I've brought along a book of poetry by Todros Abulafia that I've been working on for the duke, and I pull out a folded piece of paper on which a messy tangle of words, my first attempt at a translation, are strewn.

My thinking wove a song of purple and blue
For God, as manna and nectar were spun on my tongue.
I strung pearls of verse in his name, like a necklace...

I skim the words until I reach the end.

Your fear is over, Todros. Rise, and know
Your time and day and hour soon will come.

The voices of men walking up the path startle me. One is wearing clothing in the Moorish style—loose silk pants under a tunic
belted at the waist with a brightly patterned sash, his turbaned head
cloaked in a hooded burnoose. I float unaware to my feet. The
paper and book fall to the ground. The man must hear it, or perhaps the same force that bid me stand causes him to turn around.
His skin is bronzed, and his turquoise eyes lance me with a look
so intense I feel it all the way to my loins. My hand comes to my
heart, as if I must hold it inside my chest to keep it from escaping
with the next beat.

He comes over to pick up what I dropped. "You are a poet?"
he asks, scanning the words on the paper. He leans in toward me
almost imperceptibly, as if my answer will be news he has long
waited to hear.

"I'm a translator for the Duke of Braganza." I want to impress
him, so I switch to Arabic. "I write a little myself," I say, "but
nothing as good as this."

"We shall have to trade verses sometime." He laughs, his white
teeth flashing in the sunlight. "I hope you will not think me forward if I introduce myself," he says with a graceful bow. "Abu
Sawwar Jamil ibn Hasan. Emissary from Muhammad the Ninth,
the Caliph of Granada, and a poet with none of your modesty."
He nods in the direction of his friends. "Here I am known simply
as Jamil."

My head is spinning as I tell him my name. I don't know
whether meeting a man in this fashion is proper, and I don't care
because I know—I just know—that this is supposed to happen,
that everything in my past conspired to lead me here. My time,
my day, my hour...

Soar, don't settle. The words pour into my heart as if their force had been held back by walls in my mind as thick as those of the palace in front of me. Not like an ox or mule, I tell myself. Like a lion.

12

My body is too old and dry to waken as it once did at the thought of Jamil, but the hair on my arms rises so quickly I can almost hear it crackle as he comes up behind me.

"You're here," I whisper.

"Habibi," he says. "Yes, my love."

I rise to my feet, my heart aching with joy and sorrow. "I was hoping you might still be alive," I say as his arms envelop me. "I wrote to your wife to ask, but she didn't answer."

He doesn't reply. He doesn't need to. Only the spirits of the dead can visit the living, and I knew the moment I sensed his presence in this room that he did not survive the last days of the Christian siege of Granada. Though ashamed of my selfishness, I am glad he is here.

"Your family too?" I whisper.

"Two of my granddaughters jumped from a tower to avoid being touched by Ferdinand and Isabella's soldiers. The rest—"

It feels as if all the air in the room has been let out in one desolate sigh. "The poor had little to eat during the siege, and once disease found us, it had a taste for the rich as well. My wife…" He is silent for a moment. "I loved her, Amalia. She was a good woman."

Tears spring to my eyes. "And your sons?"

"Both dead."

Ahmad. My heart floods with memories, and the cracks in the skin of my face sting with tears. The room hums with silence, as if some barely heard music has died.

"Allah in his mercy made me welcome death." His breath is hot on my shoulders. "I am at peace now. I came to comfort you."

The skin on my back prickles like a puff of breeze passing over water. "You are always here," I whisper. "My love for you is written in my bones."

His smile warms the air as he speaks.

"What do scholars and sailors know of the shape of the world,
With their astrolabes, their spyglasses, their calculations?
The shape of the world is the fullness of your breasts,
As you lie on your side and I trace my finger between them."

The white sheets on the bed...the warm Andalusian sun pouring in from the garden...the smell of oranges and jasmine. My body, still young enough to be supple, and his so strong, so firm beneath my touch...

He takes my wispy hair in his hands and crushes it between his fingers, tingling my scalp and neck. "I remember when you wrote that for me," I tell him. "How close we came to never meeting."

His finger is on my lips, stopping me from going on. "I would have found you," he replies. "Didn't you feel it in the air the day we met? The inevitability of it?"

I remember getting up, my book falling from my lap, as if I had just caught sight of someone long delayed for whom I had been keeping watch. "I was waiting for you." I whisper.

"And I came. Perhaps your sighs were carried on the breeze to Granada and I heard you calling." He teases the laces on my dress and I look down to see they are untied. "You told me to come, and I did."

The brush of his lips on mine is as soft as the toes of angels dancing. "The barriers in life are false," he whispers. "We have always been together, even before we met. Then, now, and forever, I am with you."

QUELUZ 1451

I try to sound offhand when I ask Judah about the Muslim courtier I met at the palace, but I don't think he is fooled. I am far more interested than I should be in someone who, like many others, is passing through on court business.

I can't get my mind off him. His eyes are blue-green like the water in the coves at Sagres, in a face like glowing copper. I imagine the contours of his arms under his filmy silk tunic, the strong thighs apparent from the lightness in his step. I wonder if he has hair on his chest and whether it is coarse or fine. And then I picture it all again.

A few weeks later, I come with my daughter to Judah and Simona's house at midday for Shabbat dinner. We enter the compound gate just as an unfamiliar horse is being led away by a groom. From inside the house, I hear the boisterous sounds of men greeting each other.

"Who's here?" Eliana asks, dropping my hand and hurrying toward the open door. "It's a man," she says, coming back to me. "With a big cloth over his head."

Jamil. My hand strays to my hair, but it is too late to rush home to make myself more presentable. My heart pounds as I walk into the house.

Jamil's back is to me, but when he sees Judah look in my direction, he turns around. His eyes crinkle in a smile, and again I am not sure what is more remarkable—his teeth, white and even as a row of pearls, or his astonishing eyes.

"Our distinguished visitor from Granada has taken me up on my offer to join us for Shabbat!" Judah's voice booms with pleasure as Simona sets another place at the table.

"Are you Jewish?" Eliana asks, taking in Jamil's unusual appearance.

"No," he says, smiling down at her. "I am Muslim."

Eliana screws up her face. "What's a Moosman?"

"You aren't being very polite," I tell her, but since a child's Sabbath is not to be spoiled by criticism, I am gentle in my chiding. "You haven't even told him who you are."

"Don't you worry about that," Jamil tells her. "I haven't told you who I am either." He sweeps down in an exaggerated bow, as if he were greeting a princess. "I am Abu Sawwar Jamil ibn Hasan," he says, "at your service."

Eliana giggles. "That's a lot of names!" From the roses in her cheeks I can see she already likes him.

Jamil turns to me. "Senhora Marques. It is a pleasure to see you again."

"The pleasure is mine," I say, and feeling suddenly bold, I tease him. "No bow for me?" He grins and repeats the gesture while my daughter giggles from her new perch in Judah's arms.

Jamil turns to Eliana, who is snuggling against Judah's bearded chest. "We worship the same God, though we call him by different names," he tells her. "And I've come to share the peace of the Sabbath with you. 'Shabbat shalom,' I believe you say."

"Shabbat shalom," Eliana repeats, wiggling to signal she wants to be let down. "Would you like to see the birds in the garden?"

Jamil gives us the look of someone helpless against the wishes of a child. Taking the offer of her hand, they go off, leaving Judah and me alone.

"You are not unhappy I invited him?" he asks.

Embarrassed, I look away. "My daughter obviously likes him."

"And so do you, if I am a good judge of such things." Judah's eyes are twinkling. "He's a widower with a young child. You have that in common. And he's an honorable man too, from everything I hear. One of the caliph's most trusted diplomats."

"I—" I sigh with frustration, wishing I knew what I thought. "But he's not a Jew."

"No, and that would be a problem if you wished to marry, but is that what we're discussing?" Judah clasps his hands behind his back and rocks from the balls of his feet to the heels, as he always does when he is interested in something. "It's not my place to meddle or even suggest what you should do—unless it violates our covenant with God, and then you would be sure to hear from both me and my wife."

Simona. Had they been plotting this encounter together?

Judah goes on. "As a widow, you have some choice in your life, because—how shall I put it?—your maidenhood doesn't require protecting." He looks away, embarrassed by the personal nature of his comment. "There are ways to keep the respect of others and live one's own way with dignity. You are made by the Holy One of flesh and blood. The senses have their place, and God means us to be happy."

What is he saying? I want to rub my ears to see if perhaps I have misunderstood.

"I'm not suggesting anything," Judah says, reading the thoughts that must be written on my face. "There could be problems ahead if you were to—to mean something to each other. And you have your daughter to think about. Still, you and Jamil might have— what should I say?—an interesting friendship." His solemn eyes are offset by the teasing crook in the corner of his mouth. "I remember your poem, Amalia. You wondered what comfort there might be for you in this world, but I'm not sure you are paying attention to where you might find it."

Eliana comes back, flushed with excitement. "Jamil can—what did you call it?"

"Whistle," he says, smiling first at her and then at me.

"Whistle!" she repeats. "He made the birds come to him!"

More than the birds, I think, not daring to look him in the eye.

⁓

Eliana's glow is caused by more than excitement. She takes a longer nap than usual, and when she wakes up, her skin is hot and her throat is sore. We don't wait for the end of Shabbat to leave, and though home is only a few steps away, she begs to be carried. I am not strong enough, and seeing my distress, Jamil offers to carry her himself.

He brings her inside and lays her down, and for a moment, we stand awkwardly by my bed. "I must leave," he says. "It doesn't look proper."

Brushing Eliana's hair from her face, I kiss her forehead as she drifts off to sleep. "I think she'll be fine, if you want to stay for a moment." I look around, though I'm not sure at what. "I'm afraid I can't offer you much, since it's still Shabbat and I can't prepare food, but I do have some bread and jam, and a bit of wine." Suddenly the intimacy of the house unnerves me. "Or perhaps we could go outside and watch the sunset."

He smiles. "After cooking as good as Judah's wife's, I'm glad you don't insist I eat again."

Wisps of smoke rise from the chimneys of my Christian neighbors preparing their Saturday supper. The bark of a dog and the cries of birds readying for the night are the only intruders on the silence. The low, green fields are splashed red with poppies as they ripple upward toward the mountains of Sintra. The clouds absorb the light of the setting sun, glowing scarlet and gold above the jagged, black outline of the peaks.

"Look at the wheat," Jamil says in Arabic,

"Bending before the wind
Like squads of horsemen
Fleeing in defeat, bleeding
From the wounds of the poppies."

He turns to me. "Do you know Ibn Iyad? He was a poet centuries ago."

Can this be happening? Can I be standing where I once watched the stars, wanting nothing more than to have someone by my side, and now with a handsome man reciting poetry to me? I breathe out slowly to calm myself. "I'm sorry to say I don't know much about poetry except what I translate. My education was far more practical."

"Nothing is more practical than poetry," he says with a quizzical smile. "It teaches us how to be human."

The sun is now below the horizon. "Shabbat is over," I say, relieved to have something to tell him. I pick a poppy from the base of the wall. "We always end it by smelling something fragrant and wishing each other a sweet week. Poppies don't smell, but—"

He closes his eyes as I put it under his nose. "Have a sweet week, Jamil," I say, trying out the way his name sounds on my lips. When he opens his eyes and catches me staring at him, I don't look away. He thinks for a moment, then speaks.

"In the sweetness of this moment with you,
Fields of flowers, having only color and scent,
Hang their heads in embarrassment."

"Did the same poet write that?" I ask.

"I made it up just now. A gift for you."

For a moment, I think he is going to kiss me, but instead he turns to look at the remnants of the setting sun. "I am asking myself, 'Can there really be such a woman?'" His voice is so soft it seems he is talking to the air, and I'm not sure if I should respond. What would I say? That I don't know what he means? That the way he says the word "woman" makes me aware of the body under my clothes?

"Eliana will wake soon and need you." He searches my face. "May I call tomorrow to see how she is?"

"Of course," I say, surprised at the tremor in my voice.

He laughs. "After all, neither of us has to worry about going to church. There are some benefits to being who we are."

Eliana's cry drifts from the bedroom. "I must be going," we say in unison and laugh at the coincidence. I watch through a crack in the door as he walks away, then I crawl in next to my daughter, to fasten myself to this world by holding her tight.

༺໐

I don't see Jamil the following day. Instead, he sends a court page with a letter.

"The king has requested my company, and I cannot get away," he has written in a beautiful Arabic hand. "As I rode to Sintra last night, I recalled a poem by Ibn Hazm.

> *"Have you come from the world of angels, or from this?*
> *Tell me clearly now, for I'm perplexed and looking silly.*
> *I know without a doubt that you are the kindred soul*
> *Which had to bond with mine it so resembles.*
> *I find no logical proof of your existence,*
> *Save only that I see you here before me!*
> *And if my eye could not take in your being, I would say*
> *You are pure mind, authentic and sublime."*

I see that there is writing below, but I cannot absorb any more, and I put the letter down. Who could be that special? The stories I used to read with Elizabeth and Beatriz about the princess whose indifference breaks hearts, the aloof maiden who spurns love— perhaps they acted as they did because they knew a suitor's ardor would not survive the truth of their ordinariness.

"As I wrote out this poem, I realized I cannot lie to you," Jamil has written below. "I am staying away for another reason. If you wish to see me, I will come next Sunday, but my passions are not easily left behind, and, dear lady, I shall bring them with me or it would be best not to come at all. If you are agreeable, and the weather permits, we can go riding. Judah tells me you are quite the horsewoman. At your service, Jamil ibn Hasan."

Judah. Of course. The Zohar advises against taking a widow to wife, because the spirit of her first husband can plague the second. "Do not cook in a pot in which your neighbor has cooked," the ancient rabbi Akiba warned. There's no future Jewish husband to save myself for, no blood kin to tell me what to do, and no one who will be harmed by my going for a ride with Jamil and seeing where it leads. I pick up a quill to pen my reply.

പ

The following Sunday, Jamil arrives with a mount the same color as Chuva, who died several years ago, and I wonder again whether Judah has been filling Jamil's head with details about me. Eliana is happy to run off to the Abravanels, especially since Chana and Rahel have not yet taken their children back to Lisbon.

"I thought we might ride up to the ruins of the fort," he says. "Have you been there?"

"It's the first place I went when I got here," I tell him. At the time, I could barely contain my excitement at the thought of finding Jews evicted from Sintra living together in a deserted palace, but when I got there, the fort was a ruin, and the town's few Jews had been back in town for years.

It doesn't take long to reach an arched entrance that still has rusty bolts and splinters of rotting wood from the sturdy doors that once protected the fortress. Against the inside walls of the plaza sag the ruins of weather-beaten shacks, hastily constructed of rough stone and wood. Makeshift chimneys leading up from blackened hearths jutting through toppled roofs.

"Did you know the Jews were once forced to live here?" I ask Jamil as we water our horses from a cistern of rainwater. "These are the houses they built."

He takes in the dreary sight. "Whenever I feel insulted among Christians, I remember the many places where my people have the respect they deserve. I can't imagine what it's like not to be treated with dignity anywhere."

"Jews don't spend much time thinking how good things could be if this world were a different place," I say with a wry smile.

"We're usually just grateful it's not worse." I take my horse by the reins. "There's a lovely place near here to sit. We can have our meal and let the horses graze." Jamil's eyes are bright, as if something has pleased him. He takes his horse and follows me.

Grass and wildflowers have taken over what was once a busy square, where Moors sat on stone benches watching people come and go. Guards once paced the mossy ramparts that lead to crenellated towers looming above us. The castle is above the clouds today, and the plaza is a brilliant, sun-dappled green. Jamil takes down the food we have brought and lays a brightly patterned rug underneath a tree.

He pulls out a leather wineskin and a small cup into which he puts a little for me before tipping back his head and squirting a thin stream of red wine into his mouth. I lay out the torn end of a loaf from yesterday's Shabbat dinner, and Jamil produces two dry sausages.

"I can't eat that," I tell him. "I don't know what's in it."

Jamil smiles. "Don't worry. I have the butcher's word it's kosher. The Prophet Muhammad—ṣallallahu ëalayhi wa sallam—commands us to keep many of the same dietary laws you do."

"May Allah honor him and grant him peace?" I ask, turning his Arabic into a question.

"Muslims honor the prophets—Jesus, Moses, and the rest. When we speak their names, we ask God to grant them peace."

Jamil cuts me a piece of sausage, and the smoky taste of paprika and pungent garlic invades every recess of my mouth. I crush a juniper berry between my teeth and its resinlike flavor mixes with the sweet taste of the meat. "It's delicious," I say, as he cuts me another slice.

"You're quite trusting." He holds it out to me on the tip of his knife. "Eating sausage just on my word that it's all right?"

"Trusting?" I hope to sound lighthearted, but my voice comes out solemn and husky. "I'm here alone with you, aren't I?"

His eyes are penetrating, and my comfort vanishes. What does he want from me? Have I made a mistake coming with him? I look to my horse, grazing in the shadows of the rampart walls, and wonder if I should get away as quickly as I can.

"Yes, you are," Jamil says, "and I shall honor your trust." He smiles. "Even if that means protecting you from me." He reclines, propping himself up on one elbow, but I remain seated, my legs curled discreetly under me. "I thought if I brought you here where there were no distractions, I might find out more about you," he says. "Where you have been. What you want."

No one has ever wondered such things about me, and I am so disarmed that, before I know it, I have recounted my life as a secret Jew with my mother, my years at Sagres with Papa, my grim marriage to Diogo, and my salvation in the embrace of the Abravanel family.

He listens quietly. "You've already been through enough for several lifetimes," he says, fixing his intense and beautiful eyes on me.

I look away to avoid his stare. "I imagine you have too."

Jamil smiles. "That's for another day." He gets up to fetch something from his bag. "I brought one more treat for us," he says, unwrapping a cloth. "Something from home. You have dates here, but not like these."

The fruit is larger than any I have seen, with creased and fragile-looking folds of skin around soft, glistening flesh. "We call them mujhoolah," Jamil says, cutting one in half and removing the seed with a flick of his knife. He pinches a morsel between his fingertips and touches the silky flesh to my mouth. It dissolves and breaks away from the skin with the slightest pressure of my tongue. "Mmm," I sigh.

"Would you like more?" He puts another piece in my mouth, and then he speaks.

"Laughing, you paint your lips brown with date.
The pink tip of your tongue licks its nectar from your fingers.
Do we enter Paradise like this?
Casting off our cloaks like the skin of a mujhoolah
Our flesh melting away in sweet delight?"

His eyes are shining. "You bring out the poet in me," he says.

I take another date and paint my mouth before feeding half to him and eating the rest myself. Who is this woman, I ask myself, who does such things with a man?

Then his lips are on mine, softer and fuller than I imagined possible. He teases my mouth open and I feel sweetness mingle on our tongues. He pulls away with a smile. "Perhaps it would be wise to swallow first."

I laugh from somewhere deep within me, not just because what he said strikes me as funny, but because I am soaring, I am singing, I am shedding all the burdens of my past and beginning again.

He kisses me more deeply, cupping his hand around my neck to hold me to him. I kiss him back, yearning to find every secret of his mouth, as if I could lick through to his soul. To my surprise, I feel Jamil pull away. "Are you sure this is what you want?" he asks. "We should stop now if it isn't, and I will take you home."

I know what I want—his lips on my hard nipples, bared to the sun and the summer air, his hands lifting my skirts to give me something I have never had, never knew enough to dream of. I pull myself back. "It's too sudden," I say. "I have to think about Eliana too. About what's best for her—and me."

To my surprise, he looks relieved. He stands up, and looking down at the protrusion in his trousers, he sighs. "My mind tells me to be chivalrous," he says, "but it appears that another part of my body has a different idea." Embarrassed, I look away, secretly thrilled to have done that to him.

"I don't take these things lightly," Jamil says. "I don't make a habit of enticing women."

"You could have anyone," I say. "I'm twenty-six years old. I've borne two children—"

He pulls me to my feet. "You're right. There are many beautiful girls I can have at home by snapping my fingers." He takes me in his arms. "And I won't deny I have partaken of such pleasure, but it makes no impression on me. I'm looking for a woman who is a feast for body and mind. Someone who frees the poetry in my soul."

He pulls away to look in my eyes. "A woman, Amalia. Not a girl. Am I wrong? Is that not what you are?" He pauses. "You're trembling."

I fight back tears. "I'm not sure what I am, but I do think it's best you take me home."

"You need time to think," Jamil says. "It shows you don't take these things lightly either. I wouldn't like that." He tosses the remains of our meal to the birds and goes to get our horses.

13

That night, I lie next to my daughter, unable to sleep. What do I really know about Jamil? If there were something wrong with his character, Judah would have warned me. But Diogo was attractive and charming at the beginning too, and if I had really loved him, he would have broken my heart.

I think about the way Jamil endeared himself to my daughter and how he did not press me for more than I wanted to give at the fort. I think about his poems, and about his embarrassment at the bulge in his trousers. I remember how my body felt when he kissed me, and how surprised I was when I returned home to feel that the hair in my private place was matted and wet.

My daughter stirs next to me. I must keep my thoughts straight, I tell myself, not just for me but for her. I could never marry him— Judah is right about that—and I haven't gone to all this trouble to live as a Jew just to throw it away.

Ask yourself what you don't want to regret at the end of your life.

"Mama?" I whisper. Somehow, she's heard my distress, for I sense her beside me. "But what about her?" I whisper, reaching over to touch my daughter.

She won't always be young. She'll have her own life when she's grown. Will you be able to make up for lost time then?

"I just want what's best for her."

Perhaps what would make you happy would be best for her too.

Eliana snuffles and rolls over. "I love her so much," I tell the dark, still air where my mother's spirit hovers.

The more love you start with, the more can grow.

I lie thinking for a moment, and then I get up. Lighting a candle, I settle in at my desk and begin to write.

> *You said that wishing the prophets peace would bring that peace*
>   *to me.*
> *Our day leaves me sleepless, and I ask you this:*
> *If I wish my lips were upon yours, would you bring your kisses*
>   *to me?*
> *If I wish myself to love you, would you love me in return?*

ᑽ

The following morning, Eliana seems well enough for a ride, so I suggest we go to Sintra to buy her a new hair ribbon. At the palace, I give one of the pages a coin to take my poem to Jamil. "We'll be in town all morning, if there's a reply," I tell him.

I let Eliana dawdle over her choice of ribbon and end up buying her two. We stop at the vegetable shop to get a carrot for our horse and go into the bakery to buy a treat for Simona. Then, when I can think of no other reason to delay, Eliana's face lights up. "Jamil!" she says. I whirl around and see him standing inside the bakery door.

"I hoped I would find you." He holds out the letter. "My answer didn't take long."

Below my writing, he has written one word.

Yes.

ᑽ

A week later, Jamil meets me near the palace. "I'll take you to a side entry," he says. "I've bribed the guard." He adjusts the hood of my cloak to obscure my face. This is a mistake, I tell myself, hesitating to take the first step. And then I do. Even if it's a mistake, I am going to make it gladly and without hesitation.

"The servants know not to disturb me when the outer door is closed," he says when we are inside his quarters. He takes my cloak and stands back to look at me. "You enchant me," he murmurs.

We stare into each other's eyes until I think I may disappear altogether, like a boat slipping over the horizon into an unknown sea. I feel a tug in my belly as he pulls my hair free from the band holding it. I shake it out so that it falls down my back, and I hear his quick intake of breath.

We kiss deeply, hungrily. He pulls my dress down to my waist and cups my breasts through my chemise. I help him remove my underskirts until I am standing before him in only a single layer of thin silk. It's so unlike my wedding night that I want to laugh. My body feels glorious, and I want this beautiful person to know every part of me.

Jamil's hair touches his shoulders like a lion's mane, and I run my fingers through it. He unbuckles his belt, and soon his voluminous pants have dropped to his knees, and he stands before me, his erect penis surrounded by a nimbus of velvety dark hair.

When he is down to only a thin shirt, he takes me in his arms. I make room for his hand to slip between my thighs, and I feel his fingers stroking and separating the pink lips of my most private place. I moan with pleasure, and when he feels my knees give way, he guides me into the bedroom.

He helps me gently into bed, then spreads my legs with his knees and teases the insides of my thighs. Taking some of my wetness on his fingers, he touches his lips and then mine. He moves forward and brushes the tip of his penis against me, and I spread my legs wider, as if I could grow around him and satisfy myself that way even if he never moved at all.

Then he is inside me. His thighs are muscular and hard, and I use my own to grip his, bringing my hands down around his buttocks to move with him. A feeling grows within me, something close to pain but so glorious I want it to go on and on. Jamil drives hard into me until my body is splitting all the way to my mouth, bursting open with waves of pleasure so great I don't care how loudly I cry out.

We go on, at times with small and exquisite movements and then with wild abandon that leaves our bodies slick with sweat. I hear Jamil's breath grow shorter and more insistent, and suddenly he pulls out of me. White fluid makes an arch from his penis onto my belly. I have never seen such a thing, and then I remember that of course we must not make a baby.

With a grunt of satisfaction, he falls on his back and breaks out in soft, amazed laughter, as our breath slowly calms. Lying in Jamil's arms throws the last bit of earth on the grave of my sad and lonely marriage. I am finally alive as a woman—blessedly, amazingly alive.

ᏂᏇᏆ

"Your mind's wandering," Simona says gently, as I look down to see a few pears in the bottom of my basket and hers already full. Two months have passed since Jamil and I became lovers, and on this sultry September morning, with a hint of fall in the air, my thoughts are the only part of me that hasn't slowed to a stop.

Jamil must return to Granada soon, and he wants me to go with him. The caliph needs a tutor for his grandchildren, and Jamil has arranged for me to have a respectable life at court if I should want it. There are children for Eliana to befriend, and Jamil tells me the Muslim custom of men having more than one woman will make it easier for us to be together openly. Jamil is waiting for me to agree, but the word "yes" won't cross my lips.

"I love it here in Queluz," I say. "To be somewhere else, and know that the pears were ready to pick and you were doing it without me? To celebrate the High Holy Days without your family?" I bring my sleeve up to wipe my eyes. "I'm crying again," I say, trying to smile. "Isn't love supposed to make people happy?"

"You don't have to leave," Simona reminds me. "You can tell Jamil you won't go."

"I know," I reply, "and I've almost told him that, more than once. But being with him here in Queluz is so—" I struggle to find the word. "It's embarrassing to have you know what we're doing when Jamil's horse is outside my door and Eliana has been shooed off to visit you."

Simona's eyebrows arch as if the decision should be easy, but I know she understands. I turn my attention to the pears to keep from pouring out worries my friend has already listened to more patiently than most people would.

Jamil has been gone almost two weeks on a hunting trip near Tomar with King Afonso, a taste of what my life will be like when he leaves Lisbon. Will I then be just a woman who lives in a faraway town, someone he sees so rarely that love doesn't really matter? For diplomats, kings always come before lovers. Jamil will go where he is sent, and he might never be here again.

Then again, what would it be like to be a Jew in Granada if I went with him? Would Eliana and I light Shabbat candles alone? At whose table would we sit for the Passover seder? Where would I break the fast after our Day of Atonement?

Simona reminds me I am not leaving Queluz forever. But sometimes people don't come back. Sometimes we do, but what we want to recapture is no longer there. Only later do we realize that, without knowing it, we have already done something or seen someone for the last time. The more ordinary a thing is, the less likely we are to know the moment we lose it.

"You've stopped picking again." Simona wipes her brow. "We can get the last of the pears tomorrow. Another day will do them no harm."

One fact stares back unsaid. Jamil and I are wrong for each other as husband and wife. That thought bores holes in my heart when days pass without the sweet reassurance of being in his arms. A love that can never bring me a child? A love without the dignity of marriage? A love that, although not forbidden by either Muslims or Jews, will be viewed with suspicion and distaste by those less enlightened than Judah and Simona? Would I not live to regret what I have done if I spent—what?—perhaps years with him?

I want nothing more than that. Every dream of my future has three people in it—Eliana, Jamil, and me. Spring, fall, morning, evening, here, everywhere.

Word comes a few days later that the king's party will return to Lisbon by nightfall. Simona and I have gone to the mikveh built into the compound wall, so I can purify myself to greet my lover. Though women usually go alone to perform their ritual baths, after our first immersion in the fountain in the freezing rain, my friend and I have often done it together.

The space, stuccoed white and tiled in blue and green, is no bigger than necessary to contain a bench and seven steps leading into water deep enough to cover ourselves fully, one at a time. Simona lowers herself into the water first with a contented sigh. She chants the blessing in her lovely rich voice, and I watch the top of her head disappear under the surface. She comes up smiling, water pouring off her face and body, before immersing for the second and third times. Wiping her eyes, she moves her lips in prayer, then steps out of the pool.

"Blessed art thou, Lord God, king of the universe, who makes us holy by embracing us in living waters," I say as I step naked into the water, wiggling my toes to let it surround them. A tingling sensation travels up my spine to the nape of my neck as I lower myself into the water and lose myself in the sanctity of the moment.

Simona is wringing her hair as I get out. I sit next to her, dripping wet, enjoying the rare blessing of a calm heart and empty mind. "Jamil will want an answer about Granada when he comes," she says, breaking the spell.

"Yes," I say, sighing deeply as I reach for my towel. "I suppose he will." I open my eyes to meet her expectant gaze. "I keep thinking the right answer will come to me, but it hasn't."

"Maybe it won't," Simona says. "Maybe there isn't one right answer." She puts her hands on my towel and massages the moisture from my hair. "What do you like about going to Granada?"

"Jamil tells me I can hear poetry every night. Musicians play and women dance, and people eat and drink until dawn."

"And you would like that?"

Maybe it's human nature to hoist our sails, to climb a mountain, to get on a horse and just keep riding. To risk what we have, just to see if there might be something more. Then again, what could I see of the world that could make me happier than I am right now? I stand up and stretch my body, letting the towel fall to the ground.

Simona breaks into my thoughts, reminding me I haven't answered her. "My question is, does Jamil make you realize what you have always wanted, or does he make you want new things you probably wouldn't if they weren't part of him?"

I slip my chemise over my head, feeling it cling to my still-damp breasts.

"What do you want from your life, Amalia?" Her voice is soft but insistent. "Any decision about staying or leaving will come without a struggle when you understand what about your deepest self Jamil has spoken to." She mops her brow. "We'll never get dry in here, in all this heat. Shall we go out in the garden? We have the whole place to ourselves."

Judah left early that morning for Lisbon, taking Eliana with him for a visit with Chana and Rahel, and all the servants have the afternoon off. Unconcerned about covering ourselves, we drape our towels on a bench in the arbor and sit down, letting the dappled sun dance on our skin.

I have been trying to think of how to respond to her, but the deepest self she spoke of is a mystery, and so far a mute one. "I'll comb your hair," I tell her, to fill the silence. I stand behind the bench and lay the mass of hair down her back. I work through each strand, noticing the quiet encroachment of gray. She must be close to forty now, I realize.

"How old were you when you married Judah?" I ask.

"Sixteen," she says. "He was twenty-six and already quite a leader. I couldn't believe I was the one he wanted."

"I used to be so jealous of you when I was married to Diogo. I thought you had the perfect life. No one does, but I didn't know it then."

Simona laughs. "I was seventeen when I had Chana. I never had a chance to wonder whether there might be something more. By the time I first asked myself that, there was a baby at my breast and dinner to be made."

"Are you sure you don't mean something less? Less work perhaps? Not so many obligations?"

"No." Simona does not acknowledge my teasing tone as she gets up to change places. "That's not what I mean." She picks up a strand of my hair. "You are the freest person I know, Amalia. I love my life, but for every bit of jealousy you may have had about me, I'm sure I've had just as much about you."

"Me?"

"When Diogo was alive, my heart ached for you, but now there's so much you can decide for yourself. Go, stay, take a lover, live alone. It's up to you. Living here in Queluz should be your choice, not just something where you say, 'Oh, look where I ended up,' without knowing how it happened."

Simona works her way through another strand of my hair. "I'd hate to see you use your confusion as an excuse not to take the gift of freedom God has granted you. Stay here if that's what you want, but not because you can't decide what to do."

She touches my shoulders. "Relax," she says. "I can see how tense you are."

Her loving hands make it impossible to worry about anything. To my surprise, that's all I need.

"I have to go," I murmur.

Simona stands up straight and looks toward the door. "Did you hear horses? Is he here?"

"That's not what I mean," I say. "I have to go to Granada."

14

Jamil, Eliana, and I set sail down the Tagus River in November.
We travel south, and I strain with a tumult of emotions to see the
vague outline of the promontory at Sagres, before we turn east and
continue to the mouth of the Guadalquivir River on the southern
coast of Spain.

Passing Sagres, I told Eliana every story I could remember about
my life there, but as we near Sevilla, the city of my childhood, I fall
silent. How could I explain that I once made the sign of the cross
and stood in line for communion? But how else will she know
what wonderful women are in our family, and how important my
mother and grandmother's conspiracies were to who I became and
to who she is now?

On business in Sevilla for the Caliph of Granada, Jamil will
reside at the palace of my father's former employer, the Count of
Medina-Sidonia, but Eliana and I will stay with some of Judah's
relatives. When we dock, Jamil sends a messenger to the address
Judah gave, and before long, a young man approaches us, wearing
a yellow circle on his chest. "I am Yakov Abravanel," he says. "My
uncle Judah told us you were coming, and we've been worried
you wouldn't get here by sundown." It must be Friday, I realize.
On the water, I lost track of time.

"What's that circle on your coat?" Eliana asks.

"All the Jews wear these," he says with a shrug.

"Where are ours, Mama?" She thinks the circle is an honor. Edicts for Jewish dress were not enforced when I lived here, and I feel a wave of uneasiness at what else I might find changed.

"We need to get some circles right away," Eliana says, sounding at six like a little housewife. "We can sew them on when Shabbat is over."

She takes my hand and says no more because, as far as she is concerned, there's nothing to discuss. What could possibly be wrong with being a Jew? I say a silent blessing that she has been so well protected within the bosom of Judah and Simona's family.

Once the carts have left with our things, we set out on foot for the Abravanel's home. The Jewish quarter lies near the cathedral, whose massive towers are visible everywhere, and as we come through a covered arch next to the Alcazar, the church bells in the Giralda Tower ring out the hour.

Eliana stops to cover her ears, looking up at the astonishing mass of the cathedral. "They built a palace for God?" she asks, looking puzzled. I squeeze her hand, remembering how I stood miserably with my mother, watching with a sympathy so great it made me cry, as birds that had flown in through open doors flung themselves against the glass, unable to comprehend why they could not escape.

"I suppose that's what they thought they were doing," I reply vacantly, feeling the weight of the past pressing in around me.

We follow along the walls of the palace until we reach the tiny Jewish quarter. I expect the Abravanel's home to be large and stately, and I am surprised when we stop in front of a door indistinguishable from any other on the dilapidated street. "They're here!" Yakov says, throwing open the door, and we hear happy voices even before we pass the threshold.

An old man with a stooped back and a long gray beard clears his throat. In a gravelly voice, he intones the blessing for travelers. "The Lord preserve your going out and your coming in," he adds, "from this time forth and forever."

"Ken yehi ratzon," I whisper. "May it be so." I put my arm around my daughter's tiny shoulder and pull her to me.

"The candles, Ester," he says to a woman in her thirties who must be the mistress of the house. The moment they are lit and the blessings said, the whole family bursts into song. Eliana joins in at the top of her voice, wanting everyone to see that she knows the words by heart.

∽

The block I lived on as a child burned a few years ago, I am told, but both my sisters live not far from here—Susana, with her rock-hard soul, and Luisa, who hasn't written to me since she took vows. They don't know I am in Sevilla. We are nothing to each other except shared blood, but of course that is enough. I intend to search for them, though I can't imagine any of us will be pleased with what we find.

On Sunday, I give one of Ester's sons Susana's address, to inquire if my sister will see me. He comes back with grim news. She has been dead a month, stricken by a malady that wasted her to skin and bones within a year.

I leave my daughter with Ester and go to pay my respects to Susana's family. Her sister-in-law is a dour-looking woman with a face as long and thin as a horse but with none of its beauty. "You are the other sister," she says with no enthusiasm. I wait for her to say more, but she doesn't.

"I'm sorry I wasn't here sooner," I say. "I would have liked to say good-bye."

Before she can reply, a young man and woman appear in the doorway. It takes a moment to recognize Pablo and Ana Maria, who came to visit Papa and me at Sintra. Pablo, who was six then, is now fourteen, and Ana Maria twelve.

"I'm sorry about your mother," I say.

"Everybody dies," Ana Maria says, looking away with a shrug.

"Yes," I say, not sure whether her reaction is indifference or the shock of her loss. "But she was still quite young, and so are you, to have to go on now without her."

Ana Maria stares at the ground, her face a cold, silent mask.

"I wish I had something to give you to remember her by," I say to both of them, "but I don't have anything of hers."

Ana Maria comes to life. "Her things are ours now," she leaps to say, as if I might be suggesting that she give something up so I could have a remembrance too.

"I don't want anything," I tell her.

"Well, if you find any jewelry, it belongs to me." Realizing how harsh and grasping she sounds, she pastes on a wistful smile. "It will help me remember her," she says in a cloying voice so like her mother's I feel the hair rise on my arms.

Pablo can't wait to get back to whatever he was doing, and at the door he turns, as if he has just remembered he should say good-bye. "Thank you for coming." His tone is stiff and distant. I recognize in the curl of his lip the same barely disguised scorn with which Diogo beheld the world, and I know we are all relieved we are unlikely to see each other again.

My next visit will be far more pleasant. On the second Shabbat Eliana and I are in Sevilla, I hire a cart and driver to take us to my grandparents' house. My grandfather died a year ago, so I know it will not be the same, but I ache to see my grandmother with such intensity my heart runs ahead of the decrepit horse pulling us down the road.

Grandmother's weathered face lights up like a child's, and she greets Eliana as if she has seen her many times before. I am struck by how ancient she looks, but it has been sixteen years since I've laid eyes on her.

Suddenly shy, my daughter clings to my skirt. "Come now,"

I tell her. "This was my favorite place when I was your age."
Grandmother asks her if she wants to try some of the cookies that
were my favorite when I was her age, and I know if there's anything that can coax a response from my daughter, that's it.

She releases her grip on my skirt and allows herself to be led
into the house. "Can I see the atlas?" she asks the minute we
are inside. "Of course," Grandmother says. "After you've eaten
your dinner."

She sets a plate of cookies and a mug of cider on the table for
Eliana, and as I help her get ready for our meal, I fall in step as if I
had never been gone.

"We taste very good." Eliana jiggles one of the cookies as if it
is speaking. "Do you mind if I eat you?" she asks. "No! Eat him
instead," the cookie replies, and without further conversation, she
polishes off both of them.

Grandmother smiles. "She's a beautiful child."

"Yes," I say. "I am very blessed."

She changes the subject. "I'm glad I still have the atlas to show
her. Susana wrote twice to ask for it." Grandmother puts a serving
bowl down so heavily I am surprised it doesn't crack. "She claims
it would be safer in her house. Only after her grandfather is dead
does she worry about that? All these years, it could have been
stolen or burned in a fire, she doesn't say a word. Now she cares?
Of course, she tells me how much her children will appreciate such
a beautiful thing, and how educational it will be, but I'm sure she
plans to sell it."

No one bothered to tell her the news, I realize with shock.

"Grandmother," I whisper, "Susana's dead a month now."

She shuts her eyes. "Baruch dayan emet," she whispers. "Blessed
be the True Judge." She sits down on a stool by the hearth. "And
me talking about her that way?" Her eyes brim with tears. "I always
told myself it's never too late for a person to change, but now it is."

She looks over at Eliana's empty plate. "I think her dinner can
wait. Suddenly I'm not hungry." She goes over to a familiar chest

set against one wall. "Ven aqui, Eliana," she says. "There's something I want to show you."

I spend several hours in Grandfather's chair looking at the atlas with Eliana in my lap. After dinner, we light the candle for habdalah and end the Sabbath with a song I taught my daughter as soon as she was old enough to learn.

"Let us bless the Most High," Eliana sings in her lovely child's voice, "the Lord who raised us. Let us give him thanks for the good things he has given us." She and Grandmother sing to the end without me, as my voice is swallowed up by tears.

At the last notes, we hear a whinny at the gate. "I don't suppose I'll be seeing you again," Grandmother says.

I don't want to end the day with a protest or a lie, so I force out words I don't want to say. "No, Grandmother, probably not."

She puts one hand on my head and the other on Eliana's. "May God make you like Sarah, Rebecca, Rachel, and Leah," she says. "May God bless you and watch over you, and may He grant you peace."

"And also to you," I whisper. My heart glows with pride as Eliana returns the Hebrew blessing without prompting.

The horse nickers outside the gate. My daughter scrambles aboard the cart, and when I am seated next to her, Grandmother hands me the atlas, wrapped in a shawl and tied with twine. I clutch it in one hand while I stroke Eliana's sleeping head with the other, all the way back to Sevilla.

I tell Eliana we don't need to sew on badges because only the Jews who live here get to wear them, and I take her out with me the next morning to show her the spring. The winter sky is bright and clear, and our breath forms clouds in front of us as we go down the path through the broken, frost-ravaged stubble.

When we reach the pool, I tell her about standing guard while my mother did her mikveh, and about the day I sat with my grandmother and mother, dangling our feet and making up blessings. Eliana gets down on her knees and wets her hand. "Brrrr!" she says, shuddering dramatically. I put my fingers in the water and touch them to her cheek, saying a silent prayer. She responds by breaking into one of her favorite songs.

"Mayyim hayyim," she sings in her off-key chirp, "the gift of living water." Singing makes her want to dance, but as she scrambles to her feet, she lets out a cry. I whirl around and see two men standing a few steps away. Neither is smiling, and one has a menacing grip on his walking stick.

"Jews?" one of them asks. Eliana is clinging to my skirt, her face hidden except for the eye she is using to watch what is happening.

How could I have been so stupid as to bring her here? I have a heartbeat's time to come up with a plan to get us home unharmed, and, Baruch Hashem, something comes to me. I look confused and answer them in Portuguese. "I am from Lisbon," I tell them. "I don't understand what you said."

They hear the word "Lisbon," and their expression softens. "Foreigners," one of them says.

"We thought you was Christ-killers when we heard the girl singing. It sounded like that Jew talk to us." One of them pats his walking stick. "We know how to take care of that when we see them without their badges, don't we?" He grins at me, assuming I agree.

"We must—" I try to look as if I am thinking of a word in Castilian. "Andar a la casa?"

The men now bob their heads in a respectful bow. "We was just walking by and thought you was Jews," one of them says, gesturing to Eliana. "Sorry if we frightened the girl."

I walk past them as casually as I can with Eliana still clinging to my skirts, and when we reach the middle of the field, I gather up Eliana in my arms and break into a run toward home.

೭๑

"Why did they want to hurt us?" Eliana wails once we are safely inside.

I pull her close. "Christians don't understand why we aren't Christian too, and rather than try to get to know us, they—" I don't want to use the word "hate." Not about my daughter. "They think it's all right to be mean."

"It's not all right!" Eliana's eyes flash.

"Yes, I know. Sometimes people grow up without learning good manners, and when they think they can get away with it, they do whatever they want."

"But God watches all the time!"

"He must be very disappointed with those men," I murmur into her hair. "I suspect he thinks they should know better." Eliana relaxes on my lap as I croon a Hebrew lullaby she loves. When she has drifted off to sleep, I put her down for a nap, and Ester retrieves a bowl of sugar. She coats her finger, then draws it across Eliana's mouth. "Milizina para tu spantu," she whispers in her ear. "Medicine for your fright."

She sprinkles sugar in a path from the bed out the back door and lays down a bowl of water in which she sprinkles a little more. "Los mejores de mosotros will follow the trail of sweetness," she says. "They'll jump in the water and be dissolved, and she'll wake up as if nothing happened."

We take our places at the worktable, and Ester looks up from the onion she is chopping. "You must have forgotten the way things are here," she says, blinking her eyes. "Onions. How can something smell so wonderful when it's cooking and so awful when it's raw?"

"Actually, my mother and I were living as anusim here in Sevilla," I tell her. "Nothing bad happened to us. Nothing like today."

Ester puts down the knife in astonishment. "You're a converso living as a Jew again?"

"No one bothered me in Portugal," I add, "and Eliana was never baptized."

"Here, people die for what you're doing."

"I'll be gone from Sevilla soon." I try to sound unconcerned. "Judah told me if anything happened, the connection to his family would protect me."

"Basta que mi nombre es Abravanel," Ester says with a wry smile. "That's what our men all say. They think the family name will get them out of anything, although I think Judah forgets it's been a long time since we've been able to do any service to the crown." She gestures around her shabby home in case I wonder why.

"Judah and his family are well protected in Portugal," I say, "even when things get bad."

"May it always be so," Ester says, in a tone that implies she wouldn't put much faith in it. She gets out some cumin and gives it to me to grind, while she takes a galingale root and chops it to a paste. The peppery aroma fills the kitchen, mingling with the smell of carrots and onions sizzling in the pan.

She adds small morsels of chicken to the pan and covers the mixture with water just as one of her sisters comes in for a visit on her way home. "Good," Ester says. "There's something Amalia and I must do." She asks her to watch the pot on the hearth and care for Eliana when she wakes up. After pouring sugar into a kerchief and knotting the corners together, she puts on her mantle and borrows her sister's for me. "You'd better wear one with a badge," she says.

Puzzled, I follow her out of the house. "Show me where you went today," she demands. "It's part of the medicine, and you have to finish it."

Though I never want to go there again, she is resolute. I point the way, and she follows me to the spring. "What were you doing when you first saw them?" Ester asks.

When I tell her that Eliana was singing, she orders me to start the song myself. "Mayyim hayyim, the gift of living water," I sing, but my throat is so tight it comes out more like an anguished croak.

"Good," Ester says when I finish. "Los mejores de mosotros are here now because they know you're back. We need to talk to them." She opens the kerchief and cradles the sugar in her palm. "Tell them you didn't do evil, and evil should not be done to you."

"Ni mal ize ni mal ke me aga," I say.

She holds out the hand with the sugar. "Sprinkle it three times and walk backward. I'll tell you when to stop."

I do as I'm told, and she walks next to me, counting my steps and stopping me at fifteen. "Vos du dulsuria ke nos desh sultura," she says. "Tell them that."

"I give you sweetness that you may release us." Above me, the sun shines pale in the early winter sky. A wisp of breeze shakes the bare twigs on the poplars at the spring. "Do you see that? They're gone," Ester says. "You'll be safe now."

Not long after the encounter with the two men at the spring, Jamil sends word that we will be departing in two days. The following morning, wearing Ester's mantle, I go alone to the convent where Luisa lives. I take it off before I knock, because Jews aren't allowed in places Christians think are holy.

A peephole slides open to reveal a face. "I want to see my sister," I tell her. "I'm visiting for a few days. I'm leaving soon and can't wait until your regular hours."

"Wait here." The nun slams the peephole shut. After an interminable wait, I hear the bolt pull back, and she takes me out of the sunlight into a room so dark that at first I can see nothing at all. I pick out an iron grille dividing the space, with benches on both sides. A large wooden Jesus is slumped on a cross on one wall, his painted wounds trickling a ghastly shade of red. An image of

Mary hangs across from it, the vacant look in her eyes making me think we both wish we were somewhere else. Other than that, the room is bare, lit only by a single window where dim sunlight filters through years of accumulated grime.

A door creaks, and a nun with a face the color of fireplace ashes enters the room. Her shoulders are slumped, and she is very thin. She comes to the grille. "I am Sister Maria Teresa," she says. "I told them there must be some mistake."

She looks more closely. "Amalia!" she whispers.

I wish I could tell her she is looking well. Though Luisa is only in her twenties, the convent has robbed her of the life that once sparkled in her.

Her pallid face flushes. "Susana told me you renounced our Lord, and now you consort with the ones who killed him."

I sit back, stunned that she hasn't made any pretense she is glad to see me or even given me a chance to greet her. "I am living as a Jew, if that's what you mean,"

"You are a baptized Christian. You have no right to go back."

"I have the same right you do to follow God where he calls me."

"Comparing Jews to the servants of the Lord?"

"They are my people," I say. "Your people too, and servants of the Lord just the same. Do they know about our family here?"

"All the converso nuns have extra prayers and penances to atone for our blood. I've spent my life trying to set it right, and then you—" Her mouth twists, searching for words harsh enough for me.

Luisa's eyes take in every gloomy corner to make sure no one is eavesdropping. "You are not my sister, do you hear me? I told the nun who came to get me that it was someone from Susana's husband's family. You forced me to lie."

I've had enough. "I haven't forced you to do anything. You are responsible for your actions. Or isn't that what they teach you? It would be if you were a Jew."

I get up to leave and put on Ester's cloak. Luisa's eyes open wide and her hand flies to her mouth when she sees the badge. "Oh!" she says in a strangled gasp.

Though her words have been harsh, her lost vitality and dreary life overwhelm me, and my eyes fill with tears. "I didn't mean to hurt you," I whisper.

She looks up, her face blotchy with tears. "Were you wearing the cloak when you came in?"

"Of course not."

"I would spend the rest of my life on my knees if you had been. There aren't enough prayers for what you have done."

"We've made our choices." I place the cloak over my arm with the badge hidden in its folds, knowing that we both have equally strong reasons to keep my secret from getting out. "If you want to spend your life torturing yourself for my transgressions, I think you are doing it for nothing."

"I will pray for you." Crossing herself, she gets up as I leave.

"Pray for the soul of your church," I say over my shoulder. "That's the best way to pray for me, and for every Jew in Spain."

❦

I have one final matter weighing on my heart, and my last morning in Sevilla, wearing my own cloak, I set out for the Christian cemetery. Inside, I recognize the stone cross over the grave of my mother and her dead children. I pray quietly for a moment and then bend down to dig up some of the dirt with a trowel I carried in a cloth-lined basket.

I take it to the Jewish cemetery. When I find the tree I am looking for, my knees give way, and I sink to the ground, so weak with grief for my lost family that I cannot even cry. I stare in silence at the ground until I am strong enough to stand. Taking a handful of dirt from my basket, I bring my mother's spirit here.

"O God, full of compassion, who dwells on high, grant true rest to the soul of my mother Rosaura…" As I sprinkle the contents of the basket over the spot where the locks of my dead brothers are buried, my voice floats away from this mournful place. "May the All-Merciful One shelter her with the cover of his wings forever." I look up into a blistering blue sky. "And may she rest in peace."

15

The tents shudder and flap in the dying breeze of late afternoon as we stop near the border of the Caliphate of Granada. Pack mules and carts carry tents, supplies, and all of our possessions during the day, and though there is a carriage for Eliana and me to ride in, it bounces so badly in the ruts in the dirt road that most of the time I am on horseback, with my daughter tucked in front of me.

When the afternoon shadows grow long, we stop with our retinue of guards and servants, who set up camp before the first stars come out. The guards carry the banner of the Duke of Medina-Sidonia, and his protection keeps us safe from bandits and army deserters wandering the countryside. That and the blessing of dry weather have enabled us to enjoy the scenery, and except for saddle weariness, I am glad to be out day after day enjoying the ever-changing light and the wild beauty of southern Castile.

At night, Eliana and I share a tent, and after she is asleep, Jamil and I walk under the winter sky outside the circle of the camp, in a silence broken only by the boasting and laughter of the men around the fire and the howls of wolves in the distance. When we feel the cold, we slip into Jamil's tent. We shiver at first between the furs and blankets before our bodies grow warm with desire, and we throw off the covers, our naked bodies glistening in the lamplight.

I often sit astride him as we make love, moving my hips in slow circles, as I lean forward to brush my breasts against his chest.

We explore with our tongues every surface of our mouths, every crevice in our teeth, and then we break apart to pass our lips over bellies or arms with the delicacy of silk drawn over fine hairs, or taking mouthfuls of flesh in tender bites, as if we cannot be content until we have made each other part of ourselves.

Afterward, I slip back to my tent and crawl under covers warmed by my daughter's body. There I sleep sweetly until voices wake me at dawn.

∽

Jamil brings his mount alongside mine a few days later to tell me that we are now in the Caliphate of Granada. He points to a town perched atop imposing hills in the east. "That's Ronda. Sawwar lives there."

Sawwar. Jamil's work makes him unable to care for his ten-year-old son, and Jamil's sister Rashida has raised him from the time he was two, when Jamil's wife, Najat, died in childbirth. I had known we would be stopping here, as the route safest from marauders and bandits was along this road, but Jamil has said nothing for days, and I have had no chance to prepare myself. I look toward Ronda, upset to find myself here without warning.

He misreads the expression on my face as apprehension about the long and precarious switchback trail leading from the valley to the town. "It's best to walk, but it's not as bad as it looks," he tells me, not realizing that what I am worried about isn't the trail, but my imminent encounter with Rashida and Sawwar. As we start the ascent, I feel a childish jealousy about having to share him and anxiety so fierce it makes me not notice the narrowness of the path or the precipitous drop to the valley if we should stumble and fall.

Shortly before dusk, we stop in front of the Palacio de Mondragon, a dignified-looking house with a walled garden on both sides. The moment Jamil knocks, Rashida opens the door

"We saw you down in the valley! Come in!" Her eyes

acknowledge me with a crinkling smile that says she will greet me properly once she has embraced her brother. After we are properly introduced, she ushers us into a colorful tiled courtyard dotted with huge pots of flowers forced to bloom in midwinter, and smelling at once grassy, pungent, and sweet.

Jamil's sister, the wife of Hassan el Zegri, the Marques de Mondragon and Governor of Ronda, is older than I expected. Wisps of gray hair peek out from under her head covering, and her face is creased from the Andalusian sun. She is tall with narrow shoulders, but the contours of her ample hips are apparent under her loose tunic and short-sleeved cloak. The family's Berber roots have given her the same blue eyes as Jamil, and she is one of the most striking women I have ever seen.

Sawwar is not at home. Mondragon and he went off that morning to check on the animals to be slaughtered for Eid al-Adha, the celebration of the end of the pilgrimage season to Mecca. They aren't likely to be home until after dark.

"Just as well, because you need to go to the baths," Rashida teases, tugging her brother's dust-coated burnoose before turning to me. "Tomorrow is the day for the women. For now, I'll have the servants draw some water and bring you and your daughter some fresh clothes."

I see to Eliana's bath first, standing her in the bucket and dribbling water over her with a sea sponge until the water is gray. Fresh water is prepared for me, but I cannot linger in the delights of washing the journey from my body, for Rashida comes in to tell me that Sawwar is home and Jamil is with him.

She gives me a square garment with openings for my head and arms and a sash for my waist, and when she sees me trying to pat down my wet, disheveled hair she drapes a sheer scarf over my head and arranges it neatly around my neck. "It's the real reason we hide our hair," she says with a laugh. "Not to have to worry about it." She hands me an embroidered cloak woven in crimson wool so supple it flutters as I follow her into the courtyard.

Jamil lights up at the sight of me as he stands grinning with his arm around Sawwar's shoulders. He gives Sawwar a gentle nudge and he comes forward, bowing to me. "Salaam. Ahlan wa Sahlan," he says, welcoming me to Ronda with sober green eyes flecked with gold. "I am Sawwar ibn Jamil."

"Salaam." I say. "It's a pleasure to meet you. Ana Amalia um Eliana bint Jehuda al Sevilla," I say in the Muslim fashion, including both my father and my child in my own name, but substituting my grandfather's birth name, Jehuda, for the alienating Christian name, Jaume, he was forced to bear.

Eliana is pressing into me to convey that she doesn't like this strange boy. It's late and she's tired, but I know Eliana will never agree to go to bed unless I am with her. I make my excuses, and we go into the bedroom we will share at Palacio de Mondragon.

"What's the matter?" I ask her, settling in under the covers. "Don't you like Sawwar?"

"He's all right." She sniffs. "He's a boy."

"Since when have you cared about that?"

"Since—forever." She worms her body in closer to mine.

"You like Isaac, don't you?" I tease.

She rolls over on her back. "Isaac's not a boy."

"Well, what is he then?"

"I don't know!" She sighs, obviously annoyed that I don't understand. I look over at her, disbelieving. Is it possible for a girl of six to be in love?

"I wish he were here instead of that Sawwar," she whispers.

I cradle her in my arms. "I miss everyone too, but we'll make friends in Granada. Jamil says there's a girl in the palace for you to play with." I feel her body stiffening, and I know she is struggling not to cry. "We'll have Jamil to ourselves again in a day or two. And just think, Sawwar might be jealous of you because you have his father all the time. Have you thought about that?"

"No."

"And you know I'm counting on you to be polite to him while we're here."

Eliana exhales loudly in resignation. "All right. I'll feel a little sorry for him, and I'll be good." She pulls away and lies on her back again. "But I'm glad he's not coming with us. And I still like Isaac more."

The following morning, Jamil and Sawwar accompany us part way to the baths. At the end of town, we look down on a chasm where a river is visible occasionally through thick vegetation. We're too far up to hear the sound of water, although the air is full of the cries of birds that roost in the soft cliffs and fly out to catch insects on the wing.

"It's easy to see why the Christians haven't captured Ronda," Jamil says, gesturing from our perch to the plains below. "Although there are a few paths to the river from here." He pulls Sawwar to him. "For boys like this one, who frighten their aunt to death by climbing cliffs."

Sawwar hurls a pebble into the gorge, and we watch it glint in the sunlight as it makes its long fall to the river. Jamil throws another, and when it becomes a happy game between father and son, Rashida and I head for the baths.

Light streams through star-shaped openings in the vaulted ceiling, dappling the colored tiles that decorate the floor and arches of the entry. Potted trees and flowering baskets line the walls, and the fragrance of bark, summer meadows, and incense wafts in the air.

In a room down a short, dark corridor, light shines through high windows onto patterned tile steps leading into a glistening pool. I drop the sheet wrapping my body, and the sweet caress of the water on my weary limbs sets my mind adrift. I don't know how much time passes before I hear Rashida's voice. Barely above a whisper, her words echo off the tile walls.

"It was a terrible thing when Jamil's wife died," she says. "Najat was a lovely woman, and Jamil mourned her to a point I thought was dangerous. He didn't eat because he said food tied him to this world and he wanted to be closer to her in the next."

She looks away as if peering into the past, and I wonder why she has chosen to confide these things so quickly. "He clung to Sawwar as if the father was the child, but we finally convinced him that the boy was better off here than with a governess in Granada."

Najat's death is my gain, I can't stop from thinking, though I hate myself for having such thoughts. "I'm sorry," I murmur, and I do mean it.

Rashida pushes the water away with gentle circles of her hands. "I can see why Jamil loves you," she says. "He says you're as kind as you are lovely. Wait until you've been in Granada a few months— you'll take to Muslim ways."

I want to tell her I am not looking to change, but I know she only means to be reassuring. And that other thing she said… "How do you know Jamil loves me?" I ask.

"The way he stands, the way he holds his head. The way he says your name." She steps out of the pool and motions to me to follow to another room. "Women can tell."

When we are finished with the hot and cold pools, I slip on the loose clothing and scarf Rashida has lent me for the rest of the journey. She's right about the speed with which I will take to some Muslim ways. Already the idea of returning to my dirty and confining travel dress disgusts me.

She leads me through a baffling warren of streets until we reach the familiar square outside the Palacio de Mondragon. We sit for a moment in the shade, and she looks me over approvingly from head to sandaled feet. "Since the moment you arrived, I have been thinking how good it would be if you and my brother were to marry and have a family together."

I look away. "That can't happen," I tell her, "although I am sorry it is so."

"Because you are a Jew?"

I nod.

"And that is the end of it?"

"I'm afraid it is." I know she must be mystified why I am not willing to drop my own ways for hers, especially when marriage to someone like her brother would be the reward. I wonder how she would feel if Jamil announced he was going to live as a Jew for me. I want to tell her the story of how much I went through to be who I am, but I see her stiffen, and I keep silent.

"Well then," she replies. "Shall we go in?"

As I walk along a few steps behind, the shadow of a bird in flight draws a temporary black line across the street between us. I tell myself such things mean nothing as I follow her inside the palace.

16

GRANADA 1453

A thin veil of frost covers the plain, and our breath makes clouds in the air as we approach Granada. The sunrise casts a coral hue on the imposing walls of the Alhambra, the fort and palace that crown the city. We dismount at the gate and pass on foot amid throngs of people in wildly colorful clothing milling in narrow streets and small corner plazas. The smell of roasting meat and vegetables pungent with spices mingles with the aroma of freshly baked bread into an intoxicating perfume that I think would make anyone want to sing and dance.

"What's happening?" I ask Jamil.

"Eid al-Adha—the Feast of Sacrifice," he says, straining to be heard above the din. "We're remembering the willingness of Abraham—may peace be upon him—to sacrifice his son Ishmael because God demanded it."

Eliana looks up at me. "It was Isaac, not Ishmael," she says. "The Torah says—" A group of acrobats make a circle around us. Their back flips and cartwheels distract Eliana, and she claps in delight when they bow to her as they finish.

By now, we've reached the gate of a large and immaculately whitewashed residence on a square filled with revelers. A servant closes the wooden entry doors behind us, and though the air is suddenly calm, the noise from the streets wafts into the courtyard.

"Welcome to my home," Jamil says, looking around. "Although it would appear my entire household has run away."

"It's the Eid, Master," the servant says. "We're getting ready to feed the neighbors after the Asr prayers."

I barely have time to look around before a voice calls from a minaret. "Allahu Akbar! God is great!" The man caresses the name of God as if reluctant to let it go. "I testify that Mohammad is the messenger of Allah," he intones as Jamil pulls his prayer rug from his saddle bag and washes his hands and feet in a fountain. "Make haste toward prayer," the muezzin continues. "La ilaha illallah..."

I go with the doorkeeper to look outside. The crowd has been transformed into orderly lines of men standing shoulder to shoulder, while women cluster at the edges and in the doorways of shops. Like ripples of waves on a bay, the men bow, hands to thighs, then drop to their knees and touch their foreheads to the ground. At the end of prayers, they look to their right and left. "Assalamu alaikum wa rahmatullah," I hear them say to each other before rocking back on their heels and rising to their feet. "Peace and the mercy of Allah be on you." Though I have often seen Jamil at solitary prayer, there is something magnificent about so many people stopping at the same time to remember the Holy One, and I am momentarily envious that I am not a part of something so beautiful.

There's a momentary calm in the square, but the gaiety soon resumes, and people pour into Jamil's courtyard. Servants scurry with platters heaped high with roasted meat while others ladle cups of a brilliant pink liquid.

"Is it wine, Mama?" Eliana asks. I shake my head. Though most Muslims believe the prohibition in Islamic law is only against intoxication, I know that serving wine publicly at such a time would cause talk.

"Let's go find out," I say, glad for something to do, now that Jamil has been caught up in a crowd of people eager to greet him. We take a small, cautious taste from the cups we are handed.

"Ummm," Eliana says. "Berry?"

"Grape, maybe—or plum?" I turn to the server. "What is this?" I ask.

"Hibiscus flower," she says. "With a little clove." Flowers, I think. What a perfect way to drink in beauty.

The meats on each platter are prepared a different way—here vaguely like cinnamon and there like smoked peppers, pungent with flavors at once sour, sweet, pungent, and spicy. Eliana turns up her nose at a few, but I find the whole feast reassuring. Something tells me if they eat and drink like this, there will be much more to like about Granada.

That night, Eliana and I sleep in a separate apartment in Jamil's house. He comes to me after she has fallen asleep, her belly distended with more food than I imagined she could swallow. "What do you think of my city?" he asks, running his fingers through my hair, which still hold the dust of the road.

"It's overwhelming," I say.

"Is overwhelming good?"

"I think so." I try unsuccessfully to hide a yawn. Jamil smiles. "I have a few friends I still need to visit. It's Eid al-Adha, and I don't want to hurt their feelings." He kisses me. "Sleep well, my love."

I am so exhausted I have to muster strength to get up from the chair I collapse into after Jamil leaves. This is the first time he hasn't wanted to be with me during those precious hours while Eliana sleeps. I am here alone, without another soul who knows who or where I am. Is it because it's Eid al-Adha and his first night home, or is his life in Granada going to be full without me?

You're tired, I tell myself. *Stop imagining things to worry about.*

The candle flickers and goes out, and as I listen in the darkness to the muted sounds of revelers in the streets, I feel so small I could almost disappear. My new home. Will it ever feel that way? Numb and exhausted, I slip quietly into bed so as not to disturb my daughter's dreams.

After Eid al-Adha, Granada sleeps. A few days later, a page from the Alhambra arrives at Jamil's house with an invitation to the palace the following afternoon. Making my way during the Eid through the crowded squares of the quarter known as the Albaicín gave me little opportunity to notice anything except where my feet would step next, and I am happy for the chance to ride in a sedan chair and take my first good look at the city.

We pass through streets of low, whitewashed buildings surrounding the souk. I watch two women come out of the shadows in flowing robes and diaphanous veils, holding hands up to their foreheads to shield their dark eyes from the winter sun.

A man goes into the souk, balancing on his head a stack of folded carpets. Even though they must weigh almost as much as he does, he walks with the casual gait of someone carrying nothing at all. Another grizzled old man leads a donkey burdened with saddlebags carrying crimson and russet-colored spices and a sack of dried mint leaves still on their woody stems. A boy dashes by with a bag from which protrude the now familiar salt-washed loaves so delicious they put all other bread I have tasted to shame.

How unusual to smell such aromas in a city! The streets and alleys of Lisbon are fetid with the odor of rot and excrement. Here the pavement is swept clean, and sewers wash away the waste that would otherwise be tossed in the street.

We cross the Darro River on one of several bridges connecting the Albaicín with the palace. Looking up to the right, I see the Alcazaba, a massive fortress with rose-colored walls, windowless except for a few slits near the tops of its crenellated towers. Straight ahead is a palace of the same glowing stone but with hundreds of windows and open arches punctuating its austere walls.

Behind the Alhambra, the Sierra Nevada rise up against a cloudless, winter sky. The palace complex, impressive as it is, looks like a stack of tiny boxes against the towering snowfields and dark, jagged peaks. I try to remain calm by reminding myself that even the powerful among us are insignificant compared to mountains and sky. I tell myself I am arriving with the dignity of someone who has been asked to come, but my mind has no power over my racing heart and sweaty palms.

The sentry recognizes the carriers and waves us through into a huge courtyard with patterned gravel paving and a massive blue-and-green-tiled fountain, where a man in a rich velvet cloak and fluttering pants waits to escort me. A few men mill around conversing, while servants and grooms tend to people arriving or departing the palace.

He leads me down a long street lined with stores and workshops with upstairs living quarters for artisans and laborers, and through arbors and garden paths. Despite the snow in the distance, I'm told Granada rarely gets frost, so even in winter, the flower beds are splashed with hundreds of shades of green and every imaginable color of blossom. I hear songbirds and catch the scent of jasmine in the air, and everywhere I see and hear water. It splashes in fountains inside fish ponds and shallow reflecting pools, cascades in channels along walkways, and trickles in shallow grooves down the center of stone staircases.

We reach the palace and enter a long, open-air corridor. My jaw drops. The vault is carved as delicately as lace, dropping like a petticoat down the walls. Light streams through the arches, dappling the yellow, blue, and green tiles on the lower walls and illuminating the graceful Arabic inscriptions that run the length of the corridor. "It is the most beautiful thing I have ever seen," I say to my escort.

He smiles. "You have just begun to see the beauty of the Alhambra."

We continue through corridors and rooms and across courtyards where towering filigree-covered arches collect golden light on Quranic verses and interlocking arabesques. Eventually we come to a large double door guarded by sentries. "The Caliph's quarters," my escort says, motioning me through. "He'll spend only a moment with you. When his grandchildren are brought in, you will leave with them."

My heart is skittering in my chest, and only the knowledge that Jamil is inside with the Caliph keeps my knees from giving way. Inside I can see nothing but the broad outline of a platform on the far side of the room. Behind it, tall windows let in blinding sun, blocked only by thin lattices on the shutters. Sparks whiz across the ceiling like shooting stars from a basin of mercury that slaves are rocking in a beam of light.

When my eyes adjust, I see that Muhammad the Ninth is not on a throne but on a carpeted dais, lounging on a couch covered with silks that glint in the sunlight as if he were enveloped in a cloud of gold.

Jamil whisks me away from my escort and brings me forward to get my first close look at the Caliph of Granada. I know to expect an old man—in the complicated and cutthroat politics of Granada, he has been in and out of power Jamil's whole life—and it is his grandchildren by one of his younger wives whom I will tutor. Still, this man is so ancient his skin looks like an old saddle, and his wizened face seems disproportionate to the huge turban covering any hair he might still have.

His reedy voice brings the room to attention. "Ahlan wa sahlan. Welcome to Granada."

"Salaam," I say. "Ahlan bik. I am honored to be here, and I wish for nothing more than to have my service please you."

A disturbance on one side of the room causes me to look away. A group of young women have entered and huddle whispering among themselves. Their eyes are lined with kohl, and they are dressed in translucent silk trousers and veils, wearing nothing above the waist but a tight band over their breasts. One of them has eyes like emeralds, with hair the color of apricots. A Berber like Jamil, I recognize, but with Slavic blood as well, from soldiers of fortune who came in earlier times. I've noticed this everywhere in Granada, how some people have skin like ebony and others the creamy white of a jasmine blossom, with the most startling combinations of features—blue eyes in a dark face, or black eyes in a fair one. Their hair ranges from gold to russet to black so dark it glints of blue.

"Ah!" the caliph says. "The qiyan! My singing girls!" They start forward, carrying flutes, drums, and finger cymbals, but he waves them back and turns to me.

"Tell me," he says, "is mapmaking among your many talents?" I am startled by the suddenness of this new topic, but my voice, to my relief, comes out calm and forceful. "I'm afraid not. I tried when I was young, but my father hid his paints and inks so they wouldn't be wasted on someone with little promise."

The sultan chews on a fig, taking his time as if no one is there at all. "What a pity," he says, "and an even greater one that your family's greatest work is in France, where, I dare say, they do not appreciate the Catalan Atlas as much as we would."

If only he knew, I think, picturing my family's copy of the atlas hidden away among the possessions I brought to Granada.

A noise from behind distracts him. Two children come in—a girl around eight and a boy about two years younger—attended by a small woman with eyes like black olives behind her veiled face. "What is life for, if not to have grandchildren?" he asks, gesturing in their direction without looking at them. The boy fidgets, and the girl gives him a nudge to quiet him.

"I hope for that someday, Insha'Allah," I tell him, "but I will be waiting a while, because my daughter is still the age of these two."

A smile darts at the edges of the caliph's mouth, and I am relieved that I seem to have found the right thing to say. He looks at the children and flicks his hand in my direction. "Greet our guest," he commands.

"Are you our new tutor?" the boy asks, after bowing to me. His confident and demanding tone reminds me of Eliana, and I can't help but smile.

"I am," I tell him, "and you must be Qasim." I look to the girl. "And Zubiya."

Qasim shrinks back—shy, perhaps because a stranger knows his name. Zubiya's large, gray eyes look me over with the frank and open curiosity that is the prerogative of children. "Go with her, then," the caliph says, shooing them away with a sweep of his hand. The children back away respectfully before turning to their attendant, who has come up to stand behind me.

"I am Ana, one of the children's slaves," she says. "Please come with me to the women's quarters. The family is waiting to greet you."

As we leave, I hear the rhythmic tapping of finger symbols and the slow beat of a drum. I turn to watch a few of the singing girls seat themselves cross-legged on the floor, their trousers billowing around them. The others have raised their hennaed hands and are swaying their hips in time to the drum, making slow twirls and dips as they sweep in front of the caliph.

A small hand slips into mine, and Zubiya looks up at me. "They're very pretty, aren't they? I wish I could dance like that." Ana hisses faintly to quiet her.

"No one wants to teach me because the girls who do it are all slaves in the harem," Zubiya goes on, ignoring her. "They say it wouldn't be decent, but—" She gets up on tiptoes, and I bend down to hear her. "I dance in my room when no one is looking," she whispers so close to my ear I can smell the scent of orange candy on her breath. "Would you like to watch me sometime?"

I smile at her, remembering my own youthful fantasies. "Very much," I say.

We follow Ana through a courtyard bordered in myrtle bushes and taken up almost entirely by a reflecting pool. On the white walls, huge drapes of silk billow with every puff of air, and around the walkway, carpets and cushions are strewn for those who wish to linger. "Look," Qasim says, the first words he has said since we left the caliph. He settles on his stomach at one end of the pool. "You have to get down low, or you can't see it."

"Oh, do!" Zubiya says, lying down next to her brother. I crouch and look across the pool, not wanting to appear undignified, but Qasim insists I get so low my cheek touches the ground.

From that level, the building on the far end is reflected in the pool, down to every filigreed arch. "It seems so real," I say.

"Real water," he laughs, splashing his hand and destroying the illusion.

"Qasim!" Zubiya whines. "You spoil everything!"

We walk through more filigreed arches onto a patio Ana calls the Courtyard of the Lions. "The women and children live in the buildings around it," she tells me as the children run ahead through an open entryway into a garden I can see just beyond.

In the entry, I hear whispers from the upper floor and look up to see several windows covered with lattices of carved wood. One of the shutters moves, and I know I'm being watched. Someone giggles, and a stern voice tells her to hush.

I climb the stairs to a walkway overlooking a garden enclosed on all sides by the apartments of the caliph's chief wife and female relatives. I can see Qasim and Zubiya playing hide and seek among the sculpted bushes as Ana takes me around one corner and into a huge room.

Several women about my age come to greet me, but one who looks to be about fifty, whom I take to be Muhammad the Ninth's chief wife, Mushtaq, stays in her chair. Another woman about ten years her junior stares at me before whispering something in Mushtaq's ear.

"Ahlan wa-sahlan." The first to reach me takes my hand with her delicate fingers. "I am Jawhara," she says, "the mother of Qasim and Zubiya, and this is my friend Rayyan."

"Ahlan biki," I reply. "I'm pleased to meet you. Your children are truly charming." A girl of around fourteen has been hiding behind them, and Rayyan gestures her forward. "Don't be so shy, Noor," she says. The girl looks up through dark lashes, and when she raises her face, I have to stop myself from gasping.

She is without a doubt the most beautiful human being I have ever seen. Her eyes are the same aquamarine as Jamil and Rashida's, but her skin is much lighter, almost tawny in hue, and so flawless it is hard to resist reaching out to touch her cheek to see if it as cool and dewy as it looks. Her nose is narrow and straight and her lips, without a touch of added color, are so roselike I can imagine the scent of a summer garden on her breath.

"Fursa saeeda," she says. "I am pleased to meet you." I see a hint of color rise in her cheeks, and my heart goes out to her for being so painfully shy that even in the privacy of her home, she can barely manage to speak.

Jawhara and Rayyan bring me over to meet the chief wife and the other woman with her. Mushtaq smiles warmly, but I can see by the difficulty with which she shifts her weight in her chair that she is painfully afflicted in her joints.

"Introduce me, Noor," the other woman commands in a brittle voice.

Noor's cheeks color again. "May I present my mother, Tarab," she says.

"Tarab is one of the caliph's nieces," Rayyan adds. "Our honored chief wife is her aunt."

Tarab's eyes remained locked on me. "Fursa saeeda," I tell her. She nods and says nothing.

Jawhara takes me by the arm. "It's almost time for dinner," she says. "Would you like to see your quarters first, and the lesson room?"

My quarters? Prickles of sweat break out on my forehead. Why had I not asked about this before? I assumed Eliana and I would live by ourselves in town. Jamil can't visit me here, not within reach of the prying eyes of people like Tarab. The thought turns my ribs into claws around my heart.

What has Jamil told them? Do they know about Eliana at all? Will these strangers be her family? Will Tarab bully her with her eyes as she has already done with me? I fight the urge to run downstairs, past the fountains and pools, through the gardens, beyond the outer walls, and back to Jamil's house in the Albaicín. My mind races back further as I reverse Eliana's and my journey until we are back in Queluz, safe in our own beds, as if none of this ever happened.

Jawhara stops at a closed door. "This is where you will stay," she says, opening the latch. Like a sleepwalker imprisoned in a dream, I go inside.

VALENCIA 1492

I was wrong to fear the open door that beckoned me into my new life. What I walked into so blindly when I accepted the Caliph's invitation to tutor his grandchildren was not easy and often unpleasant, but I remember the sounds, colors, and smells of Granada with greater vibrancy and clarity—and yes, happiness—than many of the things I have experienced since.

If I were standing at this moment in an orchard in bloom, the fragrance could not compete with what comes to me by shutting my eyes and remembering the gardens of the Alhambra. The palace, the city, the magnificent mountains at its back, and the fertile vegetation surrounding it were so intoxicating that everyone there believed that Paradise hovered just out of view.

It was wonderful to be alive in Granada, and I can't imagine how those who trudge through life with downcast eyes would not feel moved to raise their faces to the sky and live more fully under that glorious sun. Still, I cannot linger too long taking in the phantom fragrances of the past, or let the city itself dance on my closed lids, without my mind going to darker things. Just as one thorn catching on a robe can tear the fabric beyond repair, remembering those years is like donning a cloak of as many colors as Joseph's, and as tattered.

The street is quiet outside my room. The setting sun will not bring relief for hours yet. I've heard that living things put in a pot of cold water set on a fire will be unaware that the temperature is rising until it is on the verge of killing them. I take a deep breath and then another to reassure myself that there is still air here, that the house has not yet been encircled by a force that is stealing my life while I am inside this room reliving it.

No, the force that wants to kill me has no need of stealth. They parade their victims to the stake. They light the kindling and from that moment, the doomed can only pray that death will come quickly. What has the world come to that the most loving thing a family can do is to add straw and dry branches to the pyre to speed their loved one from this tortured world?

The self-appointed spokesmen for God will explain with sorrowful, pious eyes that they have done the victim a favor. Such purification leaves a chance for God's mercy, however undeserved. "Who are we to know what God will do with the soul of the departed?" they ask, although there's no other time they admit any uncertainty about what God is thinking.

Besides, they will be quick to point out, God forbids the shedding of human blood, except—conveniently—in war. Arms are torn from sockets and backs are broken on the rack, but there isn't a mark on their bodies except the bites of vermin as victims are driven, or carried, to the stake. It's spectacle the Inquisition wants, and it would be prepared to make the last two people in Spain a grisly audience for each other.

I pray for the dead. How many times have I stood in the women's gallery at the synagogue and choked back tears at the words of the Amidah? "You support the falling, heal the sick, set free the bound, and keep faith with those who sleep in dust." How many times have I wondered where that whispered prayer goes?

Perhaps nowhere. I tremble at how abandoned I may truly be. Alone in a universe without a God to hear me. Alone, even when surrounded by people, as I was in Granada.

But that isn't how it felt at the beginning.

The dapple of light on shimmering veils…the voices of children… the scent of roses… I shut my eyes and surrender again to memory.

GRANADA 1455

"Try again," I tell Zubiya. Scowling with concentration, she draws her finger over a simple, two-line poem. "The spreading earth is like a—buxom?—young girl?"

"Good," I tell her.

"Cloaked in springtime, with flowers for her jewels."

I pat her hand. "It's not so hard, is it?"

"The words are too big. What does 'buxom' mean, anyway?"

"You remember what you said about how Aunt Rayyan's breasts look like melons under her clothes?"

"Oh!" Zubiya giggles. "But how can a girl be"—she consults the text again—"buxom?"

"Maybe they were more like oranges."

Zubiya looks down at her flat chest. "I wonder what mine will look like."

"You don't have too many more years to wait," I tell her, without adding that I have heard whispers among the women that her marriage is already being arranged.

Eliana is almost nine now, trailing Zubiya by a little over a year. The two have become fast friends in the eighteen months we have been in Granada. They play in the gardens of the Alhambra much as I used to with Elizabeth and Beatriz, but their romantic stories are not about wandering knights and fair maidens, but about Scheherazade and the Arabian Nights.

I see much less of Qasim than I do of Zubiya. Even at eight, he spends far more time with the mullahs and court scholars. It's just as well, for it's an effort to settle Zubiya down and get her to read. No one takes her education seriously—no one, that is, but me. She may be important to others only as a bride, but how dull her life will be with only clothing and cosmetics to amuse her. That and other people's mistakes and faults to gossip about.

Jawhara comes to fetch her daughter. "It's time for you to bathe," she says. "Your father will be here soon." I have adjusted to this strange way of life, where the caliph lives in another part of the palace, away from his wives and children, only coming for a short visit in the afternoon before going to whomever pleases him in his harem.

I wait in my quarters until I am certain the caliph does not wish to talk to me about the children. When his visit is concluded, I am free to leave. My fear that I would be trapped living in the palace proved groundless, and I come and go almost every day, having been permitted by Mushtaq to live in the aljama here.

"You need a place to follow your faith," Mushtaq told me. "You should live among your own." Her decisions are never questioned, though Tarab has ways of making her displeasure obvious. I remember what Judah said long ago about power and love, and every day the caliph's chief wife shows the compassion that comes from the balance of the two, with Tarab, unfortunately, serving as the counter lesson.

My quarters are only a place to rest while I am here and to leave the few things I need. There's a small bed, a low table for working with the children, and a few extra clothes. From the benches built into the wall below the windows, I can look out over the courtyard on one side and the Albaicín and the rocky landscape beyond on the other. The windows have latticed shutters for privacy, but when I open them, light floods in, setting the warm wood panels aglow.

The two hundred Jewish families in Granada cluster on the southern side of the palace hill, surrounded by a city of seventy thousand. I walk most days up a footpath to the palace, and in cold or stormy weather, a sedan chair is sent for me. On the worst days, I spend the night here in the women's quarters.

Eliana comes frequently to play with Zubiya, but the rest of the time she is with our rabbi's wife, Toba, who watches her during the day and sets up a bed for her when I cannot return at night. Toba makes sure Eliana completes the lessons I plan for her, and my daughter can already read and write Arabic, Castilian, and Hebrew, as well as her native Portuguese. She knows more about astronomy, geology, and botany than the caliph's grandchildren, because her curiosity is insatiable, and she learns twice as much from asking questions than is contained in the books Qasim and Zubiya open only reluctantly.

Toba's rabbi husband, Baroukh Obadia, runs a small yeshiva out of their home, and Eliana listens from a chair near the door when the discussion interests her. When she tells me what the Talmud made her ponder that day, I think of young Isaac Abravanel. How pleased he would be to have a conversation with my daughter now, and how much Rabbi Obadia's young charges are missing because a girl is not allowed to join them.

I hear noises in the courtyard and I go to the window. Zubiya and Qasim are playing a noisy game of tag while the caliph and Mushtaq sit and talk near the fountain. I haven't warmed to the idea of a man marrying more than one woman, but I can't imagine how he could love anyone more than he does his chief wife. She is kind and gentle, and it's hard to see why she would be close to someone like Tarab if they had not grown up together.

My nemesis is ten years younger, and though she is Mushtaq's niece, they grew up more like sisters. Tarab and her only child, Noor, came to live in the Alhambra when Tarab's husband died. Mother and child could not be more opposite. Whereas Tarab can terrorize a room even when silent, Noor is a cowering mouse, joining the games and conversation only when prodded.

I see Tarab now, sitting on the other side of the caliph. Though Muhammad is gracious to her, I see how he stiffens when she is near. Does he, like I do, look at her and think, "Now there is one to keep an eye on"?

I suppose not. He has little to fear from anyone. I, on the other hand, am not so fortunate. Tarab looks up toward my window. Instinctively I draw back, though no one can see me through the closed lattice. She must have been commenting about something the children are learning or my behavior around them. The only thing I can be sure of is that it is not a compliment.

Jawhara and Rayyan are seated under the arcade. The two are best friends from childhood and wives of the same man, a diplomat who is away as much as Jamil is. When Rayyan's husband and two children died in an outbreak of pox, Jawhara insisted her own husband marry her friend, but among the women of the palace, she seems little more than Jawhara's shadow.

Mushtaq seems to enjoy my company the most, for I am better educated than the other women, and she has a lively mind. She's pleased to have a Jew in her entourage, she tells me, because finally someone can answer her questions about my faith and help her appreciate her own. Despite her pain, she gets down from her chair at least once a day to pray and says the prayers from her seat the other times. Occasionally I get down on the floor and join her, reciting only the things Jews believe and remaining silent for the rest, just as I did at mass when I was a child.

No wonder Caliph Muhammad loves her best, even though her bones hurt her so terribly it must be years since they have made love. At the thought of such pleasure, my body wakens, and I wait impatiently for the caliph to say his good-byes. When he is gone, I splash some water on my face and arms and straighten my hair under the hood of my cloak before going out through the Courtyard of the Lions and down the arcades and gardens of the Alhambra to where my sedan chair is waiting to take me to the Albaicín to meet Jamil.

As I pass the souk, I see him walking with Sawwar, now twelve, who is visiting Granada. We're only a few minutes from Jamil's home, but he tells the carriers to lower the chair so Sawwar can get inside. The boy's eyes dart between us, and I know he is thinking he'd rather walk with a man than ride with a woman, but Jamil insists he keep me company.

"I'll be along in a few minutes," Jamil says. "I have one more stop to make."

Don't be long, my eyes implore. It's only a few hours until I must go home. Jamil's expression says he has no intention to tarry.

Sawwar sits beside me, exuding a boyish scent of dust and dried sweat. His face is smooth, although his upper lip is dark, as if hair under the surface has not yet erupted into a mustache. "What have you and your father been doing since I saw you last?" I ask. It's only been a few days, but Sawwar is usually full of stories of riding or hunting or gatherings of men at Jamil's home.

He shrugs. "We bought some snares at the souk and some arrows for my bow." He falls silent for a moment, then says without enthusiasm that he will be leaving for Ronda in a week.

"So soon?" I reply.

Sawwar sighs as the carriers put us down. "Father's been called away."

My heart drops at his words. "How long have you known?"

"He just found out today," Sawwar says. "He has to go back to Lisbon." Knowing Jamil hasn't simply failed to tell me makes me feel better, but not much. With news like that, how could I feel anything but miserable? He will likely be gone for months.

Sawwar goes inside the house, and I dally outside by the fountain, waiting for Jamil. He comes into the courtyard, and as usual we do not touch each other until we have gone inside. No one has illusions about our relationship, but it's still best not to invite gossip.

"Sawwar told me you're leaving soon," I say as he closes the door behind us.

"I would have preferred you to hear from me," he says. "I'll have to speak to Sawwar about keeping our conversations to himself. Are you angry?"

"No," I say. "Just sad. And worried."

He holds me tight. "Bad things can happen here too. Who knows whether my life won't be saved by not being here to fall off a balcony or drown in the river?"

He pulls away to look at me. "Insha'Allah, I will be home in a few months, but I thought I might be able to persuade you and Eliana to come with me, so you could visit Queluz for a while."

My heart leaps. Simona. Judah. My own house. How wonderful

that would be! Jamil is caressing my back under my tunic. He moves his hands slowly to my buttocks and pulls me to him. I feel his hardness against my belly. "Let's not talk about it now," I say, returning his kisses. We move to the bed, and every thought I have vanishes from my mind, as our breath mingles and our slick bodies speak the wild, wet language of love.

୧୨

I arrive at the rabbi's house shortly before dark. Eliana is eating a bowl of soup tinted red with pimentón and heaped with chunks of vegetables. I gratefully accept one too, along with a large hunk of bread slathered with a spread of chickpeas. The food and a cup of watered wine relax me, and I look around with affection at the modest home where Eliana spends so much of her time.

Like most houses in the Jewish Quarter, it has one big room with a sleeping alcove at one end. The hearth and a large table for preparing food take up one side, and a few chairs and another table for meals fill most of the remaining space. A second bed frame is propped against the wall, brought down at night, when people no longer need to move around the house.

The rabbi and his wife have four children. The boys study at the yeshiva and help Baroukh tend his garden in a field just beyond the city walls.

The other two are girls, thirteen and fifteen, who bicker most of the day over who does a better job of helping their mother, who has the more annoying habits, and who does what unpleasant thing on purpose. "It would be better to marry off my girls and have them gone," Toba tells me, "but I don't know what I would do without your little one." I know what she means as I watch Eliana furrow her brow and bite her lip as she cuts carrots and peppers as carefully as a surgeon for tomorrow's soup.

Eliana loves Granada. She has access to any book she wants from the caliph's library, she comes and goes among many who love her in our neighborhood, and she visits with her best friend Zubiya every few days. I can't disrupt her life to visit Queluz. It's best she forget about her past. I won't make the trip with Eliana, and I won't make it without her.

I lie in bed that night thinking about the other reason I cannot go to Queluz. I finally understand why Tarab dislikes me, and I know that if I go to Lisbon, she might be able to twist people's minds so they would not want me back. I've heard whispering that she set her sights on Jamil some time ago as a husband for Noor, and she makes it clear every chance she gets that Jamil needs a wife who will give him more children. Instead, she implies with furtive glances and raised eyebrows, he has me.

When I think objectively, I know she is right, though marriage to another woman would be the end for Jamil and me. The custom here allows men to keep lovers on the side, but that's not the Jewish way. I will not commit adultery with a married man, and I would honor a betrothal by refusing to see him again.

"I would rather have you," Jamil tells me. "Sawwar will carry on my name, and he can be the one to have five wives and fifty children if he wishes."

Still, something is changing in me. A chance to go home with Jamil might once have been an answer to my dreams, but I don't feel as I once did. When I left Portugal, I was prepared to make whatever choices would keep me with my lover. Now I'm choosing to stay here for myself and my daughter. Even if he isn't here—or isn't mine—I never want to leave.

18

Jamil is gone for a few months, then back, then gone again. It's late summer, and Eliana will turn ten in a little over a month. She moves effortlessly between her modest life in town and the lush world of the palace, dressing like a Muslim and chattering in perfect Arabic, while never missing a Jewish blessing or failing to be home in time to light the Sabbath candles.

Eliana is a pretty girl, but not a dazzling one. She is still narrow-hipped like a boy, with freckled cheeks from the Andalusian sun. When I look at her, I think of honey, for each hue it takes is somewhere in my daughter's hair, eyes, or skin, and its sweetness is in her veins.

I have passed my thirtieth birthday. Occasionally, I am startled by a silver hair in my eyebrows or scalp, which I pluck quickly, wondering if Jamil has noticed. He says I am lovelier than ever, but surrounded by such female beauty in Granada, it would be impossible not to have at least some doubts, especially while Noor remains unmarried and Tarab keeps hoping I will vanish from the earth.

I've let Tarab distract me again. I am waiting for Jamil in his study this summer afternoon. Later, we are going to a pavilion on the banks of the Darro River, where on warm evenings, Jamil and other poets gather to enjoy each other's company and recite their work.

I've attended several times before, although not many women do except for the qiyan, singing girls like those I saw perform for the caliph. A few weeks ago, a female poet, Atib bint Haqim, came on the arm of a new paramour and recited to great acclaim some scathing lyrics she'd written about a former lover.

"Are all women so bitter?" one of the men teased her between poems.

"Do all men give women cause?" she snapped back. I didn't like her sour views or shrill manner, but I was astonished a woman was reciting at all. With Jamil's coaxing, I have decided to counter Atib's bitterness tonight with my own poem about love. I dip my quill and write.

> *Atib bint Haqim, who could survive the love you offer?*
> *But if you go looking for another man*
> *Stay away from Jamil ibn Hasan!*
> *You'd find him with ease—*
> *His heart breathes perfume through his skin.*

I have written hundreds of poems since my first attempt that lonely night back in Queluz. I write because I want to dive deep into my own heart. I want to devour with all my senses every moment I have to be in this world. Finding words helps me believe I am not wasting any part of the Holy One's gift of life. I have wept, laughed, screamed on the page, and when I read my words to Jamil, it feels as intimate as making love. But my poems aren't always so lofty, especially when it comes to Tarab.

> *Look at your mouth!*
> *Are you trying to pull your eyes down to your chin*
> *Without using your hands?*

That's one. And another:

I whisper too low to be heard, "What a beautiful woman
  Tarab is."
She scowls at me, disagreeing as always with everything I say.

The latch opens on the door, and Jamil enters. The touch of his hand on my shoulder is better than any words. I remove the pins from my hair, letting it tumble over my shoulders in an invitation to my lover.

～

On this balmy summer evening, people in rowboats sing and call to each other as Jamil and I walk along the river to the pavilion. Above us loom the dark ramparts of the Alhambra, topped by a tiara of lights from the palace inside the fortress walls. A full moon hovers over the hill of the Albaicín, caressing the whitewashed houses with pale light.

"Granada is beautiful enough to break the heart," I say to Jamil, not sure exactly what I mean. A passing torch lights his face, and I see the glint of white teeth as he smiles.

"I didn't think I could love it more, until I brought you here," he replies. His eyes scan the dark Alhambra walls, the torchlight of the riverfront pavilion, the glittering moonlight on the water.

Granada nestles like a white-skinned woman
In a bed of dark mountains.
I make love to her with my eyes, my heart,
Though she is not true to me alone.

His aquamarine eyes are gray in the low light. "It's not a very good poem," he says, but like all the verses he makes up on the spot, I think it is perfect.

The pavilion is an open arcade surrounding a courtyard. People are milling around the steps leading to the arcade, for everyone in

Granada is welcome to listen, though only the privileged may take seats inside.

The singing girls have just finished performing, and they scurry, giggling, to several rough-looking guards, who keep the crowd at a distance. I sit with a few other women, apart from the men, as one after another recites his poems. I grow more tense as each one to sit down brings my own moment nearer. Finally, Jamil rises and gestures to where I am seated. There's no stopping this wild idea now, but oddly, the inevitability calms me, and I walk forward as if held up by a cloud.

I've changed my mind about attacking Atib bint Haqim. The night is like velvet, and I cannot hold onto hard thoughts. "Granada is beautiful enough to break the heart," I say, reciting the poem I have been writing in my head since Jamil and I walked along the riverbank.

> *"The moon above her a pearl*
> *Set in a sky of sparkling diamonds.*
> *A demanding mistress, she adjusts her white skirts*
> *As she settles back against the hills.*
> *Pointing to the peaks of the Sierra Nevada,*
> *She says, 'If you love me, bring them to me!*
> *I'm thirsty and the melting snow will cool me.'*
> *Many would die trying,*
> *Just to hear the sound in her throat as she swallows."*

I open my eyes again and I see Jamil's glowing face. Emboldened by my success, I look straight at him.

> *"How can you be so cruel?*
> *After a night of wine and love*
> *You shut your lids in sleep,*
> *Stealing my most precious jewels—*
> *The sapphires that are your eyes."*

Jamil throws his head back with a hearty, pleased laugh before replying.

"Cruel, my love?
I've put them away for safekeeping."

He shuts his eyes then opens them again.

"Here they are. I've brought them back to you.
They ask to see nothing but your beauty."

No one wants us to stop. It's a favorite pastime here in Granada, listening to two people declare their love, or sometimes their enmity, in extemporaneous verse. When my mind grows so weary that I can think of nothing more to say, I stand silently and take him in with my eyes. Jamil gives me the exaggerated bow he would offer a queen. Then he takes my hand and leads me away.

"Do you want to stay awhile?" he asks when we reach the edge of the courtyard. The singing girls have gone back in, and I hear the rhythm of the drums and cymbals and the wild, soaring voice of a woman singing an Arabic love poem.

For a moment, I want to stay to enjoy my success, but a wash of exhaustion makes me lightheaded. "No," I say. "I want to go home."

The night air cools my flushed face as we walk in silence toward the river. Stopping in moonshade under an ancient oak tree, he takes me in his arms. "You were magnificent," he says. "How can I be so lucky to have such a woman love me?"

I try to explain with my lips, my tongue, and the softest nip of my teeth that the fortunate one is me.

I come home thinking everything is perfect. I am in a cocoon that starts in my comfortable bed with Eliana, takes in the Jewish quarter, and spreads out to the Albaicín, where Jamil lies asleep. It wraps around the palace of the Alhambra and finds its boundary there—a world just the right size for me.

Before Eliana goes to sleep, we say the prayer she recites every night. "Kuatro kantonadas ay in esta kaza. Kuatro malahimes, kuatro angelines," it begins. There are four corners in this house, four angels. May they guard us from fire and flame, from evil speech and sudden death.

Four corners. Four angels. It is enough protection for two more years.

GRANADA 1458

The message to me at the palace is so stark that I know at once something terrible has happened. "Please come to my house." I recognize Jamil's hand, despite the uncharacteristic scrawl. "I need you."

I rush to the Albaicín in an early spring rain and see the somber face of the gatekeeper. "What happened?" I ask, but he won't tell me. Inside the house, I see Jamil's head buried in his arms as he slumps at his desk.

"Jamil?" He does not look up. "Jamil?" I say again, touching his shoulder. "What is it?"

He raises his head. His face is as pale as milk, and his eyes are so swollen I am not sure I would have recognized him in the street. "It's Sawwar," he says, barely able to get out the name. "He's dead."

A wail escapes from deep inside me before I can shed a tear. "He can't be," I say with the logic of fools. "He's too young." Jamil points to the open letter on his desk and I recognize Rashida's hand.

My dear brother,

I am sending this by the fastest horse and rider we have. I take comfort in the fact that until he arrives, you will be blissfully unaware of what I must tell you, and I weep that his speed will end your peace all the sooner.

A terrible accident has befallen your son. He was out with another boy setting snares and shooting partridge in the fields below Ronda. When it grew late, they took one of the shorter cliff routes instead. The other boy told us that Sawwar dropped the string of birds he was carrying. It caught on a ledge just below the trail and he thought he could get down safely to retrieve it. The rock was loose and he slipped so suddenly that the ledge could not hold him.

He lay there so perfect and quiet at the bottom of the cliff, as if he were just a dusty boy taking a nap. I pray death took him quickly before he felt pain or fear or understood his fate. We brought his body to Ronda and buried it the following morning, according to our law.

We are waiting for you when you are able to come. Perhaps grieving together will provide some comfort to us all.

May Allah grant you peace,

Your loving sister,
Rashida

I sit heavily on a stool, holding the letter in my hand. The house servants are hovering nearby, some weeping openly and others numb and still.

"Get out!" Jamil stands up suddenly, gesturing wildly. The jarring tone is so unlike him that they freeze for a moment before hurrying away. When we are alone, he holds me so tightly I would have cried out if I did not also need a way to hold on to this world.

Eventually he pulls away and, like sleepwalkers, we go into the bedroom and lie down fully clothed. He stares up at the rough-hewn ceiling, saying nothing. He's lost his wife and child already, and I wonder if all life's wounds have been torn open again. I silently drape an arm over his chest because there is nothing—not one thing—that can be said in such a moment.

I cannot imagine how he feels. To do so, I would have to picture Eliana dead. I think of a saw cutting through a rope, the last threads fraying and pulling away, sending what I most treasure into the abyss. I picture Sawwar watching as the stones he and Jamil are throwing plummet out of sight. He's smiling and happy, and then suddenly he is falling, falling, growing smaller as he nears the bottom…

I bolt to the nightstand where a pitcher of water and a wash basin are kept. The contents of my stomach splash loudly into the bowl as I retch until I collapse sobbing to the floor.

At Ronda, we go through the motions of life but find no comfort in it. I visit the baths. Jamil goes riding with the men. My daughter and I take walks and help Rashida around the house. Eliana has never dealt with death before, and every flicker of comprehension makes her cry. He must have been scared. It must have hurt. He's not coming back. I hover over her in ways she's not used to, worrying about a scratch or a flushed cheek, as if death may not yet have had its fill of children in the town.

I am grateful when Jamil says it's time to return to Granada, time to get on with life after Sawwar. On our last day, we sit in the garden together and watch the sun set over the same fields Sawwar roamed the last day of his life. "This changes everything," Jamil says. My stomach knots at what I think may be coming. "Sawwar was my heir, my only child," he goes on. "I have to think about that now."

"What do you mean?" I ask, putting off for just a moment the answer I already know.

"I must have a son." He takes my hand. "Before this happened, things were simple. I had Sawwar and you, and I didn't need anything else. Now, I have to decide what I'm going to do." Pulling back his hand, he turns away to avoid my eyes.

A blackness comes over me as my mind whirls. I take in a few deep breaths to make the awful feeling go away. "I must marry again," Jamil says. "I must have another child. Several, to ensure—" His eyes fill with tears, and he chokes back a sob. When he has composed himself, he takes my hand again. "You know I want that wife to be you."

"Jamil, I—"

I feel slain by the facts. I am too old to breed a large new family, but my other reason is even more compelling. "You know that any child I have must be raised as a Jew."

He gives me a long, searching stare, as if debating whether to try to get me to change my mind. "I know," he says with a sigh, "but as a Muslim, I could marry another woman without having to give you up. Perhaps you could be my chief wife and I could wed another as well—a younger one, to bear my children."

"I can't allow that." My heart twists with pain at what I must say. "You cannot get what you need by marrying me, Jamil. And I think—" I swallow hard. "I think we should not talk about it anymore."

We stay in our separate tents on the way back to Granada. When we arrive, he asks to be alone for a while to ponder his future. I am relieved to comply.

A week later, Jamil asks me to come to his house. His face is grim and sleepless, and he greets me with a stiff embrace. "Sit down," he says, motioning to a chair.

Any questions I have vanish in one agonizing realization. "You're getting married," I blurt out, wanting to cut short the torture of an explanation.

He looks surprised. "How did you know?"

"I sensed it. Then it's true?"

"I see no other way."

"Who is she?" The answer flashes into my mind, but I wait for him to say it.

"You know her," he says. "I'm marrying Noor."

Tarab has gotten what she wanted. The Jew from Portugal turned out to be no threat to her plans after all. I'm filled with loathing so intense I want to scream, claw, smash, tear at the hateful face I see in my mind. But I don't move. Instead, I take in one deep breath and then another, to fill the void left behind as my life bleeds away.

"I will always love you," Jamil says. "And if I could ask you to stay in my life without offending you, I would, but I know I cannot." He takes me in his arms. "I am so sorry."

I feel the tears rising, and I surrender to them, lingering in his embrace until I reach a strange sense of calm about what I cannot change.

I pull away and see his cheeks are wet and his eyes mournful and drained of life. "I can't bear to think we have already made love for the last time," he says. "Could we—?"

I feel a surge of emotion so raw that I want to say yes, to have him inside me, to pay attention as I never have before, so I will remember forever, but something in me is so close to breaking that I know I must run from this house as quickly as I can.

"No," I say. "It's better this way." Without another word, I run out the door, across the courtyard, through the gate, and out of his life.

I pull my veil over my face so no one will see me, although in this part of Granada, no one is likely to care who I am. The backs of my knees feel independently alive, pushing into my kneecaps as if to fell me, to leave me broken in the street, my grief and humiliation complete.

I should have known.

I should have known.

I am an unmarried woman who went off to be with her lover and is now abandoned. Better I had stayed at home in Queluz. Judah, Simona, Toba, Mushtaq—what will they think of me now? How will I face a gloating Tarab?

I tell myself I was not abandoned, that I chose to come, that I am the one who forced it to end, and Jamil loves me still. A slip of Sawwar's feet, and more than one life tumbled out of control.

"You're alive. You have your daughter. You will survive this," I say aloud, not caring if anyone hears. But my voice is hollow, and my heart says otherwise. I want to be swallowed up so I don't have to think, don't have to feel anymore.

I reach home, not knowing how I put one foot in front of the other, and fall onto the cool covers of my bed, letting out a cry as piercing and ragged as a blade being sharpened on rock. Over. Gone. Forever.

❦

My anguish at Noor's upcoming wedding is so great that I am certain I am dying. Tarab's happiness is so unseemly that Mushtaq scolds her openly, forcing the mean-spirited woman into an insincere apology to me, which only makes things worse.

Jawhara tells me I can stay home until after the wedding if it is too much to bear, but I don't want Tarab to have that victory. Though merely drawing breath is as painful as if through an aching tooth, I force myself to go to the palace to tutor Zubiya. One afternoon, I make a stop at the gypsy camp north of town to buy a cure for melancholy and lovesickness that leaves me so empty-headed I don't feel anything at all.

The only good in all of this is that Tarab will live in Jamil's house, and I won't have to endure the aftermath of her triumph. I stay at home the day of the wedding, and I try to picture a palace without Tarab rather than Noor and Jamil dressed in their finery at their wedding banquet, Noor and Jamil taking a festooned sedan chair to his home, Noor and Jamil going into his bedroom, Noor and Jamil…

Noor and Jamil.

❦

The scab on the wound is tested painfully when Tarab comes to the palace to visit three months later. Noor always comes with her, and I stay in my quarters, unable to bear the conversation. Today, Tarab is alone and I hear her say that Noor is feeling ill. "My daughter is expecting a child," she says, looking up at the latticed window where she knows I am watching.

Such proof of her presence in the bed Jamil and I shared is more than I can stand. I go to the window that looks out over the city, desperate for the air that seems to have been sucked from the room. My eyes light on Jamil's roof on the hill of the Albaicín.

"You bastard!" I say. "How could you do this to me?"

I don't mean it. At least, most of me does not. He offered me the place Noor holds now, and I chose my future. Still my heart is bleeding so badly I'm surprised my clothing is not soaked red. For a moment, I pity the young woman, so unable to meet him as an equal. How hard he must be working to be as happy as he was with me.

Is Jamil standing in his courtyard now, looking up at the Alhambra and wondering where I am? He knows which window is mine. "You made your choice too," I say, sending the thought to him as I shut the lattice screen.

GRANADA 1459

Noor brings her infant son, Ahmad, to the palace a month after his birth. I am afraid to look at him, for fear I will recognize Jamil's eyes or his thick, golden-brown hair. But Ahmad looks no more like one of them than the other, and I murmur along with the rest of the women, that with such parents, it's no surprise he is a beautiful baby.

I watch with odd detachment Ahmad's progress in the first months of his life. I'm as excited as the rest of the women when he recognizes me, and I smile back with sincere pleasure. I am happy for Noor, because I know what it means to be a mother, and from time to time I even forget the miserable truth behind this delightful child's existence.

By summer, another pall hangs over my life. The caliph is gravely ill. Muhammad has no son to succeed him, and in the Caliphate of Granada, the outcome would be unclear even if he did. The only certainty is that a new family and a new chief wife will take over the Alhambra, just as Mushtaq had done years before.

No one will pack anything now, so Death will not think it has been invited, but eventually Jawhara and her children will go with Mushtaq to their ancestral home in Almería. There they will live inside the Alcazaba, a fortress overlooking the sea.

"You're welcome to come," Jawhara tells me almost every day. "Zubiya will be bereft without you and Eliana. Please say yes!"

I am not tempted by the offer. Zubiya's marriage has been contracted, and in a few years, she will leave for her husband's domain near Málaga. Eliana, now thirteen, will eventually marry as well, and if she moves away, I will be alone here in Granada. But if I accept Mushtaq's and Jawhara's offer, I will serve for their amusement once Zubiya is gone, and nothing more. That's not enough of a life for me.

I could go back to Queluz. The idea tempts me, but an inner voice tells me to go first to some place where I can establish who I am on my own before I decide on a more permanent home. But where? Simona told me not to stay in Queluz just because I couldn't decide what to do with my life, and I'm feeling the same confusion now. In time, will I feel as Simona does, saying to myself, "look where I ended up," without remembering exactly when, and how, my destiny was set?

I go to the palace one morning and know from the minute I arrive that something is wrong. No one is outside tending the gardens, and the shops are empty. "Is he—?" I ask a guard.

"No, but they're saying he won't last the day." I rush to the women's quarters, but only Rayyan is there. We wait together the rest of the morning, and eventually we see Mushtaq being carried in a chair. Jawhara and Zubiya are holding onto each other, crying.

"My husband is gone," Mushtaq says as the servants lower her chair. Grief buckles her legs under her as she stands up.

"I'm so sorry," I say, my eyes welling with tears for this woman I have grown to love so deeply.

"He's better now. He is with Allah and the Prophet, ṣall Allahu ëalayhi wa sallam." She tries to smile.

The servants help her to her favorite chair, and she glances at the table next to her. "It looks as if you have received a letter." She examines the wax seal. "From Elizabeth of Castile."

She hands it to me, then turns to a wet-faced eunuch standing quietly nearby. "Please tell the servants our time here is over. We'll bury my husband and leave for Almería as soon as we can pack."

Mushtaq excuses me so I may read my letter in private. The former Queen of Castile is my childhood friend Elizabeth, whom I haven't heard from in years. She is already a widow, her elderly husband, King Juan II, having died five years ago, when she was only twenty-five.

There are rumors that her removal with her two children to the small town of Arévalo was not voluntary, but a banishment carried out by the new king, Enrique IV, who is Elizabeth's stepson by King Juan's first marriage. Elizabeth has two children of her own, an eight-year-old daughter Isabella and a son Alfonso, two years younger. The boy is second in line for the throne because Enrique is childless.

"El Impotente" people call him behind his back. After thirteen years of marriage to his first wife, Blanca of Navarre, the pope granted an annulment, based on proof that Blanca was still a virgin. When prostitutes came forward saying he had been quite the lover with them, he claimed Blanca had used witchcraft to keep him from her bed. The poor woman was sent in disgrace back to her home in Navarre.

Since his second marriage, the rumors have increased that

Enrique's member is withered, because he and Juana have not pro-
duced a child to secure the throne of Castile. Witchcraft indeed.
I'm glad Diogo never heard that excuse.

What can Elizabeth want from me? Closing the door to my
quarters, I break the seal.

My dearest Amalia,

*Although it's been years since we have seen or written to each
other, I think of you often and hold you in my heart. I understand
you have been in service as a tutor in Granada, and if you are ever
looking for another assignment, I hope you will consider coming to
Arévalo to be the tutor for my daughter, Isabella.*

*My dear Amalia, I remember our childhood together and hope
the recollection brings you the same tears of joy. Life has brought
both of us much sorrow, but there is no friend like one from that
time of youthful innocence, and I pray we will make each other
smile again.*

Your friend,
Elizabeth of Portugal and Castile

19

ARÉVALO, 1459

My first reaction upon seeing Elizabeth is to wonder whether I could possibly look that old. I am thirty-three and she is two years younger, but the sad details of her life since she left Portugal to be King Juan's second wife weigh heavily on her. Elizabeth had been plump and rosy-skinned back in Portugal, but now her collarbone juts out behind a necklace of pearls, and even the careful ministrations of servants cannot disguise her lank, thin hair and sagging jaw.

She senses my alarm and gives me a wan smile. "It's the poison," she says. "My husband's mayordomo tried to kill me with what he said was a cure for melancholy. I never recovered." She shrugs too enigmatically for comfort. "It's part of life in Castile. I guess they don't realize God sees all of the court for the fraudulent little weasels they are."

Eliana is sitting next to me, trying not to squirm in the style of dress we must now wear. The maids assigned to our quarters had to scurry to find suitable clothing for us this morning, since we'd come with nothing but our loose Andalusian robes. Later today, the tailors will arrive to begin our transition into uncomfortable Castilian wardrobes of our own.

The views from the palace are of the same glorious countryside we traveled through. Scattered among the undulating fields of golden wheat are patches of saffron flowers and orderly vineyard rows. Trees line the banks of rivers and streams like dark-green ribbons dropped from the hand of a giant. Cows and horses graze in pastures set against violet hills in the distance. The sky is blue most of the time, although massive clouds form quickly, sending shadows racing across the landscape.

Just outside the walls that enclose the town, two rivers meet. Near their juncture, a round fortress juts up to the sky, and from our window we can see small figures of guards walking the parapets. Above them, the flag of Castile waves in the breeze, next to the personal banner of Elizabeth, to mark the fact that she is in residence.

Life in the palace is turned inward, though, and the windows lining the corridors aren't open to let in light, much less a hint of the world outside. It feels like a prison here compared to the expansiveness of Granada. Is anything in this room where we now sit truly her own? Is Elizabeth her own anymore? Was she ever?

She sighs. "Do you remember I used to think being married off to an old man was the worst thing that could happen? My troubles were nothing compared to what they've been since my husband died." Her eyes cloud and she looks away, just as she used to when one of her dark moods was setting in.

I try to introduce a note of cheer. "We've been looking forward to meeting Isabella and Alfonso," I say, giving my daughter a forced smile.

Eliana doesn't smile back.

She doesn't smile much these days. At thirteen, she's not happy about coming to a place where her only company will be an eight-year-old princess. She was crushed when Jamil married Noor and devastated again at Zubiya's departure from the Alhambra. She sulked much of the way to Arévalo, insinuating that her unhappiness was, if not completely, at least largely my fault.

I've tried to reassure her this move will be for the best, even if we can't see how at the moment. I've tried to tell her my heart is breaking too, and we will both get over the pain, but there's a hole in my heart so large I feel as if my entire being will be sucked in and vanish altogether. I've lost Jamil and Granada too. I don't know where I am going, or why, and the sullen child with me, for all her desire to take her own path, still depends on me to choose well for both of us.

I haven't told Eliana how wounded I am, don't want her to know how little confidence I feel. On the journey here, I waited with such anticipation for her to fall asleep at night. Only then could I let myself go and cry for all I have lost, surrendering to the bleakness ahead, for that is all I can see.

A sound in the doorway startles me back to the present. A young girl is waiting just inside the room. The silhouette of a nun takes up most of the light, but the girl is standing in the glow from a wall torch that illuminates her blond hair like a crown around her face.

"Isabella!" Elizabeth says. "You may enter."

The little girl comes into the room followed by her brother Alfonso, who has to be urged forward by the nun. "We've come from mass, your highness," the nun says. "I hope we haven't kept you waiting." She looks at Eliana and me, and though the light is low, I see a flicker of disdain. I'm a Jew. I'm in her country. I don't expect she needs to know any more than that.

Another sour soul like Tarab. Being a nun, at least this one won't have a daughter she's trying to marry off, although the stories I've heard about some convents make me think it's best to be prepared even for that possibility.

I informed Elizabeth I was now living as a Jew, so she could rescind her invitation if she wished. "I can't say I like what you've done, but it is up to God to judge, and no one here need know you were ever anything else."

"I would get much comfort from being with someone I know to be a privada, a true friend, who cared for me when there was nothing to gain by it," the letter went on. "Such a friend can only come from the years before I became a ball to be tossed around in games others play."

"Isabella, Alfonso, I'd like you to meet Doña Cresques and her daughter, Eliana," Elizabeth says, using the Jewish family name I have now adopted. "Doña Cresques will be teaching you geography and literature." A scowl flits across Isabella's face, and I realize the nun has probably been telling her how wrong it is for a Jew to teach a princess anything. From the stubborn set of her mouth and shoulders, I can see that Isabella agrees with the nun. "And if you would like," her mother continues, "Doña Cresques can teach you Arabic as well. She speaks and writes many languages perfectly."

"Arabic?" Isabella had been examining me with her smoky eyes, but now her head turns sharply toward her mother. "Why do we need to know Arabic when there will soon be no Moors in Spain?" She looks at the nun. "I gave my favorite bracelet for the cause when we went to church today." The black-robed woman gives her a dour, approving nod.

Why learn Arabic indeed? Isabella's value lies in a strategic marriage. Whatever foreign country she goes to, one thing the little girl can count on is that they will not speak Arabic there.

I meet Isabella's stare with one of my own, tempered with a smile to show I am not unnerved by her. But I am. Something about that child is different from anyone her age I have ever met. Forget Arabic, I tell myself. Teaching her geography is going to be challenging enough.

VALENCIA 1492

I remember Isabella's face when she announced that she had given her own jewelry to fight the Moors. The intensity in her manner and expression was unlike what I expected in a princess. All the ones I had known were pampered, vacant little dolls.

God had spoken. That was how Isabella felt. The triumph of right over wrong might take time but it was inevitable. How could God be almighty otherwise?

Those raised with a modest sense of themselves acknowledge that

God loves their neighbors too and may favor causes other than their own. But Isabella did not grow up modestly. Certainly, when King Enrique didn't like something his stepmother said or did, he was not above cutting off the allowance that let Elizabeth and her children live in comfort, but Isabella's lack of modesty had nothing to do with the food she ate or clothes she wore.

The girl I tutored in Arévalo listened to what others said, but she kept her own counsel. Isabella never doubted that the Moors would be pushed from Spain, because she was sure she knew God's will. Would Isabella have turned out differently if Elizabeth had been stronger? If just one thing is altered, does a string of changes inevitably follow, or are some forces so great they plow down whatever is in their path?

I soon realized that my presence in Arévalo had little to do with Isabella needing a tutor. I can't think of anything I taught her that couldn't have been handled by someone else. Elizabeth needed a friend she'd chosen herself, and she needed to set her foot down at least occasionally, as a reminder of the person she had once been.

The kind of person who could force a doting husband to sacrifice his closest friend just to please her. Alvaro de Luna, the man who had tried to poison Elizabeth, had been assigned as Juan's page when the prince was only six years old, and as Juan grew, Luna's power grew with him. When Juan became king, Luna was appointed mayordomo, his chief of staff. Because Juan did not really want to take on the work of ruling his country, he named Luna Constable of Castile and let him make most of the decisions.

This upstart was not going to tell a royal princess of Portugal and the Queen of Castile what to do! Elizabeth used everything in her power—whining, tantrums, silences, seduction—to get Juan to sign an order of execution. The morning of Luna's death, lightning struck the palace where Juan was in residence, and in the blue flash, the king saw a vision of his beheaded friend, who told him he would be explaining to God in a year's time why he had repaid his mayordomo's faithful service in this fashion. Stricken by remorse and without Luna to restrain him, the king fell into debauchery, recovering from one illness only to come down with another. Luna was right. One year after the execution, Juan was dead.

With her husband gone, Elizabeth's power vanished. El Impotente was king. That insignificant baby we waited for Queen Eleanor to give birth to when Elizabeth and I were girls in Lisbon, the girl so quickly forgotten after Eleanor lost the regency, had become Enrique's wife, Queen Juana of Castile.

The sound of my laughter echoes off the bare walls. Insignificant baby girls have a way of surprising people. Isabella, born with little chance for the throne, turned out to be one of those. If El Impotente had managed to have a son, Isabella would not be queen, Ferdinand would not be king, and I would not be in this room.

Perhaps. Who knows? Why bother with these thoughts? Isabella happened. I'll leave the fantasies of better outcomes to others. The atlas feels so heavy in my lap I don't open it, and thoughts of that little princess in Arévalo will not go away.

ARÉVALO 1461

In the two years I've been at Elizabeth's court, I've come to understand what is going on behind her daughter's eyes. Something in Isabella seems to be lying in wait, as if she is measuring everything for how she might use it in the future. She's obedient not because she lacks stubbornness or courage but because, at least for now, listening serves her best.

She can be willful, even cruel. Her little brother is often reduced to tears by her tantrums, which always happen out of range of anyone whose opinion matters. This doesn't include either me or her maids, who mutter out of earshot about how one would think she and not Juana was the Queen of Castile, with the airs she puts on.

Eliana dislikes her, but Isabella is unconcerned. My daughter goes off every day to be with the Jewish friends she has made in

Arévalo, and she cares as little about Isabella as the princess does about her.

And yet, there's a charming side to Isabella too. In town, she enchants the merchants, claps her hands at the bands of entertainers who pass through, and gives alms to the poor and maimed. Everyone in town loves her, offering her treats and little gifts, feeding her more by their adoration than their ribbons and candied fruit.

She is second in line to the throne, after her younger brother, for there must be no male candidate before Castile will consider a queen. She will find herself further removed from power if El Impotente manages to produce an heir. Often, when we stop to survey the magnificent countryside while out riding, I wonder what she is thinking. Perhaps that it's better not to get too attached to anything or anyone, because she is likely to be sent elsewhere as a bride.

At such times I pity this little princess, who keeps her thoughts hidden behind her aloof manners and calculating eyes. For all the demands people rush to indulge, she cannot order up a future to her liking, and in many ways I am freer—and luckier—than she is.

∾

When I first came to Castile, I found it strange that when people here spoke of the infidel, they meant Muslims, because I'd just come from a place where the infidels were Christians.

People are terrified that the fall of Constantinople to the Ottomans a few years back will soon bring Muslim armies here to restore their lost glory in the land they named al-Andalus. Castilians are stockpiling bludgeons and sharpened sticks to defend themselves against Christ-hating invaders coming to batter down their doors. From every pulpit, sermons about the victory of Christendom ring forth. Church coffers bulge, and thousands of men all over Castile stand ready to march south to conquer the last Muslim stronghold in Granada.

The wealthiest of them will be in full battle dress on mounted steeds, but the poorest will be armed with little more than the pope's word that even if they drown in a creek or die of gangrene from an infected toenail before they get there, the mere act of setting out to destroy the infidel gives them a free pass into heaven. For the nobles, what could be better than returning home covered with honors, laden with booty and perhaps a new title or two, with minstrels telling of their heroic exploits to rapt audiences? Everyone wants a good war, it seems.

Except El Impotente. From what I've seen of Enrique, he doesn't care about anything except a big dinner and a fine pack of hounds. The king prefers to march south, threaten Granada, demand tribute from the caliph, and come home with most of the war chest unspent. He rewards some nobles with land, treasure, and title to ensure that the disgruntled remainder, who have nothing but debt to show for following him, don't have the numbers to form a hostile alliance against him.

The king travels around Castile most of the year, and he is now in Arévalo for a visit with Elizabeth. I've never seen a ruler so unregal. From the way the man smells, I think he must sleep with his dogs. While Enrique swaggers through the halls of the castle or sleeps off his wine, his men make a shambles of the taverns. Bar wenches are brutalized, and the churches are filled with people praying to be delivered from a pestilence that must, at least at the moment, seem worse than the Moors.

We rarely leave our quarters for fear of running into the king's retinue. Usually, after Eliana finishes her lessons, she runs off to spend the day with her Jewish friends. One of them has a handsome older brother, so I imagine they whisper and plot as Elizabeth, Beatriz, and I did, doing very little of the sewing for their wedding trousseaus that is supposed to keep them occupied. Eliana hasn't gone out since Enrique arrived, though, and stuck here in the palace with little to do, she is again the morose company I had when we first came here.

Elizabeth has been beside herself with anxiety. At the age of three, her daughter was betrothed to Ferdinand, son of the King of Aragon. Enrique broke this engagement when Isabella was nine, preferring that she marry Carlos of Navarre, another son of the same king. When Carlos died by poison on his way to formalize the arrangement, Isabella became unbetrothed. Enrique is here to take up the issue with Elizabeth again, although in the end he will make whatever arrangements he wants, with or without her approval.

As Elizabeth's privada, I sit in on their conversations, though it is clear Enrique would prefer to browbeat his stepmother alone. His huge feet and hands are visible outside the coarse and foul-smelling cloak he favors, which hangs over a corpulent body clothed in a tunic spotted with grease from his last meal. His auburn eyebrows are bushy and almost as curly as his beard, which points forward at a peculiar angle. He has a crooked, smashed-looking nose as a result of a childhood fall, and this, combined with his beard, makes his profile as concave as a quarter moon.

Colorless eyes look out coldly at Elizabeth from under reddened, crusty lids. "I must say I am rather disappointed in you," he says. "I thought you would favor a marriage between your daughter and the King of Portugal. Afonso is your cousin, and my God, woman, you still insist on speaking Portuguese here."

Enrique reached down to scratch his dingy stockings, and my eyes follow his movement. I inherited keen vision from the mapmakers in my family, and I see the tiny black specks. Fleas, I think to myself. The King of Castile has fleas.

"I love Portugal," Elizabeth says, "but the king is twenty-nine, and my daughter is eleven. She is too young to marry, and I am hoping for someone closer to her own age when the time comes."

Enrique laughs. "Afonso and Isabella are far closer in age than you and my father."

I can see Elizabeth struggling. She's been in tears most of the time since she learned the purpose of Enrique's visit, and she was so horrified by the prospect of meeting with him today that she vomited in her dressing room before he arrived.

"Yes," she replies, "I realize that such marriages can succeed, but as you see, when one person is much older than the other, the time to be together may be sadly short."

Enrique pulls himself up in his chair. "Who are any of us to say how long God wills us to be here?" I have the urge to pick up the knitting in my lap and stab him with the needles for invoking the Holy One in such an unctuous and self-serving way.

"And really," Enrique goes on, "isn't marrying for happiness a bit quaint?"

I open my mouth to reply, but I lack the status to be critical of him or even to speak at all. Elizabeth sees me, though, and says she wants to hear what I think.

Enrique leans back and drapes his elbows casually on the arms of his chair. His eyes hint of menace as he takes me in.

"I think everyone hopes to find happiness with a spouse, and parents are right to prefer that their children enter marriages with at least a reasonable chance of that."

Enrique stares coldly, and prickles of anxiety crawl down my back.

"I don't wish to speak cruelly of your own difficulties," Elizabeth says to him, "but perhaps the feelings of a parent for a child are something you don't understand."

A smile slowly curls his lips. "My, my," he says, "how delicately put." The smile vanishes. "And how reasoned. How sane." I see Elizabeth's face grow paler. Her vacillating moods are famous, and Enrique has been spreading rumors that the Queen Widow of Castile is mad.

He leans back in his chair. "And besides, I have news I want you to be the first to know."

He smirks, forcing her to wait before he speaks. "My wife is with child."

"With child?" Elizabeth's eyes widen. I manage to keep my jaw from dropping, but barely. After all these years, is El Impotente suddenly able to perform?

"And of course, if it's a boy…" He pauses to make sure Elizabeth is listening. "Your son won't be heir to the throne anymore."

Elizabeth must be stunned to the core, but she composes herself. Her voice is eerily calm. "And if it's a girl," she says, "why don't you promise her to the King of Portugal instead of my daughter? After all, you don't think age is important in a marriage."

I want to applaud. She has summoned this self-possessed person from somewhere inside her, and I only wish she could do it more often.

"I would, if it were best for Castile," he says, ignoring the acid in her tone.

Best for Castile? That stinking carcass of a man cares only about himself. When he shifts his weight to let out a loud, noxious fart, I can't help but think that is his answer to, and his true opinion of, his stepmother and his country.

With Enrique's men wreaking havoc in the town, Eliana and I leave with some reluctance to go, as we always do, for Shabbat dinner at the home of Jewish friends. I love these afternoons with my daughter. Now, just turned fourteen, she has forgotten her anger with me at leaving Granada and has become a pretty and poised young woman. After we eat, she and her friends usually go off to share secrets out of earshot, but they always return for the songs and dancing.

Eliana is more skilled than I on the castanets, and she has a beautiful voice. Hearing her sing the same melodies my mother did sometimes leaves me in tears. My grandmother is dead now too, and I imagine they are looking down, watching my daughter with the same pride I feel.

By now, the news has spread that Queen Juana is pregnant, and no one wants to talk about anything else. Sadia, our host, seems to know every rumor. "There's something wrong with his prick," she tells me when her husband isn't listening. "It's corked up at the top, I heard. That's why he can't put his seed in a woman."

"That can't be right," I tell her. "If Blanche of Navarre was a virgin when their marriage was annulled, he never got it inside her. It would have to be more than corked up at the top."

Sadia shakes her head. "It's probably what they say, then—that he likes men."

Unbidden memories of Diogo make me shudder. "I think he prefers dogs," I say. "He already smells like one."

Sadia laughs so hard she almost chokes. When she recovers, she puts her hands on her hips in mock indignation. "Amalia, you are wicked—and on Shabbat too!" She looks around and moves closer. "Tell me more!"

"I don't know anything. I stay away from him."

"Well, you hear what the servants are saying, don't you?"

"Not really."

Sadia always learns more in the square than I do in the palace.

"Queen Juana is a wild one," she whispers. "She's been having an affair with someone named Beltrán de la Cueva, and he's the real father of the child."

"Does Enrique know?"

"He must if he's never stuck it in her, don't you think?"

The importance of this hits me like a falling stone wall. Normally Beltrán would pay with his life for cuckolding a king, and Enrique's unfaithful wife would find herself banished to some distant castle or nunnery, but oddly, they have done the king a service. Enrique wants an heir so badly he apparently doesn't care if the blood of the royal house of Trastámara, the line chosen by God to rule, is replaced by some minor nobleman's. Will no Trastámara blood flow in the next ruler's veins? How will Castile pay for this disrespect of God's will?

It is getting late, and since the palace is not far, I decide I am sufficient escort for my daughter. We are in one of the narrow streets leading into the main square when two of Enrique's guards block our progress.

"Look what we have here!" one of them says. He reaches up to stroke Eliana's cheek. She struggles to pull away and hide her face, but the weather is warm and she is not wearing the hooded cloak that might have protected her.

"Get away from her!" I scream as the other one grabs me by both hands.

"What's the matter?" he says. "You're Jews, ain't you? You're the king's property, and Enrique is always"—he leers—"most generous with what's his."

Bile rises in my throat at the foul smell of stale beer on his breath. His teeth press so hard against my mouth as he kisses me that I think my lips will split. He presses me against the wall, and I feel fingers grinding one of my breasts as he tries to loosen my bodice with his other hand.

"What are you fighting for, you Jewish cow?" he snarls. "I'll just fuck you standing up while he's busy with the little virgin." He draws out this last word as a vicious taunt.

I hear Eliana cry out, and I twist my head to see that one of them has backed her against a wall and is covering her mouth with one hand while lifting her skirt with the other. "Come on," he says. "Let me show you what a cock that's not been cut off at the top feels like."

I am screaming so loud I think my throat will rip, and finally a window opens above us. "You leave them alone!" I hear a woman's voice say. "My boy's gone to get help, and my husband's coming downstairs to bash your heads in, you filthy swine!"

"Mierda!" one of them mutters under his breath. The one holding Eliana lets her go, but not before grabbing a breast in each hand and kneading it like dough. "Little Jew slut," he says. "You know you like it!"

"Hey!" I hear a man's voice and the sound of footsteps running down the cobbled street toward us. "You get away from them!"

"Mierda!" The man repeats, giving my hair one savage twist and smashing his mouth on mine before tossing me against the wall like an empty tankard of ale.

"Aw, come on now!" Eliana's assailant gives our rescuers a cocky, cruel grin. He releases her with such force that she stumbles and falls to the ground, her chest heaving silently in terror as she cowers there. "We were just having a little fun with the ladies."

"They're from the palace, you fools," the woman hisses down from her perch in the window. "Don't you get enough from the whores in the taverns?"

"The palace, eh!" The man who had attacked me shrugs, knowing Enrique will exact no consequences. "In that case, my lady, thank you for the feel." He bows with mock ceremony before joining his friend, who is ambling off down the street.

"Little Jew girl was pretty sweet," I hear the other one say. "Want to smell?" He passes his finger under his friend's nose as they disappear around the corner.

ʗ

Back in our quarters, Eliana clutches me so hard I can barely breathe. "I don't want to live here anymore, Mama," she says. "Those men!" She buries her head in my chest.

"Eliana, did he—?"

"No." I feel the heat of her exhalation. "But his hand touched me." Her eyes well with tears. "Does that mean I'm spoiled?"

I smooth her hair against her back, murmuring reassurance and resisting the urge to ask if it hurt or to check for blood. "No, it doesn't."

I run my tongue between my teeth and the inside of my lips, examining with detachment the swelling from the man's forced kisses. He touched my daughter. That's all I care about. I want to rip the world to tatters for stealing Eliana's innocence. I want to throw everything in this room against the walls, to wail at the top of my lungs to release my terrible guilt for having such bad judgment, but my child is so soft and vulnerable in my arms that I know I must be strong for her.

I venture what I hope will be a reassuring thought. "I've heard they're leaving in a few days. We'll be safe then."

"I don't care!" Eliana whimpers. "I'll never be able to walk in this town without thinking about what happened. Can't we leave, Mama?"

"But your friends are here!"

"I can't face them. He—he put his hand there, Mama. I'm so ashamed."

"No one has to know."

I can't believe what I am saying. I want to storm into Elizabeth's quarters and tell her the injustice that has been done and then march to Enrique and demand the satisfaction of seeing his men horsewhipped.

"Promise we'll leave?"

I continue stroking her hair. What can I tell her? The Queen Widow of Castile invited me to Arévalo, and it might not be easy to get away, especially when she's desperate for one person she can trust.

It's time.

The thought lances me with its absolute correctness. I couldn't shield her today, but it's not too late to protect her from what could never be enough of a life. The town is pleasant—or was before today—but there is no future for my daughter here, or for me either.

I see the faces of the Abravanel family smiling at me. "It's time to come home," I hear them say. Whatever I had been holding back has found its way to the surface, and its clarity gives me courage.

"I'll talk to Elizabeth tomorrow," I tell her. "We'll see what she has to say."

The following morning, we wake to find the servants in a frenzy. "The king is leaving," my maid tells me, "and he's taking the children with him."

"Taking Isabella and Alfonso? Where?"

"They're going to go live with him in Segovia. We were told just an hour ago."

"What does the queen say?"

Her face falls. "I'm told she's taken sick. She won't let anyone see her."

I rush to Elizabeth's quarters. A maid and a manservant are huddled together outside. The maid is dabbing her tearstained face.

"You can't go in," the manservant says. "She's locked the door."

"Well, unlock it then!" I tell him. Shaking his head as if there is no explaining people who invite disaster, he produces a key and jiggles open the lock.

The door creaks loudly, and before I have gotten through the anteroom, an object sails by my head, narrowly missing me. "Get out!" I hear her scream.

"Elizabeth?" I pick out her silhouette in the bedroom, but she can't see me because the torches are unlit where I am standing. "Elizabeth?" I repeat. "It's me, Amalia."

"Go away!" She lifts both hands to her face, and with a groan, she collapses to the floor. I rush to kneel next to her.

"I want to die," she whispers. "Why can't I just die?"

I call for the servants to help me get her into bed. The maid scurries off for a potion to calm her nerves, and the man goes back to guard the door. I sit on the edge of her bed. "Tell me what happened," I say, holding her thin, cold hand in mine.

My touch seems to calm her. "Enrique says now that his wife is pregnant, there will be a family at court, and he wants Isabella and Alfonso to be part of it." She dabs her cheeks with a soaked handkerchief, and silently I trade it for mine. "He says it's too dreary for children here, but of course it's still good enough for me." Her jaw trembles. "And now he's taking what little life there is in this godforsaken place."

"But a baby won't make a family for them. Your children are too old to be friends with someone born now."

"It's just another of his lies. He knows there are plots to put my son on the throne, and he wants him close by to control who can see him."

My flesh crawls for the mild and uninteresting boy who has the misfortune to be perceived as a threat by an unscrupulous king. Elizabeth's husband once told her it would be better to be born to a journeyman than to the King of Castile, and when I think of Alfonso going off to Segovia with someone as unscrupulous and repulsive as Enrique, I think that might be right.

"I don't know if he'll be safe," Elizabeth says, "or Isabella either. If the baby's a girl and Enrique tries to claim the throne for her, people might say that if we're going to have a queen on the throne, why shouldn't it be Isabella? Enrique might want to stop that however he can, especially since people wonder whether the baby is even his."

Two children, unaware and without allies, among the jackals at court. We both know how often inconvenient royals have suspicious deaths, and tender age is no protection. I squeeze Elizabeth's hand. "Enrique doesn't inspire much confidence," I say, "but I can't picture him harming your children."

My mind has pushed aside the terrible scene in the alley, but now it overwhelms me. A man who has such men around him— what wouldn't he do? At least Elizabeth is calm now, and after she drinks the elixir the maid brings her, she falls into a light sleep. I leave her side only long enough to fetch Eliana, and together we sit quietly by my friend's bed, so she won't find herself alone when she wakes.

The following morning, a grim Isabella urges her brother not to cry as they mount the mules they will ride to Segovia. Eliana and I watch from a window as the procession disappears beyond the palace wall before we return to our rooms to begin packing.

I spoke with Elizabeth while she lay in bed yesterday, and she gave me permission to leave. I am wracked with guilt because I know she was not fully aware of what she was saying. She kept repeating that she wanted to be left alone to die. Of course I could go, she told me. She didn't need anything—not food, not company, not even air.

It's not how I would have preferred to end my time with her, but I know what I must do for myself and my daughter. We will leave for Queluz tomorrow before Elizabeth can change her mind.

Eliana is in tears all day, between grief over leaving her friends and the lingering horror of the attack in the alley. She doesn't want to eat the meal the servants bring us at midday, and when she decides, uncharacteristically, to take a nap in the afternoon, she is not awake to hear the disturbance outside the entrance to our quarters.

Elizabeth is in the hallway wearing only a nightdress of silk so thin her nipples and the triangle of dark hair at her groin are visible underneath. Her hair is tangled, as if she had been thrashing about to escape a bad dream. Though the servants are trying to restrain her, they can't. Some hidden force is powering her delicate body, which seems to be floating just above the floor.

"He's here," she says. "He's come for his revenge."

"Who?" I ask.

"Alvaro de Luna." Her hysterical laughter echoes down the hallway. "I had him beheaded. Don't you hear him laughing at me now?"

ᏜᎧ

Eliana and I travel for weeks over the plains and rolling hills between Arévalo and Queluz. Elizabeth ordered a royal guard to accompany us, but Eliana was so fearful about being in the company of soldiers that to keep the men in line, we agreed to have a priest accompany us. He is an overweight man in his late thirties, who tipples with the guards by the campfire and tells bawdy stories as we ride along.

A jolly sort most of the time, he is grim only about the need to save Eliana's and my souls. He lectures us about the Jews' apostasy from God, and when that doesn't work, he oozes honeyed words about the love of Christ. He tries threatening us with the flames of hell, until I point out to him that as Jews, we won't be going there. Such a fate is reserved for misbehaving Christians, I remind him, arching my eyebrows to suggest that perhaps he should worry about his own fate a little more.

Finally we reach Lisbon, where we send word to Queluz that we have arrived. I dismiss the guard and the priest, and because it is Shabbat, we wait until the following day for Judah and Isaac to escort us the rest of the way.

It is Eliana's fifteenth birthday—fifteen years to the day since I made that painful ride to Queluz along the same road and gave birth to her in the house to which I am finally returning.

20

The fragrance of mown hay wafts through the branches of this year's sukkah as I sit with Simona, watching Eliana and Isaac perform the rituals of Sukkot.

I am getting used to a fifty-year-old Simona with gray hair and a sixty-year-old Judah with a beard gone almost completely white, but their children still astonish me. Isaac is twenty-four, taller than his father but still slender. His beard matches the light brown of his hair, and his dark eyes retain the solemnity of his boyhood. Chana, the oldest of Judah and Simona's children, is now thirty-two and has grown stout and disheveled, with six children between age one and fifteen to deal with. Rahel, her younger sister, is thirty and as slender as her mother, with two children and several more lost in the womb.

Simona and Judah's oldest grandchild, Chana's boy Joseph, is fifteen, like Eliana. When we left Queluz, he was a small child, and I suppose his sparse beard and hoarse, adolescent voice are the same shock to me that Eliana's womanly body is to others. I am thirty-five, and though I still have only a few gray hairs, the lines around my eyes and the furrows on my brow speak to the passage of a decade of my own life.

Eliana and Isaac are standing in front of us. "Do you remember how Eliana used to offer little gifts to the Ushpizim?" Isaac asks, his eyes crinkling with amusement.

"We decided it would be fun to do it again," Eliana says to Simona. "Do you still have the box?"

Simona gets up. "I know exactly where it is."

The covered woven basket is smaller than I remember. So many things in life are when we see them again, especially if once held in a child's hand. She and Isaac go out of the courtyard, and Simona's and my eyes follow them. We have the same thought at the same time as we turn to each other. From the day Isaac stood by my bed and touched Eliana's newborn head, they were meant to be together.

I remember being under the covers with Eliana at Palacio de Mondragon in Ronda.

"Isaac's not a boy."

"Well, what is he then?"

"I don't know!"

I remember wondering then whether it was possible for a six-year-old to be in love. She warmed to Sawwar in time, even had a bit of a crush on him, but seeing Eliana and Isaac go off to find treasures, I know that nobody has meant as much to my daughter as Isaac Abravanel.

"Are you thinking what I'm thinking?" Simona asks.

"About our children?"

She nods. "Judah told Isaac he should be getting married soon. He's almost twenty-five. The Holy One will not let even someone as important as Judah live forever, and Isaac needs to carry on after him."

"Is he spoken for?" I brace myself for the answer.

"No," Simona says. "Isaac told his father he didn't think any of the young women he knew were right for what he wants to accomplish."

"And what is that?"

Several of Simona's grandchildren come up, arguing over a game they were playing. She tends to them for a moment, then returns to our conversation.

"Isaac wants to carry on our family's leadership among the Jews, but he also wants to write—commentaries on the Talmud, the Zohar, all the things he loves to study. And it seems there's always a problem somewhere with the way Jews are being treated. He's been traveling all over Portugal with Judah, but it won't be long until he has to continue on his own."

She thinks for a moment. "He needs a woman who won't complain about his studies or his long absences. Someone with a good head and talents of her own. Someone who can be as strong as he is, whatever comes."

"It's a big burden for anyone to marry a man with such dreams," I tell her. "But look at how well you've handled it. We all grow into what life brings, don't you think?"

"True, but it's best to start with the coffers full. And I think I know the young woman he is looking for."

It's true. Eliana's coffers are full indeed. She speaks Portuguese, Castilian, Arabic, and Hebrew. She knows the Bible and the Talmud as well as many men her age. She never wavers in our practices for the sake of convenience. We arrived in Queluz with our clothes hanging on our bones because we had left Arévalo too hastily to prepare for a kosher journey. Many days, we had eaten next to nothing because she refused to break Jewish law and shamed me into a standard I might not have followed so strictly if she weren't there.

"All this time, they've being growing up for each other," I say to Simona. "Do you think they know it?"

"Let them discover for themselves," Simona says. "We are in for the great joy of watching young love grow."

Since Eliana has no father, within a few months, Judah approaches me. There's none of the usual maneuvering, just an immediate meeting of minds between old friends. Isaac has told his father he has found the woman he wants to marry, and Eliana has been so lovestruck I don't need to ask how she wants me to reply when Judah asks if I will permit them to wed.

Judah has taken the unusual step of visiting me alone in my home, and we sit by the fire on a cold February morning. "It's been almost twenty-three years since I made my first trip to Queluz," I say. "I'm thirty-six now, and it doesn't seem possible I've lived almost twice as long since that day."

Judah smiles. "You'll be surprised at how quickly life speeds up now. Then I was about the age you are now—do you realize that?"

I laugh. "It's strange how when you're young everyone seems old, but now that you put it that way, I don't feel nearly as old as I thought you were at the time." I grin to let him know I am teasing.

He laughs. "And Eliana is already two years older than you were when you went riding here for Shabbat without asking anyone's permission. Children always seem older to themselves than they do to us."

"But still, fifteen is too young. She's barely a woman."

Judah's dark eyes catch the firelight. "I felt the same way about Chana and Rahel. How would these girls who had turned into women overnight be all the things my wife is? But they've done very well. And Simona was just a year older than Eliana when she married me."

"She's growing up and leaving me," I murmur into the firelight, as if the flickering embers can clarify what to think of something so momentous. Tears make the fire a golden blur. "I can't bear the thought, but I am so happy for her and overjoyed it's Isaac she will marry."

"And we will be one family," Judah adds. "By blood, I mean, with their children. I have always thought of you as part of us, since that day you first rode here from Sintra."

I know this so deeply I don't even nod. "I'd rather they wait until she's sixteen," I say. "I'd like Eliana to settle in here first. And I'd like her to get used to being—" I don't know how to put delicately that I would like her to feel comfortable with her womanhood before it will be used as marriage entails.

"I think it would be fine to wait," Judah reassures me. "The Holy One willing, they have many years ahead to make up for the little time we ask them to wait."

"They may have other ideas though." I get up to add a log to the fire. "Do you think they know why you came here today?"

"They're probably driving my wife wild with their fidgeting. Perhaps we should go end it." He goes to the window. "We should hurry. It looks like rain."

We go out into the gray winter afternoon without feeling the cold at all.

Six months later, on a warm August afternoon, almost one year after our return to Queluz and shortly before my daughter's sixteenth birthday, she and I stand in front of the huppah in the synagogue in Lisbon to carry out the ancient ceremony that will make her Isaac's wife.

Earlier that day, I took her to the mikveh and marveled over the beauty of her young body. I suppose it's true what they say about a daughter's marriage being a passage for the mother as well, but even though my breasts have begun to sag and there are new dimples and folds in my skin, I am proud of my body, proud of its strength, proud of the fact that it bore her.

For all that strength, I am weak in the knees as Eliana steps under the huppah, a symbol of the new home they will create, made from Isaac's prayer shawl suspended overhead by four decorated poles. Wearing a kittel, a white robe denoting the fresh start of married life, Isaac does not look at her but instead stands bobbing at the waist, murmuring psalms as she circles him the traditional seven times. When she is finished, she stands with Isaac as the hazzan chants from the Song of Songs.

"*When I found him whom my soul loves,*
I held him and would not let him go.
Until I had brought him into my mother's house,
And into the chamber of her that conceived me."

Isaac places a simple gold band on Eliana's finger. "Behold, you are sanctified to me with this ring, according to the Law of Moses and Israel," he says, his voice breaking with emotion.

The rabbi recites the traditional seven blessings, after which Eliana and Isaac drink wine from a gold-rimmed glass. When they have emptied it, Isaac crushes it under his heel. "If I forget thee, O Jerusalem," he declares, "let my right hand forget its cunning." And then, because God wants us to be joyful, our voices break out in cheers of "Mazal tov!" as Isaac and Eliana beam.

We leave the synagogue and go to Judah and Simona's Lisbon house for the celebration. I hold my wonderful daughter in my arms and whisper a blessing in her ear before we shut the door of the cheder yichud, the room of privacy that newlyweds share for a few minutes before the wedding banquet. It's the first time Eliana and Isaac have been alone since they were betrothed, and before joining the celebration, they will feel what it is like to kiss and hold each other within the sanctity of marriage and talk for a while about their dreams for their new life.

The dancing and singing lasts well into the night, and when my eyelids are growing heavy, I ask Eliana and Isaac if I can have a moment alone with them in the study.

I have left a large object there, wrapped in several layers of cloth. "This is your wedding present," I tell them. Eliana's eyes widen, realizing what it is. She unties the cord, and the wrapping falls away to reveal the atlas. "I wasn't expecting this," she says. "I thought you would keep it until you—" She doesn't complete the thought.

"I gave you life," I say, "and I gave you as much experience of the world as I could. I want you to take this with my blessing and pass it along to your children."

Isaac has seen the atlas before, but he is as dazzled as a child. He sits down, and Eliana hesitates only for a moment before remembering she now can sit beside him. They exclaim over this and that as they go through the pages. I take in the aura of grace and beauty that surrounds them, and too softly for them to notice, I steal away.

21

Judah was right about how quickly time would speed up. How can it be that I can say in great detail what happened when I was eight or twelve, but now shake my head in bewilderment when I try to remember year by year what has happened since? Decades of my life are swallowed whole, and it doesn't seem possible that I have filled each day with one thing or another.

Perhaps it's because we stop centering on ourselves once we have other lives to think about. First our children, and then our grandchildren, and then, if we live to be as old as I have, our great-grandchildren come along to clarify that we are not so important after all.

And perhaps it's because I spent two decades, from the time I was thirty-five until I was fifty-six, living quietly at Queluz. Years soften into one when they are spent in the same way: the first golden leaves and a nip in the air around the High Holy Days, the blossoms of Passover, the setting of fruit at Shavuot, to autumn again and the repeating of the cycle.

Eliana and Isaac had their first child, a boy named Judah after his grandfather, a year after they were married. Four more children—two girls and two boys—followed. Chana's son Joseph married and made Judah and Simona great-grandparents somewhere in all that pool of time. Almost every year brought me another grandchild and then great-grandchild to love. Now Eliana's Judah is thirty, and she is a grandmother herself.

Time passed for others as well, and as in all families, fortune and misfortune were not shared equally. Alfonso of Castile, Isabella's little brother, died at sixteen. Civil war raged over whether the daughter Queen Juana bore was the legitimate heir to the kingdom. Enrique claimed the child as his own, but the princess was better known as "La Beltraneja," after Beltrán de la Cueva, the lover presumed to have fathered her. Rumors abounded that Enrique deformed the little girl's face to make her look more like him.

A year later, while Isabella was still Crown Princess of Castile, she married Ferdinand of Aragon, a marriage brokered by the court rabbi, Abraham Seneor. Five years after the wedding, Isabella became Queen of Castile, and they joined their two lands. Now they have Granada too, and the conquest is complete. I suppose we should have predicted our expulsion then, but no one did, not even Isaac, who as a courtier to Ferdinand and Isabella was in the best position to know.

I cannot understand what is threatening about Jews. How much more of an advantage do Christians need?

We belong here as much as anyone. I don't know when the Cresques family first came to Mallorca, but the Abravanels know they have been in Castile and Andalusia for centuries. Where do we go now? Will the Abravanel name open doors for us? Isaac has good friends in Pisa and Naples, and I suppose we will find refuge somewhere.

We? Where did that thought come from?

I still haven't decided whether to stay or go. Two weeks ago, we reached the coast after traveling on foot from the middle of Spain. There, as I waded into the sea, I felt the land of my birth disappearing under my feet. I've been floating between life and death, between here and an uncertain there, ever since.

I brush the cover of the atlas in my lap. My daughter does not know I still have it. The family library was sold for a tenth of what it was worth and the money put into the account Ferdinand and Isabella will allow Isaac to take abroad as a special privilege for his service. I rescued the book without anyone seeing and hid it in my trunk.

It will comfort me if I stay in Spain, reminding me that the shape of the world, like the fullness of time, has been decreed by the Holy One. He alone will judge their Catholic Majesties just as he will judge the rest of us. In the meantime, Jews suffer, and though I no longer think he cares, I still worship him for the power he wields over all of us

LISBON 1471

The bedroom is humid from exertion and from the water steaming in a pot hanging over the small log fire in the house in Lisbon. Eliana's face is purple with the strain of bearing down as she sits on the birthing chair. Rahel is kneeling on one side, offering encouragement, while the midwife touches her fingers between Eliana's legs to check the baby's progress. "It won't be long now," she says.

I dangle a silver hamsa near Eliana's head to keep the Evil Eye away. "I will lift up my eyes unto the mountains," I say. "From whence shall my help come?"

Eliana groans and bears down again. "I feel its head," the midwife says, as I continue the psalm.

"Behold, he that keepeth Israel doth neither slumber nor sleep."

She gulps air as the contraction subsides. I come up behind her and put my hand on her shoulder. "You're doing well," I say. She nods her head frantically as another pain wracks her body.

"The Lord is thy shade upon thy right hand. The sun shall not smite thee by day, nor the moon by night—"

Eliana lets out a loud, unearthly scream and grunts with all her might.

"Hold her," the midwife says. "The baby's coming."

"The Lord shall guard thy going out and thy coming in," I say, as she bears down again. "From this time forth and forever." With these words, Eliana's baby, my fourth grandchild, is delivered into this world.

"It's a boy," the midwife says, holding it up, its white and twisted umbilical cord still attached. It wails and turns crimson in the reflected firelight as the midwife cuts the cord and hands the baby to me. His hair is wet and streaked with blood, and his skin is slippery and coated with oily, gray paste. His testicles are two huge purple sacs, and his tiny penis points up at me as it delivers its first water onto my cheek.

"Well, well," I say. "Is that the way to greet your grandmother?"

I take him to a clean cloth we have laid out near the hearth and bathe him from head to toe while the midwife helps my daughter into bed. When I finish, Eliana asks me not to swaddle the baby. "I want to see him first," she says. I bring him to her, and she puts him to her breast as she fondles the dark hair on his head and runs her hands over his tiny back.

I know what she is thinking—that he is a healthy, beautiful child—but she will not say it while the Evil Eye is lurking. Nor will she say aloud the baby's name, though she told me several months ago it would be named Joseph if it were a boy.

I think of all the births I have witnessed, all the times I have helped say the incantations and prayers and spread the herbs and garlic that keep the Evil Eye away. Not that it helped my little brother much. It doesn't seem possible that it's been almost forty years since he breathed his last, forty years he has not shared with us. But there are happier stories as well.

To great rejoicing in Spain, Isabella and Ferdinand had their first child, a daughter, a year ago. Elizabeth is a grandmother now, although I don't suppose she realizes it, lost in madness in Arévalo.

Noor and Jamil have three sons and one daughter, and he has several by a second wife as well. I know this because he comes occasionally to Lisbon on the caliph's business. Out of sensitivity to me, he is never invited to break bread with us, but I hear from Isaac that he is well and that he always inquires after me.

I'd like to tell him that I think he did the right thing in marrying Noor. I could not have borne him so many children, and perhaps his wives are not yet finished presenting him with sons to carry on his line. More than a decade after our parting, my mind is no longer wracked with pain, but my heart is still tender enough that I am grateful he stays away, even though I'd like to tell him how pleased I am for him.

Eliana is dozing with the baby at her breast while I go ask one of the servants to run to Chana's house with the news. Leaving, she collides with Isaac, who is responding to the message we sent to the palace.

He's a barrel-chested man in his mid-thirties now, with the same moon-face he had as a child. Though his beard is not yet gray, his brow is already furrowed. "My wife?" he asks. I tell him she has delivered and is doing well. "And the baby?"

"A son. Besiman tov." He sighs with relief, and his lips move in a private prayer of thanksgiving.

I follow him into the bedroom. Eliana is sleeping but the baby's eyes are open. Isaac leans over him, stroking his face. He looks at Eliana, and I see how much he loves her, even after a difficult nine years for both of them. His father is almost seventy now, and the mantle has passed to Isaac not just in business, but in advocacy for the Jews. "He needs a woman who can be as strong as he is, whatever comes," Simona had said before he and Eliana were betrothed, and my daughter has become just that for a husband who seems to belong to everything and everyone else before her.

Isaac leaves her bedside to go to his study to pray, and I wait for him outside the door. I want to know the latest news about the crisis that has alarmed the Lisbon aljama. King Afonso V, at the urging of his uncle Henry the Navigator, continued the effort to drive the Moors from North Africa, and the recent conquest of the fortress town of Arzilla resulted in the capture of several hundred Jews. The captives were given as rewards to the nobles who had supported the cause and our people are now slaves all over Portugal.

Jews do not stand by while other Jews are enslaved. We were captives once in Egypt, and the Holy One took us from there with a strong hand and outstretched arm. It is now up to us to be the instrument of God's command that our people be free.

"What did the king say?" I ask Isaac when he has finished his prayers.

"He says he can't favor the Jews over other captives. The Cortes is already angry at how well we have been treated during his reign, and Afonso knows he can't risk helping us by intervening now."

"So what do we do?"

"He says he will not oppose private efforts to free the Jews. That will take money—a great deal of it—and time." He thinks for a moment. "It's getting to be fall already. Travel will be more difficult when winter sets in."

The words we say every Passover come to me. "This year we are slaves; next year we will be free people." I turn grave eyes to him. "If anyone can accomplish that, it's you."

Isaac pledges a small fortune of his own money for ransoms, his reimbursement to come from contributions by Portugal's Jews. He probably won't get it all back, but that's a small matter. "I'm a wealthy man," he says. "Perhaps the Holy One has seen to that because he wants me to be his treasurer."

A few of the nobles keeping Jewish slaves live close to Lisbon, so for the first months he is not gone more than a few days at a time. Then, the estates where the Jews are still held are at a greater distance, and Isaac is rarely at home.

The toll on Eliana is clear, though the children have grown accustomed to his absences. Leah turns seven and Hadassah four without a father to tell them stories or to hear about their accomplishments. Judah, at nine, spends his days at the yeshiva studying the Torah and Talmud, where the son and heir of Isaac Abravanel has an entire community of men willing to put an arm around his shoulder.

"The better things get for the Jews in one way, the worse they get in another," Eliana says one afternoon at the mikveh next to the synagogue. Isaac has sent word ahead and she is expecting his arrival any day. She has been so busy with her four children that she has not made the time to end niddah, her ritual impurity, after her monthly flow.

The Lisbon mikveh falls somewhere between the tiny pool at home in Queluz and the elaborate Arab baths at Ronda. There's an entrance hidden from the street, because it is no one's business when a wife is ready to resume sexual relations with her husband. Women usually come alone, to protect their privacy even from each other, but I've carried on Simona's and my tradition by going to the mikveh from time to time with my daughter. Today, she is so distracted that our usual intimacy is lost. "You've been gloomy all day," I say as we leave the water. "Especially for someone whose husband is on his way home."

She wraps a cloth around her body and tucks the end in above one breast. "Isaac is planning to use the papal election of a new pope to argue for better treatment of Castile's Jews. He says he may need to travel to Rome with the envoy going to congratulate the new pope." Tears well in her eyes. "It's too much, Mama. He'd be gone so long, and what if—"

"Every trip has its dangers," I point out. "Even if he's only going to Évora or Tomar."

"Sometimes I wish he weren't so confident everything will be fine when he's not here."

"Would you want to be weak, just to keep him home?"

"Of course not," she says indignantly, her voice echoing off the damp brick walls. "I just don't want him to go to Italy. I have nightmares about it." Her voice grows husky. "I see him standing on a boat sailing out to sea, and in the dream, I know he's never coming back."

"Have you told him this?"

"No." She gives me a rueful smile. "I just try to be brave."

"You have to assert yourself," I say, remembering Judah's words to me long ago. "Don't snuff out your own light." I help her into her dress. "Isaac could be a better man. Don't you think he would want to be if he knew how? When you don't tell him how you feel, you deny him the chance for compassion toward you." I give her what I hope is a reassuring smile. "Perhaps it takes a wife to help even a wise man understand the meaning of what he reads in the Zohar."

Power and love realign, and Isaac does not go to Rome. After a private talk I hear little about, he is still gone much of the time, but his trips are as short as he can make them. At Queluz, Judah and Simona move back into the small quarters they lived in when I first met them, to make room for Isaac and Eliana to live year-round in the main house. "Now that consulting my husband takes a long ride here rather than a walk down the street," Eliana says with a wry smile, "it's interesting how much of the aljama's business can be handled without him."

No one needs to say the other reason to be in Queluz. Judah is seventy now, and though Simona is ten years younger, not many people live even to her age. Judah's beard is white, and he seems shrunken under his clothes. Simona is no more than a twig, and her gray hair frames eyes made narrow by drooping lids. They are still surprisingly strong, but they accept help now with things they used to do easily on their own. Though Eliana's children assume their grandparents will live forever, we know better.

In May, one week before Shavuot, Simona, Eliana, and I are sitting together mending the light summer dresses the girls will need now that the weather is getting warm. Isaac is away on what we hope will be his last mission to free the Jews of Arzilla, and my grandson Judah is in Lisbon at his yeshiva. I can hear seven-year-old Leah and four-year-old Hadassah chattering with their grandfather in the courtyard. Judah's eyes are too weak to read, and he spends most of his day dozing in a chair and watching them play.

Joseph fusses in his cradle, and Eliana lays down her mending to put him to her breast.

Simona lays down her work as well. "I should see to dinner," she says, getting up stiffly. The first steps pain her, and I stand up to give her an arm, though I know she will wave me off. "Don't treat me like an old lady," she tells us with a wink, "or los mejores de mosotros will turn me into one."

While Eliana nurses Joseph, Simona and I cut vegetables. "Shavuot's coming up," she says, breaking the silence. She knows it is my favorite of the Jewish festivals, for it honors the story of Naomi and her loyal daughter-in-law, Ruth.

"'Entreat me not to leave you or to turn back from following you.'" I repeat the familiar words. "'For wherever you go, I will go, and wherever you lodge, I will lodge. Your people shall be my people, and your God, my God.'" My eyes fill with tears. I put my knife down, and Simona hugs me.

"You see? It's made me cry again," I say through the lump in my throat.

"It's just the onions," Simona teases.

"If it weren't for you taking me in…" I don't know how to go on. I wipe my eyes with the edge of my apron and fall silent, wondering where I would be if she hadn't been Naomi to my Ruth.

Eliana lays a sleeping Joseph in his cradle. The three of us continue with our work, but after a moment I stop. "It's too quiet outside," I say, just as Leah and Hadassah come through the door.

"Grandfather fell asleep while we were talking to him," Leah says.

Hadassah giggles. "He fell out of his chair. He's sleeping on the ground."

"Oh, no," Simona whispers. Wiping our hands, we rush out into the courtyard, where Judah lies crumpled and still.

❧

The May sun hangs in the afternoon sky as the men of the village dig a grave on the flowering hillside. Judah will be buried with his feet pointing toward Jerusalem, where the Day of Judgment will begin, and he and all the dead will rise to face our Maker.

Word has been sent to Lisbon and a rider dispatched to the town near Évora where Isaac is at work. He will not make it back for the burial. Rahel and Chana's families will assemble before a full day has passed, so Judah's body may be laid to rest according to our law.

I take the first turn guarding Judah's body, for it must not be left alone before he is buried. Sometime in the middle of the night, Eliana takes my place, and when I wake up, Simona is sitting by the body again, as serenely as if she has just slept by his side.

When everyone has arrived, Chana's and Rahel's husbands carry Judah's shrouded body on a litter up to the grave. When we get there, we tear our clothing near our heart in the ritual of kriah.

A rabbi has come from Lisbon, and once we have lowered Judah's body, he begins to chant. "O God, exalted and full of compassion," he prays, "grant perfect peace in your sheltering presence to the soul of Judah, who has gone to his eternal home."

Eliana's daughters are clinging to her skirt while her son, Judah's namesake, bobs with the other men offering prayers. "The Lord is his portion," the rabbi concludes. "May he rest in peace."

"Amen," we say, amid sniffles and soft weeping. I hold my arm around Simona's shoulder to keep her knees from buckling. "Blessed, glorified, honored, and extolled, adored and acclaimed be the name of the Holy One," we pray. "Let he who makes peace in the heavens grant peace to all of us. And let us say amen."

22

I opened my eyes this morning and gave thanks to God for restoring my soul, which escapes to wander all night in the land of dreams. Modeh Ani was the first prayer, after the shema, that my mother taught me, and though I could no more forget to say it than to open my eyes, I don't like the words anymore. If my soul leaves my body when I sleep, I would rather it stay away. Not to wake up at all would be something to praise God for.

The afternoon shadows are deep now, and a breeze is rustling the curtains. It won't be long until my grandson is here. I will sleep on the ship tonight, and when my eyes open tomorrow, I will say *Modeh Ani* into the stifling air of the hold and bend to God's decree that a soul be restored to someone old and helpless in the middle of the sea.

When Judah died, I ached not just for my loss, but from watching Simona go through her days without him. She managed to be contented again in time, with grandchildren and great-grandchildren to occupy her. Being Simona, even when she grieved, she praised God for the blessing of having had Judah so long, and her strength helped me find my own.

In the ten years after Judah's death, my granddaughters Leah and Hadassah were both married. My grandson Joseph reached his tenth birthday, and Samuel, who was Isaac and Eliana's last child, grew into a stocky eight-year-old.

My fingers stiffened by the time I was fifty-five, but I had lost interest in writing poetry by then, preferring to watch life flow past without plumbing its deepest meanings. A hug from tiny arms or a limp flower brought from the garden in muddy fingers was a poem of more value than any of mine.

Isaac passed his fortieth birthday and became King Afonso's chief financial adviser and a member of his inner circle. Wealth poured in from his businesses, investments, and gifts from the king. As a Jew, Isaac could never have a title granting him noble status, but Afonso considered him a true and trusted friend and those who tried to harm us paid the price. Those were good years for all the Jews—as good as it gets for people who, despite the king's tolerance, paid exorbitant taxes and lived by decree behind the aljama's walls.

We felt somewhat secure, unlike the Jews in Spain. Ferdinand was crowned king of Aragon after his father's death in 1479, and Spain was united, except for the throbbing thorn of Granada. Would conquering the Muslim caliphate lead to a crusade against the Jews too? Doomsayers said so, but most of us ignored them.

We should have listened. From the time Ferdinand became King of Aragon, conquest fever brought anti-Jewish riots all over Spain. Then, a decade ago, the first inquiries were held at their behest by Tomás de Torquemada to determine whether Sevilla's conversos were secret Jews. Like my mother. Like my grandparents.

Is anyone alive who saw me wearing a crucifix? If so, who would recognize me after half a century? Still, can a church and its records burn down thoroughly enough? Ferdinand and Isabella will stop at nothing to get Isaac to stay in Spain, for some Jews are too valuable to lose. If they knew my story, would they tie me to a stake as a Judaizer, hold a lighted torch, and tell him the price of saving me was a trip to the baptismal font himself?

I have no doubt they would.

Families are coming out in the cool of the early evening. It's calmer now, as if having made a feast of our belongings, they now want to work off the meal by taking a pleasant stroll.

I stare at the door, imagining my story is out and soldiers' boots are pounding the stairs. Much as I don't care about living, I don't want to die the horrific way Torquemada thinks people like me should.

I shake my head and tell myself I am a foolish old woman. I'm safe here in this room.

Safe? My laughter sounds disembodied, so harsh and cackling that it raises the hair on my arms. I am almost the last Jew in Spain. Safe indeed.

LISBON 1481

The church bells of Lisbon peal a somber dirge as the funeral cortege for King Afonso V passes from the bright August sunlight into the gloom of the cathedral. As Jews, we cannot go inside, so I stand in the crowd with my family to pay respect to the king I knew as a little boy when I played with his cousins at the palace.

Afonso, at forty-nine, was dead from loss of will to live as much as from the plague that struck him down. Six years earlier, he married his thirteen-year-old niece Juana, the girl known as La Beltraneja, born of the affair between El Impotente's wife and the courtier Beltrán de la Cueva. His plan to bring Castile under the Portuguese crown did not succeed. His forces were defeated by King Ferdinand, and soon afterward, Afonso's marriage to La Beltraneja was annulled by the pope. Even though he remained king in title, he faded away, dying in a monastery near Sintra.

Such a sad end, I think, watching his coffin pass into the cathedral. Such a sad family. His cousin Elizabeth, mad at Arévalo. His sister Juana married to El Impotente, disgracing herself with other men. And La Beltraneja, married at thirteen to a man more than three times her age—who could not be moved to pity by the heartlessness with which she had been treated? Her marriage annulled and stripped of all her titles, she's gone off now, before her twentieth birthday, to live in a convent, wondering how it could be that just a few years ago, she was fawned and fought over.

Or did she grow up knowing, as Elizabeth did, that she would end up a pawn in a game played without a thought for her?

Later, Isaac arrives at the Lisbon house, where Simona and I are staying to help Eliana prepare for the High Holy Days. His face is as grave as the pallbearers' earlier that day. "The Duke of Braganza is preparing for a showdown," he says. "King João is saying outrageous things, with his father's body barely cold."

"He was saying them while Afonso was still alive," Eliana reminds him. Indeed, since his father's decline, João's swaggering has been kept in check by the nobles, who made sure he understood that he had no authority they did not wish to grant him, at least while his father still lived.

Isaac nods. "He's been telling us how things would be different when he became king, but I don't think anyone was expecting trouble to start so soon. He's asking the nobles to show proof that lands and titles are legitimately theirs. He intends to strip them of what they can't document, even after hundreds of years in their families."

"What about Queluz?" I hear the worry in Simona's voice.

"I have papers," Isaac says. "This is really about the Duke of Braganza. He owns more than a third of the land in Portugal, and he tells me many of his possessions were never formalized." He looks down, stroking his beard, as he always does when he is thinking. "João doesn't stand a chance of toppling Braganza, or any of the other nobles, unless the Cortes backs him, and we all know that turning on the conversos and Jews is the easiest way to get their support."

"Look at what's happening in Sevilla," Simona murmurs, her voice so soft it can barely be heard. The first convictions for Judaizing have been handed down by the Dominican inquisitors, and dozens of people have been tied to stakes and burned alive.

"There's talk about inviting the inquisitors here." Isaac's voice trails off, and the room falls silent. No one notices the stew scorching to bitter black as we all look away so as not to have our own fears heightened by what we see in each other's eyes.

QUELUZ 1482

The next year brings slow suffocation. The Holy One takes both Chana and Rahel, along with several of their children, when plague sweeps through the crowded streets of the aljama. Eliana and Isaac's daughter Hadassah's wedding to Reuben, a young rabbi and Talmudic scholar, is the only thing that raises our spirits. When she becomes pregnant within a few months, we hover in her radiance like moths drawn out of darkness to even the faintest light.

At seventy, Simona's health is failing. A few years ago, she scoffed at our worries, claiming she intended to live until she crumbled into dust before our eyes. Now she wonders aloud whether she will live to see Hadassah's baby. We ask ourselves the same as we watch her steps slow to a painful creep.

Isaac is suffering at court, and though he doesn't talk about it much, it shows in the deepening furrows in his brow and a beard growing translucent and colorless. "João is greedy and deceitful, and one of the greatest tyrants ever to rule," Isaac says, and for a man who knows history as well as he does, that is quite a statement.

João's father, King Afonso, was so generous in currying favor with the nobles that he gave away much of João's patrimony. All that was left him were the highways of Portugal, the new king complains, and he intends to do something about it.

"He thinks his father was weak," Isaac explains to me one summer evening as we sit in the courtyard at Queluz. "He doesn't see anything wrong in taking back what was given by someone else. After all, how is he to have power in a land other men control?"

Isaac brushes away an insect buzzing around his head in the dimming light. "João thinks Braganza had a hand in his mother's death. She was married at fifteen and dead of poison at twenty-three, so João lost his mother at what? Four or five? He has grievances to settle with the House of Braganza, and he can't wait to start."

The situation soon darkens when one of the Duke of Braganza's brothers is exiled from Portugal for a trivial insult. Our good friend, Gedaliah Yahya, the royal physician, having had enough of the new king, has decided to go to Constantinople to protect his family from what he fears are terrible times ahead for the Jews.

"I was Afonso's physician, so João despises me," Gedaliah says at a farewell Shabbat dinner at Isaac and Eliana's home. "I'm tired of the looks he gives me, as if his hangnails and headaches should be treated better than his father's were. I removed a splinter last week, and he glared at me the whole time. A splinter! Is there an old way and a new way to deal with that?"

"He wants to get rid of everything associated with his father," Isaac adds. "None but the most blatant panderers have his favor now." He hesitates, as if debating whether the peace of the Sabbath should be disturbed by thoughts that are too private, or perhaps too painful, to share.

Finally he speaks. "'He's after the Jews too," he says. "Not publicly yet, but that will come."

Gedaliah has had quite a bit of Shabbat wine, and he sets his cup down noisily. "Before Passover, one of João's new favorites asked me where the Jews were planning to lay in wait for a Christian child to murder. He said they all wanted to know so they could keep their children safe." Everyone exchanges glances. The blood libel, the belief that Jews murder Christian children to use their blood in our Passover matzoh, would die if people understood that Jewish law requires us to throw away any food with even a speck of blood in it. But lies are hard to kill when they make a better story.

"Last week, I overheard two of them discussing whether they could see the outline of my tail against the back of my robe or whether I walked with it between my legs," Isaac adds. "They kept their voices just loud enough to be sure I couldn't miss what they were saying."

He gets up from the table and retrieves a piece of paper from a book. "And then, there's this." It's a sketch of Isaac and Gedaliah, each with one hand on a large bag of coins, while behind them lurks a horned devil. Its face is drawn with the same evil grin and narrow, sneaky eyes as the two men. Peeking out from beneath their cloaks, their hooves match the devil's own.

"What is this?" I ask, stunned.

"Something I found lying on my desk at court," Gedaliah says. "No one has claimed it, but that's likely from embarrassment over the lack of artistic skills." He tries to smile but fails. "Hatred is in the air, and I don't intend to let it feed on me."

Gedaliah's wife has been silent until now. "We're rich. We're Jews. How long until João sees how easy it would be to take everything from us?"

Eliana stiffens, and a hush settles over the table. Of all the Jews at court, only Isaac would have more to lose than Gedaliah if the king were to turn on him.

Isaac speaks first. "We are not honoring Shabbat," he says. "We will worry enough about it tomorrow, but for now, I must insist we stop." He turns to my grandson Judah, now a tall youth of nineteen. "Will you get the guitarra?" he asks. "It's time to sing."

By the time the green hills hint of a new spring, Isaac has left the king's service all but officially. He finally has the time he long dreamed of to write, and his commentaries on the biblical prophets spill out onto the pages. Some of the old joy returns to his spirit, and he, like the rest of us, lives happily in seclusion in Queluz.

The courtyard is filled with the voices of children, and Eliana and Isaac preside over their home just as I remember Judah and Simona doing long ago. Simona has lived more than ten years without Judah now, but from the way she talks, it seems as if he has momentarily left the room. Perhaps to her he has. Perhaps they were so close he still lives in her.

It saddens me that I never had such a partner, but I don't think of Jamil very often now. When I do, I remember him as a friend more than a lover. Perhaps it's been too long since my body cared about such things.

Simona seems barely of this world. Her skin is as brittle and translucent as onion skins, and her hair is as light as tufts of dandelion drifting in the breeze. She sits without moving most of the day, a sweet smile on her face as she watches her great-grandchildren at their play. Sometimes, to their annoyance, she calls them by the names of her children, as if she were traveling back in time. She eats almost nothing. The nourishment she needs comes from somewhere else now, a place only she can see.

Then one morning, she doesn't come out from her bedroom. Eliana and I go to see if something is wrong, and we discover her body, as peaceful as if she were taken away in a beautiful dream.

I mourn her with great abandon, as if every other death has been heaped on top of this one to be grieved afresh. At the end of shiva, the period of formal mourning, I go alone to the mikveh built into the courtyard wall. There, I examine my wrinkled thighs and arms, my sagging breasts, the soft folds of my stomach. "You're next," I tell myself.

I am fifty-six years old. My daughter is a grandmother. Where once I might have found death a gloomy prospect, I don't now. Though there is always something new I want to live to see, I understand how the old might feel that they don't have the strength to face what lies ahead. Perhaps this is why we die, more than the failure of our limbs or heart.

I feel the water lap at every inch of me, under my fingernails, into my eyebrows, and among the shrunken folds of my most private part. I feel Simona's presence and sit down with her beside me in this place of changes, where so many times before, she and the living water helped me find the grace and wisdom to move on.

23

VALENCIA 1492

I wake to find my body and face wet. I trace my finger across my arm and touch it to my tongue. It is pure and clean, not tasting of sweat at all. I catch in the air the faint odor of ripe pears and cloves. "Simona?" I ask. "Judah?"

A puff of breeze brings the room to life. "We're here. We knew you were afraid, so we came."

"You found me," I whisper. Just like they did so many years ago. Found me, took me in, and loved me.

I cast my mind over the ten years that have passed since Simona died. "I'm almost as old as you were when we buried you," I tell her.

I feel the radiance of her smile. "You are lucky indeed to have lived so long."

"Lucky? Here?"

Judah is standing behind me, and his laughter ruffles my hair. "There are no books where I am."

"Or a mikveh," Simona adds.

I gesture around the room. "I have no books or mikveh either. I have memories—nothing more."

I am at the spring, washing the grease from my hands, racing across the beach with Chuva, climbing the green mountains of Sintra...

A tattered boy drops his coin while Diogo leers behind him... my dead child baptized while I sleep on sheets red with my blood... Susana's bitter voice and her children's cold eyes.

Sawwar falling...falling...

Jamil is crying, Luisa is crying, Eliana is crying, we all are crying. Suddenly tears are all I can remember, and I feel as if I could fill this room with mine.

"I want to die," I whisper, surprised at the simplicity of it.

"Amalia," Judah says. "Go to the window."

The sky behind the rooftops is smeared with scarlet and orange so intense the remaining blue is tinged with green. "Can you still enjoy that?" he asks. I hear the same annoyance in his voice as when he thought one of his children was not trying hard enough to understand a lesson.

"Yes," I whisper.

"Now shut your eyes. Which do you like better?"

There's peace in the darkness behind my eyelids. Still, I open my eyes again, because who would not want more of that sight?

I want to sit down, but Judah's power holds me where I stand. "You don't want to die. You aren't ready to say good-bye."

"You don't know how things are," I say. "You haven't had to see all the suffering..."

"Who says we haven't been watching?"

"You've seen Isaac grow old before his time."

"He would be this old if he lived in better times. My grandson is almost thirty. It's his turn to lead now."

Judah. Our lion. Isaac and Eliana's first child, bursting with talent beyond that of his father and namesake grandfather, with the personality of a diplomat, the mind of a scholar, and the soul of a sage. Why was such a man born when there is no Jew left in Spain to lead?

Simona senses my question. "He's living now because this is when he's needed. The Holy One wants us to survive. We can't do that here. This is the beginning of our journey home—the dead can see that."

Our. For a moment, that sounds odd, until I realize that Judah and Simona will be leaving too. All Jews, past, present, and yet to come, will be going with the exiles out of Spain.

How could I ever have doubted that I will go too?

Instinctively, I reach for the atlas. "I'd have to leave this behind," I say. "I can't bear that. It's all I have left."

"Do you ever wonder why you have it?" Judah asks. "Why, after all these generations, it's still in your hands? Why, despite your journeys, it has never been lost?"

"I don't know." I sound like a frustrated child, ready to be fed an answer or give up trying.

"Don't ask me," Judah says. "Maybe you should look at it again. Perhaps what you want to find out has always been there."

QUELUZ 1483

The year that would change our lives forever begins like any other, with a family celebration of the High Holy Days at Queluz. My grandson Judah is twenty-one now and lives in the Lisbon house, near the yeshiva where he studies. Isaac writes endlessly over the course of that winter, pausing only to receive visitors like the beleaguered Duke of Braganza. Sequestered in Isaac's study, they discuss the ugly turn João's reign has taken, while Eliana preserves the peace in a bustling home.

At thirty-seven, she is still robust and lovely, but a few white hairs spring loose from the dark tangle of her hair. I want to pluck them, more for my sake than hers. To have a daughter old enough to go gray is a shock. Has she noticed them herself? Women as busy as her have little time to wonder how they look.

The situation in Spain grows more worrisome as well. Last year, Ferdinand and Isabella began a crusade to conquer Granada, the last Muslim stronghold in what they perceive as rightly their kingdom. I imagine Jamil and his family with a hostile army at their doorstep. What does he look like, nearing seventy? Would he choose to fight? When I lived there, I heard stories of heroes dying gloriously in battle when they were older than he is.

Isaac's relatives write to tell us about the chaos around them in Sevilla. When the Inquisition began two years ago, conversos left in droves, abandoning so many businesses that trade was disrupted for lack of sellers or buyers. Shortly after the executions began, plague broke out in the city, and of course it was blamed on us.

Soon worse news reaches Queluz. Ferdinand and Isabella have ordered all the Jews of Andalusia into exile. Thousands of conversos in Sevilla and all over southern Spain are secret Judaizers, the Inquisitors claim, and since they say Jews encourage the baptized to return to the old ways, the only way to save new Christians is for all of us to leave.

The Sevilla Abravanels are on their way to Toledo. Isaac arranges with a business acquaintance to find them a house in the aljama and pay for it with money he owes Isaac from last year's sale of textiles. "I told him to find the largest house he could," Isaac says after supper one evening. "There's no telling how crowded the aljamas all over Spain will become when the Jews start arriving. For all we know, others in our family may need to be taken in as well."

Eliana thinks for a moment. "What problem does this solve? Don't Ferdinand and Isabella think there are anusim practicing Judaism secretly in Toledo too?"

"They must realize that," Isaac says. "I think they don't really want to convert all their Jews. They couldn't gouge us with special taxes if they succeeded. They're still new on the throne, and they may just want to look tough." He shrugs. "Perhaps in a few years, all the Jews will be back home. We'd best concentrate on what's happening here. Our problems are bad enough."

Bad enough indeed. When disaster strikes, Isaac is in Évora visiting with Jewish scholars before returning home from his latest business trip. It is late May, and Eliana and I are weeding rows of beans. The day is hot, and the sounds of insects buzzing around our sweating faces is so loud we don't hear the sound of galloping hooves until a rider pulls up in front of our stables.

My grandson Judah, now twenty, is handing the reins to a groom. Dust from the courtyard swirls from his frantic arrival. Not expecting to see us yet, he does not have time to wipe the alarmed expression from his face.

"Is Father back?" He gives a hopeful look in the direction of the house.

Puzzled, Eliana studies his face. "We don't expect him back for a week. What's wrong?"

Judah is more agitated than I have ever seen him. "Perhaps we'd best go inside," I say, to get him away from the curious ears of the stablehands.

Once inside the house, Judah drops onto a bench at the table. "They've arrested the Duke of Braganza," he says, burying his forehead in his palms. "King João is accusing him of treason."

"Treason?" Eliana and I gasp together.

"Spies intercepted correspondence between the duke and King Ferdinand, and João says the two are hatching a plot."

Eliana puts a hand on the table to brace herself. "Braganza visits here all the time. What if the king thinks Isaac was involved?"

"I've heard talk that Father lent money to Braganza recently," Judah says to his mother. "Is it true?"

Eliana sits down heavily. "He gave Braganza a loan about six months ago, and again just before he left for Évora…"

Her fear buzzes through the room like charged air before a lightning strike. Isaac has been tainted by his friendship with a man accused as a traitor, and it may not matter if he had nothing to do with the plot. He can't have been involved, I tell myself. Isaac would never question whom God chose to rule. Even if he did, he would know how much suffering a Jew's disloyalty would bring down on all of us. No, Isaac would never have plotted against King João. Never.

A week after Braganza's arrest, the news is grim indeed. The duke is to be executed tomorrow. When his brother went to Évora to plead with João, he was stabbed to death, and some are saying the king himself wielded the knife.

A few days later, another rider appears at Queluz with a letter. Eliana recognizes Isaac's hand and pries at the seal so frantically that the vellum rips.

"*My beloved wife,*" Eliana reads. "*I was a day and a half's ride from home when I received a summons from João. I had not yet heard of Braganza's arrest, but that night, people spoke of nothing else. João's summons can only mean that he intends to move against me as well. I left my host's home before dawn to avoid the spies, and I am now inside Spain in Segura de la Orden…*"

"Spain…" Eliana's voice trails off. She hands the letter to me.

I read on. "*I forsook the woman whom the Lord designated for me and the children whom God graciously bestowed upon me, and I only pray that someday the success of my plan to rescue my family will merit your forgiveness for what now must seem a cowardly act. Many times I have considered turning myself in as a way of protecting you from João's anger, but if I am dead, I can offer you nothing. I have decided the best course is to bargain for your safety from where I am.*"

"At least he's safe," I say. He is for now, but are we? I resist getting up to bolt the door, not wanting to convey my fear to my daughter.

"*You must immediately begin packing to leave Queluz,*" I continue aloud. "*Leah must do the same in Lisbon. Her husband has been accused as a co-conspirator with Braganza, and he should leave immediately to join me here. The rest of you should wait until I can arrange safe passage or, if necessary, your escape.*"

Escape? I picture fording streams and creeping through the night across pastures and mountain passes. I can't do that, I tell myself. I am too old.

Eliana takes the letter from me. "He says we should pack only valuables that can be easily carried and as many of his books as possible. You are to stay in Lisbon with Hadassah to wait for her new baby and leave together after we have settled in Toledo in the house he bought when his family was forced from Sevilla. When he negotiates our passage, he will hold back a final payment to João until the rest of you are safely out of Portugal."

Eliana rarely cries, but she is dabbing her eyes as she struggles to continue reading the letter to me. "*I fear it is unavoidable that we will lose almost everything. My heart aches that I have seen Queluz for the last time, but we must never stop praising the One who has given us such blessings over the years and will sustain and strengthen us now. I am his servant, and your loving husband, Isaac.*"

We stare at each other without speaking. A gust of wind slams a door somewhere in the house, and we jump to our feet. It is too much for us, and we dissolve into sobs in each other's arms.

The atlas is nestled among other books and carted off to Lisbon. Joseph arrives safely in Segura de la Orden, and none too soon, for the king's police do show up at Leah's door to arrest him. Finally word comes from Isaac that King João has granted us all safe passage, in exchange for an exorbitant sum of money. Soldiers will take Eliana and the others to the border, and from there, Isaac's own hired guard will bring them to Segura.

João is apparently feeling magnanimous. After all, how does the loss of Isaac's service compare to the gain of all his property? Even better, he will not have to repay Isaac the small fortune he borrowed for the latest expedition to Africa. Isaac has some letters of credit he will use to establish a modest living in Spain, and we have been busy sewing gold and small valuables into the hems and linings of our clothing to help us begin again in a country whose Jewish population is already uprooted and in despair.

Eliana and I have an unspoken agreement not to discuss our losses aloud, for fear the Holy One might interpret our commiseration as ingratitude. We agree that when we are finished at Queluz, we will walk around the house to shed all our tears at once and then go for the last time to the mikveh.

When the trunks are full, there's nothing more to do but go to Lisbon and wait for word that it is safe to leave. There must be something more to keep us here, I think as I scan the rooms, unready to face that awful, final moment. I run my hand over the top of a cabinet, and as I look at the gray coating on my fingertips, Eliana reads my mind.

"We should clean," she says, casting a glance at a little triangle of matted dirt in one corner of the room.

I shrug. "What does it matter? We don't live here anymore." My voice cracks, and I cover my face with my hands, feeling the hot sting of tears. Eliana puts her arms around me. "I'll get the rags," she says.

For another day, we put off the inevitable as we honor the house by dusting, sweeping, and polishing. I want to touch everything we are leaving behind—the furniture, the window sills, the walls—to imprint memories on my fingertips. "It's like preparing for Passover," I say, which in a way we are. We are beginning our own exodus, and like the Israelites, most of what we take away will be in our minds.

"Perhaps we should paint a red mark on the door to keep the Angel of Death away," Eliana says, attempting a laugh.

Or figure out a way to fool it into looking for us here, I think to myself, remembering a precious and vulnerable party that will soon be on the road to Spain.

Finally we acknowledge there is no more to do, and we begin our good-byes. We start with the hardest part—the original house, where our oldest memories lie—and my whole body shakes with emotion as we go in the door.

It's already not the same, with trunks and wooden crates filling one corner of the main room, and the menorah, spice box, and many of our most beloved things packed inside. The furniture is still there—the long table and benches where I shared Shabbat dinner all those years I was hiding as a Christian, the kitchen work-bench where Simona and I sealed our friendship by doing chores.

I brace myself against the door frame of Judah and Simona's bedroom. "This is where I gave birth to you," I whisper to Eliana. I sit on the bed in a flood of memories. Nine-year-old Isaac is standing solemn-faced as I show him Eliana's wet and matted hair. "I can't tell you her name," I remember saying. "We don't want the Evil Eye to know she's here."

I go like a sleepwalker to the other bedroom, where I used to nudge aside Chana and Rahel's sweet, soft bodies to make room to sleep next to them. *They're both dead.* I reel at the impossibility of it. In the study, Judah's spirit sits at his table poring over the Zohar while I translate poetry and little Eliana tugs at my dress to come share Sukkot with her.

Eventually we go into the courtyard, and I stand silently in front of the fountain. Though we had planned to share our thoughts when we were finished, now that the moment has arrived, it is too intense for either words or tears.

Eliana speaks first. "Shall we go do our mikveh?"

"Yes," I say, trying to smile as I gesture to the fountain. "But let's not do it here." Eliana has always loved the story of Simona's and my unconventional ceremony on that cold and rainy night so long ago. Something about my attempt at humor releases our pent-up anguish, and we start to laugh just as I did then—hearty laughter from a place so deep we are scarcely aware it exists, a place where we store our most profound thoughts, our griefs, and our sustaining joys.

Once in the mikveh, Eliana steps into the water first. When she comes out, I notice that her belly is soft and her breasts are flat and fallen from having nursed five children. I came to this house long before she was born, and here she is, a grandmother.

I go into the water, and my world constricts to the present. I submerge three times, saying the blessings that are as familiar to me as breathing. Eliana helps me up the steps out of the water, for with bones growing fragile with age, I have a fear of falling.

"They will desecrate this place," my daughter whispers.

"I know," I reply. "Whoever takes over this house will have no use for a mikveh."

We dress in silence. Eliana goes to tell the groom to prepare the carriage to take us back to Lisbon. She returns with a small knife. Going to the outer door, she puts the blade under the edge of the mezuzah, which has announced for decades that this is a Jewish home.

"There's no blessing for taking this down," she says as she pries it off. "I asked the rabbi." She gives me a wry smile, for the rabbi we now consult is Reuben, her young son-in-law.

She lets out a cry as the mezuzah falls into her hand. She has cut herself on the thumb, not badly but enough to leave a smear of blood on the tiny scroll that has fallen into her palm. Seeing Eliana bleeding on the threshold of this house, I am overwhelmed by the incomprehensible magnitude of what leaving means.

Eliana presses her bloody thumb to the dark spot where the mezuzah was, leaving behind a stamp like an oval etching. "We identified our houses with blood before we left Egypt," she says. "It was a mark of our salvation. Perhaps this will be the same." She puts her thumb in her mouth to suck the rest of the blood away.

I hear the voice of the driver and the sound of hooves. As the carriage bears us off to Lisbon, neither of us has the strength to prolong the agony by looking back.

Within a few days, only Hadassah's family and I remain in Lisbon. We receive a letter several weeks later telling us that everyone has arrived safely at Segura de la Orden, and soon they will head for Toledo. King João seems to have forgotten about the Abravanels who remain in Lisbon. We wait through the winter storms, and when the roads are clear and the weather has grown mild again, we prepare to rejoin our family.

A few days before our departure, I make one last journey to

Queluz. I tell the driver to go into the village for a few hours, because I want to be alone in my own house for a while. I don't enter right away, but head for the small hill where Judah and Simona sleep under an ancient oak tree.

I want to spill everything in my heart, but I feel empty already. I lower myself to the ground, wincing at the pain in my knees and hips. I wonder how I will get back to my feet without a hand to help me, but I want to be as close to the earth of Queluz as I can.

I sit quietly, and then I start to sing. It is one of Simona's favorites when we worked in the garden. "Lababi ya'ireni kaso'el lasha-harah," my voice rings out.

"My heart awakens me as one seeking the dawn
And my eye watches out for morning,
With my mouth's utterance, his glory I shall tell,
And so long as my spirit is in me, I will sing."

I laugh until I am crying too hard to go on. "I'm singing," I tell my best friends. "My spirit is in me, and I am still singing."

I remain under the tree for a while, quietly sitting with them, and then I go back to my house, stopping for a moment to remember how Jamil carried Eliana home the first time he came to Queluz. The first poppies are beginning to bloom, and I wonder if he remembers the few lines he made up for me that day. I do. I have cherished them always.

In the sweetness of this moment with you,
Fields of flowers, having only color and scent,
Hang their heads in embarrassment.

I recall how I gave him a poppy to hold to his nose, relieved to divert our attention from the attraction between us. "Have a sweet week, my love," I whisper to him again over the distance of land and time.

I go inside my own small house. The things I packed are already in Spain, and I cast my eyes over my empty desk and the table where Eliana and I had our meals. I lie down on the bed and shut my eyes, remembering the feel of her body, the little noises she made in the night, the times I sat by her side cooling her fevers or calming her after a bad dream...

I wake to the sound of men's voices and go to the door, thinking the driver has returned. Three or four men dressed in the livery of King João are standing in front of the compound. They laugh at a joke before they head inside. I feel as if I am witnessing my own death as they come out one at a time, bearing the possessions we left behind.

"Donha Cresques?" the driver says. I did not hear or see him come up alongside me. "Are you ready to leave?"

Is this how death creeps up on us? Are we ready to leave, and then we simply go?

24

"It's a mapmaker's job to leave people unsatisfied." Papa's spirit whispers as I feel him take his place next to Judah and Simona. "Look at what is not there. Don't be distracted by what is."

Bartolomeu Dias has rounded the bottom of Africa now. If my father were alive, he would no longer have to draw a vague line to the south, nor guess at legends like islands of gold, but I don't think that is what he means.

"Look at the interiors, look at the faraway places. See how little we know?"

My fingers touch Asia and drift north. The map seems full because of all the pictures of kings and travelers and mythical beings, but he's right. There is little to rely upon in it.

I feel his hand on my shoulder. "The empty spaces are why we go on. They're why people explore. We want to know the world, every last bit of it."

Only four years ago, almost thirty years after Prince Henry's death, Dias's ships were blown far out to sea in a storm. They headed east to find the coast again, and when they had sailed too long without sighting land, Dias turned the ships north and discovered the Cape of Good Hope.

The air vibrates with my father's excitement. "With Columbus setting out west for India, there will be maps of everywhere before long."

"But ignorance will continue," Judah says. "The best we can do is nibble away at it, but if we don't try to do at least that, we waste the spirit breathing in us."

"And there's never enough time," Simona adds. "There will always be babies you don't get to hold, husbands and wives you never meet, graves you won't visit, things you won't understand. People will dance without you, drink Shabbat wine, sit in the sukkah, quarrel and make up, whether you are there or not."

"But you will be there, as long as anyone is alive to remember you," my father says.

"To call out to you," a new spirit whispers.

"Mother?" My heart sings at the sound of her voice.

"Live as long as you can, for those who need you now and those whom your example will strengthen later," she tells me.

I shut my eyes and feel the room fill with ghosts. Chana, Rahel, my grandmother and grandfather, all the lost children, and those who lived before my time. Abraham and Jehuda Cresques, their wives, their parents and grandparents. The walls of the room dissolve as it fills with the soul of every Jew who stood at Sinai and accepted our covenant with God, those who sleep in dust and those not yet born.

"The success of old age is to die while you still wish to live," Judah says. "To take your last breath still wanting more."

TOLEDO 1484

By summer, I am settled in the Toledo aljama. We live up a steep street, just beyond the only remaining synagogue, in a space far too small for the thirty Abravanels who have found no other place to go. We are no more crowded than anyone else, for Toledo has taken in exiled Jews from all over Andalusia.

There is no room for books, so the rabbi has given Isaac a small space to write in a nearby yeshiva. If we were still in Portugal, my son-in-law would be looking forward to retiring into a life of contemplation. As it is, at forty-five, he will try to build the family fortune again.

The Abravanels have no special privileges here. We wear badges like everyone else, and we must be inside the aljama before the gates close at night. In some ways, exile is harder on us than others, for we are used to having plenty of room, and most Jews have been in cramped city quarters all their lives. Tempers flare from time to time in our home, and alliances shift almost daily. Eliana and I are pained by the loss of our loving little nest in Queluz, and the only solution is to find a house of our own, which will take money we no longer have.

It doesn't take long for Isaac to improve our lot. Ferdinand and Isabella have no permanent home for their court, and they spend the year here and there in their realm. Within a week of their arrival in Toledo, they summon Isaac. When he returns home that evening, he brings the stupendous news that he has been offered a job as the collector of a tax on sheep. The Abravanel's reputation for making and lending money has followed us, and the king and queen are desperate to get money to continue the fight for Granada.

Isaac's plan is to use his profits to buy army provisions to sell to the crown. We'll be back on our feet before we know it, and best of all, in a house of our own. For the first time in ages, I believe, at least a little, in the future. I am too old to adjust well to the noise and the crowds. Change is for the young, and I only want to be left in peace.

TOLEDO 1485

Isaac needs less than two years to make us one of the wealthiest Jewish families in Toledo. Ferdinand and Isabella's need for money is inexhaustible, and the king and queen already find him indispensable. "It's easy to be valued when your pockets are bulging,"

Isaac says with a sardonic grin as he extends one loan after another for food and armor for their troops.

By now, we live a few steps outside the aljama. It's a mark of Isaac's royal favor, although we must abide by all other rules for Jews, staying inside after nightfall and wearing our badges when we go out into the streets.

I look out the upstairs window on a beautiful morning in May and watch a little girl and her mother on the way to market. The girl pauses to look down the tiny street leading to the aljama gate, and her mother pulls her by the arm, her lips moving in a terse scolding.

I watch them every market day. I know what her mother is saying because I know that girl—not her name or where she lives, but I know her all the same. She's a secret Jew. She is drawn, as I was, to where she knows she belongs. Do she and her mother buy pork sausages and throw them away? Do they light Shabbat candles in their cellar? I see a crucifix dangling around the little girl's neck, and I wonder whether her mother adjusts it when they leave the house, as my own mother did, to make sure it is always visible.

Nailed to the door of a church across the street is a sheet of paper, printed on one of those new presses invented in Germany. I've seen the same notice all over town. The bottom end has torn away from the nail, and the paper has curled up, but no one needs to read it because we all know what it says.

The notice from Tomás de Torquemada gives those engaging in practices condemned by the Church forty days to confess. Anyone who can incriminate another is required to give evidence as well, to save the souls of those who do not comply. The Inquisition has come to Toledo.

Across the city, printed leaflets identify thirty-seven ways to detect secret Jews. Do they refrain from cooking on Saturdays? Is the family clean and well-dressed by Friday sundown? Do they keep Jewish fasts? Are they never observed eating pork? Such suspicions are enough to send the people in Toledo to the chambers of the Inquisition, to give confidential testimony against their neighbors.

In the first two weeks of the grace period, not a single person—Jew or Christian—came forward, so great is the antipathy toward these outsiders strutting in and announcing they will decide the fate of Toledo's people. A converso plot to assassinate the inquisitors and their chief supporters was discovered the evening before it was to be carried out. Apparently the inquisitors are so confident they see with the eyes of God that they didn't hold trials until after the bodies of the accused, stinking with decay, were finally cut down.

The conversos have been debating what to do. Should they ignore the call to confess because they believe their practices are well hidden? Should they come forward on the suspicion that they have already been secretly denounced? Many have already fled Toledo, but I wonder where in Spain they will find any lasting safety.

I've watched the street every morning with an uncomfortable flutter in my heart, wondering if the girl and her mother will reappear. Tomorrow, all chance for mercy will vanish, and the arrests will begin.

In the aljama, feelings are high. Some say conversos should expect punishment for abandoning our covenant with God. At the moment, it seems that those who remained Jews have proved the wiser, for the Inquisition has power only over Christians, although we all know that whenever conversos are targeted, Jews won't be far behind. I say nothing, because no one other than Eliana and Isaac—even the younger generations of my own family—realize that I am one of those the Inquisition is looking for.

The following morning, black-robed Dominican monks take down the tattered notices, ending clemency in Toledo. I watch for the girl and her mother on market day, but they do not appear. "What happens to the children?" I ask Isaac one evening. "Are they burned at the stake too?"

Isaac has heard that one ninety-five-year-old woman was burned somewhere in Spain, but he suspects that leaving children orphaned and impoverished will be seen as punishment enough for their parents' sins. For the next few weeks, I lie sleepless with worry about that little girl, knowing how easily, in another time and place, she could have been me.

The Inquisition concludes its first trials a month later. Torquemada expects the whole town to turn out for the auto-da-fé, but I intend to spend the time in the synagogue saying the Mourners' Kaddish for the victims. As I go down into the aljama with my twelve-year-old grandson Samuel, who attends yeshiva next door to the synagogue, armed guards sweep down. "All Jews are to come with us," the priest with them shrieks into the street. "Come see what damage the dead faith of Moses has wrought."

A guard puts his hand on the sword tucked in the scabbard at his waist to show he won't tolerate any excuses or delay as we are herded through the narrow and winding streets to the Plaza de Zocodover. Workers are unloading wood from carts in the clear, cold air of a winter afternoon, piling it around seven stakes erected near a platform holding gilded chairs with red velvet upholstery.

At first, the sound of drums is faint, but it grows louder as the procession makes its way from the cathedral. The crowd, to this point waiting in quiet agitation, erupts in a roar as a group of Dominican monks comes into view, holding aloft the banner of the Inquisition, with its olive branch on one side and sword on the other. I read the Latin embroidered there. "Exsurge, Domine, et Judica Causam Tuam," it says. "Rise Up, Master, and Pursue Your Cause."

God's cause? I begin murmuring the words of a psalm that lodges in my mind.

"Pride is their necklace;
they clothe themselves with violence."

Samuel adds his voice to mine.

"From their callous hearts comes iniquity,
the evil conceits of their minds know no limits.
They scoff, and speak with malice;
in their arrogance they threaten oppression.
Their mouths lay claim to heaven,
and their tongues take possession of the earth."

By now, the local magistrates are passing by. I see sugared piety on some faces and bloodlust on others, and both disgust me equally. Behind them march six men and one woman in yellow robes, wearing nooses around their necks and carrying candles. Samuel and I continue the psalm louder now, in hope it will comfort them. One of the men turns to us, his terrified eyes flickering as he recognizes the Hebrew.

"My flesh and my heart may fail,
but God is the strength of my heart, and my portion forever."

The woman must understand Hebrew too, for she lifts her eyes to look at us. My heart lurches. It is the mother I watched in the street. Acid rises in my throat, and I fight down the urge to vomit. My eyes scan the procession for her little girl, and in a group of people following the procession, I see her being carried by a man. She is rigid rather than clinging to him for comfort, and I think perhaps a stranger picked her up when she lagged behind, calling for her mother.

Samuel and I fall in with the families of the victims, and we all huddle together in the square as the condemned mount the platform. A tall and extraordinarily pale man with a bald pate rises from his chair and holds his bible aloft. "Scorn of our Lord Jesus Christ has made this Inquisition necessary. It is a painful burden to see these unrepentant souls before us and to think of God's eternal judgment on their souls."

After a long rant of which I hear nothing, Tomás de Torquemada drops the hand carrying his Bible to his side and slumps his shoulders, as if he has done all he can. "It is the Word of the Lord that condemns them, not us." He turns to a magistrate. "Describe the crimes and pronounce the sentences." He gives the prisoners a dismissive wave before going to his chair.

Eating meat on Good Friday, refusing to eat soup made with a ham bone, not cooking on Saturday—the magistrate drones on and on. The knees of one man buckle. A guard helps him to his feet, but he cannot stand without help. Has he been tortured, I wonder, or is it pure terror that has taken away his strength? "I—I wish to confess," he says.

Torquemada gets to his feet. "Confess what?" he asks, leaning his head forward as he skulks toward him like a wolf sizing up prey.

"I—I kept the fast on Yom Kippur," he says. "I wore a torn shirt when my wife died."

The man next to him moans. "Mordechai, you are dead anyway. Be strong."

"I can't," the man says, looking again at the piles of wood around the stakes. A dark, wet circle forms at his groin on the front of his yellow robe.

"Take him," Torquemada says, and a guard leads him away, tying him to the nearest stake. Then, without a word, the guard takes a leather strap dangling from his belt, puts it around his victim's neck, and as the crowd gasps, he strangles him.

The others are led from the platform, and each is tied to a stake. An older man shuts his eyes as his arms are tied behind him. "Shema, Isroel," he calls out at the top of his voice. "Hear, O Israel, the Lord is our God, the Lord is One," he repeats. "I am saying aloud what I have only whispered for years! And you shall love the Lord your God with all your heart, soul, and might. And these words that I command—" A guard stuffs a cloth in his mouth to stop him.

Samuel and I move closer, and we continue his prayer, in a voice loud enough for him to hear. "And these words that I command you today shall be in your heart," we say, and the man responds by bobbing his head. "You shall teach them diligently to your children, and you shall speak of them when you sit at home, and when you walk along the way, and when you lie down and when you rise up…"

I am sobbing too hard to go on, but Samuel continues to recite as the girl's mother is tied to the stake. She looks over at the man next to her, and I realize like a hammer stroke to my chest that it must be the girl's father. "Be brave," he says to his wife. She nods, her eyes wild with terror.

"Mama!" I turn to see the little girl stretching out her arms. "Papa!"

A cry comes from deep within me. There is no individual sorrow now, only one universal grief—now, then, forever—reaching out to drown us all.

The mother's eyes lock on her child, and I see her mouthing to her to run. Oblivious, the girl moves closer until she is pushed back by one of the guards.

"Run!" her mother cries out, as torches are placed on the kindling at the base of each stake.

The flames start softly, innocuously, but as the smoke begins to rise, the screaming starts. At first, the victims thrash in a futile effort to free themselves, but soon they grow rigid with pain as the smell of burning flesh fills the air. Their pleas for death pierce the air as the flames lick their legs, their hips, their chests. The woman slumps and her hair bursts into a halo of fire. One by one, the rest grow quiet, and then the pyres go up in one mighty conflagration that hides the bodies from sight.

Dazed, the girl takes a few steps forward, but is stopped by a guard. She wriggles free and darts off through the sea of legs around her. "Get her!" I say to Samuel.

He reaches her on the edge of the crowd, and by the time I arrive, she is biting and kicking like a trapped animal. Eventually she crumples in exhaustion, and I cradle her in the crook of my elbow and brush my lips on her mussed hair.

Her breath squeaks with fear and confusion as we lead her to the privacy of a side street. "We won't hurt you," I tell her. "Is there anyone to take care of you now?"

She shakes her head. "Then we will take you home," Samuel says. It is exactly what I was going to say, what any Jew would say to one of our own, and I am so proud of him.

"What's your name?" I ask her.

"Dolores," she whispers.

"No," I say. "I mean, what is your real name, your Hebrew name?"

"I don't have one!"

"It's all right," I tell her. "We live on that street you always look down."

"You live there?" She stares at both of us, and I think she understands only then that we are Jews.

I have to ask her to repeat what she whispers, because I don't think I could have heard correctly. "Eliana," she says. "Mama and Papa baptized me Dolores, but they told me it wasn't my real name."

Eliana.

Torquemada's stark vision of divine retribution rises in smoke above the crowd in the square, while in this dark and narrow street, every wall, every cobblestone, every doorway is charged with the sacredness of God's presence in this moment.

"God has answered," Samuel says, taking her by the hand. "That's what your name means."

I picture her parents' blackened corpses as we lead the girl away. What happened to her parents was not God's response to anything, but perhaps we are the answer to this child now for the wrong that has been done in his name.

ᔿ

"We need to raise her ourselves," I repeat behind the closed door of our home.

"She is a baptized Christian," my daughter says. "We'll be accused of kidnapping her. We could die at the stake for that."

I can't expect anyone else to understand how I feel. This girl is me. The woman at the stake was my mother. Regardless of how crazy anyone else thinks it is, I am determined to take this new Eliana in. "We have the power," I tell them. "Will we lack the love? Will we walk away from compassion?"

I know that an argument from the Zohar will win Isaac to my side, and Eliana too. The first step, he tells me, is to find out whether the little girl really is alone in the world. If family steps forward, there will be no choice but to abandon my plan. Perhaps her relatives will place her in a convent or sell her into servitude if they cannot keep her, but in their eyes, they will have done their duty by ensuring that she not live among people like us.

While Isaac inquires, we hide her, which isn't hard to do because she barely moves. We comfort her when she awakens screaming in the night, and during the day, we sit with her for hours while she stares at the walls. As the months pass, I feel both relief and sadness that no one comes forward to claim her and that I have a chance to honor her mother's wish that the little girl live as a Jew.

Then, to my joy, Isaac announces that his service to their Catholic majesties requires that we leave Toledo. That fall, shortly after Yom Kippur, we pack again. We will be moving to Alcalá de Henares, near Madrid, with a new member of our family, my grandchild Leah's daughter, Eliana.

25

My five-year-old grandson studies the long feather in his hand as his brother Samuel supports him on his hip. "Take the feather and put it up there," he says, in the husky voice of a young man one year past his bar mitzvah. "We need to see if there's any hametz left."

Hadassah's five-year-old daughter holds Nita's hand and watches solemnly as the little boy makes a clumsy pass with a long quill feather over the top of a cabinet. "There's something there," he says. Samuel reaches up and offers him a cookie he planted earlier, then taps his hand again to find the one he left for the girl. Both children examine their treat solemnly before taking a bite.

"Oh no! Some crumbs fell on the floor!" Elianita—or Nita, as we now call her—says in mock horror when they have finished, and together she and the little ones wipe the spot clean.

Passover begins this evening, and all traces of hametz, unleavened bread, must be removed from the house before sundown. The children are too young to know how unlikely it is to discover a cookie—and an undusty one at that—atop a cabinet any time of year, but the women have worked so hard there would be nothing for the children to find now unless it was planted. Despite the rain flooding the streets and the mud encroaching on the entryway, the feather will be as white at the end as when the ritual started.

Nita is eight now, and already she is so much a part of our traditions that it is hard to remember that she once wore a crucifix.

Three years after witnessing the deaths of her mother and father, she receives her new father's blessing at the start of every Shabbat, as if she has been with us her whole life. Perhaps it is the love of a merciful God that makes children's memories fade, but I am still haunted by the screams coming from the human torches that were her parents and the animal ferocity with which she fought off Samuel, unable to imagine anyone could mean her any good.

She has a special affection for Samuel, who from that terrible day took her deep into his heart. Samuel and his older brother attend a yeshiva in Guadalajara, where they live with my daughter. Though Samuel and Nita do not see each other often, when they are together, they form a community of two, just like Eliana and Isaac did.

When I see them building our sukkah, lighting the candles at our Festival of Lights, and wishing each other a sweet week with a sniff of the spices and a taste of membrillo, I can't help but imagine the future. Wouldn't it be strange if their story ended up like my daughter's—a second Eliana taken into a family and ensuring its legacy through the children she bears?

Isaac comes out of his study and laces his boots on a stool near the door. "It's time to go to the synagogue for the minyan," he says to his youngest son.

"I found some hametz on the cabinet," my little grandson says, patting the feather.

"No, you didn't," Nita tells him. "The feather's just getting ragged." She looks worried. "Can you check, Nonna?" she asks me. Just as with my Eliana, everything needs to be exactly according to our law.

As he waits for Samuel to lace his boots, I watch Isaac with the same admiration I always feel for him. During the bleak days of our escape from Portugal, we sewed gold coins and jewelry into our hems and left with a few boxes on a cart. Now, thanks to Isaac's acumen and the will of the Holy One, the Abravanel family has several houses in Alcalá and another in Guadalajara, where Isaac can be closer to his patron, Cardinal Mendoza. Eliana and Isaac's house in Guadalajara is small because only they and two of their sons live there. Their three older children, Judah, Leah, and Hadassah, have their own homes in Alcalá. Judah and his wife Samra have no children yet, but Leah and Hadassah have five between them.

We are happy now, and safe from want, but no Jew is foolish enough to be certain any day will end as well as it starts. We all understand that a time in which the only problems we face are keeping a curfew and wearing a badge must be counted as a good one.

I feel at peace in Alcalá, living in Judah's house, surrounded by my grandchildren and my first great-grandchildren. Perhaps these little ones will live in a better world than I have known, a better one than Nita witnessed.

"Ken yehi ratzon," I whisper in Hebrew. "May it be so."

ALCALÁ DE HENARES 1492

Church bells clang as heavy flakes of snow drift to the stones of the plaza and melt under our feet. It is almost five years later—the sixth of January, 1492, the Feast of the Epiphany. We knew that the Caliphate of Granada would not survive Ferdinand and Isabella's resolve to destroy it, but the reality stuns us. Granada has fallen. The Catholic Majesties have entered the city and settled themselves in the Alhambra.

For years, a civil war raged in Granada between two rivals for the caliph's throne. Their armies were so busy inflicting damage on each other that the border slowly inched in, as one village after another was claimed by Spain.

When, after a long siege and great bloodshed, the port city of Málaga fell to the Spanish army, the last supply route for the Caliphate was cut off. Renegados, Christians who converted to Islam and fought for the Caliphate, were tied to stakes while mounted Castilian soldiers used them for target practice, throwing spears made of cane stalks into their bodies. Every Muslim—old and young, male and female—became a prisoner of war. Those who could not pay ransom were sold as slaves.

All the conversos were burned at the stake. There were no accusations, no trials. Being anusim was enough to warrant death. The Jews were all taken prisoner, and of course, we ransomed them.

I have had one thing on my mind since the fall of Granada. Where is Jamil? Is his family safe? There are so many valiant men among the Muslim dead, and I know he would prefer to be one of them than live with dishonor in a defeated Granada.

For the Jews of Spain, there's not much in the fall of Granada to celebrate. As the Inquisition drags on, the mood of the country has become more hostile. Absurd stories inflame hatred against us. In LaGuardia, a Jew was burned at the stake, accused of having participated in the crucifixion of a four-year-old boy. Though there was no evidence the boy ever existed, under torture, the poor man admitted all sorts of vile acts, and he died for no other reason than being a Jew with the bad luck to have come to the authorities' attention.

As Judah and I watch people dancing around bonfires on this winter day, we stand at the top of our street so we can escape quickly if the celebration turns hostile. Though the townspeople seem joyous today, there's no way to know about tomorrow. The church has always fanned hatred, and the monarchs have beaten it down, insisting Jews are their property and demanding the rule of law.

Ferdinand and Isabella are friendly to the Abravanel men, both Isaac and Judah. I would go so far as to say they are sincerely fond of them. They behave the same toward Abraham Seneor and his brother, who have been financiers and royal advisers for decades. Seneor is the chief tax collector for Castile and one of the wealthiest men in Spain, owning houses, estates, and land throughout the country. His family and ours are among the few exempt from the restrictions on Jews, and though the Abravanels don't flaunt their wealth, Seneor lives in a mansion in Segovia and travels like royalty with a retinue of thirty servants and guards.

Secretly we wonder whether Seneor's wealth and power has made him drift too far from his people. He's the official court rabbi, the supreme judge of Jewish law in Spain, appointed not by Jews but by the crown. He's friendly with the most rabid Jew-haters at court, and recently he bought a house for next to nothing after its Judaizing owner died at the stake.

I give my grandson a sidelong glance. He's twenty-nine years old and a physician—a royal physician no less, for when the king or queen are here, he attends them. Judah is the most striking member of our family, although, as with all Jewish men, his face is covered with a beard. His nose and cheekbones give him the appearance of a hawk, and from a distance, he has the fierce look of an ancient prophet.

Close in, the ferocity vanishes. He has the same gentle ways I remember in the Judah for whom he is named. He is a worthy successor to his father Isaac, and with the birth last year of his first child—named Isaac like his grandfather, according to our custom—he has begun to ease into his role as the future patriarch of the family.

"What do you think will happen now?" I ask him.

He shrugs. "Isabella promises to unite all Spain as a Christian country," he says, looking across the plaza. "These people won't be thinking any more about Muslims in some little part of the south they've never seen. They'll be thinking about the Jews in their midst now."

"Anusim, you mean."

"It's beyond that. Ferdinand and Isabella want to be popular—and they are at the moment, because of Granada. But this popularity won't last beyond their first big mistake, and I suspect Torquemada is trying to convince them that allowing Jews in Spain is just that."

"Allowing us? We've been here forever!" I splutter with astonishment. "Surely they can't hope to convert us, not after we've seen how they treat the anusim. How else will they get rid of us? Kill us? Make us leave?"

"They expelled all the Jews of Andalusia. That didn't make sense either." Judah takes in a deep breath and lets it out slowly through his nose, a habit when he is thinking. "I think we're safe, though. Jews pay more taxes than anyone. Just our family adds millions of maravedis to the treasury every year. The king and queen may wish we were Christians, but I suspect they're resigned to letting us be what we are."

The bonfires bathe the square in a golden glow as evening settles in. The falling snow fills my mind with images of ash fluttering over corpses tied to stakes.

"But you never know," Judah says. "You never know." He looks at me. "You're shivering, Nonna. Let me take you home."

୦ᴥ୦

The winter of 1492 passes uneventfully in a euphoric Spain. Bards compose poems extolling Ferdinand and Isabella, nobles claim their spoils, and churches fill with music praising God for the victory. Even the Inquisition seems to die down as the country celebrates. Then, the thunderbolt.

Shortly before Passover, Isaac arrives unexpectedly in Alcalá, his face ruddy from his gallop through a cold rain. It is Friday, and although he left Guadalajara at dawn to make sure to arrive before the beginning of Shabbat, the roads are muddy, and he gets here with only a few minutes to spare.

"Where's Judah?" he asks without greeting us.

"At the synagogue for the minyan," Judah's wife Samra says. We look at each other, puzzled.

"Isaac, what's wrong?" I ask.

"I must find Judah."

"My daughter—" I insist, grabbing his sleeve as he heads for the door. "Is she all right?"

"Eliana is fine. She and our sons will be coming here when Shabbat is over." Isaac pulls his arm away and leaves without saying more.

We stare at the closed door and then at each other. Isaac is mild and contemplative, rarely abrupt, and I am astonished that his behavior toward me would ever cross over into rudeness, as it just had. "What in the world...?" I ask, my voice tinny with concern.

"We'll know soon enough." Samra holds her year-old son Isaac in one arm and lays out silverware with the other. "They have to be back before sundown when we light the candles." Though she is only twenty, Judah's wife amazes me. I know many women who would be out in the cold right now, beseeching Isaac to share the news right then before they died on the spot of worry. Not Samra. She's strong and resilient, taking the bad and the good with an even temperament. What women we have in this family, I think, and what a lucky man Judah is to have such a wife.

"We'll know, unless your father-in-law decides that the news will disturb the Sabbath, and he makes us wait until tomorrow."

"Would he do that?" Underneath her calm, I can see she is worried.

"I suppose he knows our Sabbath peace is already disturbed by whatever brought him here," I reply. "I imagine he'll tell us."

Leah and Hadassah's families arrive for the evening meal before Isaac and Judah return. The children get out the Shabbat box, which is filled with special toys, while we tell the women about the unexpected visit.

"What could be so bad?" Hadassah wonders, holding up her pregnant belly with her hands. "The church bells would be tolling if the king or queen were dead."

We hear men's voices outside, and Judah opens the door. Isaac comes in next, followed by Leah's and Hadassah's husbands. They scrape the mud from their boots and rub the soles on the fresh straw by the door, studiously avoiding the anxious faces of the women.

"Tell us, Isaac," I demand. "We're faint with worry."

Isaac shakes his head. "Shabbat will not wait for us. Samra must light the candles."

Samra's arms tremble as she puts the flame to the wick, and Leah comes to her side to help her finish the ceremony. After the last child has received its father's blessing, we turn to Isaac.

"I will share my news before we bless the wine and bread. Then we will have our dinner as if nothing has happened. Shabbat is a time of joy. Is it agreed?"

We all nod. The children, sensing the mood, have not drifted off as usual. The youngest beg to be picked up, and the older ones nestle in their mother's skirts. Nita, now twelve, comes to stand by my chair and puts her hand on my shoulder.

Isaac pulls a piece of folded paper from his jacket. "I spent several hours copying this last night," he says. "Cardinal Mendoza received it yesterday. It won't take long for the news to spread, and since people look to our family to lead them, I thought you all should know about it first, rather than being surprised in the street."

I see Judah's lips moving in silent prayer.

"It's an edict of expulsion," Isaac says. "Ferdinand and Isabella have given the Jews four months to leave Spain."

I'm not sure what happens next. The room swims in front of my eyes, and my mind goes blank. When I can focus again, Leah and Samra are sobbing in each other's arms, and Hadassah has been helped to a chair to keep her pregnant body from collapsing to the floor. Baby Isaac is screaming, and Nita is doing her best to comfort him until Samra is ready to take him again.

Isaac is speaking. "They say the only way to save the anusim is to get rid of the Jews." He consults the paper in his hand. "'They steal faithful Christians and subvert them to their own wicked belief and conviction,'" he reads, "'persuading them to observe the law of Moses, and convincing them that there is no other law or truth except for that one.'"

He lets out a deep sigh before continuing. "'We commanded

them to leave Andalusia, but neither that step nor the passing of sentence against the guilty has been sufficient remedy. So there will be nowhere to further offend our holy faith and by diabolical astuteness wage war against us, we must banish the Jews from our kingdoms.'"

"Four months," Samra whispers. "When we've been here for centuries." She looks down at her son, who is calm now and growing droopy-eyed at her breast. "What has this baby done to them? What have any of us done?"

Isaac holds up his hand. "Enough! Talk will change nothing. The king and queen will listen to reason. We must have faith in that. I have already written to Abraham Seneor asking him to go with me to try to persuade them."

"Dinner smells delicious," Judah tells Samra, "and Father has been riding all day." His shoulders are squared and his voice is unwavering, but even as an adult, my beloved first grandchild cannot hide his fear from me.

He helps me to the table. "Look at me," I command him, but he will not.

⁓

Hadassah's baby comes into the world scarlet and howling. He roots at his mother's breast and falls asleep quickly, while we admire his thick black hair and beautiful features wordlessly, to fool the Evil Eye. Isaac and Judah miss the circumcision because they are still at Madrigal, where Ferdinand and Isabella are currently in residence, but our celebration has added joy, for they have sent word that the edict has been temporarily suspended.

"Ferdinand wants time to think it over," Judah writes. "Father spoke as I imagine Moses must have, and I could not help but smile at the thought that the Holy One has so inspired him that this time, the pharaoh may be persuaded to let our people stay rather than go."

From Madrigal, Judah and Isaac travel from court to court, soliciting nobles to support the lifting of the edict. The next we hear is from Guadalajara, where Isaac has returned to discuss the situation with his patron.

"Cardinal Mendoza thinks we are wasting our time," Isaac writes. "Ferdinand may yet be swayed, but only by money. I am willing to offer our family treasure, confident that the Jews of Spain will repay us if we are successful, but Mendoza tells me Ferdinand is unlikely to accept such tribute. Taking money to let the Jews stay might make people think their majesties care more about gold than Christ."

Are the Abravanels to be poor again? At least this time, it would be our choice and, knowing our men, it would not be for long. The women discuss these things as we work together to ready each of our homes for Passover. My job is to watch little Isaac, who is just learning to walk and must be kept from underfoot. No wonder I feel something special for him. He is the first son of my first grandson—the boy who, if it is God's plan, will carry on the family legacy. He's a beautiful child, with his father's dark eyes and his mother's calmness, and of course I am sure he is the smartest baby in all Castile.

When we finish the other houses, we return home to clean our own. Samra goes into the study to dust the bookshelves, while Eliana heads for the kitchen. I take Isaac into the courtyard, turn him on his belly at the fountain, and laugh with him as he splashes his chubby fingers in the water.

When he starts to fuss, I bring him inside. The house is unnaturally quiet, and I find Eliana and Samra in the study weeping. "We were talking about how we may be doing this for the last time here," Eliana says.

"I don't think I can bear it," Samra whispers. "I started moving Judah's books to dust underneath them, and I thought—" She dissolves into tears on Eliana's bosom.

"Do you remember cleaning before we left Queluz?" I ask my

daughter. "We did it for—" I think a moment. "For the sacredness of it. I was touching everything like a blind person, using my hands to print that house in my memory." I shut my eyes. "And that's what happened. I can call that house up in my mind right now, to every last detail, as if I will open my eyes and be standing in it."

I stroke Samra's shoulder. "It may be our family's lot to lose everything again, but let me show you how to keep from saying good-bye."

⤳

Isaac and Judah arrive home the day before Passover with news we don't want to hear. Ferdinand turned down Isaac's money. "The only glimmer of hope," he says over supper, "is that the edict is still suspended. Apparently they aren't sure what to do."

"He says Isabella feels more strongly than he does," Judah adds. "If we can convince her, Ferdinand says he will go along."

Isaac and Judah will be here only for the first two days of Passover, before going back to Madrigal to see Isabella. "Perhaps all this time, we've been talking to the wrong person," Judah says.

Isaac strokes his silver beard. "And then again, perhaps the king's dinner was waiting, and he just wanted to get rid of us." He thinks for a moment. "Torquemada has his claws sunk into her. It's hard to imagine getting much help there."

Samra and Eliana get up to clear the table, but Isaac asks me to stay behind. "Isabella reminded me that you had been her tutor years ago. I don't think she liked realizing so much time has passed that you have a thirty-year-old grandson."

"The queen's a grandmother herself."

"Yes, but I suppose even queens wonder where the years have gone. She said she'd like to see you and Eliana again, and I think she meant it."

"Why don't the two of you come with us to Madrigal?" Judah asks. "Perhaps if she sees the fate she's decreed for an old friend, she might decide she doesn't want to go through with it."

"I'm sixty-six," I tell them. "Why can't Eliana go for both of us?" I can see Judah's idea taking hold in Isaac's mind, and my heart sinks. He's going to tell me to do it for the Jews. He'll say how much his bones have ached from these weeks of traveling and make me feel guilty for not being willing to suffer the same way for our people.

But he doesn't. "If you don't think you can do it, that's the end of it," Isaac says. Still, I know they are disappointed, and I go to bed wondering if I can bring myself to take on such a journey even if they aren't going to ask.

❧

We have just doused the flame from the habdalah candle at the end of Shabbat a few weeks later when there is a bang on the door. Judah opens it to see a soldier of the Santa Hermandad, the Inquisition's police. "You are ordered to come to the synagogue," he barks. "His Reverence Tomás de Torquemada will speak to you there." The guard looks over Judah's shoulder. "All the Jews must come."

Isaac stands in the doorway, shaking a fist and thundering at the soldier sauntering down the street. "What is this about, that you disturb the peace of the Sabbath?" It's not really true—Shabbat ended the moment the candle was put out—but Isaac does like dramatic effects. Besides, it doesn't really end like that. Shabbat lingers, even as we get back to the ordinary work of cleaning dishes and stoking fires.

"We should refuse to go," Eliana says. "Torquemada has power only over Christians."

Judah shakes his head. "It's unwise to provoke him, especially with the king and queen pondering our fate." He's right of course. We throw on our shawls and go out into the damp chill of the early spring night.

Upstairs, the women's gallery is so crowded we can hardly breathe. Eliana, my granddaughters, and great-granddaughters are squeezed against the rail, looking down. A buzz grows among the men, and they turn to see the Grand Inquisitor's guards clearing a path toward the tebah. Torquemada's burning eyes, obscured by his hood, look out from under thick eyebrows. Dangling on his chest is a massive silver crucifix, the only thing distinguishing him from the two priests flanking him.

He ascends the steps of the tebah and, tossing back his hood, he glowers at the crowd. His flattened, lumpy nose disfigures his face, and his bald pate, fringed with a circle of dark hair, looks oily in the golden light of the lamps.

"The hour is growing late!" He shakes a clenched fist at the men. "Your days are numbered. Leave your dead faith behind, and embrace salvation!"

With a pleading smile, he holds out his arms, as if he wishes to embrace them all. "Why do you turn your back on God?" He sees the men's impassive faces and sighs loudly. "How can you bear to live with his scorn?" he whines, as if he has been personally hurt by each of us. "Come to mass tomorrow and I will baptize you, for the sake of your immortal souls."

He takes a deep breath and without warning raises his voice to a scream so loud it lifts the hair on my arms and makes one woman behind me burst into tears. "He has abandoned you just as you abandoned his son. There are no Jews—only heretics!"

He storms down off the tebah and heads toward the ark containing the Torah scrolls. As if they are sidestepping a runaway wagon, the men clear a path for him. He rips the embroidered velvet curtain aside and flings open the carved wooden doors of the ark.

The women gasp, and an angry murmur rises up from the men. The ark is never opened without ceremonies befitting the word of God. Torquemada swats at a silver filigreed crown that tops the scroll case. "Baubles! Do you think you can impress God with such things when you turn your back on him by your wickedness and lies? Do you think he will stand by and watch you lure Christian souls back to darkness?"

Torquemada makes his way back to the tebah as we watch in hushed silence. "My children," he says, his tone again unctuous as he stretches out his arms. "Come to me. Come to the Savior who died for you. Come to the hope of eternal life."

Eliana pulls her shoulders up tall beside me. "If I forget thee, O Jerusalem, let my right hand forget its cunning." Her strong voice floats across the synagogue. "Let my tongue cleave to the roof of my mouth, if I remember thee not."

Everyone looks up at the balcony, and I see Isaac's eyes lock onto his wife. Samra is pressing against the grille now too. "Be thou my judge, O God, and plead my cause against an ungodly nation," she sings. I recognize the words of the forty-third psalm and I join her.

> *"Deliver me from the deceitful and unjust man.*
> *For thou art the God of my strength…"*

Leah, Hadassah, and Nita join us, and our rich women's voices have a force so profound I am shaking. All Jews who ever suffered for their faith seem to be offering their strength to me, to my family, to the women crowding behind me, and to the men below. I feel our power bursting through the walls of the synagogue, like Samson breaking his chains.

What a small matter my old bones are, compared to the force of my heart. I will walk to Madrigal to see Isabella if I have to. I will crawl. I will put myself in God's hands and let him use me as he wishes.

Torquemada's face is scarlet with rage. "Who are those women?" he thunders.

"They are our wives," Isaac says, "our sisters, our mothers, and our daughters." His voice breaks, and as he looks up at us, I see tears streaming down his face.

"Bring them down here," Torquemada growls in a low and menacing voice. Behind me, the women gasp. Does he not know what he is asking? Women do not mingle with men on the floor of the synagogue.

I hear the rabbi call up that it is necessary to obey. Our worried murmurs echo off the stone walls of the narrow staircase as we make our way down and assemble in front of the Grand Inquisitor.

"Who sang?" he demands.

"We all did," Samra replies.

"Who sang first?"

"I did." Eliana steps forward.

"And what did you mean by it?"

She looks confused. "We sing to the Holy One all the time. To praise and honor and thank him."

"'Deliver me from the deceitful and unjust man?'" Torquemada sneers. "You see, I know the words too."

"You praise God with the words of our people then," Eliana says. "The psalms are our prayers. Perhaps we have more to teach you."

"How dare you?" Torquemada's face mottles with rage.

Samra and the other women of our family have stepped up to stand with her, and Eliana slips her hand in mine. "We may fear the punishment of man for singing, but not of God," she tells the glowering priest, "for he has not abandoned us and he will not, regardless of what you do or say."

I hear Nita next to me, taking huge, gulping breaths. I turn to look at her ashen face. "He was there!" she gasps, staring at the Grand Inquisitor. "He was there when my parents—"

I wrest my hand from Eliana's and cup it quickly over Nita's mouth. "Don't!" I tell her.

Torquemada steps forward. "Who are you?" His eyes narrow with menace as he looks from Nita to me. "What are you keeping her from saying?"

My eyes plead with Nita to understand that she mustn't let him know she was a converso and we took her in. We're dead if she does, I think. All of us.

"You can tell me," Torquemada's tone is unctuous as he comes nearer to size up his prey.

"I—" Nita gets no further. Her body heaves, and she covers his robe with the pink contents of her supper.

He lets out a cry of shock and indignation and steps back. The guards try to wipe the vomit from his robe, but he shoves them away. "This is how the devil speaks to the servant of Christ!" His shrieking is as shrill as that of his victims at the stake as he gestures to his soiled robe. "You are evil! The devil makes his home in you. You shall see what God has in mind for such enemies!" Without another word, he storms out of the synagogue.

Nita sobs in Leah's arms as we leave. When everyone is on the street, Torquemada looms out of a darkened doorway. "Lock it!" he says to his guards, pointing to the synagogue door.

One of them brandishes a large padlock while the other throws the bolt. The lock closes with a loud click. Torquemada snorts in derision and walks away, leaving the Jews of Alcalá speechless in his wake.

26

There's not much to say on the road to Madrigal. We aren't cer-
tain Isabella will see us, especially after she's heard how the Grand
Inquisitor was treated at Alcalá. In the emptying of her stomach,
Nita had spoken with an eloquence surpassing language. "This
is the mess you left when you murdered my parents," she told
Torquemada, "and this is what I think of you."

We settle in the home of a rabbi to wait for the queen's summons. To our surprise, she writes personally, saying she has time
for us the following afternoon.

Eliana and I are escorted into a large room that, despite the tapes-
tries on the walls and thick carpets on the floor, has the chill of disuse,
for the king and queen have only recently returned from Granada.

"My goodness," Isabella says. "Isn't it a surprise how easy it
is to recognize people one hasn't seen for decades?" Her voice,
though deeper, has the same lilt as it did when everyone in Arévalo
stumbled over themselves to offer her cakes and hair ribbons.

"I am so happy to see you," I say, and I mean it, brushing aside
for a moment the doleful reason we have come.

"And you married well," she says to Eliana. "One of the most
influential men in the country, and your son is following in his
footsteps." Her words are gracious, but perplexing. What footsteps? Soon there will be no Jewish feet in Spain.

It's worth a gentle reminder. "We are proud of what our family has contributed," I say. "And we hope to continue for generations to come."

The flush in her cheeks tells me she still catches nuances easily. "Ah yes," she says, forming her face into one of those well-practiced smiles that are second nature to women at court. "I want you to know that it's not me but the Lord who has put this thing into my husband's heart." She gives a casual glance away. "I don't think there's any more hope of swaying him than asking water not to follow the bed of a stream."

I am stunned. Ferdinand told Isaac and Judah the opposite, that the queen's will had driven the edict. Are Isaac and Judah, and the others pleading for the Jews, being tossed back and forth in the hope that they will eventually give up and go away?

"You know," Isabella says, "we truly don't want all the Jews to leave. Nothing would please us more than to have families like yours accept baptism and follow the one true faith. That is all it would take." She holds her hands palms up and arches her eyebrows to underscore just how simple it would be.

"If it please your majesty—" Eliana says, but before she can say more, a side door opens. Without requesting permission to enter, Tomás de Torquemada is standing by Isabella's chair, scowling at us with his intense, reptilian eyes.

"Do I know you?" he asks. Isabella seems taken aback by the presumption with which he came into her quarters and took over the conversation, but she says nothing.

"We live in Alcalá de Henares," I tell him, certain he will need no further help remembering us.

"Yes," he says, drawing the word out with a hiss as he stares at Eliana. He crooks the corners of his mouth in a menacing smile. "And you," he says, turning so suddenly toward me that I am momentarily startled. "Where are you from?"

His demand is bluntly personal, and I respond more out of surprise than anything else. "I was born in Sevilla," I say, "but I spent much of my life in Portugal."

"And what brought you there?"

"My father was a mapmaker. He worked for Prince Henry and King Duarte."

"A mapmaker?" His eyebrows arch with curiosity.

"I am Amalia Cresques. My family is among the most renowned mapmakers in Europe."

"Cresques—there were conversos among your family, were there not? You did not take your husband's name?"

"I was married only briefly," I say, hating myself for telling him anything at all. "My husband was a sea commander and drowned off the coast of Africa. I returned to my family name because I am proud of it, and I had his for so short a time."

Torquemada is kneading the silver crucifix hanging from his neck. "That's odd," he says. "A Jewish commander? I've never heard of such a thing."

My heart stops. I have walked into a trap of my own making. "He wasn't Jewish," I admit disconsolately.

"Who would marry a Christian and a Jew? Certainly not a priest."

I could say Diogo and I were married by a rabbi, but he won't believe it. If I say I was married in a church, he will know I used to live as a Christian. I blurt out the only reply I think might save me from a charge of Judaizing and a trip to the stake. "We were never married. Not formally, I mean."

The horror of what I've said dawns on me when Torquemada begins to cackle. "The wife of Isaac Abravanel a bastard child?"

Isabella's face grows scarlet as his derision rises to a roar of laughter. "Stop it," she says. "This is most unseemly. Leave me now." The glee on his face is unmistakable as he strides out the door.

The world collapses in around me. I have dishonored my daughter, and there is no way—no possible way—ever to make this right.

∽

We leave at daybreak and celebrate the end of Passover in a make-shift camp on our way back to Alcalá.

"The bread of affliction indeed," Judah says, as we break the last of our matzoh. Isaac smiles wanly. "Perhaps our exile from Portugal was practice for this one," he says. "After all, Moses had to escape to the desert when he killed an Egyptian, and what he learned in those years served him well when he led our people out of slavery."

We try to take cheer in this, but there is little to be had. The only concession Isaac got from the king and queen is to let him get home before word comes that the edict of expulsion is final and again in effect.

He called my daughter a bastard...

If I could grab Torquemada's crucifix, I might beat him to death for what he has done to the two of us, to Nita and his other victims living and dead, and to all the peaceful and loyal Jews of Spain.

Eliana doesn't seem troubled by what I told that shriveled soul. "It isn't true anyway, so why should I care what he thinks?" she told me as I wept in our quarters. "I wish I had asked him why, if his religion is right and true, he had to resort to such ugliness."

Despite her casual demeanor, I could tell she was unnerved, and I spent much of yesterday torturing myself. By the time night fell, her patience had turned to annoyance and then to anger.

"We'll never see him again, remember?" Eliana rarely snaps at anyone, and I couldn't recall the last time she had been cross with me. "He won't get far with such talk when every noble either has bastards in the family or is one. We have to leave Spain. It's time to think about that."

She's right, I tell myself, as I watch the embers crumble and release their glow. Eliana and I huddle together in the damp, chilly air of early spring, while Isaac strokes his white beard, deep in thought.

"'I am a man of unclean lips, and I dwell in the midst of a people of unclean lips,'" Isaac says in Hebrew.

Judah picks up the verse from Isaiah. "'Then flew unto me one of the seraphim, with a glowing stone in his hand, and he touched my mouth with it.'"

The calming, luxurious sound of our ancient tongue makes a cocoon around us, and moved to tears, Isaac wipes his eyes. "The Holy One asks, 'Whom shall I send?' Isaiah says, 'Here am I; send me.' But I am no prophet. He sent me, and I failed."

"You've done all you can, father." Eliana's voice cracks with emotion. None of us says aloud the words that follow, how people will continue to be blind and suffer until cities are without inhabitants and the land is laid waste. No one says what we all must feel, that we are in that time now.

We sit silently for a while. Finally Isaac speaks again. "It was not God's will that the Jews be rescued with money. Much as I hate to say it, perhaps Torquemada was closer to the divine purpose than I was. We are a stiff-necked people, and I am among the worst. If God wills us to leave this land, I pray that the Holy One is not angry with me for trying to stop it."

When Judah and he met with Ferdinand and Isabella yesterday, they saw that the pair had been toying with them by saying the other was in charge. When Isaac asked if his offer was irrevocably refused, Torquemada held out his heavy crucifix while the king and queen cowered. "Judas Iscariot sold our Savior for thirty pieces of gold!" he screamed at them. "Here he is! Barter him away again!" Any chance for the Jews ended with the clatter of that crucifix at Ferdinand and Isabella's feet.

Judah's voice is soft. "'Depart, depart, touch not. They hunt our steps, that we cannot go in our broad places; our days are fulfilled, our end is come.'"

Silently, I continue the verses from Lamentations. The joy of our heart is ceased. Our dance is turned into mourning.

∽

We arrive home the same day the news spreads through the aljama. We have three months to leave Spain. The only positive note is that Isaac has the queen's permission to reopen the synagogue. All the Jews gather there that evening to hear Isaac and Judah speak about what is to come.

"Take what you wish, but the journey will be very long, and even your most valued possessions will become burdensome," Isaac says. "Any mule or other animal you take with you cannot cross the border, and you will have to shoulder your load from there. The king and queen wish to keep all useful animals here for the Christians who remain." A shocked murmur rises up from the crowd. Apparently their majesties have placed us lower than beasts of burden and are more prepared to lose us than one donkey or horse.

"Valuables will be confiscated at the border," Judah adds, "but the roads will be thick with bandits, and you may already have been robbed of what is easy enough to carry."

"Where are we to go?" one woman cries out.

"We are promised safe passage out of the country," Judah says. "The King of Portugal has agreed to take in Jews, but only for six months, for a head tax that will be collected as you enter. And the ports will be full of boats willing to take you anywhere for money."

"Money?" An angry voice rises. "Where do we get money?"

Isaac takes a deep breath and sighs. "Anything you cannot take, you should try to sell. It will be worth nothing to you if you leave it behind. May we hope that our Christian neighbors offer us fair prices, but…"

He doesn't need to say what everyone knows. With desperate sellers, a house might go for the usual price of a cart, or a vineyard for an extra pair of shoes for the road.

"Better to convert and keep everything," I hear a woman mutter behind me.

"How can you say that?" Samra wheels around to face her.

"Now more than ever, we must not lose faith." Her voice crumbles as she dissolves in tears in Eliana's arms.

The air is silent except for a few muffled sniffs, as the synagogue empties and we go home to contemplate the tasks that await us.

The first weeks after the edict is enacted, the aljama is a mix of frenzy and torpor, as people are struck down with melancholy so deep they are unable to rise from bed, only to be overtaken by agitation, as if they are leaving tomorrow. Within a month, many families are gone, some heading for North Africa or Palestine, saying that even if the edict is rescinded, they are tired of living among people who hate them.

Most are going to Navarre or Portugal, because they can get there on foot. For our exiled family, Portugal is not a possibility, and Isaac rules out Navarre because he believes once Ferdinand and Isabella rid Spain of its Jews, neighboring countries are likely to follow. We will go by boat to Pisa, Genoa, or Naples and hope one or another of Isaac's Jewish friends at court will take us in.

Priests roam the aljama, exhorting Jews to be baptized. One barged into the synagogue to preach last week, and the rabbi was jailed for shouting to those present to remain strong. When he was released, he was given one day to leave town.

While the rest of us walk like the dead among the ruins of our lives, the newly baptized live as they always have, gritting their teeth and reminding themselves they will not have to endure our cold shoulders much longer. One neighborhood shrew has scoured the aljama since her baptism, offering to take goods off her friends' hands, but not for a penny more than a Christian would offer.

She doesn't contribute to our fund either, and we don't know which is worse. The Jews of Alcalá have pledged that no one will be left behind, forced to convert for lack of money. This fund adds to our burden, as does the order to pay two years of taxes in advance, so the crown won't suffer any loss of revenue from our departure.

One sweet and impoverished widow was baptized at her grown

children's insistence. Afterward she came to our house, and when she saw we had not packed a pair of Shabbat candlesticks, she offered us a fair price for them.

"What will you use them for?" Samra asked.

"I'll light candles on Shabbat," she said, "so I can remember you."

When we reminded her that following Jewish practices after being baptized will bring the Inquisition down on her head, she looked stunned and took to bed with such a deep sickness we thought for a while she might have taken poison. She stays inside now, except when her son comes to take her to mass.

Isaac and Judah will not leave Spain until the last moment, so we wait, suspended in time. Some shred of hope lingers that Ferdinand and Isabella will renege when they see Jews, including the wealthiest and most influential, choosing to leave rather than abandon their faith. Eighty-year-old Abraham Seneor and his even wealthier son-in-law are packing, and with the Abravanels going into exile too, the crown will suffer a palpable loss, not just of scholarship and expertise, but of ready sources of loans for their adventures. Isaac and Judah wait here to press the moment if their majesties waver. No one expects it, not with Torquemada daily spewing his poison.

The neighborhood is half-deserted now. The border of Spain is far away, and time is running out. No one stops by to fill our house with gossip and laughter. No one needs flour, or a poultice, or help with a difficult spouse or a laboring daughter. No one knocks on the door asking if we have anything to sell, for we have made the decision to keep our house as it is for as long as we can and then to walk away.

We are luckier than most. Isaac and Judah have arranged for some debts to be paid to them after we arrive in Valencia, and we have enough money for the bribes we are sure to need at the border. We are sewing everything we can into our clothing and will hide other valuables among the items we pack, but other than that, we try to maintain a normal life for the children while we wait.

One afternoon, I bring out the atlas from a box of books Isaac plans to give to a Christian friend in Guadalajara. "Would you like to look at this one last time?" I ask one of my grandchildren, Aya, who is playing with baby Isaac on the floor. No books are going except the religious tomes Isaac needs for his writing. Those have no beautiful lettering and illustrations in gold and lapis lazuli, and they will be unimpressive to greedy soldiers on the docks at Valencia or bandits on the road. One way or another, I am told, the atlas will not make it to the boat.

"Why take it, in that case?" Eliana asks. She loves it as much as I do, but she has gotten fiercely practical. The atlas takes space that should go to a warm cloak to wear at sea or extra shoes to replace those that may wear out before we get to Valencia.

I bring it to the table, and Aya sits next to me on the bench, holding baby Isaac in her lap. He gives me a happy smile. "Mermer!" he says.

I know what he means. I turn to the page with the mermaid, and he laughs that beautiful, full chortle that comes from somewhere deep in the heart of innocence. I give his hair a tousle because I no longer bend well enough to kiss his cheek.

"Do you wish you were her?" I ask Aya. "I did when I was a child."

"She's very pretty," she says, "but I'd rather be on land." She burrows in next to me. "With my family."

My eyes burn at the thought of how little time we have left for moments like this. "Do you know where we are now?" Of course she does. She has seen the atlas countless times since she was baby Isaac's size.

She points to Alcalá de Henares, in the heart of Spain. "And here is where we're going." She draws her finger down to Valencia, on the coast, then looks up with a shrug. For her, it is an adventure, much like mine to Sagres when I was her age.

She doesn't understand that Valencia is where the journey truly starts, a voyage that will take us so far from home that we would have to turn the atlas page to see the first possible resting point. I know that even what is around the next corner may be menacing, but maps give comfort, especially to the young, making us think the world is known, familiar, safe.

As she points to this and that and baby Isaac listens solemnly, the realization comes to me as surely as my next breath that I will not leave such a thing behind. I must keep it for them, for the future, and though it might be lost along the way, I must do my part to preserve it.

Samra is calling her niece to help with something. The baby fusses at the sound of his mother's voice, and Aya holds his hand as they walk into the kitchen. I bring the atlas to the one small trunk I am taking, and pulling away the top layers of clothing, I whisper a prayer to the Holy One to keep this treasure safe, to keep us safe, so that someday I will be able to pull it out and say to my daughter, "Look! It isn't lost to us after all!" and see her weep with happiness.

I lay the book down and put a hamsa on top of it, hoping the silver charm will protect this and everything I love. I replace the clothes on top and hold my breath as I press the lid down hard, sighing with relief when it latches.

The fragile peace of our dwindling hours in Alcalá ends in mid-June with two staggering pieces of news. The first is that Abraham Seneor has been baptized by Cardinal Mendoza in a ceremony attended by Ferdinand and Isabella. We hear that Isabella told the court rabbi that if he did not convert, the retaliation against the remaining Jews in Spain would be swift and brutal.

Perhaps Seneor is just being practical about not wanting to lose everything at his advanced age. Still, I wonder what went through his mind as Torquemada and the others watched to make sure he finished his bowl of pork stew, which is served after many baptisms to complete the humiliation. I wonder what he thought when forced to answer to his new Christian name, Fernando Nuñez Colonel.

Fernando. He will be called for the rest of his life by the name of the man who fashioned his disgrace. Angry as I am, I can't help but pity him.

Seneor has a new name among the Jews as well. Abraham Sone-or, many call him now—Abraham, the Hater of Light. Out of loyalty, Isaac doesn't call him that, nor does he ask his friend for an explanation of his decision. "He must at least pretend to be sincere," he says, "and that lie would break both of our hearts."

Isaac has endured the same kind of pressure to which Seneor succumbed. Isabella even offered to let our family stay in Spain as the only Jews in the country. "Who are we without our people?" Isaac says. "And who will my grandchildren meet under the huppah on their wedding day if all the Jews are gone?"

The second piece of news is so horrifying that Seneor vanishes from our minds. One afternoon, Judah receives in his study a nervous and agitated visitor. When he comes out, his face is drained of blood as he slumps at the table. "They plan to kidnap my son," he says. "Ferdinand and Isabella are going to baptize our Isaac and hold him for ransom."

"My baby?" Samra's voice is small and vague, as if she doesn't understand. Then she gasps. "My baby!" she shrieks, sagging into Eliana's arms.

"No!" I say in a voice as hoarse and raw as a threatened animal.

"Ransom?" Eliana asks. "They'll get everything we own when we leave Spain. Can't they wait?"

"They don't want money," Judah says. "They mean to force us to stay. It's illegal to take a Christian child out of Spain, so once Isaac is baptized, anyone who wanted to remain here with him would have to convert. We would get him back at the church after we let them put their water on us."

I remember the story of a desperate mother hiding Moses in the bulrushes, and my mind runs wild as I imagine living with Isaac in a cave, riding madly across the border with him in my arms, throwing myself over him and being torn apart rather than let him loose from my embrace.

Wordlessly, we all move toward the bedroom where Isaac has been napping in his parents' bed. His beautiful long lashes flutter over shut eyes, and his soft lips make sucking motions as he sleeps. Someone lets out a muffled sob, and he opens his eyes. "Mama?" he says, sitting up to look around.

"Pick up," he says, holding his arms out to his father. Judah holds his only child tight and nuzzles his tiny neck. Samra comes to his side and strokes the baby's back as tears roll silently down their stricken faces.

ᐃ

We confer with Lev and Yehudit, two of our neighbors still in Alcalá, and we decide to leave together after nightfall the following day. They are going to Portugal and will take Isaac with them, pretending he is their own baby's twin. We will send for him when we reach our new home.

We need as much secrecy as we can manage, for the kidnappers may be close and waiting their chance. We talk casually with our remaining neighbors about all the work left to do and point to our few paltry boxes as just the beginning of our belated packing.

That night, we steal from our homes, leaving one lit candle, as if we have gone to bed by its light. As we pass down the dark and deserted streets of the aljama, Samra holds the baby so tightly that he wakens, and she covers his mouth to muffle his wails of apprehension.

The stablehands Isaac and Judah have bribed for their silence receive part of their payment for packing our belongings onto a cart and finding the donkeys that will pull it. The rest of the money will come only if we are not tracked down for several days. There is no time to think, no time for regrets, no time to look back in the night. The animals plod their way along a trail unfamiliar in the dark, as we begin the first steps of our exile.

We travel until midmorning over flat, undulating fields of wheat as lush as pale-green velvet in the hazy light of early summer. The women have been riding in the cart with baby Isaac, taking turns holding him. Hadassah clings tight to her own infant son, torn between relief she will not be the one facing such a loss and the knowledge that no one, ever, is safe from the lurking gaze of the Evil Eye.

Samra sits beside me, wearing the key to her house around her neck, as are all the women of Alcalá who have left homes behind. We won't be returning, but wherever we are, the key will keep alive the claim of the heart to what was once ours. None of the women have spoken at all, and the few exchanges between the men walking alongside are as jarring as noises heard while drifting off to sleep. We are hovering outside of life, outside of time, in a world where we still have what we know we have already lost.

"Cry?" Isaac asks as he reaches up to examine my face with his perfect little fingers.

"Yes, my love," I tell him. "Nonna is sad today."

"I love you," he tells me, wiggling up in my arms to plant a kiss on my cheek.

We reach the road where our friends will turn west for Portugal and we go east to Valencia. Judah comes to the cart and holds out his hands. Samra shrieks, thinking he intends to tear her baby from her, but for now, he simply wants to help us all get down.

I see pastures with grazing sheep and cattle, the purple-gray hills beyond, the cloudless sky darkened with huge flocks of birds that whirl across the fields. But it is not the same in both directions, because our Isaac will go one way and we another. We will not be like Joshua at Jericho, stopping the course of the sun to battle our way back from defeat.

"We will take good care of him," Yehudit, our neighbor, says, jiggling her baby on her hip. "I'll have enough milk for him and my own, I'm sure of it." Her husband, Lev, shifts from foot to foot. He is a quiet man, shy even among friends, but now there is truly nothing to say. We know they will keep our beloved child as safe as they can, but it is in the hands of the Holy One whether that will be enough.

Baby Isaac will not let his mother keep him close any longer, squirming to get down to examine something lying in the road. She puts him down, and the inevitable sinks upon her as her arms lie useless at her sides.

The child is making lines in the dust with his finger. I crouch down next to him as much as my old bones allow. "Go bye-bye now," he says, and I wonder how he knows.

"Yes," I say, choking on my tears. "Isaac is going bye-bye now, but only for a little while."

"Bye-bye with Nonna."

My heart rips from my chest at the betrayal to come. "Yes, my love," I say. "You will always be with me." *In my heart*, I whisper too softly to be heard. *In my heart*.

Lev is helping Yehudit into their cart, and he hands baby Isaac up to her. We are standing nearby with our faces locked into smiles so he will not think anything is wrong. Samra is working so hard not to let tears break through that her breath is coming out in shallow pants.

Nita is with us. Nearly thirteen, she is the only grandchild who knows what is happening. We have sent the others to run after butterflies and fight mock battles with stalks of wheat. We could not bear to deal with their misery as well as our own before the deed was done.

Now that baby Isaac is in the cart, they must sense something is wrong, because they all come running. Lev gives the reins a shake to get the horse moving. Isaac stops smiling. "Mama come too!" he says, his face crumpling. He is screaming now, and as the cart moves father down the road, we succumb to our own grief with wails and sobs.

My grandchildren run after the cart, but Lev sees them, and he picks up the pace to keep them from catching up and prolonging the agony. Nita picks up a wailing cousin to comfort her. The children turn around and run back toward us, horror written on their dirt-streaked faces. We watch together as the cart grows smaller and disappears from view.

I have never seen the senior Isaac look broken, even on the road back from Madrigal, when he nursed his defeat at the hands of Torquemada. Now his shoulders are slumped, and the corners of his eyes are shriveled with grief. He is fifty-five, and from this day forward, he will be an old man.

He clears his throat, and to my surprise, he begins to chant one of the Psalms, exhorting us all to join in. Only Samra is silent. Her eyes are like dead coals in her impassive face. Samra—the steady one, the one who exhorts us all to rise up and be strong—is gone into a world of pain.

Tears wet the top of Judah's beard. "We must trust in the Holy One and know that His will is always done." He shuts his eyes, and I see his jaw tremble as he tries to compose himself. "We must remember that even now, God deals bountifully with us, and we will…" He looks up toward the heavens, and I see his astonishing strength breaking through his grief. "We will rejoice that he will never abandon us. Or our son," he says, gently shaking Samra's limp body as if to restore her to life. "Or our son."

We keep our heads pointed down the road, trying to think of nothing but the next hill, the next patch of shade, the next endless hour. By nightfall the following day, we reach a camp where about sixty Jews are resting for Shabbat. Yesterday and today, I have been looking behind us for a cloud of dust rising from soldiers in pursuit, because I cannot imagine that Ferdinand and Isabella would give up so easily.

I haven't said aloud what I fear most—that Isaac has six more grandchildren, including Nita, whom he loves equally well. Jews are all the same to Ferdinand and Isabella, and one kidnapping would be scarcely different from another. I am relieved that we have other families to travel with now. Fellow exiles will offer not just companionship but a measure of safety. Already my four oldest great-grandchildren have disappeared with others their age to explore their surroundings. How would anyone pick those few out as ours?

"They assume baby Isaac is still with us, and whoever comes to take him will not want to go back empty-handed," I tell Eliana when I can hold in my fear no longer.

"I know," she says, shaking out a blanket. "We should tell the children if anyone comes looking for us, they should mingle with the other families rather than standing with us." She smiles faintly. "Christians think we all look alike. Perhaps this time, their ignorance will work in our favor."

By the time we settle in to sleep, all the children and grandchildren know what to do if we are caught by royal emissaries on the road. Hadassah and her baby will disappear into the crowd, and the children will stand with the temporary families to whom they have been assigned.

None too soon, for the day after Shabbat, two men in the colors of a local lord ride along the road calling out for Isaac and Judah. "You are to come with us," one of the men says.

Judah shakes his head. "Any business you have is with my whole family. You will say what you have to say to all of us or be on your way."

Having lost as much as we have makes it easier to be fearless. What punishment is left except death, and who, I wonder, other than the young hasn't thought that would be preferable?

"It is their majesties' decree that we be gone from this country," Isaac adds in his ponderous voice. "Surely they will not wish us to be delayed."

The men exchange glances. It is obvious they expected this to be simple, and they have no instructions if it is not. "Very well," the leader shrugs. "We'll be back." By the time they are specks in the distance, we are breathing again.

That afternoon, a well-dressed nobleman rides alongside us on a beautiful mount caparisoned with a richly patterned saddle blanket and a polished and bejeweled harness and bit. The two soldiers from this morning point out Isaac, and the man dismounts. "I am Juan Enrique Montevera, the Count of Tarancón," he says. "Their majesties have asked that I come see how you are faring." He looks around our group. "Where are your children? Are they all well?"

My body freezes, and I stifle the urge to check if they have mixed in with the others who have gathered around.

"We sent our children elsewhere," Isaac says. "We are going by sea, and our prospects are uncertain. They will live with family in"— he hesitates for a moment—"in Navarre." Navarre. The opposite direction from where baby Isaac is traveling. I marvel again at the dignity of my son-in-law. "When we are settled, we will bring them to us," Isaac goes on in a voice so authoritative it would be difficult not to believe him, even though the story is preposterous.

"Really!" The count arches his brows as he casts his eyes over the crowd. I tremble with dread, but Samra has already drawn herself up and taken a step toward him.

"I know who you are looking for," she says in the strong, clear voice I remember. "My baby is not here. The king and queen you serve forced me to send him away." She gestures to the front of her dress. "Do you see I am wet with milk? Would that be so if he were here to nurse?" She has bound her breasts to ease the pain of their engorgement, but every time Hadassah's baby cries, milk seeps through her bodice. It's been soaked and dried so often since she was separated from baby Isaac that the stains have made twin haloes on her bosom.

"Come! Walk with me," she tells the count. "You will not find one baby here who reaches out for me." Her voice quavers, and her face flushes with the onset of tears she is too proud to shed. The count seems unnerved by the talk of leaking breasts, but Samra's tone is so demanding, he follows in her wake.

She steers a path through the group, keeping her eyes straight ahead as she passes her nieces and nephews. She goes up to one small child and then another, plucking this one's chin and pinching that one's cheek, and the count sees how each child shrinks away deeper into its mother's embrace.

Samra turns to the count. "Are you satisfied?"

"Well then," he says, shifting uncomfortably from foot to foot as he clears his throat. "I will tell their majesties I found you all safe and well and making good progress." He remounts and stares coldly first at Judah and then at Isaac. "Without your children." He touches his horse's flank and is off, kicking up dust that swirls around us as they disappear from view.

Perhaps he pitied the fate that Ferdinand and Isabella's loveless and calculated piety has ordained for us. Perhaps he saw bedraggled people who had done him no harm and decided to do none in return. He didn't believe us about leaving without our children, but whatever the reason, we are safe.

Every day, the road becomes more clogged with refugees heading for the ports of Alicante and Valencia. One group merges with another until we are a ribbon of bodies pressing forward across the plains of Andalusia. Villagers sell us food at high prices, while the local priests move among us offering baptism. Those who can go no farther accept and stay behind.

Women bang on tambourines and boys beat drums to keep our spirits from flagging. People die, babies are born, muscles cramp, bones creak. Still we press on, singing hymns and chanting psalms.

We stop several times during the day for the men to pray. The women in our family form our own group and honor the Holy

One as well. "Ashrei, yoshvei veitecha," we call out to the huge sky above us. "I will extol Thee, my God, O King. The will of those who fear him he will do, and their cry he will hear."

So many have already left Spain, so many are following behind us, so many are on other roads. Is Isaac right, that perhaps we are going home? I wish I could believe that, but all I can do is wonder if God knows or cares, or is listening to our cries at all.

We follow the path of the Júcar river until it turns sharply east. There, the people going to Alicante will head south, while we continue along the river, which is now flowing in the direction of Valencia. We mill together where the roads diverge, saying good-bye and praying for each other's safety.

"When I first knew we would be exiled, I was so full of despair I wanted to die," Isaac says as the two of us stand watching clouds of dust rise up from the group on the road to Alicante. "I even wondered whether the prophets had been wrong to put such faith in God. But I see now that there never was such a people in beauty and in pleasantness and that God is with us."

I cast a glance at him. Once a great courtier, he stands in torn shoes, ragged stockings, and a soiled cloak. He is not wearing his usual skullcap but a larger hat to shield his eyes, and it is limp from days of sweat. Only a man with the deepest store of goodness could have such thoughts now.

We fall in with a smaller party headed our direction, among whom are two of Abraham Seneor's nephews leaving Spain with their families. "Please don't speak of him," one of their wives tells me.

I wonder what Fernando Nuñez Colonel is thinking, as he rides between his new houses, orchards, vineyards, and mansions, bought for nothing from departing Jews. Will he be like Midas, thrilled to have everything he touches turn to gold until his greed destroys him, body and soul? I wonder whether, after realizing no one remains to keep him company but Christians who despise and suspect him, he may realize he is still Abraham Seneor and follow us out of Spain. Not today or tomorrow, perhaps, but someday, unless the grave claims him first.

Perhaps it's not greed though, but exhaustion. I understand that well enough. Perhaps he felt as I did about going to Madrigal— that my bones ached too much to serve any cause. And after all, my effort changed nothing.

Sone-or. The old man now alone with his riches is not a Hater of Light; he is a sad, lost soul, more bereft than anyone on this road. I will not judge another, and I say a silent prayer that Isaac's old friend will find peace.

∽

We travel for several more weeks, parting from the rest of the group only when we near Valencia. We head north to Sagunto to stay with friends of Isaac's until the deadline to leave Spain. It's a short distance from there to Valencia, where our ship awaits.

Leah's husband and Samuel travel ahead to let our hosts know we are coming. When they come back, they bring no news of baby Isaac. I imagine a ship bearing a letter from Lisbon heading into port just as we are sailing out. I picture it gathering dust in Sagunto until we can write to say where to send it.

It is not proper to pray for what has already been decided. A letter will arrive before we leave, or it will not. Our beloved Isaac is either safe, or he is not. Prayer cannot change the facts.

Despite being at our journey's end, a heaviness settles over us as we enter Sagunto. We walk between whitewashed houses, up steep streets, and through the arched gate of the aljama, as close to dead as people can be while still on their feet. A bed, a table, and a comfortable place to sit await us, but our hearts are too burdened with sorrow and apprehension to care.

The women take a short walk to the ocean to wash off the dirt before going to the mikveh, which many need after weeks on the road. We set up a tent in minutes after all the practice we've had, and after undressing inside, we emerge with only a cloth draped around our bodies.

As we walk across the sand, a gray horse gallops at the water's edge, and for a moment I am confused. "Chuva?" I whisper. A sudden puff of sea breeze blows back my loose hair. The horse slows and makes a wide circle, watching me the whole time, before heading off again.

I am not the young girl I was at Sagres, and the ache in my feet is only slightly soothed by the lapping water as we go out through the gentle surf. The swells caress our legs and rise up around our breasts, but we go no farther, for none of us can swim.

I'm not sure who has the idea first. Perhaps it is the touch of living water on all of us at once. Nita had her first blood on the road from Alcalá, and though she does not require a mikveh until she is married, we decide she has earned the right to be seen as a woman after all the courage she has shown. Who needs the mikveh in the aljama when here, under God's sky, we can honor her and ourselves for making it this far?

We all gather around Nita and offer the blessings as she immerses. When she comes up the third time, our women's voices mingle with the sounds of shore birds and the gentle pounding of waves on the sand. "Blessed art thou, Lord God, king of the universe, who has created us, sustained us, and enabled us to reach this day."

Turning my back to the shore, I take away the cloth and let it float on the water. I say a prayer on my first immersion for my mother, on the second for Simona, and on the third for my daughter, the greatest joy of my life.

Under my toes, the land of my birth is disappearing. I am buoyed up by the swells, but still rooted here, sustained by so many things—people, places, memory. I say a prayer for myself as well as I pull the cloth back around me, acknowledging that I am in the hands of the one who made the sea, the journey, and the life I have lived.

The mikveh has worked its magic again and granted me peace. The little girl we saved on that horrible day in Toledo is a woman now, part of us forever. I am part of her too. Perhaps she will carry on my Eliana's legacy, marrying Samuel, who loves her, and bringing more beautiful babies, more leaders of our people, into the world.

I don't know how many more of these moments I will share, but I will be watching even when they and their families can no longer see me, and when they need strength, I will give them mine.

On the beach, the gray horse is coming back, stretching its long limbs as it strides along. It stops and looks out at me. "Are you coming?" I feel it saying, and in my mind, I climb on its bare back and ride away.

VALENCIA 1492

"Do you ever wonder why you still have the atlas?" Judah asks me again. "Why, despite all your journeys, it has never been lost?"

"I am saving it for your children, for their children," I tell him. "For those long after we have been forgotten."

"You have been caring for more than a book." The voice is a new one.

"Grandmother?" I ask.

"The atlas will not leave this room with you. It will be found, and lost, and found again, and each time, people will be astonished that there was a time and place where people who made things of such beauty could be exiled."

"My son and I made this atlas," my great-grandfather Abraham Cresques tells me. "It was always for more than our family. Though we didn't know it at the time, it has its own reasons for being."

"And you have done your part by keeping it safe and leaving it here," my mother says.

A lifetime of journeys with my daughter, my grandchildren, and great-grandchildren flood my mind. "Kaminos di leche i miel," I think to myself. "Kaminos buenos." Paths of milk and honey. Good paths.

I hear footsteps on the stairs and the creak of the door. Judah and Samuel look confused, as if they were expecting to find me in the dark instead of this glow of love and light.

"Were you all right here alone?" Judah asks me.

I smile. "I wasn't alone. I have never been alone."

I put the atlas on the chair and close my trunk. "I'm ready," I say, feeling the souls of my people as they follow me down the stairs and out into the dying light toward the ship that will take me somewhere.

READING
GROUP GUIDE

1. The Jewish community depicted in *The Mapmaker's Daughter* is divided between those who have given up Judaism for Christianity, those who pretend to be Christians but secretly practice Judaism, and those who live openly as Jews. What are their reasons for what they have chosen, and how do they view the choices of the others?

2. In her first musings while she waits in Valencia, Amalia says, "There's a knowledge deep in our bones that some lines cannot be crossed without becoming unrecognizable to ourselves— the only death truly to be feared." Does this resonate in your own life?

3. As Amalia matures, how does the meaning of the atlas evolve emotionally and philosophically for her?

4. Have your relationships with your own mother and father and/or your children's relationships with you been as different as Amalia's are with each of her parents? What does Amalia want from her mother? From her father? Does she get it?

5. *The Mapmaker's Daughter* is set among people who think very differently about many things than people today do. What has changed the most? The least?

6. Amalia's naïveté in her early years sometimes makes it difficult to see people for what they really are. What clues enable you to see what she fails to understand about Diogo? What other characters do you think you see more clearly than she does?

7. Both Judah and Simona function as friend and counselor to Amalia. What advice do they offer that makes the most sense in your own life? Have you had someone who filled the same role for you?

8. Amalia is uncertain whether her father would want her to perform Jewish rituals to prepare his body for burial. What do you think he would have wanted?

9. Judah explains that love and power must be in balance to reach the highest form of compassion. What does this mean? Do you agree?

10. "Anywhere you can be a Jew is home…and exile is anywhere you cannot." Does this apply to any aspect of one's identity?

11. Amalia's reaction to Jamil is immediate and powerful. Have you ever had an encounter like that?

12. How does poetry, both their own and that of famous poets, help Amalia and Jamil build their relationship?

13. Though having different religions ultimately divides Amalia and Jamil, are there are ways in which their religious identities strengthen their relationship?

14. The ritual of the mikveh occurs numerous times in *The Mapmaker's Daughter*. What does it mean for the women who practice it?

15. When Amalia can't decide if she should stay in Queluz or go to Granada with Jamil, Simona tells her, "Living here in Queluz should be your choice, not just something where you say, 'Oh, look where I ended up,' without knowing how it happened." Is there anything about your life that illustrates what Simona means?

16. What does Amalia offer her daughter that was missing in her own childhood? How does that influence the kind of adult Eliana becomes?

17. What does Amalia find most surprising about Granada? Was the Muslim culture also surprising to you? How?

18. Did Amalia do the right thing ending her relationship with Jamil? Is there any way they might have been able to salvage it?

19. Elizabeth's husband, King Juan, has been quoted as saying it was "better to be born to a journeyman than to the King of Castile." After reading about the Castilian court, do you agree?

20. Amalia wonders, "How can it be that I can say in great detail what happened when I was eight or twelve, but now shake my head in bewilderment when I try to remember year by year what has happened since? Decades of my life are swallowed whole, and it doesn't seem possible that I have filled each day with one thing or another." Do you see your life the same way?

21. Amalia and Eliana cope with the loss of their world in Queluz by cleaning house. Have you found ritual ways to console yourself in times of great turmoil and grief? Were you surprised by what gave you comfort?

22. "The success of old age is to die while you still wish to live," Judah says. "To take your last breath still wanting more." Do you agree?

23. When Nita's parents are killed, Amalia describes "Torquemada's stark vision of divine retribution ris[ing] in smoke above the crowd in the square, while in this dark and narrow street, every wall, every cobblestone, every doorway is charged with the sacredness of God's presence in this moment." Why does she view the moment of Nita's rescue as being so sacred?

24. Based on what you learned by reading *The Mapmaker's Daughter* and what you already know about Ferdinand and Isabella, Torquemada, and the Inquisition, what do you think Ferdinand and Isabella were trying to accomplish by expelling the Jews from Spain?

25. *The Mapmaker's Daughter* is intended as a showcase of the frequently unsung strength and courage of women. At what points in the novel did you feel that most profoundly? Do any of the characters stand out in particular for you in this respect?

26. The ghost of Amalia's grandfather, mapmaker Abraham Cresques, says of the atlas at the end of the novel, "Though we didn't know it at the time, it has its own reasons for being." What reasons for the atlas' existence are revealed during the novel? What future reasons might there be?

SUGGESTIONS FOR BOOK CLUB ACTIVITIES

1. Look up online images of the Catalan Atlas and discuss its characteristics and how these are brought into the novel.

2. Look up the rituals and blessings involved in the mikveh and/ or Shabbat, and discuss how these might reflect and shape the world view of people who observe these practices.

3. Read the poems in the book aloud.

4. Get a CD or download of medieval Sephardic music and discuss how it influences the way you view the culture described in the book.

5. Look up "Judah Abravanel, Poem to His Son" to read online what Judah Abravanel wrote after sending his infant son to Portugal to foil the kidnapping plot.

A CONVERSATION WITH THE AUTHOR

Q: Why did you choose to write a novel on this subject?

A: Like everyone, I wonder how the human race is going to figure out a way to move beyond the ignorance and hatred that so polarizes our world. When I was first exposed to the term "Convivencia," or "living together," the label given to medieval Iberia during the centuries it was populated by Jews, Christians, and Muslims, I naively thought I would find a shining example of a diverse, multicultural society that had created a community of tolerance and mutual gain.

After months of study, I began seeing the Convivencia as containing more warnings than answers for our time. I hope readers will benefit from reading about people long ago who encountered some of the same issues we face, whose behavior holds up a mirror by which we can confront the awful results of religious and other forms of prejudice, as well as look with new appreciation at our incredibly diverse society and affirm that it represents the kind of world we want to live in.

Q: Is there a personal connection between you and the story of the Jews in medieval Iberia?

A: I have written a number of books on Jewish themes (most notably *Until Our Last Breath*, my 2008 nonfiction book on Jewish resistance in the Holocaust), so choosing a Jewish subject was nothing new. I have identified with Jews and been drawn to Jewish culture on a very deep psychological level since I was a young girl. A number of years ago, I became what I suppose might be called a reverse converso—a Jew by choice (that's the preferred term today). Though I am not conventionally religious, I feel a great sense of connection and community with other Jews, and I enjoy promoting knowledge and understanding of Jewish history among Jews and non-Jews alike. I am a novelist and a Jew, both by choice, and the two came together in *The Mapmaker's Daughter*.

Q: What particular challenges did you face writing this book?

A: The biggest challenges came about as the result of early decisions I made about the structure of the book. I wanted to include both Henry the Navigator and Queen Isabella as characters, and to do this, I needed to have my protagonist live across a number of generations. This was new for me, since my previous novels have ended while the protagonists are still fairly young.

Having Amalia look back at her life as she is going into exile meant I had to choose a first-person narration, and that can be tricky. I had to write as Amalia, avoiding anything she couldn't have known or wouldn't have thought. I had to see things through her eyes, which, in this case, meant I had to write many religious sentiments I don't agree with. She believed in an omnipresent and omnipotent God, and that's what matters.

Another challenge was that the flashbacks had to be told in the present tense, because she is slipping into reverie. She's not telling someone else her story; she is reliving it herself. Add to that the need to switch back and forth between her present situation and her past, and I think it should be obvious why I view this book as the most complex I have written to date.

The character of Diogo was also touchy for me. Amalia is

my only voice, and early in the book she doesn't see Diogo for what he is. I had to find a way to slip in some clues for the reader without giving Amalia insights she didn't have. I tried to do this by veiled allusions to Henry's homosexuality (which, by the way, is strongly suggested by the historical record) and his unusual favor toward Diogo, as well as by Diogo's self-centeredness and indifference toward Amalia even as he is asking her to marry him. Only Amalia should be surprised to find her marriage is a disaster, because the reader should have seen it coming.

Diogo is cold, calculating, and unethical, faults that have nothing to do with his sexual orientation. It makes no difference if he is gay or straight. He is reprehensible as a human being, period, and knowingly dragging a naive young woman into a loveless and unfulfilling marriage simply adds to his ugliness.

Q: Historical novelists frequently have to make adjustments in the facts to make their stories work. What did you have to invent or change?

A: Of all my books, I had to invent the most and at the same time change the least in this one. First, I had to create from scratch all the Jewish and Muslim women in the book. In occasional references to his wife in his writings, Isaac Abravanel never mentioned her name. For me, this lack of concrete information is both the dilemma and the driving impetus to be a historical novelist. These women existed, despite the fact we must now invent them, and because they existed, I feel compelled to do what needs to be done so that their lives can be celebrated.

All the women in the Alhambra are my inventions, but the Christian princesses, queens, and other of high rank are real people, although in some cases with minor adjustments in their names. Elizabeth is the Anglicized version of Isabel or

Isabella, because I thought it would be too confusing to have Amalia's childhood friend have the same name as the queen who will figure so prominently later. I kept the Portuguese or Spanish versions of most names, with a few exceptions. Henry the Navigator and Ferdinand of Aragon will be more recognizable that way than as Enrique and Fernando.

What I mean by having to change the least is that there is very little deviation from what I know to be true about the events I describe. With one exception, events happened when, where, and how I wrote them. The exception is the description of the Inquisition in Toledo, which I condensed to preserve the narrative pace. The period of grace would have ended in the early fall of 1485, but the first auto-da-fé was not held until the following February. At that time, 750 people were paraded before the public, where their "crimes" were read aloud, fined up to one-fifth of their fortunes (used to fund the war against Granada), physically punished, and humiliated in various other ways. None were killed. Executions began in August, almost a year after the events I describe.

Likewise, an auto-da-fé was an all-day event, with long sermons and the reading of the crimes of each of as many as 750 victims. My research indicates that the burnings at the stake sometimes were held in Plaza de Zocodover, but in most places, the condemned were taken outside the city walls for their executions, so it may have been only the ceremonies that were held in the plaza.

In some cases, sources are inconsistent as to where the Abravanels lived at particular times, so I chose what worked best for the story. Also, because it helped the story, I left out many family members because there was no role for them to play, and I thought there were already enough characters to keep track of.

Q: Are there any aspects of this book that gave you particular pleasure to write?

A: I enjoyed working in Jewish ritual practices and customs wherever I could, and I also particularly liked writing the scenes set in Muslim Granada, because it was such an enticing culture. Most of all, I reveled in the Hebrew and Arabic poetry that is part of Amalia's relationship with Judah and Jamil. Iberia was one of the great centers of medieval poetry, due in large part to the great and longstanding tradition of secular Arabic poetry. It was my pleasure to introduce readers to some poets they probably haven't heard much about and to write poems of my own for Amalia and Jamil, imitating the contemporary styles.

Q: This is your fourth novel, and all four have been about different places and eras. How do you choose a subject?

A: It may seem as if I am all over the place, but really I'm not. The unifying drive and focus of all my work is forgotten or underappreciated women and their stories. I'm a professor of humanities at San Diego City College, and my textbooks briefly mention a number of women. Writing a book is a huge investment, and one has to be far more than merely interested in a subject to take it on. I wait until someone gets under my skin, until I find myself thinking about her during the day and already seeing scenes and hearing dialogue in my head. Then I'm a goner.

ACKNOWLEDGMENTS

I have been blessed with a small and capable group of people willing to read *The Mapmaker's Daughter* in manuscript and offer critiques and suggestions. First, as always, I want to acknowledge my sister, Lynn Wrench, who is tireless at finding things that need to be more real, more powerful, more vivid, and just plain better.

Pamela Lear, Honey Amado, Saul Matalon, and Hillary Liber have my sincere gratitude for reading all or part of this novel in draft and helping me make it not only accurate from a Jewish perspective but supportive of a culture I love. The late Gail Forman used some of her life's last energy to read and comment on an early draft. May her memory be a blessing.

Shokran to my lifelong friends Katharina Harlow and Aisha Jill Morgan for their assistance with the portions of the book requiring a deeper understanding of Arabic and Islam.

Sincere thanks also go to Dolores Sloan, whose book on the Sephardic Jews of Spain and Portugal and personal efforts to track down details made a huge difference in the quality of the finished product. Also many thanks to two more lifelong friends, Reverend Nancy Pennekamp and Reverend Mark McKenzie, who helped me figure out Eucharistic practices of the time, and to Rabbi Zoe Klein for her support throughout.

Many thanks go to my editor at Sourcebooks, Shana Drehs, and assistant editor Anna Klenke, and once again, I want to lavish praise on my agent, Meg Ruley of the Jane Rotrosen Agency, who shepherds me through the process with grace, good humor, and much patience.

A belated thank-you also to Claudine Efthymiou Yin, whose assistance on previous novels has gone unmentioned until now.

I leave for last the one I most want to honor. I wrote *The Mapmaker's Daughter* before my beloved husband, James Fee, was diagnosed with metastatic prostate cancer. He did not live to hold the book in his hands. I would like to go on record with my feelings here, but he would only be embarrassed. I will just say I don't think I would be a novelist without him.

ABOUT THE AUTHOR

Laurel Corona is a professor of humanities at San Diego City College. She is the author of *Until Our Last Breath*, a Christopher Medal winner about Jewish resistance in the Holocaust, and several award-winning historical novels. Learn more at www .laurelcorona.com.

Olga Gunn Photography